BOUND & FREED

the complete collection

NIKKI SEX

BOUND AND FREED

Copyright 2013 by Nikki Sex

BOUND

1

Chapter 1

André's Case *Difficile*

−−− ✕ ✕ −−−

The naked man was face down and spread-eagle, with all four limbs cuffed to the St. Andrew's Cross. Tilted at a 45 degree angle, the X frame was custom made, and built for safe play. Pressure points for the sub's head, ankles, wrists, hips, and shoulders, were all lined with soft padding.

"I said, *come for me.* You will come. Now," the stern female voice rang with power, combined with sensual, yet merciless dominance. Her small, soft hand stroked her sub's erection, while her riding crop welted his slim, youthful thighs, and a butt plug vibrator buzzed in his ass.

The man's back and buttocks glowed bright red, contrasting dramatically with his normally pale skin. His swollen shaft was a cross between red and purple, and it dripped with pre-cum. The young man was erect to the point where it must've been a source of great pain. The Domme massaged, fondled, and caressed him skillfully; and still, he made no sound, except for his measured, yet ragged breathing.

"Mistress Diana, that is enough, if you please," said André Chevalier, as he came into the room.

Merde, André swore to himself, astounded by the sight. *Was John Taylor incapable of achieving orgasm? Or stubborn? Whatever the reason, he couldn't, or wouldn't, allow himself release. But why?*

The whipping stopped, and Diana removed her hand from the twenty-two year old man's straining cock. The extent of his arousal was no surprise. Mistress Diana was one of the best.

What kind of man could withstand such an overwhelming physical and sexual assault? André tilted his head and carefully

1

studied his client. John's lungs heaved, sucking air rapidly into his slim chest. His entire body trembled and he was covered in a thin sheen of sweat. André observed only bodily responses; his facial expression was remote. Detached. The young man's mind, heart and soul seemed incapable of being touched.

The young man is cut off from others. André knew this already, but bearing witness to such misery caused a wrench in his own heart.

At around six feet tall, the young man had attained his full height, yet his lean, well-cut form still needed filling out, to complete his development. Not long out of his teens, his youthfulness showed in his face and form.

But not in his eyes, André thought. *The eyes have seen too much. More than others ever would. More than anyone ever should, in this world. There is vast experience in those distrustful, dark eyes.*

Physically attractive to an impressive degree, John Taylor could be described as being 'male model' handsome. He had physical beauty and emotionally detached control. These attributes, combined with his high IQ, and almost omnipresent skills of observation would serve him well. In time, and with training, he'd become a highly skilled and sought after Dom.

Mistress Diana's gaze met André's and her eyebrows rose, along with a sardonic smile and slight shrug. André read much from just those small physical tells. The Dominatrix clearly had no idea why she couldn't make her sub achieve orgasm. As an experienced mistress of heterosexual males, Diana had been totally baffled by John's resistance.

André hid a bubble of amusement. The consummate professional probably hadn't been perplexed or challenged by a man, for many years… if ever. This experience wouldn't harm her. Her lack of success in this situation had nothing to do with her skills, which she was well aware.

John Taylor is burdened with powerful inner demons, André Mused. *But how to exorcise them?*

André frowned. Was it a shadow, or had John's balls actually turned blue, in color? *Merde!* Such inhibition! Or was it restraint?

The young man panted and trembled with need, as every part of his body demanded release.

John would simply not let go and permit himself to orgasm, despite the extreme discomfort involved. He refused to surrender. In his mind, submitting to another was as serious as life and death. John never lost control, nor did he give control to others.

André approached the X frame.

"Release him, if you please, Mistress Diana," André said. Then he gestured toward the butt plug, "and remove anything else upon his person." As she did so, John started to push himself up and began to move away from the cross. André put his hand on his back, and the youth become rigid and stilled.

"Remain on the cross, without the cuffs," André directed him, quietly. "Rest comfortably. Do me the honor of remaining by my side, John. Stay, for we shall talk."

As Mistress Diana moved toward the door, to leave the room, André softly reminded him, "Thank your Mistress, John."

"Thank you, Mistress," came a deep, deadpan voice.

Once they were alone, André began to stroke and pet the back of John's head and neck. Not many days before, John would've been rigid with displeasure. When he'd first contacted André for help, he'd been repulsed by any touch, with a passion that bordered on hatred. André had taught him to endure his caress. So far, he both loved and hated his touch.

He ran his fingers through John's thick, black hair in soft, fond caresses. Gently and rhythmically, using the healing power of human contact, André attempted to calm and soothe him.

"Shut your eyes, *mon ami*," André said, making the tone of his voice low and hypnotic. John obeyed him. "Listen to my voice. Relax now and be comfortable, for you are safe here with me."

André continued his caress. John's tension lessened, yet only slightly. "You are not a submissive, *non*. Yet, as a Dom who I am instructing, I wished for you to fully participate and comprehend the submissive experience. This is an important aspect of training, to embrace the experiences of both the Dom and the sub. You must do nothing to a sub that has not first been done to you. In this way, you will become the best Dom that you can be."

"I failed," John said, in what André was now able to recognize as his careful, emotionless voice – the dispassionate tone that he used when he was hiding an ocean of feeling.

"*Mais no,*" André said, delighted to find that the young man held no anger or resentment for Mistress Diana's treatment of him. For unless André was mistaken, John's flat response concealed feelings of utter despair. "You have only exposed more of yourself to me. This is very good. I am pleased with you."

John's eyes were dark pools of pain, yet André's genuine appreciation stirred the coals of his misery. A momentary flare of hope kindled in those eyes, warming André's heart. He sympathized with the young man's desolation, for John Taylor was truly a tortured soul.

"I tell you now, that I understand you. And I comprehend more and more each day," André said. "Shall I flatter you? Shall I tell you that I grow to like and respect you, *mon ami?* For it is true, *oui.* Brenda was wise to send you to me. She wants you to listen to me, and to do as I say. She knows that I will place your feet on the right path. We both care for you. We wish you to find peace, John."

John's entire body gave an uncontrolled shudder. For a moment, there was the light of conscious awareness in his cold, remote detachment. There was pain, loss and longing in his eyes.

Ah, tres bon! André thought, with satisfaction. *Love and trust are the keys.*

"Hush now. Relax. Imagine that it is Brenda stroking your hair. Imagine that she is here, with you. You are the most important person in her world. Have you done this, *mon ami?*"

There was a long pause, and the young man's breath caught. "Yes, André," John finally said, in an even voice. The man's self-restraint and control was remarkable.

André pet him affectionately for a few more strokes. Then he lowered his voice, "Brenda loves you very much, *mon ami*. She wants you to be happy. She knows that I will help you, if only you would bow that stubborn will of yours and submit to me. You know this is true."

John's body quaked under André's hand, and his breath hitched. Like an animal caught in a trap, his eyes were wild and fearful. He displayed an instinctive, and overwhelming need to escape. This was the crossroads. He was at the exact point, the possibility of soul-freeing catharsis. John was on the precipice now, looking into the abyss. But would he have the courage to jump?

"You trusted Brenda, and you should trust me," André urged him, with confident self-assurance. "It is my wish for you to climax, John."

With one hand remaining firmly on the young man's nape, André flexed his grip slightly. This was a reminder of who was in control. It was a physical show of possession, ownership, and the intimate bodily restraint of his sub. Right now, this young man belonged to him.

"Come for me, John." André placed the fingers of his other hand lightly on John's cock – just barely a touch. "Come. Right now."

John exploded. With his hips thrusting sharply and repeatedly, his long body convulsed violently, and he sprayed, and sprayed, and sprayed. Yet, throughout this immense orgasm, John made barely any audible sound.

Inside this young man, is truly only a boy, André thought. *What was the-oh-so crass American saying? Ah, yes. 'Young, dumb, and full of cum.'* Well, that much was true, for he was astonished by the huge amount of ejaculate that could issue from one man. When his climax finally subsided, John's penis remained erect and his entire body trembled.

"Shush, shush," André said, still stroking John's hair. "Well done, *mon ami*. Very well done. I am oh-so-very pleased, and I know that Brenda would be pleased also. I am not Brenda, no, but you can trust me, as she did. And as for me? *Eh bien,* you are most important to me, John. For I have learned to care for you."

How could one recover when trust was broken? André thought. Not only broken, but shattered. Crushed beyond redemption. This young man's physical, emotional and mental constraints were too deep-seated. He was always tense. Always on guard.

John expended so much energy watching and seeking inconsistencies. He was forever trying to predict what people would do, and was at all times prepared for, and expecting to be disappointed, injured or hurt. It was this hyper-vigilance that had helped him to become the gifted observer that he was.

André gave the back of John's hair a quick little tug, not with enough force to cause pain, more in a compelling, commanding manner. He wanted the young man's full attention.

"You need to let go now," he said, "for you have been holding everything inside for much too long. Stop worrying. Stop thinking. You must trust me, and leave yourself in my hands. I am here for you. Do not hide from me, John, for I know who you are. I understand the depth of your grief. I too, loved Brenda. *Oui,* it is true. I loved her for who she was – a kind soul and a sensitive, caring submissive. Brenda knew you, John. She was probably the only one to ever do so. She loved you very much."

A deep, throaty sob came from the young man. It was a feral, animal sound, raw and brutal, as if it had been torn from his throat. The dam broke and John began to cry – not with normal tears, André realized, no. He sobbed and keened with agony. It was as if his very heart was pouring out from within him.

John Taylor's life had been ripped apart. The only one in his tortured life who he loved and trusted, the one person who loved him freely, and who made him feel safe, was gone forever. Now he was lost and absolutely alone.

Chapter 2

Broken

❮❯

At this moment, I am the only one in the world who knows and cares about this tormented young man, André thought. And it has been a difficult journey. We have come far, but there is still much farther to go. Yet he will no longer hide from me. Not now. Not anymore.

"Sit here with me, my friend," André said, taking John's hand. Breathing raggedly, the naked young man stood on shaky legs. He stumbled toward his mentor, with tears streaming down his cheeks.

They sat together on the couch. André wrapped his arms around John and held him, with his head against his chest. He patted and soothed the grief-stricken man, as he sobbed and sobbed. He cried as if there was no end to his pain and despair. John's slim, young body convulsed. He was wracked with a sorrow that was so profound, so deep and palpable, that it was almost like a separate presence in the room.

Mon Dieu, such loss, André thought. His own heart constricted painfully beneath his ribs, from bearing witness to such an intimate and moving display of passion. *This vulnerable young man is like a child in his grief. He cries as if there is nothing left. As if everything that had made his life worth living has been taken from him.*

Until this day, and almost this very moment, André had been extremely concerned that John Taylor might be a sociopath. He'd been so detached, emotionless and without proper human feeling or responses. The impassive and almost clinical way that he'd dominated a sub seemed like callous disregard.

André had also been worried that the young man had no capacity to love. Instead, it became clear that John had been so tormented by the depth of his passions, it seemed that the only

7

way he could endure life was to become emotionless. By shutting down and detaching himself, the young man had discovered a way to cut off his feelings.

John had shown André his willingness to learn, as well as a high level of intelligence. In fact, the young man was probably a genius, in many ways. He was also an excellent actor and could be superficially charming, when he chose to be. No wonder André had been worried.

It was imperative that a Dom care about his subs, and fully appreciate their gift of submission. John was hyperaware of his subs. He noticed their every response, the slightest nuances, as well as the most subtle of changes physically, mentally, or emotionally. Yet, he didn't seem to bond during a power exchange. Would he use that potentially dangerous, intimate knowledge to break a sub down completely?

André had been apprehensive. Was this handsome boy as cold and unfeeling as he appeared? If André taught him dominance, without impressing upon him the importance of his connection with a submissive, the youth would increase his knowledge and experience, yet still, he would have failed. For what would be the point?

Educating the mind without educating the heart is no education at all.

André patted and soothed him for some time. John's anguished tears were especially touching, because up to now, he'd buried and hidden his feelings so deeply. That the young man felt safe enough to display his honest emotions to him, was a testament of how far this damaged soul had come. This was the start. Now they could move forward.

Patting and soothing, André embraced his grief stricken client. In time, the young man's tears and wracking shudders lessened, and eventually stopped. It was a long while, before he gradually came back to himself.

John Taylor is not heartless, au contraire. André thought, with immense relief. *He has been overwhelmed by the vastness of his passions.*

He had hidden his emotions deeply, a protective action, no doubt learned as a child.

But for John to prevent ejaculation to this degree? To have such impossible control of his body? André now knew the answer to that mystery. The young man could climax in the presence of another if he cared for them; only someone that he trusted and with whom he felt safe.

The fact that André was connected to Brenda, the only person that John had loved and trusted, helped immensely. Devastated, betrayed and alone, the young man had taken a leap of faith. Life had taught John to *never* trust anyone. Yet Brenda had trusted André, and John had no one else.

After the amount of time that they'd spent together, John was only now learning to trust André, and perhaps to even love him.

André allowed himself an internal wry smile. He felt strangely paternal toward the lost and damaged creature in his arms. There was only a ten year difference in age between them, but it may as well have been a hundred, so different were their life experiences.

André took a deep breath, patting John's shoulder comfortingly. John's childhood was grounded in consistent betrayal, a lesson which was proving difficult for him to unlearn. Dependence upon another wouldn't come easily for him. For this, one needed trust, openness and love.

André frowned with distaste. The scars that covered the young man's back, buttocks and thighs were thin, numerous and white with age. John's reaction to pain, in a similar situation to what he'd experienced in his past, had been important to determine. Thus André had set up this scene. This session could very well have ended with violence. The security team was on guard, even now, watching them closely. Yet it had been illuminating, and had proved a necessary point.

For at least part of his childhood, John had known fondness, affection and love. His mother's older sister had loved him. She'd taken care of him before her death. André had received a long letter from her, along with finances toward the boy's tutelage.

She'd sent that money, five years earlier, well before her death. But John had refused to come to him initially.

The woman had recognized the traits and inner nature of a Dom within the boy. But had she known the extremes of which he was capable? Six months after she'd passed away, John had finally come to André, lost in hopeless misery.

André smiled once more at the young man in his arms. He was both warmed and amused by the fatherly feelings he had for him. A sadist without empathy could only be a monster, and yet André had discovered a human being hidden inside this man – child.

Ma cher, André thought, shutting his eyes. *I have taken on this case difficile, oui. Your nephew is lost without your love. But with assistance from the Bon Dieu, we shall help him find peace.*

André frowned, and took a considering look at the young man, who had wrapped himself tightly around André's torso, unwilling to leave the shelter of his arms.

John was an extremely challenging case. While André's intervention would help him a great deal, it could not bring full resolution. The young man's scars went far beyond the physical. His greatest need for healing was deep within his mind, his heart, and soul. There was a long journey ahead of him. Yet the progress John made on this night, was a significant step toward that goal.

André stroked John's hair, generously giving him the human contact that was so vital for him, the connection that the young man craved and needed. The absolute solution to such a broken spirit, André realized, was for John to discover trust and love, once again.

But how long would it take for such an injured soul, with a heart so deeply broken, to find love?

Chapter 3

Four Years Later

⊰⊱

Twenty-four year old Kelly Flynn took the elevator down to the underground entrance to The Basement, a local fetish club. It was a Saturday night and the place would be jumping. Unfortunately, she was running late. Her mother had been nagging her to come home for a visit, so out of guilt and a sense of obligation, she'd gone. Unfortunately her family lived in Dunthorpe, which was a long drive from where Kelly lived in Hillsboro, as well as from the club. The Basement was located in the heart of downtown Portland. Traffic had been rotten, and of course it was raining.

Getting to the club was what she looked forward to all week. When she was there, she didn't want to leave; and when she was away, she couldn't wait to get back.

Following a succession of boring and unfulfilling jobs, after completing her Arts Degree, Kelly seemed to have found her niche. Now she organized and ran a speed dating service, which she worked at three evenings a week.

She still had no idea what she wanted to do with her life. Sadly, despite Kelly's wishes made upon stars and blown out birthday candles, her love of cooking, singing, flowers and everything French had yet to solidify into any particular profession. Being a Speed Dating Coordinator was fun however, and the pay was great. Unfortunately, she had to work from three pm to midnight, which severely curtailed her time at The Basement.

She'd heard that there was more than one opening for a 'club sub' – a Basement employee who'd be available to partner with guest Dom's in the club. But Kelly didn't want to go there, either.

She smothered a giggle. *I'm not **that** submissive*, she thought.

While she liked to be topped, she also liked the freedom to choose. That included deciding who she'd spend her time with, and what she'd willingly do, or wouldn't do with a Dom. The thought of losing that level of control didn't turn her on – it disturbed her. She wasn't nearly as open or kinky as most of the other people she'd observed at the club.

Regrettably, her super expensive, month-long trial membership would soon run out. Although membership fees were expensive, she felt they were worth every cent. Kelly had learned so much about the BDSM lifestyle, as well as about herself. While she'd enjoyed herself immensely during her time at the club, she was no closer to finding a Dom boyfriend.

For Kelly, finding a Dom was a matter of trust, really. It was so difficult for a sub to rely on anyone. The last bastard she'd trusted enough to be with, hadn't used a condom, once he'd tied her up. He'd said that he'd accidently forgot! Bastard. To top it off, the lying jerk turned out to be vanilla, anyway.

Luckily, Kelly would never risk an unplanned child, so she was on the pill at the time. She believed in being safe, and always used protection.

After that vanilla jerk-bastard had unprotected sex with her, it had been embarrassing to have to tell her doctor and get a full battery of tests to ensure that she hadn't caught anything. Ironically, not long after that experience, in order to join The Basement, she'd had to take the tests once more. She smiled. It had been easier for her to ask the second time. Her doctor's expression had remained professional, he hadn't even blinked.

The elevator doors opened smoothly and she exited into a small entry room. A large man with gray hair sat behind a desk, reading a "Four Wheel and Off Road" magazine, while drinking freshly brewed coffee, from the smell of it.

"Hey, Tom-boy!" she said, cheerily.

"Kelly, as I live and breathe. How are you, gorgeous?"

"Better for seeing you, handsome," she said.

Tom laughed. An ex-cop, he worked security at the club, most nights. Kelly drew out a small white paper bag from the pocket of her knee-length jacket. "For you," she said, and put it on his desk in front of him. "Chocolate chip cookies. I made them today."

Tom opened the bag and took one out. Kelly watched as he drew in a deep, appreciative smell. "Yum. Are you sucking up to me, young lady?" he asked her with narrowed eyes, and a wry grin.

"Of course," she replied with a smile. "Seriously, it's the least I could do, after all of the help you've given me."

Tom shook his head. "Anyone can change a flat tire. But bake cookies? Not so much. Hey, what about my girlish figure?"

Kelly arched her brows. "I'm assuming you'll bring some of them home to Mary."

"Fat chance. Uh, oh, there are seven cookies here, an uneven number. I'll have to eat at least three, possibly even five." Kelly laughed, because with his growing paunch, she knew that he'd do just that. "You have a good night, honey," he added as she went through the left hand door.

There were two doors in the entry room, one to the male dressing and changing area and one to the female. Kelly went in and snagged a locker. After putting her valuables inside, she clipped the key to her corset. She refreshed her red lip gloss in the restroom, taking a quick peek in the mirror, to make sure she that looked her best.

Kelly wore dark eye shadow to set off her pale blue eyes. Her blue-green satin corset with a black lacy overlay, accented her eye shadow. Short black underwear, thigh-high fishnet stockings, and black high heels completed the ensemble.

Kelly stared into the mirror, looking at her wavy, orange, shoulder-length, hair with disgust. If she didn't condition it and constantly pamper it, it would curl and frizz up like Little Orphan Annie.

She smiled at her reflection, because she *had* played Little Orphan Annie in school, singing her heart out and stealing the show. Hell, if she'd had more discipline, maybe she could've been an actress or singer. But really, it wasn't discipline that she lacked, but motivation and passion. At twenty-four, she still had no idea what she wanted to be when she 'grew up.'

She frowned. Why was her hair orange and not red? Probably for the same reason that rust-colored freckles covered her pale complexion – sprinkled over her face, arms and shoulders. Kelly had freckles all over; in fact, *all over*. She'd never have the unblemished skin that she'd always longed for. There was nothing that she could do about her freckles, unless she covered them up with make-up. However, that would involve applying foundation from head to toe with a paint roller.

At five foot six, Kelly was of average height. Her figure was pretty average, too. Her mouth was just too damn big for her round face. Actually, her mouth was too big for pretty much anyone's face! Both that, and her manly, square jaw, were the features that she hated most about her appearance. When she smiled with her big mouth and orange hair, she felt like a jack-o'-lantern.

I should have been a man, she thought. *Prince Harry looks great, and he has orange hair and freckles.*

Kelly figured that she although wasn't really pretty, she wasn't ugly, either. At least she had a great ass! Lots of people had told her that, so it must be true. She could probably be considered striking, she supposed, when she was her animated, happy self.

That's right, idiot, she mused, with a skeptical grin. *No need to be gorgeous – not when you've got 'personality.' But does any man really go for that?*

Girlish sounds of laughter and giggling came to her ears. The restroom door burst open and two women came into the room. "Kelly!" They chorused.

"Hey girls, what's up?"

Gina and Rosslyn were Kelly's friends, and were also subs. Gina was ten years older than she was, and Rosslyn, fifteen years older. They'd both been out in the club, checking over the landscape. They happily filled Kelly in.

"You won't believe it," Gina said. "Father John's already busy entertaining the troops."

A delicious thrill of anticipation and desire coursed through Kelly. "Really?" she said. "I didn't know he was doing a scene tonight."

Kelly's heart sped. She'd be able to spend at least a portion of her evening staring at the guy that she had a huge crush on, and he'd have no idea that she was watching. It didn't get much better than that.

John Taylor. She closed her eyes, imagining him, and sighed. *Mmmm.* With lovely firm lips, and a commanding presence – he was the best male eye candy, *ever*. Too bad that he never smiled. Kelly, in her secret heart of hearts, would love to be the one to make him smile. He'd have a sexy smile.

"Oh, I think this scene was impromptu," Rosslyn said.

"Woo hoo!" Kelly yipped, tossing her lip gloss back in her bag. "Well, finish up in here, girls. We don't want to miss *that*, do we?"

Chapter 4

Kelly's Crush

Why oh why do I have to be so fascinated by such an unattainable man? A seriously dangerous guy, who's into intense shit that I'm not into. Jeez, he scares the crap out of me.

She sighed and supposed it was most likely the combination of his 'bad-boy' allure, along with knowing that she'd never have him. Women often seemed to fall for unattainable guys. Maybe it was because it's 'safe' to do that. I mean, how badly can you get hurt, if you never even stood a chance with them?

As far as relationships go, hooking up with John was about as practical and likely as being asked out by a famous movie star. Having him as a fantasy lover was as close as she'd ever get to being with the super sexy Dom. Kelly wasn't the only woman in his fan club – she was one of many. However, her fascination for him bordered on obsession.

John Taylor, also known as 'Father John,' was a bit of a celebrity at The Basement, and he was seriously HOT. Word had it, that his membership fees were waived because of the crowds he drew, and the lessons he sometimes gave to less experienced Dom's.

Once every two weeks or so, he'd put on a public show for the guests of the club. John was not much older than Kelly, but the rumors that had spread about him were endless.

Some of the more popular rumors included that he'd 'lost his true love,' and that he really *had* 'once been a priest.' Many people assumed that he must be gay. John Taylor had gotten the strange nickname of, 'Father John' because his subs always seemed to confess to him after he'd skillfully tormented them into a blissful state of euphoria.

Then, just like a priest, John forgave them.

No one called him, Father John, to his face, of course, that was just the nickname that the club gossips called him. Although sometimes his subs used that title, during a scene. He didn't like the standard appellations of "master" or "sir," insisting that he simply be called his given name, John.

Other than the fact that everything about the man, from his voice, to his entire persona, screamed 'Dominant,' he also had a flawless, sculpted body. John exuded masculine power and control with every fiber of his being. He had a compelling allure. A magnetism that affected her and drew her to him.

Something about John Taylor just made Kelly want to go to her knees before him, and kiss his feet – as well as any other places he'd allow. What the hell was that about?

It was so unfair! He was broad shouldered, with cut abs, narrow hips, a great ass, and was male model good looking. The man was perfect, well, at least externally. He defined alpha male perfection, and was easily the sexiest and most desirable hottie that she'd ever seen.

The one of the most interesting and well-established facts was that Father John never had sex with any of his subs, male or female. He'd never even let them go down on him! During a scene, he was the giver, never the receiver. Although he was responsible for his subs' countless orgasms, he'd never climaxed with anyone.

Was he gay, hetero or bi? Whatever he got from his scenes, it sure wasn't sex. The man was such a mystery. No one knew anything concrete about him, really, outside of what they'd observed in the club.

In fact, no one at The Basement had ever seen the man's penis. Although it did not go unnoticed, that the outline of a long, thick bulge in his black leather pants could be observed, virtually whenever he was in the club.

Clean shaven, no visible tattoos or piercings, and no sex. Despite the very naughty, sadistic kink that he engaged in, Father John seemed as pure as freshly fallen snow. The man didn't even kiss anyone! Chaste, almost fatherly pecks on the forehead or cheek were all he'd ever given, and these were only to encourage or coax some poor, suffering sub to accept even more pain.

Kelly sighed. She'd fantasized about the sexy Dom all the time, but she'd never have the nerve to approach him or scene with him. It was unfortunate, but John Taylor liked dispensing pain, and other than a sexually inflaming spanking, Kelly wasn't into that. The intensity and severity of the hurt that he delivered went away beyond what she was into. Frankly, it scared her.

"He's working over *two* subs at the same time, a man and a woman." Gina gleefully informed her.

"No shit? With his bullwhip?" Kelly asked.

Gina snorted. "He hasn't gotten to that yet, but I'm sure he will. Man, I'm sooo never going to go there."

Both Kelly and Gina looked questioningly at Rosslyn, the oldest and most experienced of the group.

"C'mon Rosslyn, you *went* there with Father John," Kelly said, curious beyond words, and more than a little bit jealous of her older and more courageous friend. "He topped you once, not too long ago. What was it like?"

Rosslyn's thin shapely blonde brows drew down, making a serious little crease in her forehead, as her brows furrowed. "You two have asked me that before, and I still can't tell you. It was indescribable. Sorry, but how can I explain it? There's nothing else to compare it to, I guess."

"Did it hurt?" Kelly asked.

"Fuck, yes! Like the fires of hell. I told you that already."

Kelly bit her lower lip, barely able to imagine the experience. "But did you enjoy it? Was it good? Was it worth it?"

"Yes."

"Would you do it again?" she asked.

"Yes, if he asked me. It's impossible to say 'no' to John Taylor," Rosslyn said quietly. Kelly was amazed to realize that the usually open and outgoing submissive was almost shy when it came to talking about Father John. This was obviously a subject that was close to her heart. It meant something to her.

"How about marks? Did you get any scars from that whip of his?" Gina asked.

"Nope, not a one. The man's a skilled professional."

"You know," Gina said, pensively. "I haven't met a sub yet, who didn't rave about their time spent with Father John. How does he do it? He hurts people. I mean, he really tortures them, and yet they love him for it."

Rosslyn sighed. "The man doesn't kiss, he doesn't fuck, and he won't even let a poor, desperate sub go down on him. He says very little, and that deep seductive, well-educated voice of his, even on its own, is more than enough to make a girl orgasm, I swear. Oh, speaking of swearing, he never swears either. Can you believe that? "

"Really?" Kelly said, astonished by the hypnotic magnetism that the man seemed to have over the entire population of The Basement. Even older, more experienced Dom's were in awe of his skills. He was captivating to everyone, regardless of their sex, age, or experience. His allure held no bounds

"Oh, for sure. The guy's a perfect gentleman, too," Rosslyn said. "He's always unattainably reserved, formal and polite, throughout an entire scene. He's never mean, and isn't into humiliation. He's respectful, at all times. I think he has a high opinion of his subs. To John Taylor, pain isn't about punishment."

Rosslyn's eyes clouded for a moment, and her lips tugged up with what looked to be a joyous memory. "It's a reward."

She pulled a compact out of her clutch, and began to apply its contents, in front of the mirror. "He made me feel cherished." She looked meaningfully at their reflections in the mirror. "It was as if I was the only person in the entire world to him. Father John's touch – his few heartfelt words of praise or appreciation – it was like nothing I've ever experienced. He treated my submission like it was a priceless gift that he treasured."

Shutting her compact, Rosslyn turned back to Gina and Kelly. "It was all about me – the entire scene, every part of it. I've been topped hundreds of times, but I've honestly never had anyone be so aware and totally focused entirely on me. I think his goal was to bring me to sexual release and spiritual bliss."

Rosslyn swallowed and it sounded loud in the hushed, empty bathroom. "He did it, too," she added in a soft, reverent tone.

Kelly remained quiet, silenced by the heartfelt devotion that Rosslyn conveyed towards Father John. Gina didn't seem to have anything to say, either. They both just gazed silently at their friend, in awe of her experience.

Rosslyn stared at a blank wall for a long moment. Kelly could see that her thoughts were far away. "I flew somewhere with him," Rosslyn said, and her voice took on a transcendental, dream-like quality. "To a place I've never been before. Or since. The entire experience was incredible. Life changing."

Kelly mentally shook herself. She snapped out of her stare, and gave a snort, breaking the charged atmosphere. "Yeah, well. As amazing as that sounds, I don't think I want to go anywhere that involves enduring that bullwhip of his."

Rosslyn smiled. "Father John can also read minds. Honestly. He knows exactly what a sub is thinking."

"Really? So, did you confess anything to him?" Kelly asked.

Both girls stared at their friend, as Rosslyn's cheeks reddened. Finally she drew in a deep breath. "Yes. I told that man more about myself than anyone on this earth knows. He's a magnet for secrets. It's impossible to hide anything from him. But he made me feel happy, and even honored, to confide in him. He's probably fifteen years younger than I am, but I'm shy and seriously horny around him, even now, weeks after our session. Go figure. John Taylor is the ultimate Dom. I had the most amazing orgasms I've ever had in my entire life with that man..."

"But?" Kelly asked. "I'm sensing a 'but' in there, somewhere."

Rosslyn shrugged and gave them both an ironic, crooked grin. "But I just wish he'd fucked me."

Chapter 5

The Basement

Kelly loved the Dungeon atmosphere in The Basement, which was enhanced by a mix of murmuring voices, laughter, the crack of whips, floods of floggers and pulse pounding music. This moody tapestry of sounds was occasionally enhanced by moans and orgasmic shrieks.

Gina had a Dom for the evening, so she returned to him, but Rosslyn and Kelly went up to the sub gallery together. The sub area was cool. It had a safe feeling to it, serving as a 'time out,' place of sorts. It was a little raised up from the ground floor, so Doms and Subs could check each other out from a distance.

The gallery was close enough to the action that almost everything could be easily observed. There were three roped-off play areas in the main room, near the bar. Complex specialty furniture that catered to various kinks, including spanking benches and crosses, were placed there for public use.

Hooks, chains, and eyebolts were everywhere. The Basement offered a wide variety of options to cater to and happily satisfy everyone. There was a mix of every kind of kink imaginable.

Kelly could spend the entire night just watching from the sub's gallery, and in fact, she often had. Enjoying the shows and marveling at the costumes, characters and outfits people wore was all part of the fun.

From the gallery, she could participate in the festivities from the sidelines, socialize with her fellow subs, or just sit back and watch the floor show as it unfolded before her eyes. There were different levels of appreciation, to entice her during her visits to the club. So much appealed to her, depending on her mood.

Nearby, were coffee tables and seating areas. Wrought iron sconces with realistic looking flickering electric lights were arranged in an eye pleasing manner around the walls, adding to the dungeon atmosphere. Numerous places to sit, including stools, chairs, loveseats and sofas were scattered carelessly, but with artistic flare.

The bar usually had a few people gathered around, and both male and female bartenders kept everyone happy. Subs sat at their Doms' feet. Mistresses and Masters paraded their half-naked male or female subs around, on display.

It was all yummy and erotic to Kelly. While everyone was fun to look at, she much preferred watching the men. What was not to love about a beautiful male body?

"I'm glad I'm a sub," Kelly said to Rosslyn, while seated on a comfortable couch. "I think being a sub is so much fun. And I don't get why people think it's demeaning. I mean, everything's really geared to the sub's side, in my opinion. They have all of the power and most of the pleasure, as far as I can tell."

"Is that so?" Rosslyn asked skeptically, her blonde bob haircut bounced, as she leaned against the balcony railing.

"No, seriously," Kelly said, speaking loudly, to be heard over the sounds of music and people laughing and talking. Typical for Saturday night, the place was packed.

She continued, "The Dom comes to me, and I get to say *yes* or *no*. I have a safe word and I don't have to do anything I don't want to do. If the Dom doesn't please me, I can say, *'see-ya-later-bye.'* As far as I can tell, I have all the power in the relationship."

Rosslyn laughed. "Out of the mouths of babes. So true, yet so *not* true." Her expression changed. Her eyes became distant, as if she'd suddenly been transported far, far, away, to another time.

"You won't sing that tune anymore if you ever really fall for someone." An odd smile curled Rosslyn's lips, and her voice softened. "You'll see. There's nothing you won't do for your Dom, then. You'll want to surrender any power you have completely, and let him do anything – just to see his approving smile."

"Anything? Really?" Kelly asked.

Rosslyn gave a rueful snort, snapping back into the present. "Yes! And I hope I'm there to see it. You'll have no control in *that* scary roller coaster ride. Haven't you ever been in love?"

Kelly wrinkled her nose up in distaste. "You mean that stupid, insane, sickly infatuation that people get when they can't eat and can't sleep because they can only think of *him?*"

Rosslyn laughed. "Yep! That's the one."

Kelly looked away, and felt her traitorous cheeks heat. Her stupid, pale complexion couldn't hide anything. The way she flushed bright red, no one needed to have Father John's impressive intuitive and observational skills to read her. She was virtually an open book, and she hated that about herself. Her emotions were on display for anyone who cared to look at her.

"Oh my, God!" Rosslyn laughed, shocked by her noticeable flush. "Are you in love?"

"No," Kelly said irritably.

Rosslyn sat down next to Kelly on the couch. "C'mon, give it up, girlfriend. Something caused that pale skin of yours to turn scarlet. Lord, girl, your face and neck, and even your breasts are red. Damn! Does that blush go all the way down, covering your entire body? I've never seen anything like it."

Kelly sighed. "Yes, it does. It's soooo humiliating, whenever I get embarrassed! It's like one of those feedback-loops, you know? The more embarrassed I am, the redder I get. Then I become even more self-conscious and embarrassed from my bright red complexion, which only causes me to blush worse, and so on. I feel like a freakin' neon sign of humiliation flashing, 'look at me! I'm embarrassed!' It's truly tragic."

"Well, I like it," Rosslyn snickered. "It's kind of cute. Sweet, actually. But don't think you're going to distract me from the more important issue, girl. Give. Who's the lucky guy?"

"It's really nothing," Kelly assured her. "It's just that I've got a silly crush on Father John."

Rosslyn exclaimed loudly with a rude word, a snicker, a giggle, and then she really started laughing. Kelly ignored her and just kept talking. She really needed to unburden herself, and finally get this off of her, currently bright red chest.

"There's just something about him that's gotten under my skin," Kelly said. "Actually it's *everything* about him. He intrigues me."

Agitated, and unable to hold still, Kelly stood up and began pacing. "I want to know more about him. I want to touch him, kiss him, and make him smile. Just the thought of him gives me butterflies in my stomach, and makes me feel kind of giddy. I feel like a giggly, teenage, schoolgirl. "

She stopped and turned, meeting Rosslyn's eyes. "Have you ever had that before?"

Rosslyn nodded. "Sure."

Kelly frowned and shook her head. "I can't control it. Just thinking of him makes me wet. When I see him, I think of sex – hot, sheet ripping, back scratching, bed biting sex. I'll never act on it, because I just don't like pain and frankly, he intimidates the hell out of me."

She shrugged. "He's probably gay, anyway. So it's pretty much a big joke that my mind is playing on me. Really. It's an exercise in futility. I'm like a freakin' hamster on one of those wheels. I run and run and get nowhere. Maybe that's why I'm so obsessed with him, because I know, deep down, that I could never have him. But I swear, I can't get him out of my mind."

Rosslyn shook her head sympathetically, and Kelly knew her friend totally understood. Rubbing her face, she expelled a deep breath and said, "You know what? John Taylor's driving me crazy."

Chapter 6

'Triple F factor

Rosslyn patted Kelly's arm and tsked pityingly. "In love with Father John? Well, you and every other sub in this place is, too, hon, including me. Why? Who can say? It's just not fair. Father John oozes the 'Triple F factor,' crushing and breaking the heart of every woman who comes near him. The man's beyond everybody's reach. He's untouchable, but he's also utterly captivating, you know what I mean?"

"Triple F?" Kelly asked.

"Yeah. You know, 'The Fatal Female Flaw.' It's when ordinarily sensible women fall madly in love with an unattainable man who can't, or won't, love them back. I also call it the Triple Fucked Factor. "

Kelly let out a bark of laughter. *Yep, that's me*, she thought. *I've got an incurable case of Triple F for Father John. It's madness. I simply can't seem to think about or want anyone else.*

A couple of Dom's climbed the few stairs, coming up into the sub area together. Master Ron was a thirty something, lighthearted Dom, who was really good fun. Kelly had played with him before. With him, was Master T, an older, salt and pepper haired man, who was solidly muscular, and a very experienced Dom.

Master T's deep blue eyes were locked on Rosslyn. They radiated pure male power, as well as a rather disconcerting level of intense heat. Rosslyn immediately looked down. Kelly watched in amazement, as it was apparently Rosslyn's turn to display a tinge of red in her cheeks.

Not a word was said, but Rosslyn instantly held her arms out toward Master T, her wrists together, palms up, in submissive obedience. Kelly saw that her hands trembled slightly.

Master T secured her wrists with the colorful tie the Club provided, capturing her, and indicating that she was taken. The large man effortlessly pulled her to her feet. Without a sound, Rosslyn stood up in front of him, her eyes cast downward. Then both Master T and Rosslyn left together, her bound wrists firmly grasped in one of his large hands. Her eyes remained meekly looking down, as they walked past Kelly and left the subs area.

Kelly looked up at Master Ron, the man who'd stayed behind with her. Their gazes met, and they exchanged wide eyes, head shakes, and knowing smiles.

"My, oh, my," Kelly said, making a show of fanning herself. "That was a hot little interlude. I swear, I could see steam rising off of that man."

"You got that right," Ron said. "You could cut the sexual heat with a knife. Looks like Rosslyn has a big night ahead of her."

"Tell me about it."

"Hey Kelly," Master Ron said. "Are you wanting to be topped tonight?"

She grinned and then put her index finger to her lips in a pensive manner, teasing him. "You mean with *you*? I don't know, Master Ron," she said playfully, her voice a sultry purr. "Do you think if I hang around up here, I might get a better offer?"

He laughed out loud, apparently not surprised or even disturbed by her comment. "Jesus Kelly, you're so much fun. Why don't we just stay together for a while? We could explore the scene, enjoy each other, and have some laughs. I swear, I honestly think I could fall in love with you."

Kelly tapped her lips again. "Hmmm. Well, you do give a good spanking," she said, pretending to be undecided, yet considering the matter.

"Yeah?" Ron asked. He bent closer, and his voice lowered,, as his expression became a bit more serious and intense. "That's good, because I feel like giving someone a good spanking tonight. And I'm expecting that whoever I discipline will climax from it as hard and fast as a speeding train."

Kelly giggled. "Like a train?"

"Don't laugh," he said. "That's what it seemed like to me when you came the last time we were together. Christ, it was amazing. You blew my mind."

"It *was* amazing," she said, and the familiar feel of lust rolled through her, at the memory. Her eyes met his with a smile, as they both recalled the last time they played together.

She sighed, well aware that the sweet, older Dom had a bit of a crush on her. "I really don't know, Master Ron. I guess, I'm fickle. You're perfect, you know," she added looking him up and down.

He was big, blond, and seriously cute. Unlike her white skin, Ron could actually tan. He was a cheerful guy who was an attentive lover with a toothpaste ad smile. Ron was a lot of fun, and he wasn't one of those Dom's who made her look down or remain silent all the time. Kelly preferred to look at a man and to be able to talk freely, at least while there was no domination sex going on.

For a moment, she imagined how well he'd fit in with her life and her family. They'd love him. Images of marriage, children, and an easy-going life together rolled out in front of her. It actually wasn't a bad vision of one possible future that she could choose. Life would be fun with Ron. Pleasant, with lots of laughter, and even great sex, but…

So where was that *thing?* That euphoric rush of "wow factor" that was so elemental in a real love affair? Because that rush was the lightning bolt that she was looking for so desperately, being the idiot that she was.

Kelly knew that Ron was the perfect match for her. They were compatible in so many ways. They had a similar sense of humor, laughed often, and usually at the same jokes. They chatted together happily about almost any topic, had compatible sexual kinks, had like-minded temperaments, and very similar personalities. So, why couldn't her stupid heart just be practical and fall in love with him?

The answer was simple. Incredibly stupid, but simple.

Ron wasn't Father John.

I'm such a bitch! I don't deserve Ron. He needs someone who can love him and appreciate them for who he is. He's so damn nice. Maybe too nice? But love is just something that I can't give him. I'm too hung up on a guy who doesn't even know I exist! Argh!

"Never mind," Ron said with forced composure. "I'll grow on you. Give it some time. But hey, want to play tonight? I think you've been through everyone else around here."

She giggled. "What a thing to say! Not *everyone*. And anyway, you're one to talk." She put her hands out for him to bind her wrists and stood up. "Sure. Let's go see what you got, big boy," she said with a sexy lilt to her voice as she eyed him up and down again, part jest, part genuine sexual interest.

"Oh, but hey," Kelly said. "Can we go by, and check out Father John, first? He's apparently beating the crap out of a couple of subs tonight, and I want to watch for a bit. The man's really creative in his tortures."

Ron crossed his arms and studied her for a moment, in a considering manner. There was an odd mixture of curiosity and apprehension in his expression. "Would you want anyone to get that creative with you?"

"Hell no!"

Utterly in tune with each other, they both laughed, and wandered off together, to watch Father John at work.

Chapter 7

The Scene

Kelly strode through the crowded main room of The Basement, side by side with Master Ron, while he held her bound wrists in one firm hand. As she was passing a woman who had an intricate scarification of the Virgin Mary that covered her entire, fully exposed back, Kelly stopped in her tracks to look at it, stunned.

Ron was forced to pause, as well, since he was holding her wrists. They both stared at the woman's receding figure, as she continued walking away from them.

"Wow," Kelly said, in awe of the scars that graced the woman's body. The details and clarity of the design were astounding. A talented professional had used her flesh as a canvas, combining pain with beauty, to create an aesthetic work of art.

"Yep," Master Ron added. "That's some serious body artwork, right there.

"It's quite beautiful, but soooo not for me," Kelly said with a laugh, and Ron agreed wholeheartedly.

They sped up, trying to reach Father John's scene as soon as possible, knowing that they'd already missed some of the show. But the crowd that had gathered to watch, was too dense for them to be able to see what was going on behind the roped off area.

Ron jumped up onto a nearby coffee table and pulled Kelly up to stand next to him. It was solidly built, like something from a peasant's hut in the twelve-hundreds. It was made of heavy wood that was at least six inches thick, with six inch thick table ends, rather than legs.

"Man, they have to do something about this," Kelly said. "Everyone wants to watch that man during a scene. They need to rearrange things to accommodate more people, so that everyone can see what's going on."

It was then, from their higher vantage point, that they noticed a huge flat screen on the wall right past the bar. A number of other people had collected there, all drinking while watching the extremely popular event unfold before them. Father John's efforts were being projected upon the big screen.

"Now *that's* more like it," Ron said, and hopped down. He turned and grasped Kelly around her waist, picked her up, and set her down on the floor beside him.

"That's new," she said, with a broad grin. "Excellent."

Ron and Kelly walked closer. There, they met up with another Dom/sub couple who were clearly captivated, both of them watching the show on the big screen.

Kelly looked silently, but imploringly, at Master Ron. It violated a number of taboos and rules, for a sub to talk any old time she wanted. She could speak to a Dom other than her own, or to his sub, while on the club floor. This rule was a challenge for Kelly, who was a bit of a chatty, social butterfly. However, having made this mistake previously, she'd learned her lesson. While she was still a little unsure of the correct protocol, now she tended to keep her mouth shut and let her Dom talk for her.

Ron smiled at her, knowing exactly what she wanted from him. He said to the other Dom, "We've missed it. What's happened so far?

Ron is really great, Kelly mused. *Look at him, going out of his way to please me, even when it has nothing to do with sex. You just gotta love that guy! Yeah right. If only I could love him. And why can't I? Man, I'm such a picky, self-destructive, bitch.*

The Dom had his arm around his sub, idly caressing one of her large but firm breasts, and occasionally pulling her nipple ring. "Well, he's finished with the woman. She left the scene and is out back. Her own Dom is attending to her after care. Father John was showing him a few interesting tricks. I think she must have been allowed to climax four or five times, the last one was rather spectacular. It happened when that bullwhip of his managed to flick right on the woman's clitoris."

"Honestly? Directly on her clit? Ouch," Ron said, wincing slightly.

"I swear, I wouldn't have believed it myself, if I hadn't seen it with my own eyes. He talked to her first. Of course, no one knows what he said, but apparently she was up for it. When the whip struck her clit, the woman's body jerked violently. It was as if she'd been hit with a hundred and twenty volts. She screamed like she was on fire. I couldn't see the color of her eyes anymore, her pupils were *that* dilated. Her hips pumped like a piston, so hard and fast, when she came. It looked like she was hopped up on amphetamines or something. It was unreal."

"I wish I'd seen that," Ron murmured.

"I think she passed out right after she came. She was carried away by her Dom, dead to the world. Yep, that little sub came harder than I ever knew anyone could come, just like a runaway train."

Wide-eyed, she and Ron exchanged a look.

Trains again! Kelly thought, barely curbing an overwhelming impulse to giggle. While Ron obviously attempted to maintain his outward composure in front of the other Dom, she could see that his eyes were bright with amusement.

"Really?" Master Ron asked. "Like a train, you say?" he added, encouraging the man with a tongue in cheek smirk.

Hiding her smile with a hand over her mouth, Kelly looked down at the floor to stop herself from laughing out loud. She faked a little cough, and glanced up to see Master Ron, was also struggling to hold back his laughter. Why couldn't she just fall in love with Ron? He's so much fun. They were so in sync. Why must she have this impossible attraction to a serious, dark, super scary guy like John Taylor? A man she'd never seen smile, or laugh.

Ron felt more like a *friends-with-benefits* type of arrangement, for her, at least. They were good buddies who could hang out, have fun and enjoy great sex. It wouldn't be fair to Ron, or herself, to try to go through the motions, and pretend that she could offer him anything more than what they had together. He was lovable, but for some reason, she just wasn't 'into' him enough. Not in the way that she needed from the man in her life, and not in the way Ron felt about her.

She hid an internal derisive snort. *Because I'm into Father John, the sadist. Silly me. If only I could choose who I fell in love with, I'd happily have a crush on Ron.* Until then, Kelly wanted it all. She wanted to be swept away by love, passion, and the intensity of her feelings. Just like she was by her unrequited, obsessive longing for John Taylor.

"Oh yeah," the unfamiliar Dom continued speaking, "but she'd been flying in the zone for some time, anyway. That's one experience that little sub will never forget. "

"What about this guy he's working on now?" Ron asked.

"Oh, you arrived just in time for the finale."

Ron studied the screen. "How can you tell?"

The Dom laughed. "This isn't my first party, you know. Father John had his sub on the X frame for some time. Now, he has him in classic strappado bondage. No one can maintain that sort of binding for long, especially while being tormented."

Kelly saw the unfamiliar Dom's shorter sub grin up at him at that comment, while he playfully ruffled her short, bottle bright red hair. There was a subtle communication, and sexy energy between the two of them. It was because of his tormented comment. Kelly smiled. His sub was probably looking forward to experiencing a bit of sensual torture herself.

"Take my word for it. This is the finale," the Dom said. "Father John put him there because he's almost ready to reach the pinnacle of his scene."

Damn, Kelly thought. *It's almost over.*

She stared over at the big screen and her eyes locked on Father John's image. He was facing away from her, so Kelly was treated to a terrific view of him from behind. She studied his powerful shoulders, tight ass and muscular frame.

Yowza. Oh. My. God. That man is always so freakin' hot! But he's even more sizzling and intense, when he's working a scene. Kelly wondered what it would be like to have all of John Taylor's attention focused on *her. Wow. What a concept.*

A tiny whimper escaped from her.

That idea alone almost had her panting, and it caused a flood of moisture and heat to pool low in her belly and between her legs. A thrill of both delicious fear and intense sexual need rolled over her entire body.

Chapter 8

Angelic Smile

Kelly saw that the sub, who was the sole focus of Father John, had his arms bound behind his back. A rope ran from his full forearm cuffs, to a securing point on the ceiling. The man's arms were lifted until he'd been forced to bend forward. She knew that this particularly agonizing way of binding someone was called strappado bondage. The position was torturous in and of itself and couldn't be maintained safely, for too long. It would be an interesting balancing act for Father John.

A spreader bar kept the subs legs stretched widely apart, and a vibrating butt plug completed the picture. The man's cock was huge, dripping from extreme arousal. Usually he'd be wearing a condom, but management probably figured that it made a better show without one.

Kelly studied the scene intently. Numerous objects were carelessly strewn around on the floor nearby, after being used; paddles, floggers of different shapes and sizes, canes and riding crops. Man, Father John must've been really riled up tonight, because this guy was getting the works.

Her brow furrowed and she pursed her lips in thought. Maybe some of those objects had been used on the female sub, before she was carried away by her Dom. However, the fact that Father John had chosen two people to scene with was interesting.

Also, his performance was impromptu, when they were usually scheduled ahead of time. Scenes with Father John and his bullwhip always boosted attendance at the club, and drew the biggest crowds.

John's sub had vivid red welts distributed all over his body. Certain areas were more heavily concentrated with these marks, like on his chest, especially around his nipples, his upper and inner thighs, and buttocks. Those marks were clearly from the attentions of Father John's infamous and beloved bullwhip.

To think that anyone could be skilled enough with a whip, to be able to strike a clit. Wow. That was a true testament, to Father John's mastery. It was also a declaration of trust from the sub. Why would anyone allow that degree of potential pain and physical danger?

Kelly shut her eyes for a moment, because the answer was obvious. She could imagine herself going past her own limits for John, just from her insane longing to please him. She shook her head, reminding herself again, to keep far away from the fascinating but dangerous, Dom.

Sweat was dripping from the sub, his entire body was soaked, and he was breathing heavily. His upper torso rose and fell with each breath, and to his swollen cock throbbed visibly. How had he been able to prevent himself from climaxing after so much stimulation?

A close look at his face and expression showed that he was feeling no pain. His appearance was so at odds with his uncomfortably bound and battered body. She admired the sub's courage. But did she even *want* to be brave enough to go *there*? The man was blissed out, off somewhere in super sub space. Maybe even outer space.

Although Kelly was terrified, and even disturbed by this type of scene, at some level, she yearned to be in that man's place. What would it be like to be the sole focus of Father John's attention and care? A pang of jealousy went through her, because she wanted John Taylor so badly.

It always came down to this internal mental struggle, whenever she thought about her scary dream Dom. Although she thought about him all the time, and wanted him intensely, was he worth *that? Was anybody?*

Kelly's focus shifted to Father John's face, where she saw… *satisfaction!* The man was usually impassive and detached, so this obvious show of pleasure surprised her.

Father John's persona – in fact, everything about him, remained expressionless, calm and in control. His thoughts and emotions were nowhere near the surface, they seem to be buried completely. Mind you, it was difficult to meet his eyes. Maybe that was part of the problem. Was that why he was nearly impossible to read?

John approached his sub while holding his bullwhip. He lightly brushed the man's shoulder, resting his hand there. The sub responded like a newlywed lover, trembling with sublime ecstasy at only one small touch from his tormentor. John spoke to him, lifting three fingers, and the man nodded.

Father John stood back, and raised his arm and shoulder, then slammed the whip hard onto the floor.

"Crack!"

The sound was chilling. He did it once again, but this time, the tip lightly touched the sub's buttocks. The next time, it slammed into the butt plug, causing the man to jerk. On the third strike, Father John flicked the sub's left testicle – just a small kiss with the tip of the whip.

A red welt appeared instantly. The man's balls drew up as his entire body stiffened. He screamed. It was a bloodcurdling cry of pain – or pleasure – or both. Kelly wasn't exactly sure, but it was an animalistic shriek that really scared her. It sounded like the trumpets of Gabriel, a frightening portent, signifying the end of all things. Instinctively, she leaned into Master Ron for support.

The sub's cock began spurt like a fountain, as the man's hips bucked and thrust. The muscles of his back and buttocks rippled rhythmically while the man spewed – pulsing, copious strings of ejaculate onto the floor. The sub was crying, with a flood of tears trailing down his face. All the while, he kept sobbing and calling out, repeatedly, "Father! Father! Father!"

Father John moved quickly to the man, loosening the spreader bar so he could regain his balance. Then he lowered the tension on his arms, and unhooked his cuffs. While of average height, John was muscular and strong. With biceps bulging, he effortlessly picked up the larger, now boneless sub, tenderly carrying him in his arms, while looking down into the man's face.

Father John had slowly, with careful encouragement and consummate skill, brought his sub to a state of bliss. Despite the endorphins coursing through his system, and the mindless, transcendent ecstasy of sub space, the man was wholly conscious of his Dom. The sub's emotional response to him was transparent. The look on *his* face was easy to read: devotion, adoration, and even love.

Motionless, silent and entranced, Kelly stared.

Hundreds of people watched this extremely intimate moment between them. Many of the spectators had become quiet and still, just as she had. Due to the amount of people in the club however, there was movement, talking, laughing and discordant noises everywhere. Yet, the two men appeared to be unaware of anyone, or anything, but each other. To them, in this moment in time, they were the only people on earth.

Kelly felt extraordinarily drawn to the scene before her. The handsome young Dom of her dreams had always seemed to be so intimidating, dispassionate and implacable. Right now, he displayed an array of possible emotions, as he gazed at his sub. She could tell that he'd been affected by his sub's submission. She could see that he'd connected to the man he cradled in his arms.

Yet, unlike his sub, John was still not easy to read.

Kelly tried to interpret and comprehend, from his body language, what John was feeling right now. Protectiveness? Appreciation? Love? Whatever he felt, Kelly was stunned to recognize that it was *truly beautiful.* There was a palpable connection between the two men, a bond that couldn't be seen with one's eyes – yet anyone with even a drop of humanity, would recognize it.

Just being a witness to such a sacred joining, affected Kelly. She got caught up, transported by the beauty of such a connection. There was something thick in her throat, making it difficult to swallow. It choked her up, and touched her deeply.

Father John looked down at the sub in his arms. This man who'd willingly given him everything that he'd been capable of giving, and then he'd reached further, digging deeper, and given him even more. John's handsome face was serene, almost angelic. His lips curved infinitesimally into a subtle, blissful smile of contentment.

He is so beautiful, she thought.

Kelly had observed John every chance that she could. She tried to glean as much information about him as possible, from her covert observations. Until now, he'd never given Kelly the impression that he was a happy soul, at peace with himself. She'd never seen him smile before, but he did so now.

Was this Dom space? Was he experiencing his own endorphin rush from his physical and mental efforts during that long, intense scene? He hadn't experienced sexual release, but it didn't seem as if he needed anything more. He looked fully satiated.

Kelly couldn't hear Father John, but she saw him speak to the man in his arms. She wasn't a lip-reader, but she could swear that she saw him mouth the heartfelt words, "Thank you." And then he added what looked like, "… forgive you."

Had Father John said, "I forgive you?" Or had he named someone else, maybe even God, and said that whoever it was, "forgives you?"

Kelly's curiosity burned. It seemed important to know exactly what Father John had said. The man was surrounded by mystery and mystique. She had so many questions. She was dying to know so much. Her curiosity was overflowing. But she'd never have the courage to ask him anything.

Chapter 9

Close Call

In excellent spirits, Kelly left the ladies dressing area, shutting the door behind her. She smiled and said good night to the friendly guard, Tom. Not meeting her eyes, he looked a little sheepish as he said goodbye. Kelly assumed that he'd probably already finished all seven of the cookies she'd given him earlier.

Grinning, she got into the elevator that was already waiting. It had been a great night. Watching Father John transport his sub off to paradise had been awesome. After that, bondage play with Master Ron had been off-the-charts hot, and unusually satisfying. Of course, the mental and emotional foreplay from witnessing John's scene, hadn't hurt.

Alone in the elevator, she smiled to herself, as the doors started to slide shut.

Long, white, male fingers stopped the elevator doors from closing. Kelly immediately looked up... and then stopped breathing.

John Taylor, with unconscious, confident, animal grace, strode into the elevator like he owned the place. He looked so masculine, so dominant, and tough. The man was wearing his black leather Matrix-style trench coat, black leather pants and black swat boots. John's dark hair and eyes, combined with his Matrix look, reminded her of Keanu Reeves in that movie. Only Reeves, who Kelly considered to be an undeniable hottie, could never be as attractive to her as John Taylor was.

"Oh," Kelly said, thoughtlessly, reacting reflexively out of disbelief and shock. The current star of all of her fantasies had materialized unexpectedly, so up close and personal!

John nodded to her, and a zing of pulse-pounding lust went straight to her core. The man was seemingly oblivious of her consternation, while she could feel her traitorous pale cheeks heat with awkward discomfort. Kelly became aware, at that point, that she was openly gawking – staring stupidly at him, with her mouth open. Quickly, she shut it and looked away.

Holy Mother of God, she thought, as the elevator doors closed with finality. *I can't believe this! I never thought I'd be **this** close to him! I never thought I'd be alone with him. Yet, here he is, bigger than life. He's so close that I could reach out and touch him. We're alone. And "oh" was all I could say? Well, that and staring at him like a freakin' idiot with my mouth open. Man, I'm sooo lame! This is mortifying!*

Kelly kept her eyes trained to the front, a task that was difficult for her to achieve, much less maintain. She loved looking at John Taylor. When visiting The Basement, she did so as much as she could possibly contrive.

Somehow, her eyes automatically sought him out. The compulsion to look at him was almost beyond her control. Kelly stood perfectly still, eyes front, staring at the brushed metal doors. It like she was a flower, and he was the sun. Kelly wanted to turn toward him. His magnetic pull was so compelling and consistent.

The force is strong with this one, she thought whimsically, and restrained her desire to giggle hysterically.

Fascinated and incurably drawn to the hot Dom of her dreams, she'd always taken care to stay away from him, or to at least keep at a safe distance. It was a strange combination of behaviors and urges, at war with each other. Feasting her eyes on him whenever possible, yet still dodging him and hiding like a rabbit.

She was so conflicted. Avoiding him was like trying to escape a healthy, feral wolf. There was a natural desire to look at, and to even touch such a beautiful, wild animal. Yet, being so close to such a creature would be taking a stupid risk.

The man was dangerous, especially to her. What would she say if he came for her at the sub's gallery? Would she even have the ability to refuse him? How could she resist *him*? Kelly knew that she'd be as pliable as sculptor's clay in his hands.

She took a deep breath and bit the inside of her cheek. *Clay in his hands.* Even that simple thought made her instantly wet. Her brain went completely out of gear, shifting into 'neutral.' Or was it in 'park?'

Her mind flashed back to the fantasy he starred in, that she'd masturbated to, the night before. Kelly shut her eyes, unconsciously imagining the feel of John's kisses and his hard male body thrusting inside of her.

Mentally, she gave an internal curse, and thrust those unwanted images away. This was so stupid. None of this would ever happen. Kissing on the mouth and sex were both things John never did with anybody, male or female, as far as anyone at The Basement knew.

What was wrong with her? She was losing her mind. But the answer was obvious. *I'm alone in a tiny room with Father John!* Kelly wasn't sure if she was scared stiff or ecstatic, and both emotions battled with each other for supremacy inside her mind.

But damn, if the man didn't smell great. What was it? Sandalwood and healthy male sweat? She risked a glance at him in her peripheral vision.

Oh God! Kelly's hands went into fists as she suppressed a burning desire to touch him. John Taylor looked as if he might've had a shower, as his short straight hair was wet. Of course, it could just be sweat. Wielding a flogger or a bullwhip over a period of time was pretty damn physical. Kelly felt her heart speed up and nervously licked her lips.

Dark and dangerous, John Taylor was the kind of man that her mom always warned her about. Of course, Mom had no idea that Kelly was a sexual deviant. The thought of her mother finding out about her kinks cooled her ardor for a moment, as if she'd been dunked in cold water.

Of course, this sensible slap of reality couldn't last. Not with the guy she had an enormous crush on, standing right beside her, making every female hormone she had come to life and start singing with boundless, lustful, and procreative joy.

Not long after the elevator doors shut, the lifting mechanisms began to hum. Thankfully, the elevator began to move upwards. Just standing next to Father John, Kelly could swear that she could feel his male heat radiating an intense energy against her flesh. What was this irresistible pull that this man had? Nobody should have that much power over another, at least when they weren't on the verge of orgasm. Was it pheromones? Jeez Louise, even her legs felt weak. Couldn't this elevator hurry up?

Kelly didn't know how much more she could take. Being in this situation was wreaking havoc in her mind and body. It was intense. Too intense. Once this elevator stopped on the ground floor she'd make a quick exit and escape the inexplicable masculine allure of Father John.

Or at least, that was what she thought would happen.

She couldn't have been more wrong.

Chapter 10

Disaster

The overhead light flickered. Then suddenly, all light was extinguished, as the elevator jolted to a stop, falling with a frightening jerk.

The darkness was complete.

Kelly froze to utter stillness, as if she was sculpted of ice. A familiar wave of nauseous fear flowed through her. Instantly, her skin dampened into a cold, cold sweat.

Just then, a number of things happened, all at once, in an instant of mind-numbing insanity.

Kelly felt a heavy pressure in her chest. Her heart seemed to skip a beat, no – it skipped a number of beats, or perhaps stopped altogether. After that, her heart sprinted without pause – it fluttered in her chest like hummingbird wings. She felt her racing pulse pounding in her neck and head. It was as if a living thing was hammering within her body, trying to get out.

She was confined in a small, dark place. Imprisoned. *Trapped!* And she'd been trapped like this before. Suddenly dizzy, and incredibly faint, Kelly felt as if there wasn't enough air in the small, dark room.

I can't breathe! I've got to get out of here!

Primal, animalistic panic caused a frenzied explosion of terror from deep inside her. Kelly simply couldn't breathe! She couldn't breathe! Her concept of time altered. A minute became a second. A second became an hour. Kelly suffered unspeakable horror, and her torment seemed to last a lifetime. She was caught in a nightmare, engulfed by dread.

A weird sense of detachment took over, and her ears rang. She heard a terrifying, blood curdling scream, then, from somewhere far away. It was a sound that she'd imagine someone might make if they were going to die, or maybe the sound of someone actually dying.

Seemingly out of nowhere, her face was slapped *hard,* once, then twice. It was then that she realized an astonishing fact. *Oh,* she observed with an oddly blank indifference. *It's me. I'm the one who's screaming.*

"Kelly? Kelly! You will speak to me *now,*" a demanding male voice said.

She was too confused to make sense of anything. It was pitch black. There was screaming, her body was on shutdown, and she couldn't breathe. Then there was that compelling voice. The sound of those word echoed sternly through her head, yet they weren't combining into something that had any meaning. What was happening?

She felt her arm wrenched backwards in a bone breaking twist, which slammed her up against the wall, face first. It really hurt! Then strong fingers wrapped around her neck. It came to her then, in a flash of shock and awareness.

John! Oh my, God. Father John! He's here. Father John, the sadist, is here. He's hurting me!

It was still dark, and she was still trapped, but this new terror commanded her attention. Her arm was painfully twisted behind her back, her face pressed against cool metal. A strong hand was around her neck, taking control. Kelly couldn't move. This new impending danger returned her mind to the present.

"Oh," she sputtered and gasped breathlessly, "I'm sorry."

"Good girl," John said dispassionately. He tightened his fingers on her throat, his thumb pressing firmly against her jugular. She could feel the rapid hammering beat of her own pulse against his thumb. Dread rolled through her. Her entire body shook uncontrollably.

What is he doing? Jesus, is Father John going to strangle me?

"Kelly," he said softly into her ear, with his long heated torso pressed firmly up against her back. "Are you more afraid of this small, dark room, or of me?"

The tone of his voice frightened her. He sounded as if he was barely holding back a mountain of restrained violence. Kelly could feel the energy of it, and she had no desire to upset him and feel his wrath. Her mind and body were caught up in a stunned daze. Being trapped in the dark scared her. Being trapped with him scared her even more.

Her already incapacitating fear reached a whole new level. Confused and afraid, she opened her mouth, but no words came out. She couldn't speak, much less frame a sentence.

"Answer me, now," he snapped, in a stern voice. Lost and confused as she was, Kelly, was unable to defy that dominant ring of command.

"You…you, Sir," she stammered. "I'm more afraid of you." Her hands trembled, so she closed them into tight fists.

"Good girl, that's correct," he said in a deceptively mild tone. Apparently he'd been mollified by her capitulation. "I'm much more dangerous, I can assure you. You will call me, John. You're going to sit down here, on my lap."

Sit, yes, she thought, because she seemed to have lost all of the strength in her legs. One of his hard, strong arms slid around her, for support. Like a rag doll, she collapsed into him, letting John's self-assured, powerful arms position her as he desired. They slid to the floor together, and then she was sitting across his hips and thighs, exactly as he wanted.

Her mouth felt as dry as sand. Kelly swallowed, and felt her throat muscles work underneath the strong grip of his fingers. Her arm throbbed from being twisted behind her back, and her face stung from those slaps. The room was still dark, and airless. Yet all of her attention was fixed on Father John, and what he might do next.

He was so much stronger than she was, it would be a simple task for him to throttle the life out of her. Stretched out across John's lap, he had Kelly's arms behind her back. Both of her slim wrists were tightly confined by one large, strong male hand. His other hand moved from her neck, to press her head firmly against his chest.

The man radiated a comforting heat – it felt incredible! Kelly had no idea, until that moment that she'd been shaking with cold. She became aware of his leather trench coat, as he folded it around her. In the back of her mind, she realized that John must've taken it off, at some point. It was warm and smelled so good. It smelled like him. Being cocooned in his jacket, soothed her frazzled nerves. But when had he taken it off?

"You're hyperventilating," he said, in a tone that was utterly devoid of compassion, or any other emotion, for that matter. "Slow your breathing down, Kelly, or I'll slow it down for you."

His compelling threat pushed into her mind, forcing her brain to wake up and start working. *Shit,* she thought wildly. *Will he choke me again?* Warm male fingers brushed along her throat, a potent reminder of her vulnerability, and his total power over her. She suddenly discovered that she could control her breathing.

"That's right. Good girl," he said in a soothing, seductive whisper. "Now, listen to me. Can you hear my heart beat?"

With her ear held firmly against his chest, she could hear it when she focused. "Yes," she whispered. It was slow and quite loud, pounding away with vitality and health, in a steady, even rhythm.

"Pay attention now, Kelly. I want you to count the beats for me. Count them out loud. Do you understand?"

"Yes." There wasn't much that Kelly thought she could manage, in her current witless state, but counting was certainly one of them. *Oh, okay, I can do that,* she thought, unaccountably pleased. She began, "One, two, three, four...."

When she'd counted to a hundred and eighty he said, "Stop now, Kelly."

She stopped counting and took a deep breath. Her anxiety level was still off the charts, but she felt much more in control of herself. John stroked her hair, and slowly traced her eyebrows, nose, cheeks and lips. His warm fingers were both gentle and calming.

"You've done very well," he said, in a warm and steady voice.

The ridiculous sense of joy that she felt in response to his praise, was beyond anything. That feeling alone warmed her.

"I'm going to ask you some questions now, and you will answer, yes or no. Just *yes* or *no*. Do you understand, Kelly?"

"Yes."

"Good. Was there an event in your past, where you were trapped in the dark?"

"Yes."

"It was when you were a child?"

"Yes."

"And you feared for your life?"

"Oh, God. Yes," she said, as vicious, frightening images and emotions bubbled up from somewhere deep within her mind. Evil memories began spewing forth, as fierce and as hot as burning lava. Without making any conscious decision to speak, words tumbled out of her, pouring from her, in a frantic rush, "It was so terrible! You see, I was playing hide and seek…"

Kelly's speech cut off abruptly as John grabbed her breast, squeezed and twisted it *hard*. She gasped and cried out with the sudden pain of it. Yet it shocked her into silence. The terrible memories that had begun to boil up into her mind disappeared, just as fast as they'd entered her consciousness.

"Stop, Kelly," he admonished, with a final painful pinch to her nipple. "I told you to answer yes or no. Do you remember?"

"Yes," she replied. "Sorry, John." Her voice sounded pitifully meek and frightened, even to her own ears.

"Very good, Kelly. Here and now is not the time to speak of childhood fears. You're in shock. This is clearly a case of Post Traumatic Stress Disorder. Now that I know what's going on, we can begin to manage it."

"Oh!" she said. Although he'd scared her, and caused her physical pain, she really appreciated that he'd made those unbearable memories go away. The man was so confident, and he'd said that he could manage it.

Thank God! Kelly expelled a deep breath of relief. If anyone could help her, Father John could.

"Drink this," he advised, and held a flask up to her lips. It tasted sweet and heady. She took a long drink, and then another. It went down warmly, in a comforting wave of heat that quickly spread throughout her chilled body. Kelly could almost feel John smiling in the dark, as she made no attempt to hide the allure that the drink held for her.

There'd been gossip around The Basement, that Father John had his own tonic that he'd use after he'd tortured some poor bastard into a mindless state of euphoric ecstasy. That must be what she was drinking, and Kelly had to admit that it really helped.

"What is this?" she asked, swallowing more.

"It's a mixture of my own, but mainly brandy. It's rejuvenating after a shock, I find. Better?" he asked.

"Much better. Thank you," she choked. She was better, but she still had a long way to go, to be back to normal again. She was still completely freaked out. She could barely wrap her mind around the fact that was she was sitting on Father John's lap. She was trapped with him, in a small metal box, in complete darkness.

For the moment, just barely, she was able to keep her mind numbing panic in check. Yet, hysteria continued to build within her, and her body continued to twitch and shake in occasional, uncontrollable spasms. It was as if intermittent gun fire sporadically slammed into her flesh. Her mind and thoughts were reeling.

John's fingertips rested lightly against the pulse in her neck, and she realized that he was counting the beats of her heart.

Somehow, having his one hand binding her arms together behind her, and the other holding her firmly against him, also had a steadying effect on her. It was strange to feel so safe and so cared for in his powerful embrace. Especially, when just a short time earlier, she'd thought he'd intended to strangle her.

Father John, the sadist, scared the hell out of her. But in addition to his ability to deliver extreme amounts of pain, he could also be kind, it seemed. She'd seen a glimpse of this part of him earlier, when he'd been carrying his sub away, after their scene. It felt amazing to be the focus of his care and attention.

A light suddenly glowed from John's cellphone, as he called 911. When the operator answered, he calmly reported the malfunctioning elevator, where they were, and their circumstances. Their situation didn't seem to bother John in the least. Did anything stress him out?

When he put his phone away, Kelly whispered, "Do you think we'll be trapped in here much longer? Did they say when they'd get here?" She knew that her unsteady, quavering voice betrayed her panic. Father John was holding her in his lap, and taking control during a very stressful time.

Kelly had a huge crush on this man. From the moment she'd first set her eyes on him, during her initial visit to The Basement, Kelly had longed to be held in John's arms. But she didn't want to be in his arms like *this*. Not here, trapped in a tiny, airless box that was shrouded in darkness, as black as a tomb! This was wrong. So wrong!

"They're sending someone, Kelly. I suspect that there's a power outage of some sort, something severe enough for the backup generators to also be off line. Or perhaps, some safety protocol has kicked in. Either way, we may be stuck here for some time."

Kelly shuddered, as a wave of dread rolled through her at the thought of being trapped, unable to get out of this nightmare. The darkness surrounding them pressed thickly in on her, seeming to slam against her body with a physical force. She trembled and shook with renewed force, as she began to feel that creeping dread of not being able to get enough air in her lungs.

Animal panic was gathering within her once again, ready to overtake her mind and body. She fought to control it.

"You...you'd said that now that you knew what it was – that you could begin to manage it. What...what else can be done? Because honestly, John, I'm...I'm still really freaked out."

"Distraction is the only thing that will work in a situation like this," John informed her calmly.

"Oh." The word hung there, just like it had when John had first walked into the elevator with her. *I'm still lame*, she thought. Yet it was all that she could think of to say.

In a clinical, dispassionate tone he added, "So I'm going to make you come."

.

FREED

2

Chapter 1

Distraction

⚯

"Mon ami, may I recommend you to read, "The Little Prince," by Antoine de Saint-Exupéry. It is a beautiful tale of loneliness, friendship, love and loss, in the form of a young prince fallen to Earth. It states, "One sees clearly only with the heart. What is essential is invisible to the eye." To me, John, you are the lost Prince, searching for your rose. Have faith, *jeun homme.* Trust your heart, and trust hers, for all is inevitable. You will find each other."
--- André Chevalier, (email to John Taylor)

Kelly Flynn's evening started well, even though she arrived late to the local fetish club.

First she'd met up with two of her friends, and then she watched John Taylor, aka 'Father John' do what the man did best, which was to torture a willing bottom into euphoric bliss. Even though Kelly missed most of that demonstration, just seeing the finale had been worth it. Viewing those moments of trust, where the man submitted completely to his Dom, had been a real privilege.

Kelly had been witness to the ultimate in power exchange. During that scene a priceless gift had been freely given. And the generous largess had been accepted. Yet intense gratitude from the exchange had gone *both* ways. Kelly felt it would take time for her to work through it, to fully comprehend what she'd seen. Tears had filled her eyes as she had watched the lines of power blur. In taking, Father John had given. In giving, the submissive had taken, and both men had become richer through the experience.

What had her friend Rosslyn told her? *"Father John's goal was to bring me to sexual release and spiritual bliss. He did it too."*

Something profound had occurred, but understanding what had happened seemed just out of Kelly's reach. Yet to watch them find connection, to forge the unique, almost spiritual bond as they had…well. It really had been a wow moment. For the first time she was beginning to really understand the attraction people had to S & M.

After that Kelly had enjoyed a sexy entertaining adventure with Master Ron, a playful Dom who made her laugh, gave her multiple orgasms and was an excellent Top. What could have been better? The evening had been perfect, right up until the moment that Father John, the man she had an irrational and foolish crush on, got into the elevator with her.

After the elevator doors had shut, and they started to move upwards, the lights went out and the elevator stopped working. This unfortunate series of events triggered Kelly's terror of small, dark enclosed spaces. John Taylor had brought her back from sheer panic, but they might have a long wait before rescue.

Distraction was the only solution now. "So I'm going to make you come," Father John had calmly informed her.

Kelly giggled and couldn't help laughing, although the brittle sound of her laughter seemed rather hysterical to her. *Scary, hot, intimidating Father John – the man who is the subject of all my fantasies – is going to make me come?* she thought. *Well of course he is. That'll certainly be a distraction.*

"Shush, shush," John soothed, no doubt picking up on her panic. He cupped her face with his free hand and kissed her forehead, a chaste, gentle kiss.

John seemed so unlike the person she'd thought he was. Kelly had been terrified and he had been so understanding, so kind and sweet that she simply wanted to melt. How many personalities did Father John have? The Sadist? The kind Dom? And his own personality – whatever that was. She had to wonder, did anyone really know John Taylor at all?

Having a crush on him had been one thing, and fantasizing another, but the real man was way hotter than Kelly had expected.

She'd known John was beautiful, but in the dark she was attracted to his warm sensual touch, his masculine scent and the way he took control of everything. God. If she'd been alone in this elevator when it broke she honestly could have died, or at least certainly she'd have gone mad with terror. The thought ratcheted up her anxiety levels so her pulse increased, too.

"Shush, Kelly," he directed her in a reproving voice. "Stop thinking." He gave her hair a firm tug to emphasize that order. "I'm going to touch you now, and I want all your awareness on that. My skin – in contact with your skin. Do you understand?"

"Yes... John," she gasped out, the skin to skin comment made her pulse speed for another reason. Strong male fingers skimmed lightly over her lips and cheeks, trailing down her neck and shoulders, stopping just above her breasts.

"Do you feel my fingers?" he said.

"Yes, John," she replied, and Kelly found that as he had instructed, she was no longer thinking. Truthfully, just now she didn't feel even capable of thought. All her concentration was right *there*.

He folded down the cups of her corset, exposing her in the darkness. Kelly found herself straining toward him and holding her breath – waiting for his touch. When his warm rough fingers began to explore her tender breasts, she sighed, in a little ummmm sound of.

Anticipation, anxiety, panic and pleasure... she felt completely out of her depth in these circumstances, trapped in an elevator with the man of her dreams. Almost impersonally John explored her breasts, plumping and squeezing, smoothing over the contours of both. Inhaling in short, shallow breaths, Kelly shut her eyes in the darkness, absorbing every sensation.

The effect this man had on her! She quivered in response to his touch, helplessly making desperate little sounds of need, despite trying to hold them back.

John took some time, rolling and tugging on her nipples, apparently gauging every reaction. Then his hand went lower, resting on the edge of her underwear. "Lift up, I want to take these panties off," he ordered.

Kelly immediately obeyed and John removed them, leaving her sitting on his warm leather pants, her legs parted. Her giddy head-spin of residual terror, anticipation and apprehension settled with this dominant demand. John Taylor was in control. Simply knowing that made her feel safer. On some primal level, Kelly trusted him. She expelled a deep breath, unaware that she'd been holding it. Giving herself over to this man was a huge relief, causing her uncertainty and confusion to vanish.

"That's right, Kelly," he said, no doubt registering that the high-strung tension in her body had eased. "I've got you."

His confident conviction was like a balm, eliminating the last remnants of her doubts and fears.

His warm fingers soothed over her cool thighs, and then cupped her pubic area. Kelly was glad she was smooth and hair free, because she felt ridiculously eager to please him. But John, a man of notoriously few words, said nothing.

His probing fingers moved lower, until they rested enticingly between her folds, right outside the sensitive nerves of her entrance. "Try to sit up for me, Kelly," he said.

With instinctive obedience she immediately attempted to raise her torso, but John's hand gripped her wrists firmly behind her, securing her tightly. She couldn't move at all, as long as John restrained her.

Oh, God, he's so much stronger than I am! He could do anything to me, and I couldn't stop him!

That thought caused a flash of fear to roll through her. She struggled and strained against him. Restrained and helpless, she felt an accompanying gush of wetness between her legs. Sensation and lust drowned her consciousness.

Kelly became aware of the soft movement of male fingers. Father John had registered her slick spill of arousal due to being held down, captured and bent to his will.

"Good," he said, again with no more than a clinical appreciation for what got her hot.

Kelly was speechless and embarrassed. A familiar flush of heat spread over her, and she knew her whole body was blushing red. For a moment she was actually glad it was pitch dark. Good Lord. Talk about a distraction. Well, he had all her attention now. John didn't seem to expect her to say anything, which was just as well, because she had no idea what to say.

Jesus. All this time Kelly had been at the club, thinking she knew what it meant to be submissive, but everything before this moment seemed like role playing or pretend. There was no comparison. Father John controlled her easily and absolutely. It was instinct or natural law for her to submit to him. And not just submit, more like surrender unconditionally to his will – whatever his will might be.

Freely and without reservation she gave all of her power to him. Liberated from her burdens, she was thankful to do so.

John Taylor had mastered her completely.

Her core pulsed with that thought and she realized something else. More than anything she longed to please him. She felt as if she was unable to deny him whatever he may wish for. Kelly felt she'd do anything for John Taylor.

She swallowed and thought, *I just hope that he doesn't want to hurt me.*

Chapter 2

Lessons

∝—∝

I'm alone with Father John, Kelly mused, alternating between anxious anticipation and rapture. And shit! Even trapped in an elevator, can this man get a girl riled up, or what?

His hand and fingers explored her sex in a heated, erotic caress, stroking delicately, circling, but always careful not to brush against her clit. He played with her for some time, a teasing assault to her senses that made her breathless and needy. Moving his fingers down between her legs, he delved between her folds, invading her hungry feminine entrance. He slipped one tantalizing finger inside her moist depth, just up to a knuckle.

"Um, ah, oh, God," she murmured, shifting restlessly, unable to stop her sounds of enjoyment.

He paused for a long moment, until she'd collected herself, and then asked softly, "Do you like pain, Kelly?"

"Not really," she replied surfacing quickly from the intoxicating bliss his finger provided. "I like a spanking. Sometimes I can climax with a spanking," she offered, nervously hoping to divert him from whatever torturous action he might be imagining for her. She soooo did NOT like pain.

Her less than enthusiastic response to the pain issue had no apparent effect on Father John, which was a relief. He continued as he had, calmly asking questions or giving orders.

"Spread your legs further apart, Kelly. Wide as you can," he said. Her instant obedience surprised her, and once more she knew that it was instinct that drove her, not logical thought.

John ran his hand from one thigh, over the sensitive cleft of her sex to the other thigh, feeling how open she had made herself to him. "Thank you. That's right, Kelly," he said, with formal civility. "Keep them like this." His deceptively soft, cultured voice was a huge turn on in itself. Just the way the man kept saying her name made her wet. She found herself burning with desire. A heavy aching need settled between her open legs and exposed pussy.

"Now tell me, Kelly," he murmured. "When did you last masturbate?"

"Last night," she replied immediately.

"Good girl," he said, sliding two digits between her damp folds and slipping them deep inside her. Kelly moaned. John took his fingers out and lightly brushed her slick essence over her swollen clit a number of times. She understood then. This was an instant reward for her honesty. Rapturous pleasure spiked through her body and her core tightened at his perfect touch. Oh Lord! His thick male fingers felt sooo much better than she had imagined.

"What did you fantasize about when you were masturbating?" he asked.

Her thoughts paused for just a split second, as she wondered how to reply. The truth was she had been thinking about him. How could she tell him that? No way! Instead she said, "Uh, just the usual, you know, hot guy, intercourse."

The acute pain was instantaneous. John slapped the open skin of her pussy *hard*, three stinging sharp swats that sent a tingling wave of hurt rippling throughout her whole body. Kelly cried out in astonishment and surprise.

"Oww!" In an unconscious reaction she closed her legs, bringing her thighs together.

John followed this agony up by grabbing her clit and squeezing it, then giving it a cruel twist, just like he had done to her breast when she was hysterical earlier from a childhood memory of being trapped in the dark.

"Please! Please!" she begged, thrashing in his arms. He easily held her, just by continuing to restrain her wrists behind her back. She could do nothing except endure this terrible punishment.

He didn't let go of her beleaguered clit. Instead he said coolly, "Keep your legs spread, Kelly."

"Ahh!" she cried out but quickly put her legs back to where they'd been, far apart. John released her swollen aching clit, and she felt immediate relief as he released it. It burned and throbbed in protest at its treatment.

He soothed her then, with soft, tender strokes. His gifted fingers relieved her abused flesh, fondling her with gentle, almost apologetic caresses. "I ordered you to spread your legs, Kelly. They must stay that way until I tell you otherwise. That's why I hurt you by pinching your clitoris. I always punish noncompliance."

"Oh," she panted breathlessly.

"I spanked your pussy for another reason. I need to you to understand, Kelly. I'm going to be very clear. You must never, ever, lie to me. I don't have to see your face to recognize when you're hiding the truth or when you tell a lie. Even in this darkness I'll know. I punish disobedience and I punish lies. Do you understand?"

"Yes, John."

"Good girl." The soft circular touches that John was generously giving her sore, tender pussy and clit felt sublime and nothing short of marvelous. Her whole body trembled uncontrollably with sharp, fierce arousal.

What was that about? How could he draw such pleasure from her after giving it such pain? The entire lower half of her body throbbed and tingled. There was no question that she craved Father John's touch. She needed it desperately. It was all she could do not to arch up toward his hand, and she found herself once more making soft, unintentional whimpers.

"That's right, Kelly," he said in that calm, sexy voice of his. "It feels good. When you obey me I shall reward you. Now. What did you fantasize about when you were masturbating last night?"

John's large palm traveled down between her nether lips, spreading them open with his fingers, and then trailing deliciously along her empty, needy slit. His clever thumb, slick with her arousal, moved to circle around her swollen clitoris.

Whenever he rubbed the aching nub, Kelly jerked and moaned, drunk with sensation. She didn't care what he knew anymore. As long as he continued to finger her with his devil blessed hands she was happy to tell him anything he wanted.

"I, uh, I was thinking of you John. I was fantasizing about you."

"Good," he said calmly, without noticeable surprise in his composed voice. "What was I doing to you exactly? Tell me while I masturbate you now. If you're honest and give me exact details, I'll let you come." As he said this he encouraged her by putting one long finger inside her needy feminine sheath.

"Oh! God, yes. God that feels good. Um." Kelly swallowed and licked her lips, trying to recall. "Okay, I uh couldn't go to the club last night, because I was doing this Speed Dating job. Ahhh!" She said, as he dexterously put two fingers inside her and began to swirl and scissor them. Totally blissed out with sensation at his touch, her eyes drifted shut.

John drew his fingers out again, coating her clit with her slick moisture. Then he began to masturbate her wet swollen clit with his thumb, pulling the velvet skin of the hood back to expose the nub, then bringing it up again, back and forth, back and forth in long firm strokes.

Kelly had never experienced that before, and whimpered with pleasure. It was divine! A flood of arousal gushed from her core, and she panted breathlessly as her back arched and her toes curled.

He paused in his attentions and said, "Continue, Kelly. Details, remember?"

Kelly cleared her throat. "Ah, I just used my fingers, I don't have a vibrator, because I can climax pretty easy as it is. You um, wanted to use that damn bull whip on me, and I let you. I don't know why – no wait, I do. The thing is I kind of have a crush on you, John. You're just so attractive to me. You're probably the only guy even close to my age at The Basement, too, but it isn't that. You're so scary though. So I've been avoiding you."

"Tell me the fantasy, Kelly," he said in a compelling smoky voice that was even more seductive in the darkness.

She felt herself dripping on his fingers as he pushed them back inside her, drenching his hand. He was skillfully using all her moisture, rubbing that slickness all over her. Wonderfully wet, she arched and moaned as he deftly fingered her. He stopped once again, cupping her pubic area, giving her a break so she could talk.

"Um, God, John. That felt amazing. Okay. The fantasy. Let me see. We kiss, and you play with my breasts, and I suck you off somewhere in there, and then you spank me – I can't recall why, but you let me come from it. Then you press me to do the whip thing and I really don't want to – but I do it anyway, because… because…

"Because?" he said in an encouraging tone.

"Because it seemed really important for me to please you, alright? To let you do whatever you want. Because I need to make you happy." She cleared her throat again. "You just don't seem happy, John, and for some reason or another I can't let that go. It bothers me. I need to see you smile."

The silence seemed more intense in the dark, and when he said nothing, she continued speaking. "And then afterwards you were so caring and loving, and then you made love to me. I imagine that you, the guy who never kisses and never has sex with anyone, makes love to me. That's it. Honestly. That's the fantasy."

"How many times did you come?"

"Oh crap," she said, hoping he wouldn't have asked her that. "Three times." Sometimes masturbating helped her get to sleep. She'd come home a bit tense and wound up that night, and that's what it took to exhaust her mind and body. Her last thoughts as she drifted off were of John Taylor, of course.

"When?"

She sighed and said, in a frustrated tone, "When you kiss me because it feels so good to me, when you whip me because it feels good to you, and when you screw me, because it feels good for both of us, alright? Does that make you happy now? To know that I really get off on the idea of having sex with you?"

"Yes," he replied calmly. And then he kissed her.

Chapter 3

A Kiss

John held her arms, tight behind her, and pushed her body up against his.

Kelly was so wired and aroused that she moaned the moment his mouth met hers. His kiss was so soft! Gentle but commanding, his sweet lips erotically brushed against hers. In the dark, she had only an instant to feel his heat coming toward her. To find him kissing her was both a shock and a thrill.

Oh God! The darkness had terrified her, and John had resolved to distract her from her fears. It was a gift, and she was so grateful, that the man who never kissed anyone, was willing to kiss her.

Emotions overwhelmed her, tears stung her eyes and she began to cry. Not sobs, not sighs, just tears of joy running down and across her temples.

John had warm sensual lips, just as she knew he would, but he was uncannily aware. Even in the total darkness he traced her tears with the fingers of his hand. "Beautiful girl," he murmured. "Put your arms around me."

Kelly felt him let her go, and she curled trustingly around him, her arms around his neck, her face nuzzling into him. His own arms circled her.

"Oh, thank you," she said, with a hitch in her breath, her tears were falling down her cheeks now that she was sitting up. It felt so good to be held close against the warmth and strength of his hard male body. So many emotions – they were overflowing! She had been terrified, and then turned on, and now she was so very grateful. Honestly, she felt she could die with no regrets in his solid embrace.

With his arms around her, John caressed her with his soft, supple lips. Slipping into her mouth with a French kiss, he delved into her, probing every part of her from the inside. His greedy exploration made her moan. When he caught and sucked on her tongue, the sensation and pleasure of it went lower. Liquid heat pooled in her belly, and tingles of need arrowed straight to her clit and her womb.

This first kiss went on for some time, each exploring and enjoying the other uninhibitedly. Soft sounds of pleasure came from Kelly, but John, she noticed, remained strangely silent. One of his hands reached down to fondle and squeeze her breasts, rolling her nipples and pinching them to the point of exquisite aching tenderness, making them stiffen with pleasure.

His mouth left hers to move to her nipples. He took one between his teeth, his bite making her back bow with the sharp hurting twinge. But then he suckled, swirled and lashed her breast with his hot velvet tongue, and the throb of pain turned to rapture. Her other breast received the same treatment, and her core contracted with need for him.

John then sucked each breast deep into his mouth, one at a time. It was as if the man wanted to eat them. His teeth held them inside while his tongue licked and he pulled her flesh right to the roof of his mouth. He nursed and sucked, not just her nipple in his heated mouth, but what felt like her entire breast. To Kelly, it seemed as if he was swallowing each tit whole.

"Ah, ah, ah! John!" she moaned. It was so erotic, the way he nuzzled and nursed her. This was her fantasy, only better. John Taylor was the perfect Dom, the ultimate lover.

HIs fingers continued to roll and tug at the nipple of one breast, while his tongue, mouth and lips hungrily devoured the other. Then his mouth moved across her shoulder, and up her neck. He paused to kiss and lick behind her ear, blowing warm breath over her moistened skin, creating goose bumps.

"Oh, um, good. So good," she murmured, her breath ragged.

John nipped her earlobe, and then his lips traveled across her throat, neck, and cheek, leaving hot trails of fire as his mouth returned to her lips. She panted breathlessly, her buttocks and molten core clenching in an instinctive bid for sexual relief.

He sucked on her tongue then, while squeezing and caressing her heavy, swollen breasts. Hypersensitive and horny, Kelly felt a familiar heated pulse low in her belly and her sex. She feared that she'd climax just from what he was doing and nothing else.

As if reading her mind, but more likely reading the signals of her body John said in a dangerous, admonitory tone, "Don't you dare come, Kelly. I will be very displeased if you do. You don't have permission to come."

She moaned and held her breath, getting back under some sort of control once more. It helped to imagine that she belonged to him. If she was his, it would be easy to do as he asked.

"Lay back, arms over your head," he commanded her. She sprawled backwards, lying across him; legs wide apart, arms outstretched her body trustingly open in complete submission, and surrender.

I'm spread out like a human sacrifice she thought, and that idea gave her only pleasure. *A sacrifice for you, John. Only for you.*

"That's right. Thank you, Kelly," John approved, running his hands from her wrists and arms, down across her shoulders, breasts and torso, brushing lightly right down past her legs to her ankles, almost to her toes. Eyes shut tight, she shuddered with pleasure from the sensation. His every touch was divine.

"Perfect," he said. "Open and ready to submit to my will. Now I can play with you exactly as I wish. I'm sorry to inform you, Kelly that I'm in no hurry. I'm just getting started. You don't like pain yet I really do want to torment you."

Her speeding pulse quickened. Why did this erotic threat turn her on so much? Because there was no question about it, the dangerous menace in his voice really did it for her. John bent over her, and with a hand on her hip he circled her belly button with his warm tongue, nibbling and licking his way down her body.

Kelly trembled and squirmed as he moved lower. God she wanted his tongue between her legs! Thankfully, he must have read her mind again because he parted her folds and began licking her clitoris.

She gasped and her back bowed, instinctively thrusting toward him. He responded to her ardor by drawing that swollen, sensitive bundle of nerves right into his mouth, sucking on her clit in a steady pulsing rhythm. Crying out, she moaned and squirmed with pleasure, but John didn't let her climax.

He let her clit slip out of his mouth and said, "Tell me what you need. I want to hear you beg."

Chapter 4

Finger Fucked

―――――∝∾――――

"Please, John," she said. "Please may I come?"

"Not yet," he murmured. His teeth returned to her breasts, and he placed one pussy moistened finger in her mouth.

"Um, um, um, ah!" Kelly gave a strangled sort of moan, instantly imagining it to be his cock. She sucked his finger fiercely, tasting her own essence. John's other hand caressed her, from her breasts, along her flank and hips, teasing and brushing her clit and cleft, then carefully pushing one finger just barely inside her. She gasped.

Moving his finger in and out of her quivering slit, John pressed deeper inside, a little further each time, pulling and stretching her warm swollen flesh as he went. At the same time, with exact synchronization, he finger fucked her mouth.

She sucked and thrashed and moaned. One finger in her pussy, one in her mouth – and both needy holes sucked him in. Two fingers in her pussy, two in her mouth. Finally he buried three fingers deep in both holes and she cried out, and almost came.

Kelly endured a wave of sharp, pulsing contractions that gave her no relief or sexual release. They felt good, yet they were also agonizing because she needed to climax. How else could she ease the buzzing tension that was building inside her?

He paused, letting her pre-orgasmic convulsion settle, but then he began again. This process continued for some while, John penetrating her pussy and her mouth with his fingers exactly as a man's penis would, sometimes deeper, sometimes shallow, and sometimes rimming her slit and the lips of her mouth. But always together exactly the same he worked his way in and out of both her needy holes.

Kelly bucked and whimpered, her wanton sounds of desire reaching a fever pitch when he finally stopped. "Please, John," she pleaded in a shamefully craven whine. "I beg you! Please will you let me come?"

"No," he said, taking his fingers from her mouth only.

His lips and mouth went back to the column of her throat then, as his fingers continued their sensual assault between her legs. She obligingly tilted her head, giving him full access as he sucked on the tender skin of her neck, marking her with nips of his teeth.

Then his head dipped back to each nipple. His tongue flicked, his mouth working with gentle suction in the same pulsing rhythm as he penetrated her cleft and worked her clit. It was just like when he had finger fucked her mouth and her pussy, the pace once more in an erotic, rhythmic sync.

Kelly felt her arousal dripping down her thighs as he brushed her clit with his thumb. It pulsed. It was as if her womb and her clit throbbed in time with her rapid heartbeat. An overwhelming orgasm was building, and then stopped, building, then stopped and each time an irresistible mountain of sexual need was reaching new heights. These pinnacles of pleasure were actually quite painful.

I'm in hell! I need to come! Kelly thought wildly, for never in her life had she experienced such exquisite suffering. *If my tormentor ever does let me climax, it will be quite the explosion.*

"Oh John, please! I'm begging you," she mewled in a plaintive whimper. He obligingly swirled his fingers, stabbing just near her G spot. Yet the man continued to be diabolical in his ability to bring her right to the edge of an ever expanding, earth shattering orgasm without letting her go over.

"What do you want?" he asked, and Kelly thought she heard a smile in that seductive whisper of his. By toying with her so cruelly, Father John was thoroughly enjoying himself.

"More! Please more! I've got to come," she sobbed, and wept because her need was so overwhelming.

Kelly thrashed and jackknifed mindlessly now, and somewhere she understood that this was how John controlled his subs so completely. Now even his bull whip didn't scare her. There was nothing she wouldn't endure to enjoy such heavenly moments of pleasure, even with the painful ache of non-completion.

Never had sex been so amazing. She'd begged and pleaded, whimpered and moaned. Greedy, needy and desperate, she arched toward shamelessly. Nothing she'd experienced previously compared to this. It was as if her body had been waiting for John all her life.

Suddenly she had a tiny vestige of insight into why addicts stole from others, or fell into prostitution. Kelly craved John like an addict ached for drugs, she wanted him that badly. Just then she felt that she'd do anything to have him.

She needed him just like she needed air to breathe. The man was ruining her for sex with anyone else.

"John," she moaned. "Please, John! Uh, uh, ah, ah!" Kelly made a constant keening sound now – she could hardly recognize the noises coming from her own throat. Her entire body felt as if it was on fire. The man was a sadist, and this was proof of it. How long had he been tormenting her? Being on a pitiless razor's edge of orgasm for so long would surely send her mad.

Oh God, she thought. *The man is killing me! If I don't come soon I swear I'm going to die!*

"You're doing well," John said, probably aware that she was in a frantic mental fog and needed encouragement. "You're able to take much more from me now, and still prevent climax. Thank you, Kelly. I know that this is difficult, and that you're restraining yourself from orgasm by my command. I'm proud of you."

Somewhere in her raw animalistic state, Kelly registered his praise. It only increased her joy. *John is proud of me,* she thought, and even without orgasm her elation was complete.

Her entire body throbbed and burned. Every inch of her skin tingled, and her eyes stung, she was crying again, hot tears rolling down her temples. It all added to her total surrender to the man who had mastered her. To the Dom that controlled her so completely. She was *his*.

The scent of her arousal filled the room, mingling with his enticing sandalwood musk. John continued to fondle her clit, pulling back the hood and rubbing the naked nub with his slick wet thumb, flicking his fingers in and out of her dripping channel with delicious friction.

"You are the perfect submissive, Kelly," he told her in a calm, composed voice. "I feel fortunate to be here with you right now."

This final tribute was all too much. Too much sensation, too much emotion, too much pleasure, too much pain. She didn't want to disobey him, but she was helpless now. A pang of regret at the thought of displeasing John caused her oncoming orgasm to momentarily stutter. She couldn't bear it. Disappointing him would create an entirely different kind of pain. But really, she was going to climax!

"Do you want to come for me, Kelly?" he asked quietly, idly fondling a breast and tugging hard, then gently, then hard once more upon on one nipple.

"Oh yes! Please, John, please!" she gasped breathlessly, scarcely able to prevent her resounding climax. "For you. Only for you." She'd no idea why she said that, it just bubbled right out of her mouth.

"Very well. Come then. Right now," he said in a firm voice, driving his fingers deep against her G spot, impaling her with short, fast strokes that simulated the thrusts of a man in climax. His lips came down right on her clit at the same time. With waves of suction John drew it inside his hot mouth, tugging it all the way in, nursing it with hard suctioning pulls. His rhythmic bursts pounded upon her sensitive, swollen clit, like the thrusts of a lover hammering into her flesh.

Flicking with his tongue and sucking, John bit the outer edges of the skin of her clit *hard*. The combination of all this sensation created a simultaneous clitoral and vaginal orgasm like Kelly had never experienced before.

"Ahh!" she screamed and wailed. Somewhere in the back of her mind she knew she was probably shrieking like an emergency services siren, but she simply couldn't stop herself.

Her entire body stiffened and she convulsed on John's fingers, squeezing them hard – with the force of a clamp. A warm gush of fluid came from her, coating his hand. Kelly bucked, screaming, thrusting and thrashing like a wild animal. Every synapse in her brain seemed to burst with all this stimulation. It was too much!

A rolling wave of sensual bliss enveloped her. All the ecstasy to be had in the entire world filled her body from the tips of her fingers to the tips of her toes.

In the darkness Kelly saw colorful flashes behind her eyes. *Yep, emergency services, ambulance lights,* she thought in a moment of hilarious glee and all the while her hips rocked and her body pulsed with orgasms.

One after another, each climax came in wave after wave, like being on a calm lake beach after a huge boat had passed by. Then slowing, slowing, slowing, until all the waves stopped and there was only still water and peacefulness once more.

In her jubilant mindless stupor she felt John hold her close, controlling her movements, and continuing to finger her throughout her orgasms, bringing her down slowly, through her aftershocks. Her limbs shook with exhaustion. When he pulled her into his embrace, stroking her soothingly, she gratefully curled up against him, nuzzling her face into his neck.

And in all that time, the fact that she was trapped in a small dark elevator had not once crossed Kelly's mind.

Chapter 5

John Taylor

John couldn't really believe it. Kelly Flynn was in his arms. So soft, so vulnerable and so beautiful. Jesus. Right now she belonged to him.

He'd intentionally caught up to her in the elevator, having considered that he might actually ask her out. It was an insane scheme, but he couldn't think of anything else. He'd never gone out with a woman in his life, and had no idea what he'd do with one if he did. Try to make small talk at a restaurant like they did on TV? But about what? Was there anything he could have in common with the purity and innocence that was hers? Yet, strangely compelled, he'd been willing to try it.

In the entire time Kelly had been coming to The Basement never once had John been so physically close. Hyperaware of her, he knew the minute she arrived and the moment she left, but he had easily managed to camouflage his own interest. Yet, he'd also been conscious of her eyes upon him, following him wherever he went.

Why did she seek him out? Why did she watch him? Because of gossip? He'd hoped that maybe she might actually be interested in him.

John knew why now. As an astute, trained observer of both sexes, he couldn't miss the signs. When he'd entered the elevator, and stood beside her he saw her pale skin flush, her mouth open, her breaths increase, and her pulse speed up. The woman had also shifted restlessly, with unconscious sexual need. Kelly Flynn had been aroused by his presence.

Kelly Flynn had been aroused by his presence!

The hollow emptiness in his chest eased at the thought. For the last month he'd watched her take up with one new Dom after another, telling himself that it was better this way. That she needed the experience. That he didn't have to be first, as long as he had her eventually. And perhaps, just maybe he'd be her last. Yet he couldn't work up the nerve to ask if she would let him Top her. Because what if she said no?

It was obvious that Kelly didn't recognize him, and yet he could *never* have forgotten her. When he'd first seen her at the club, he'd thought that he'd finally lost his mind. He was sure that she was a hallucination, something from his own subconscious coming to life.

Kelly wasn't a child anymore, but she was still the same amazing person. She was the opposite of himself: cheerful, happy and naturally kind. The woman tried his emotional control, and had done so from the first. Why was that? Was Kelly Flynn the dream? He already loved her – he always had, in his peculiar dysfunctional way. But could she love him? This was crazy thinking and he knew it. For how could he ever have a real relationship with anyone?

His own subs had suffered and his sadism had reached new heights. Every time Kelly went with another Dom he had to fight not to push his poor subs too far too fast due to an unfamiliar jealous rage. But here she was now, in his arms.

"Have faith, *mon ami* for the universe will provide," André Chevalier had told him. Well, he'd never truly believed that, but right now it held an aspect of truth.

Thank you, universe, for disabling this elevator, came the ironic idle thought. But he really was grateful.

John mused over the recent events. When Kelly had started screaming after the lights went out he'd almost gone ballistic himself. Always controlled, this immediate reaction had shocked him. Never had he been consumed by such wild and uncontained emotions, and such bizarre ones for him, too.

He *had* to help her, he needed to protect her and save her from whatever was happening – all quite foreign feelings, unless he was deep in a scene with a sub. The only time he felt connected was while dominating a scene, and of course to a lesser degree with his friend, André Chevalier.

And now, here with Kelly Flynn.

Luckily John's instincts had kicked in, and his understanding of the human body. First, control the incident and then find what the hell had happened. Christ he was glad that he'd taken pre-med. No one understood human anatomy, what the human body could take and what it couldn't, or how to manage trauma better than he did.

André Chevalier had taught him everything there was to know about pleasing a woman or a man. He'd also made John have sex with his subs, bringing them to climax in various ways, all for their gratification – and certainly not his own.

"Pleasure, pleasure, pleasure, John," André continually reminded him. "Always your goal is pleasure – *c'est très important! Oui,* pain, yes of course, as much as you wish without causing permanent marks or physical damage. Even if the sub desires such scars, I do not recommend this. With time, people change their mind, John. But pain must only be used as a means to ultimately add to your sub's sensation of pleasure, *mon ami.* To do otherwise is *un péché noir* — a black sin. It will tarnish the soul. You are a good man, John Taylor, and such is not for you."

Under André's tutelage, he'd become a master in both pleasure and pain. Thus it had been a simple matter for him to divert her from her terror with sex. Kelly had simply been in shock. The small, dark, enclosed space of the elevator had triggered a childhood PTSD event.

John felt a sudden need to swallow, for he'd been affected by her panic. Always physically in control, he decided to allow himself to swallow, and did so. Yet the significance of the need was not lost to him.

Kelly was important. He was a sadist, yet it had hurt him to know that she was suffering. The irony of this didn't escape his notice – it was such an odd problem for him to experience.

He continued to softly rub Kelly's back, as she rested from the extreme violence of those multiple orgasms of hers. He hadn't seen them of course, but he'd felt every one when her body thrashed and her cunt had tightened in convulsive waves around his fingers. The woman was dripping with arousal.

The candid details of her fantasy of him had his balls tingling. His cock throbbed and twitched the more she revealed.

But he hadn't been only physically moved. Something in his chest hurt, too.

All this time he'd been masturbating, dreaming of her. And all that time she had been thinking of him. God, he wanted to fuck her. He really did, and this surprised him, because he never wanted that.

He never even thought about that.

What he really wanted to do was to hurt her.

Chapter 6

Off the Cliff

~⋈~

Kelly doesn't like pain, he thought, and disappointment stabbed at him. *But maybe, like many others, I can teach her to enjoy it.*

John found it difficult to be emotionally involved with the rest of the human race, except through pain. But with pain there could be in his experience, no greater bond. There was always a point, a moment of surrender when torturing someone. It was the ultimate joining, when the eyes met and two souls linked in a place far above the physical realm.

Correctly done, pain was profound. It was a spiritual release, and an honest connection like no other. The reward of torment, the subs willing submission, the agony, then mercy and forgiveness. Such was a gift from each to each other. Kelly liked a spanking and some hurt, but could she like it enough to meet the heights he wanted to take her to? For he'd never ever take her anywhere she didn't want to go.

God, that kiss. He never kissed, but he'd longed to kiss her. It was as if her goodness flowed into him with that kiss. Kelly was all lightness to his dark, all radiant white to the dirty black hole of his own darkness. He wanted to kiss her again.

"John?" she murmured, stirring from her trance-like state of release.

"Yes?"

She sat up. "I know you never allow anyone..." she cleared her throat, "I mean do you mind if I suck you off?"

"I don't do that," he replied instantly.

"Oh," she said in a forlorn voice, clearly saddened by his response.

With logic and observation, John was attuned to others. These were ingrained skills he'd trained into himself on purpose. He noticed everything, but even more so with Kelly. She was submissive, and most submissive women found real pleasure through serving a Dom in that way. This was a natural part of Kelly's makeup. He hadn't wanted to wound her. Hurting her felt like hurting himself. What was that about? Why was that?

There was a long pause while he considered granting her wish. Could he climax with Kelly? He'd tried with other submissives both male and female, but was utterly incapable. Only twice had he been able to climax with another.

Once had been on his eighteenth birthday, when he'd begged his Aunt Brenda to take his virginity. That had been a terrible day. Brenda had been kind and understanding. She knew his history by then, and felt responsible. His aunt had been the only good thing in his life *ever*. Nothing had been her fault. Aunt Brenda had been a beautiful woman. But it had taken him most of the day to finally achieve a climax with her, and it had given him no pleasure.

John grimaced. Sex had always been such a problem to him. It was a hateful bodily need. He'd learned something of what wanted to understand about it, but the entire process had still been hideous.

The other time he'd been able to orgasm with another was with André Chevalier, four years ago. Back then, the terrible shame he usually felt afterwards had been overridden by grief for Aunt Brenda's death.

John's mindless cock was constantly erect – it was a real problem to him. Masturbating was safe and regular, particularly after a good session where he and his submissive had brought each other to soaring euphoric heights. At those times he had to relieve himself in the shower even before leaving the club, and those orgasms always produced some small enjoyment for they felt clean and pure.

Sexual release otherwise was a shameful, dirty, necessity. It was something his body had to do, like urinating, or eating, but less pleasurable than either of those things.

If he understood the problem he'd be able to fix it. That was why he'd completed a psychology degree after all – but there were no answers there. John couldn't climax in the presence of another, for he could barely climax on his own. Was it a question of vulnerability? Because he was unable to show how he felt? Or give himself over? Or was it simply overwhelmingly negative associations with the entire process?

André told him that the ability to climax with another would come to him eventually. He had suggested that perhaps it was a matter of the heart and soul, and that John just needed to find someone to love and trust.

John gave an internal snort. It seemed an endless, impossible task. But maybe because it was dark, and because for some strange reason he really cared about this girl? Could her purity be a key to find enjoyment, and the ability to actually climax with another?

With his arms encircling Kelly's torso, John squeezed, noticing that this was an impulsive affectionate touch. Usually every action he took when near others, except during a scene, was pre-thought out beforehand. He didn't feel affection for anyone unless he'd brought a submissive to release through pain, yet he was fond of Kelly.

Was it karmic? Was it meant to be this way? But what if she couldn't make him climax? How could he face her again after exposing her to his own personal shame?

André Chevalier had assured John that someday he'd find someone, or they would find him. He wondered if Kelly could be that someone. It felt right, but how could he trust feelings? Especially when he preferred to cut his emotions off all together and live without them entirely.

John's jaw clenched with indecision. He should just say no and forget the whole thing. That would be the easiest course to take, but he couldn't do that. Because he didn't want to upset Kelly.

I'm Father John the sadist, but I don't want to hurt her!

God dammit, the woman was messing with his head, yet he was incurably drawn to Kelly. Could she be the one who could make him whole?

John took a slow deep breath. He'd simply have to be brave enough to try. "Courage, *mon ami*," he could hear the words of his mentor say in the back of his mind. It was madness, and it was well beyond daring, but he wanted to risk everything. Because of her. *'Yes, I'll do it,* he decided. *For her.*

"I don't have a condom," he suddenly said, realizing with both relief and agony that he may not be able to throw himself off this cliff after all.

Chapter 7

Queasy

John wasn't frequently surprised, but even as a child Kelly had stunned him with the unexpected. Irrepressibly cheerful, even trapped in a small dark room, she laughed out loud.

"The man with brandy in his jacket doesn't have a condom? Well, don't worry, I've got one in my purse," she said, "but I'd rather not use it, if that's okay. I mean, we both have had all the tests for the club, and I always use condoms. But because it's just oral, and because..."

She stopped talking suddenly, and John knew then that she'd found something she didn't want to tell him. And since she didn't want to tell, he would force her to do so. That was just who he was.

"Tell me, Kelly. You said because..."

"Because sucking you to completion will be special for me. I want to do something nice for you, John. I really do. I don't know why. I know you never do oral, or even sex with anyone, but will you let me? Just this once?"

"I'll allow it, Kelly," he said, as if granting her a privilege, which, in fact, he was. No one ever touched him there. *Never*. His body reacted. He wanted to tremble and move but he automatically suppressed those urges as he always had, with rigid self-control.

"Oh, God, really?" she said, her voice leaping with enthusiasm.

In the darkness, he permitted himself to smile. It was something he'd never do otherwise. John avoided showing emotion, hell he didn't even *allow* emotion. It was a habit, and a survival mechanism, he knew that. It was difficult to change. Yet here in the darkness Kelly had made him inexplicably happy, and he felt comfortable grinning as broadly as he liked.

He stood up, and Kelly moved toward him, resting her trembling hands on his hips. She reached up for his buckle, and undid it and his zip, pulling his leather pants down past his thighs, allowing his hard cock to spring free. It ached, and dripped, but he was used to that.

It was as easy for him to disconnect from his own cock as it was to be detached from people, or even himself. He moved his legs apart, making himself the perfect angle for the height of her mouth.

"Um, do you want or don't want anything particular?" she asked.

"No," he said dispassionately. For some reason he just couldn't be involved. Even with Kelly. Yet his cock was certainly interested, so perhaps nature would take its course.

She said, "Um, John?"

"Yes?"

"Um, before I start, I just want to say, I like to do it, but I really don't know if I'm any good at it. I just want to say, if you think I can do it better, or if you want me to do something differently, will you tell me?"

He heard an odd catch in her voice. John put his hand down to her face, and felt her hot tears once more. What did it mean? Why was she weeping now? She was so hard to understand sometimes. "Tell me why you're crying," he ordered.

"I don't know if I can explain," she said with a hitch in her breath.

"Try."

Kelly blew out a breath of air. "It may be a woman thing that a man can't appreciate. I just feel so emotional. You," she sniffed loudly, "You've been so kind to me tonight, and I just never expected it. You made a horrible experience the most memorable event of my life."

She was weeping even more, John could tell even without an ability to see her. Her voice was raised and her turbulent emotions flowed over him like a river racing through a rocky gorge. Her feelings were fresh, honest, and purifying. Something inside his own chest stirred.

"I'm honestly so glad this stupid elevator broke," she said, and she sniffed loudly once again.

Her childlike, snuffling runny nose touched him. The woman really was just so damn sweet. He reached into his jacket, pulled out a handkerchief, and gave it to her.

Kelly laughed, "Oh my God! Who has a handkerchief in their jacket?" She blew her nose loudly. "You have everything. Brandy, handkerchief. What next?"

"My Aunt Brenda always had a handkerchief," he said musingly.

"Really? Do you like her? Is she a good Aunt?

"She's dead," he said flatly. "But I loved her very much."

John was surprised at the automatically truthful response he'd given her. Not that he usually lied. More that he never told anyone about himself. Never. Such was his habit and unbreakable rule. But somehow here in the shelter of darkness he'd wanted to remember Aunt Brenda, and he'd wanted to share that memory with Kelly.

"I'm so sorry. It's hard to lose someone you love."

"Yes," he agreed with finality, dismissing the painful subject of his aunt's death. He skimmed his fingers lightly over her face, stroking her cheeks affectionately. Kelly didn't think she'd that much experience in going down on a man. Well, he hadn't much experience in receiving such attentions.

Honestly, even the idea of it made him feel a little queasy.

Chapter 8

Only You

John's thumb wiped her hot tears, but more were coming. Kelly had so many feelings, while he had none. My God, she was his opposite in every way. But the fact she was shedding tears for him touched him, and he found he wanted to climax for her sake, if not his own.

For her happiness – not his own.

They were unfamiliar feelings that Kelly was rousing within, and they swelled with terrifying uncertainly, but he didn't crush them down or deny them as he normally would. Like he had with her emotions, he let his own flow over him, deciding to simply experience them.

The words from his mentor, André Chevalier came to him then, "You are cut off *mon ami, oui*, but you are not an evil man. Your past has taught you to hide, even from yourself. But do not despair. You came to me, *n'est-ce pas?* That was an act of valor. Continue with such courage, *jeune home*. Life, for all its trials, is a healing process. Trust in what I tell you now. All will resolve in the fullness of time."

He recalled Kelly's words, when he'd asked her if she wanted to climax for him. She'd said she did, *"For you. Only for you."* It was as if she'd reflected herself right inside of him, more perfectly than a mirror, because he felt exactly the same way toward her.

John decided to be brave enough to tell her that.

He withdrew his hands, placing them passively beside his thighs. "Suck me off, Kelly. You can't do it wrong. Anything you do will be right. There's no one else I want. Just you. Only you."

The sound she made was between a sob and a sigh, and he knew the emotional woman was no doubt crying again. It made him want to cry, too, which of course was impossible, and was just another step he was taking on the road to total madness.

He leaned against the wall of the elevator, as he needed the support. *I can do this,* he thought, with this hands clinched in tight fists upon his thighs. But then she put her mouth to the head of his cock. In the safety of darkness, with a woman he was fond of, he tried to forget everything and force himself to *feel.*

Kelly softly curled one small hand over his shaft, and the other caressed his balls. John felt his cock jerk as she brought him to her mouth. He'd never been circumcised, and he wondered if that fact made a difference to her. She seemed to take this in her stride however, sliding his foreskin back and licking around the rim, her tongue dipping in delicately to taste him.

He was hard and dripping and this was no surprise. That detail seemed to be a product of his age, not his interest. In fact, John felt incredibly uncomfortable. *Oh God! I can't do this,* he thought desperately. *No. That's an unproductive thought. Best to wonder, how can I do this?*

The answer came to him, and it was so obvious that he began to relax. All he had to do was concentrate on Kelly, and on the pleasure she was taking from giving him a climax.

"Your focus should be upon your sub. Your sub's pleasure is your primary concern," André had told him over and over, and it had been his golden rule ever since. He'd given Kelly an orgasm, and she wanted to return the favor.

John subdued an overwhelming impulse to laugh out loud. Wouldn't she be surprised to know how much he hated even the idea of it?

Kelly was humming. She was happy, and this made him happy – an abnormal circumstance in itself. But the woman was working too hard. Her need to please him was making him feel an emotion he rarely experienced: anxiety.

"Slow," he said, and her frantic movements ceased. Kelly's tongue caressed him languidly then, in a soothing manner.

"Yes. That's right," he said. Somehow, while relaxing into her movements, John's mind drifted. He thought of his mentor, André Chevalier.

The memory came back to him and he felt he was there.

Chapter 9

Instincts

John remembered that day so clearly.

It had been a bad morning, a terrible morning. He'd overstepped his bounds with his sub. The woman had been forced to call her safe word more than once. Somehow with an implement of pain in his hands John simply became mindless with the need to hurt someone, anyone. It was as if a lifetime of anguish could be exorcized by causing agony to another.

"It is not about pain," André continued to remind him. "It is all about pleasure." Depressed and defeated, John doubted if he'd ever get it right.

"Come, *mon ami*," André said with a cheerful smile. "We are going out."

He got into the elevator with his mentor, moving down into the basement where André kept his Bugatti Veyron. It was a beautiful red and black sports car. They'd both jumped in, after André put something in the back.

At John's curious look, André explained. "We are going on a picnic, *mon ami*."

Of course, John thought, yet he admitted that the prospect cheered him.

They drove to Red Rock Canyon National Park. André had an annual pass, and after they arrived he'd gotten out of the car and let John drive. John had never driven a high powered vehicle, much less a Bugatti, and he was flattered that André would let him. When he had asked about it, André had shrugged his shoulders in that French way of his.

"It is only a car, my friend. A very nice car, *vous comprenez*, but still a car. You are much more important to me right now, John. Crash it if you must, but do not kill us both if you do so, *s'il vous plait.*"

The comment had surprised a laugh out of John, which he knew full well, had been André's intention.

They stopped at Willow Springs for their picnic, surrounded by cactus trees, sage bush and chattering ground squirrels. The view was awe-inspiring. It was an astonishing contrast to the bright lights and hype of the Las Vegas Strip. The desert had its own dry beauty, with towering red sandstone cliffs.

André's chef, who John was beginning to really appreciate, had packed everything. André shook out a large plaid blanket for them to rest on, and they enjoyed fantastic French cuisine. In this open, natural environment John found that he'd gotten his often temperamental appetite back, and had seconds, and then even thirds. André had laughed over his greed, but in such a way that John couldn't feel insulted.

"It is very pretty, *n'est-ce pas?*" André asked looking out to the vista, while lounging languidly on his side with his head propped on one elbow.

"Yes," John replied.

André had laughed again, no doubt amused by how few words John used. André was forever telling him to stop his constant chattering. Such was his odd French humor, and John was only beginning to understand it and find it amusing. He found himself so attracted to the man that his mentor was. André was such a happy soul. How did he do it? John wanted to be just like him.

He found himself staring at André, and André lay back with his arms behind his head and shut his eyes. John knew that his mentor had done this intentionally. His friend had felt John's eyes on him, and wanted him to go ahead and uninhibitedly look his fill.

André was considerate that way, and when he did little things like this, John did feel something. It was a little pang in his chest, possibly even his heart. For even though John doubted it, André had assured him that he did have a heart.

André was about ten years older, but a million years more experienced than he was. John wondered why the man tolerated him, although he knew that André genuinely liked him. Why he couldn't imagine.

John didn't like himself.

Unmoving, he studied his mentor. He was wearing blue jeans, but on him they looked like Armani. André loved to dress well. The man was very fit, with a flat stomach, broad shoulders, dark hair, cut short around his neck and ears. His skin was naturally tan. He had brown eyes, and was always clean shaven.

John frowned. Other than his fancy clothes, and fit body the man looked fairly ordinary. There were pock marks on his face, yet they didn't detract at all. When he looked at his mentor he didn't see those marks anymore.

He only saw André, and he trusted the man completely.

It was the way André spoke, or the self-assured way he walked, he smiled, or he looked at you, he decided. André Chevalier oozed confidence and good-humor. John didn't like anyone, but he liked André very much. How close had his mentor and his Aunt Brenda been? Was André looking after him for the money or for the love of his Aunt? But John was sure that money wouldn't be André's biggest motivation for anything.

After a while André sat up. John didn't flinch or look away, but just continued staring at André, absorbed in the man who had already made his life so much more endurable.

André laughed, good-naturedly. "*Mon ami*, you have been watching me for a very long while, *oui*?"

"Yes."

André chuckled. "Well then, tell me what you study so intently. What do you see?"

"I'm curious about you, André. I wish I was more like you."

He laughed. "This is not a goal I would have had for you, John. I wish for you to find who *you* are, and be more like that."

John ignored André's comment. "When I look at you I see confidence, not arrogance. I've learned to trust you in a very short time, and that's something I never do with anyone."

"Trust?"

"Yes. I was trying to understand, what is it about you? Why do I trust you so completely?"

"*Merci.* You flatter me, John. And what have you decided?"

"You're comfortable in your own skin. Your actions come naturally. You don't second guess yourself all the time. It's integrity. I'm not talking about strong moral principles, although I'm sure you're a man with those. I mean by definition "the state of being whole and undivided." Honesty, probity. You're not divided, André, – you wage no war against yourself."

"And you, *mon ami?*"

"I'm divided in every way, and very uncomfortable in my own skin. It's not natural to me. My parents didn't teach me…I never learned. I don't know how to do it." John ran his hand through his thick hair, aware that by such an action he was displaying his agitation. Yet he was becoming accustomed to being more relaxed around André. Despite his inbuilt inclination to hide behind an emotionless mask, he was able to expose himself to the man.

André gestured to him, pointing toward the red and green plaid picnic blanket. "Look at this fly, John. Do you see it there? It is enjoying a little crumb of our French bread, I think. Study it now for me, and then tell me what you see."

John watched the fly intensely for some time. When he finished he looked up at his friend.

"And so? What did you see?"

Ever observant, he gave André a detailed account of how it had been sitting, ready to fly off, alert and prepared for danger. But when the tiny creature had decided that all was safe, it had stretched its long tongue out, and eaten bread. And after eating, the fly had cleaned its head and wings in a very exact and particular way, first one side, and then another.

"Have you seen a fly do these things before, John?"

"Yes. Every fly I've ever seen does exactly what I just saw this fly do."

"Exactement! So, do you think the mother and father fly taught this fly to do these things? Or do you think these actions came naturally?"

"It's instinct."

"Just so." André sat up. "Your parents had no need to teach you, John. You were born with natural instincts and inherent personality. Your parents harmed you. If they had not interfered, you would have become who you are meant to be. Because of them it will take longer to find yourself. But the person you truly are is there, *mon jeun ami.* There is integrity. *Je vous assure,* you will become whole, John. And I will help you to achieve this."

Chapter 10

The Blind See

Kelly had her hands on him, and the queasy feeling John initially experienced exploded into full blown nausea, suddenly making him want to throw up.

No hand! No hands! No hands! he thought frantically.

"Stop," he commanded.

She did immediately, and he reached for the club tie he had in his pocket. He found both of Kelly's wrists in the dark, and pulled them together behind her back, binding them there. His movements were quick and thorough, because he had to get her hands away from him. But after she was safely restrained, he instantly felt better.

John cupped her face, and gave her a brisk yet reassuring kiss, licking and wetting her soft lips. "You *are* pleasing me, Kelly. Thank you. Yet I prefer to have you bound. I only want your mouth on me, alright?"

"Of course, John" she said, "Whatever you want, whatever you need, I want to give it to you." Then she took him into her warm wet depths once more.

Kelly's simple honest words struck him more forcefully than a fist to the gut. They were profound. *Whatever you need. I want to give it to you,* she'd said. The woman was a mirror again, reflecting his desires. Because more than anything, he wanted to do the same for her.

Instinct and integrity, he thought. *My body wants to climax, and I really want to please Kelly. This is who I am. I can do this. It's the natural purpose of a man, to procreate, and to please the one he loves.*

With those few thoughts a wondrous sensation surprised him – an intense spike of pleasure radiated along his spine, buttocks and balls. John's mind and body reeled with the heady, overwhelming sensations which flowed on the heels of that truth.

I really do love Kelly Flynn, he realized in a blinding white light of certainty, *and I always have.*

Suddenly he connected with his cock and he jerked, his hips thrusting uncontrollably. At first it felt painful, that odd joining to something he hated – to something he'd cut himself off from so many years before. But that was then. Everything felt completely different now. *This is who I am. I need to please Kelly Flynn. I love her.*

An amazing pleasure rolled through John Taylor's body, all the enjoyable, electric sensation coming from his lower belly and his cock. *Oh!* he thought with wonder and sudden understanding. *This is what my male subs feel.* His flesh awakened, as if after a long sleep. It was like bright light flashing on, illuminating the darkness, or opening one's eyes and seeing the world after a lifetime of blindness.

Awed, John understood for the first time the exquisite joy of a woman going down on him. The human need for skin to skin contact. Love, trust, and the sharing of an intimate moment with someone that he cared for. Just then he felt he'd do anything for Kelly Flynn. Anything to make her happy. Live for her, die for her – it didn't matter. She was the most important thing in the whole world to him.

Sensations, emotions and *feelings* woke up, bombarding him, firing his soul: hunger, intense yearning, excitement, insatiable ferocious bliss.

"Ahhhh, ohhh!" he gasped with astonishment and pulse-pounding pleasure. "That feels good, Kelly." The words were inadequate, but John was surprised that he'd been capable of uttering anything at all. Not with the barrage of sensation that was currently frying every synapse he had.

With his response she began to work his cock faster, and he didn't mind, in fact he welcomed her enthusiasm. She wasn't anxious to please him now, for she instinctively knew she *was* pleasing him. Kelly was enjoying giving him actual pleasure, because *she cared for him, too.*

His muscles bunched and flexed, as a fierce and violent orgasm took him unexpectedly. With a guttural incoherent shout, he cried out and lost all control. Hips jerking ruthlessly forward, he drove hard into Kelly's wet, willing mouth.

John couldn't stand up to such ecstasy.

The man who mastered others, and had complete mastery of himself, suddenly experienced helplessness – a sensation he'd avoided since he was a child. Right now, Kelly was in command of him, because he was lost in pleasure. Yet, somehow, that was okay. He felt safe with her, so he had trustingly jumped off that cliff. John let himself go – for he knew she was there. Kelly would catch him as he fell.

"Oh my, God!" he shouted.

Soundless at all times when masturbating, this uninhibited expression of sexual gratification was far out of the norm for John Taylor. Usually he was disconnected from the entire process, quietly trying not to be a part of it. Yet, here in the dark, with Kelly, a woman he cared for, he suddenly found he could experience an orgasm.

His head flew backwards as he arched and thrust, spurting inside her in violent spasms. His balls shot their load and his sperm erupted, jetting from his cock, in blinding pulses of release.

Nothing in his entire lifetime had ever felt so good.

Nothing. Ever.

Silent now, except for his ragged breathing, he continued to ejaculate into Kelly's mouth, marveling in the shear, uninhibited joy of it, and the fact it felt good and right and pure. With her mouth tight around his shaft, Kelly ravenously continued sucking and swallowing his semen as he climaxed. As the last of his cum spewed from him, his happiness overflowed.

André! John thought. *André my friend! I understand now! I understand!*

It was the first time he could recall ever having an orgasm without feeling nausea, shame or discussed. For once he wasn't at war with himself. It was the first time he'd simply been there and experienced sex.

John went to his knees, embracing and kissing Kelly with all of the passion and unbridled joy he was feeling, tasting his own musk in her mouth, combined with the feminine scent and flavor that was uniquely hers.

Arms bound behind her back, she pushed up against him, making small sounds of what? Triumph? Happiness? Joy? She deserved it. John had never felt so happy in his life.

Framing her face in his hands he said with absolute sincerity, "Thank you, Kelly. Thank you."

He was surprised to find that his eyes stung. He never cried, and didn't think he could even now, but he wanted to – so vast and uncontained was his joy. John was totally overwhelmed and not a little confused from discovering how to let go and to *feel*. But now that he'd escaped, he wasn't going to allow anything to push him back into the dark box he'd lived in for so long.

A tendril of fear curled through him, because so much could go wrong. But right here, and at this moment, Kelly was his. He was alive, and in love. No matter what happened, at this exact moment he was truly happy.

John came twice more in that elevator, and each time he had Kelly suck him off. In-between times he fingered or licked her also to orgasm. Now that he'd discovered the key to such natural completion, he wanted to ensure he really understood and didn't forget how it had happened, so that it could happen again.

His need was great, for the more pleasure he received, the greedier he became, hungry for the physical act that represented trust and affection and all the finer emotions. At last he had a glimpse of the joyfulness in the union of love that poets wrote of. Until this night he'd never understood.

John's ever erect cock was hard, tireless and insatiable. That was nothing new. But for the first time in his life he was quite in harmony with the damn thing.

I've had three orgasms, he thought. And unlike what usually happened, all three felt *good.* No disgust, no shame – he'd only enjoyed ecstasy. At twenty-six years old John Taylor was only just beginning to understand the pleasure and essential intimacy of the sexual act.

But would it last? What would happen after the firemen came and he and Kelly escaped their dark sexual haven? He clenched his jaw.

Somehow he had to make Kelly Flynn his, and in a way that he could keep her forever. But he had not the slightest idea of how to go about it.

STRIPPED

3

Chapter 1

Rescue

⚭

"Parents are supposed to love their children. One could imagine this fact to be a genetic imperative. Your parents, *je suis désolé*, were quite mad, *mon ami*. You have seen how pain and pleasure can become confused, for your own body's natural gratification was turned to pain. Yet the opposite is also true. It is a strange paradox that if you love someone so hard that it hurts, your pain will disappear. You must find someone to love, John. For she will take your pain away."

- André Chevalier, conversation with John Taylor

⚭

Kelly Flynn had been knocked completely on her ass – both figuratively and literally.

It had been quite a night. If someone made a list of human emotions, from the worst feelings in the world to the highest possible states, Kelly figured in this one evening she'd experienced pretty well all of them. Terror, panic, dread, fear of death, shock, embarrassment, shyness, anticipation, excitement, longing, joy, happiness, euphoria, and heart-stopping, soul soaring love. She'd felt the full gamut.

All because she'd been trapped in an elevator with an unattainable man that she had a crush on. A man that she was obsessed with, and had fallen in love with. But John Taylor seemed to want her, too. Or did he? Did he feel as close to her as she did to him?

The building that The Basement was in, was an older one. Because they were unable to immediately fix the fault, firemen came and pried open the external elevator-well doors at the first floor. John then boosted Kelly up through the ceiling man hole, so that she could be pulled to safety. With the aid of a rope, the firemen pulled John up and out, after her. They'd spent an hour and twenty minutes inside the darkness of the elevator.

I had five orgasms during that time, Kelly mused. *That's like, what? One climax every twenty minutes or so? And John had three.* She realized her jaw was a little sore from going down on him, and smiled. The man who never had sex, and never kissed had done so with her. *Lord in heaven. First I had a crush, but now I'm gone. My savior. I'm completely in love with Father John.*

The way that man kissed alone was enough to make her love him!

The paramedics checked them over, and gave them water. John kept his arm possessively around Kelly the whole time. His steady hold both supported and charmed her. She still wore his long leather matrix jacket, thrown casually over her shoulders. The scent of him was embedded in it. The warmth of John, the feel of him holding her, and his smell engulfing her, all combined to make her feel safe, protected, and cared for.

"Come with me," he said, guiding her with a firm hand, placed on the curve of her lower back.

They took the stairs to the ground floor car park where John had left his silver Mercedes sports car. It was brand new, and expensive. Kelly hadn't ever considered what kind of car he might drive, but this sleek and powerful vehicle suited him. He hit the unlock button. and it beeped cheerfully.

Opening the passenger door, he guided her in. Once he got into the driver's seat he said, "I'm going to stay with you tonight, Kelly. Do you want to sleep at my house or yours?"

Thinking of the mess her small apartment was in, she gave a shaky laugh. "Yours."

"Good. I live closer, too."

Kelly thought it an odd comment, but didn't question it. How did he know where she lived? She had a fleeting thought about her car, but it was safe in a parking lot. John drove with the competence she'd expected from a man like him. There was a full moon out tonight, peeking in and out of the clouds of rain. He stopped at the 7-Eleven.

"What kind of pop do you like?" he asked.

"Diet Coke," she replied.

He left the car running, and told her he was getting just a few things. Then he opened the door and ran through the rain and into the shop. Alone with her thoughts, Kelly waited. What exactly about him held such devastating appeal?

She'd had a crush before but now she was really in trouble. Man, oh, man what a guy. He spoke and moved with total confidence. She imagined what his hard muscles would look like under his clothes and her stomach fluttered, because she was going to find out real soon.

When John returned he handed her a bouquet of flowers – not roses – pink and white daisies. Kelly laughed out loud, but inside she was touched. "Daisies," she'd told him, was her safe word. Was he trying to reassure her that she was safe with him?

It was still raining, so there were drops of water on his neck when he hopped back in. She looked at him, wanting to lick it off. Jesus, five of the best orgasms of her life and she was still horny. She wondered if either of them would get any sleep tonight, and decided probably not.

John also handed her a paper bag of stuff, which she immediately looked through. Two Hershey's chocolate bars, a large cold bottle of Diet Coke, a pink, up-market toothbrush (a thoughtful touch) and a large box of condoms.

She felt her lips curl with a broad grin of delight when she saw the box of condoms. Kelly slid a look at John. To her delight, he smiled back at her. *¡Ay, caramba!* She'd never really seen him smile. It was all she'd hoped it would be. Father John smiling, took her breath away.

"Do you think we have enough condoms?" she asked, daring to make a little joke.

"I'm not sure. Do you have anywhere to go tomorrow?"

"No."

"Good," he said in a neutral tone. "Then we can spend the day together. And in that case, we may need to go out for more."

She snickered, because it was funny. But she also wasn't sure if he was actually making a joke. John always appeared so solemn. Kelly wondered what she was doing going home with him, but only a moment. The man had saved her life. Seriously. She could have died in that little elevator. Not only that but he had probably exorcised that phobia of small dark spaces forever. Now when she thought of tiny, black, airless rooms she'd think of *him* and not be frightened at all.

Kelly licked her lips and grinned. From this day forward, each time she entered an elevator, she suspected that she'd become instantly wet.

Chapter 2

John's House

John lived in Aloha about fifteen minutes away from The Basement. It was kind of a rundown old suburb with older homes and even older people. His house had a detached garage that they drove up to by way of a driveway alongside the house.

He entered his block, and hit the automatic door. An upward-acting garage door raised but this was the only evidence of modernity that Kelly could see. Long boards were through the rafters of the garage, and she could see odd assorted, stored stuff up there, like a rusty red children's bike, and garden stuff like hoes and rakes. The garage was pretty basic, with no heat, no obvious insulation, and one bare bulb for electricity.

When Kelly stood at the doorway she noticed two strips of concrete spaced for car wheels, with grass and gravel alongside and between. It seemed so odd to have this modern, expensive car, housed in such a lowly garage. It was like having a champion thoroughbred racehorse put in a back yard garden with a handmade wooden lean-to for shelter.

They both made a run for it in the rain, in through a side entry and into his home. He tapped numbers into a keypad, turning off an alarm as they entered.

John lived in a bungalow, a house built probably back in the 1940's. It was small but quaint with a front porch and transverse roof slope to the street-front and a dormer window in the roof. Older area. Older home. Kelly was even more surprised when she walked inside.

This house belongs to an old lady, not a strong, masterful Dom like John, she thought.

It was a small house with probably two or three bedrooms and a modern-feeling low ceiling. They'd entered directly into the kitchen, family area. The ugly tan armchairs were from the 1970's, and the kitchen hadn't been renovated either, or rather it had been, but the countertops were still that weird orange that was all the rage years ago. A really old overstuffed chair sat in front of the antique TV, covered by a blanket made with colorful crochet squares. Definitely old lady.

When she looked up at him with a question in her eyes John shrugged and said, "This was my Aunt Brenda's house."

Kelly wanted to ask how long had he lived here? And why hadn't he modernized or redecorated? Yet some renovation had been done as the room was warm and comfortable, centrally heated.

Irrepressibly curious about John, Kelly had a million questions but bit her tongue. He was notorious for being a man of few words. In her case, it was hard to keep her mouth shut. Still a little shy of John, and his overwhelming presence, she managed to keep quiet, having decided that if he wanted to talk, he would. So she sat on a wooden stool at the kitchen counter and simply watched him.

John made them both hot chocolate in mugs, tossed a couple marshmallows in each, and heated them in the microwave. Then he got out homemade spinach and ricotta cannelloni and a fresh salad from the fridge. Kelly could see it was home made. Did John cook it? Did he, like her, enjoy cooking? But again, she didn't ask.

When the microwave finished, he handed her a cup. "Careful," he cautioned. "It may be too hot."

Kelly blew on the dark liquid, and smiled when she took her first sip. Marshmallows. What man would think of that wonderful little touch? Seriously? Meanwhile he got out red wine, a Bordeaux, corked it, and brought it and two glasses over to the kitchen table. Kelly was willing to bet money that Bordeaux was the exact wine that one was supposed to drink with cannelloni.

John put the cannelloni in the microwave on re-heat. Then he got a clear crystal vase out of a cupboard, and a box of aspirin. He crushed an aspirin between two spoons and put it in the vase, stirred and added water. Kelly had left her daisies on the counter and he put them in the vase. She figured aspirin must add to the life of the flowers, and she thought it was such a weird thing for someone her age to know, or even to care about.

Complete silence was no longer an issue, mainly because John was such a pleasure to watch, as he confidently and purposefully moved around the small kitchen.

The microwave finished with a ding. Putting both cannelloni and salad on separate plates, with a hand at her lower back, John escorted her to the 1960's wooden kitchen table set. He courteously pulled out a chair, and she sat down.

"Are you hungry?" he asked, setting a plate of food in front of her.

"Now you ask?" she said with a smirk, looking up at him.

John gave her that slow smile again, and Kelly just wanted to melt. He was sooooo freaking beautiful with those dark expressive eyes. He'd a strong jaw, thick dark hair and a symmetrical face with strangely soft, almost feminine features. No wonder everyone wondered if he was gay.

John's usually smooth shaven face showed the shadow of a growth from the stubble of a beard. Kelly found herself caught, staring once more because he simply took her breath away.

"I want you to eat," he said. Then he added in a low, suggestive voice. "I think we're both going to need our energy, Kelly."

Chapter 3

Bedroom

∝ ∾

Kelly felt her cheeks heat and bit a lower lip while her mind whirled. What was it about John Taylor?

Never had she felt such sexual chemistry with another person. It was completely overwhelming. She wanted to shout with joy, or dance naked in the moonlight – even in this rain. She needed him to screw her silly, to be inside her, to spill his cum all over her body. She wanted to listen to him climax with those amazing male sounds of pleasure he made. She wanted to hear his courteous "Thank you, Kelly," after he shot his load and she'd swallowed every drop. She wanted to feel all those wonderful sensations she felt when John showered her with his grateful sensual kisses.

Man, I've lost every brain cell I ever had, she thought, and she knew her heated cheeks were as red as a strawberries. Kelly cleared her throat, got hold of her emotions and nodded. Then she picked up a fork.

Using a thumb and finger from his hand, John raised her chin, to look at her. "I love this blush. It's such a wonderful display, to let a Dom know something is going on. But I don't understand it. Are you embarrassed after all we've done together?"

Her gaze never left his, as she shook her head sheepishly. "You said we need energy, and I know why we need it. Then I imagined you and me in your bed, and the idea of more sex sounded so great that I just blushed because I was seriously turned on. This is my 'I'm turned on' blush," she said with an irrepressible giggle.

She shifted back in her chair and pressed her thighs together, trying to camouflage her desperate need. "It's probably not much different from my 'I'm embarrassed' blush. I go red a lot, John, so

I hope you can get used to that. But right now I want to have sex with you. And I want it with the lights on, because I want to see you this time. I'm looking forward to lots and lots of hot, back scratching, toe curling, mind-blowing sex."

His lips firmed into that implacable look she was beginning to know so well. "Me too," he said, in a quiet voice. "Thank you for telling me. I want us to always be honest with each other, as much as we can be. I feel so honored by your trust Kelly."

There were so many things she wanted to talk to John about, but he was so reserved. For once she decided not to wreck the mood, with her famous idle chatter. She didn't want to risk it just at the moment. Because if she talked too much maybe he'd just get sick of her and take her home.

They both ate silently, without attention on their food. If she slowed, he gave her narrowed eyes and a, 'If I can eat when all I can think of is sex, so can you,' look. John poured them each some wine, and they both sat across from each other, just staring.

Kelly thought it was the single most erotic meal that she'd ever had. Watching him put each forkful of food in his mouth, and knowing where that mouth had been, and where it might yet go later on tonight.

John stood up suddenly, picking up the box of condoms. "Had enough?"

"Of food, yes," she said, making it clear that she was still hungry in other ways. She reached for her plate.

"Leave it," he said. With a firm hand on her back, and the tips of his fingers resting on her butt cheeks, John escorted her into his bedroom, and flicked on the light.

"Oh," Kelly said, and stood back in shock. Now this was more like it. She'd imagined something minimalistic and super well ordered, judging by what she knew of John, but that wasn't the case. This room was warm and inviting.

John's bedroom was huge, big enough to be a bedroom and large living or study area. He must've renovated this section completely, taking over the living room, but that wasn't the most interesting thing about his bedroom. It looked like something out of Merlin's Cave. A large chandelier brightened the entire room that had dark wooden floors, and an interesting red, green and yellow oriental carpet. Olive green velvet curtains covered the windows, sheltering them from prying eyes.

The room was filled with elaborate patterns and natural textures. It had an air of sophistication, yet the materials seemed simple and often antique or made by hand. There was a large fireplace, with a stone hearth. The bed was king size of dark barley twisted oak, with a matching dressing table. There were two oak desks in the room, and rows of book shelves with hundreds, if not thousands of books.

An ereader rested on a bedside table with three other books. A plastic full size skeleton hung in the corner. At least she hoped it was plastic, and there was a world globe and a set up with four computer screens – so the man was certainly computer literate. The walls were filled with everything from Indian tie dyed wall hangings to a quite stunning Greek Orthodox religious Icon of the Virgin Mary with a child.

He'd placed the box of condoms on the bedside table, and since then had been studying her intently, no doubt gauging her reactions. Kelly turned to him and said in a gush of enthusiasm, "Oh, John, this room is gorgeous!"

There was no change in his expression, but a smile lit his eyes.

She brushed her hand over the handmade broken star quilt, made in the masculine ocher, olive greens and dark yellows of the room. Had some Amish lady somewhere quilted it?

John was such a unique and enigmatic man. What strange circumstances had made him the way he was? And what man of his age would consider making such a comfortable, unique space for himself?

"Did you decorate this room?" she asked,

"Yes," he said. "I spend a lot of time here."

Kelly had been surreptitiously looking for floggers, paddles, even ring bolts or cuffs – but there was nothing. So what did he do with his sexual partners?

"You're the only person that I've ever brought to my home, Kelly," he said.

Jesus, she thought. *How had he known what I was thinking?* She knew then that her friend Rosslyn had been right. Father John could read minds.

For one weird moment, she felt violently jealous of Rosslyn, for the time she'd spent with him, and for the connection they'd forged. It was an odd emotion for her, because she wasn't the jealous type, but John was different. Kelly had never had such an incredible attraction to anyone, like she had with this sexy Dom. And was she really the first woman he had ever brought home?

"Am I really the first?" she said, echoing her thought out loud, and on catch in her heart with that idea.

He brushed her cheek with the back of his knuckles. "The one and only," he replied with a smile that would make angels weep. John was achingly beautiful but all she could think was, why her? Why would this man, who could have had anyone, want her?

John strode purposefully to the bedhead. Then he pulled back the quilt, blanket, and top sheet, dropping them off the end of bed. "Have you seen enough?"

"Yes," she said, and her mouth went dry.

"Good," he said quietly, but his voice had the tone of command. "Then take off all your clothes please, Kelly."

Kelly felt like all the air had left her lungs suddenly, and she couldn't speak. She stared at him, mesmerized. Then she simply nodded, and started to unlace her corset.

Chapter 4

Examination

There was not one hesitation as Kelly instantly obeyed. John, still in his black leather pants, swat boots and black T shirt watched her undress with a firm no nonsense, intent look. When she was naked he said, "Thank you, Kelly. Now stand here in front of me. Spread your legs wide apart, hands clasped behind your back."

She complied.

Unmoving, standing about three feet away, John studied her for many long moments. The look he gave her was calculating and heated, and her breath and pulse quickened. He looked over every part of her body until Kelly wanted to squirm away from those hot intense eyes of his, or jump his bones – she wasn't sure which.

"For tonight you're my sub, agreed?" he said.

"Yes, John."

"I don't have a lot of rules, Kelly, so don't worry. I'll tell you what I want. No lies and obedience are the main things. You will use your safe word if you have any hesitation, on anything at all, do you understand?"

"Yes, John."

"Remain perfectly still now, Kelly. I want to inspect you fully, to discover just exactly how lucky I am," he said in a deceptively mild tone. She felt he was holding himself back, trying to start slow, to give her confidence, and set her at ease. His consideration made her heart ache because it was so thoughtful and sweet.

John came close to her, and put his hands lightly on her head, and began playing with her hair. Bringing it close to his face, he breathed in deeply. "I love your hair, Kelly. I know you hate the color, but I love it. I think it's really striking and unique."

How does he know? she thought wildly, her body tensing. *Shit. And what else does he know about me? The man is psychic. I can hide nothing from him.*

His fingers moved to her face, tracing her cheeks, eyebrows, and forehead. "I love the color of your eyes, too. So pale blue." He cupped her chin. "Your jaw is square, and I bet you hate that. But I like it, Kelly. Do you know why I like it?"

"No, John," she whispered, and her body quivered for he had struck the truth once more. Jesus he was freaking her out. She did hate her manly jaw. This Dom scared her, and excited her in a way that no one had ever done before.

"Because it's yours, Kelly. I like everything about you."

Impossible, she thought, fighting against the need for a physical response to such a ridiculous statement. *Why is he lying to me? He doesn't even know me! He only met me tonight in an elevator.*

John must have seen the surprise and anger in her face, despite her attempt to hide it, because he gave a soft chuckle. "Did you think I didn't notice the way your eyes have been following me for the last month? You've been watching me. Well, I've been watching you, too. I think you're drawn to me, Kelly. You want me. And you've had no idea, have you? That all that time, I've wanted you, too."

She drew in a shocked breath, and her heart thumped loudly with that disclosure.

One warm hand cupped her jaw, and he pressed his lips against hers in one short, bruising, passionate kiss. "God, I love your mouth," he whispered, because he was so close to her. "Open up, Kelly," he said, and while she did so she wondered at his interest, why he wanted to look inside her mouth, like she was a horse for sale or something.

John's sensual fingers caressed her lips, and he put his fingers inside her, touching and seeking for the end of her throat, feeling her tongue, and the roof of her mouth, rubbing his index finger around her gums. Taking his time, he intensely studied her *there*.

The entire process made her wet and needy, and not for one logical reason could she imagine why. Unless it was simply the fact that she was letting him do exactly as he liked. The idea of John taking her over, and doing whatever he wanted, was the turn on after all.

"You may close now, Kelly," he said, taking his fingers away. "I just wanted to see," he added by way of explanation. "To understand how my cock fit so well inside you. You gave me so much enjoyment, just from your beautiful mouth," he kissed her again, and brushed his warm fingers along her throat, cupping her chin and jaw. "A large jaw is supposed to represent strength of character, Kelly, did you know that?"

"No, John." She couldn't believe the intense physical reaction she had when he said her name. His deep, cultured voice, was soothing yet commanding; focused and in control. Her heart skipped a beat, and her whole body came to attention with arousal and need, every single time he said her name.

John stroked down her neck and shoulders, and along her arms. "Give me your hands," he said, and she did. To her surprised he brought both of them to his lips and kissed them. "Such feminine little hands." He studied them, too, and finally said, "Clasp them again, behind your back," he ordered. When she did so he said, "Thank you, Kelly," politely, as he always did.

Kelly, Kelly, Kelly, she thought, feeling an urgent need to climax. *All my life I've heard people say my name. But no one has ever said it in the dark, seductive, and sensual way that John does.*

His fingers trailed down her skin to cup her breasts, weighing them and inspecting them. With thumb and fingers of both hands he gently rolled each nipple. Kelly felt them stiffen further at his touch. He looked into her eyes then, and pinched each nipple *hard*, both at the same time.

Kelly didn't move, but she did gasp slightly.

"Good girl," he said. He tugged and lightly fondled her, caressing her abused flesh. She found it difficult to remain still. "You liked that, Kelly." It was a statement, not a question.

"Yes, Sir," she admitted, absently agreeing with him. A wave of fierce energy, recalled her to her mistake. The suppressed violence of John's expression, combined with his flashing eyes, made her unintentionally flinch.

"I'm…I'm sorry," she stuttered quickly. "I meant to say yes, John."

He exhaled a sharp breath. "Don't ever call me that," he said in a stern voice, his face implacable, and his eyes *hard*. "I'll disregard this incident this once, but if you make this mistake again I'll punish you. And I'll do it in a way that you will never forget," he added ominously. Kelly blinked under his fierce stare. "Do you understand?"

"Yes, John," she said, her body shivering with dread. *Crap! I've got to remember,* she thought. *He's a powerful Dom, and he has a bullwhip! I sure don't want to cross him. But what's the big deal about using the appellation, Sir?*

Incident forgotten, he ran his fingers caressingly through her hair. It made her scalp tingle, and sent sensation down her spine. It seemed a soothing apology for his unexpected reaction.

"Good girl," he said. John came to one knee before her then and clinically examined her sex. It was amazingly erotic, to have him fondle her in such an objective manner, softly stroking her mons, spreading her labia wide, impersonally examining her clitoris, pulling back the hood, and even stroking her perineum.

All the while he made scientific comments, almost muttering to himself saying, "A pale, well-formed vulva," and when putting a finger inside her, "Such a snug, tight vagina, but it will swell and loosen with arousal."

She could feel his hot breath tickling her sensitive skin as he spoke, and wondered if she'd go mad with lust.

Finally he leaned back and looked up at her. "Your sex is gorgeous, Kelly. So pink," he said. "So soft and swollen and pretty. And all mine. This pretty little cunt is mine, isn't it Kelly?" he said, firmly cupping her mound.

"Yes, John," she gasped.

"Good," he said. "Then I'll tell you what I plan to do with it."

Chapter 5

Mastered

~⟡~

Kelly waited, desperate to know what he intended.

John put two fingers inside her, moved them in sensual, circular motions and then removed them. With his fingers dripping, he splayed them around the small bundle of nerves of her clit, rubbing back and forth with firm slick strokes. Kelly became aware of how aroused she was from the unintentional little sounds she was making. It was becoming more and more difficult not to move.

"You're very wet for me, aren't you?" he said.

"Yes, John... God, yes," she breathed. Well, that was an understatement because she could feel her arousal trickling right down her thighs. Kelly's mind whirled. This man didn't need BDSM trappings of cuffs or crops to master her. Right now she was his willing slave. He dominated her completely, with just his voice and touch. She'd never been so turned on in all her life.

He chuckled, his straight white teeth gleaming. "Listen to me, Kelly. I love having my mouth on your cunt. I'm going to taste you. I want to lick up every drop, and make you climax."

A strangled moan escaped her lips.

John noted her response, but continued speaking. "This is the point. I've decided that I want you to stand right where you are without moving. And I don't want you to make a sound either. You may not be able to do it, but if you can it will please me very much. Do you want to please your Dom, Kelly?"

"Yes, oh yes, John, I do."

"Very good." He snorted. "My mouth is going to be too busy to order you to climax, especially as I want to feel you come with

117

my tongue deep in your cunt. I want to feel that, you milking and bathing my lips, my mouth and tongue. Do you understand? Don't come until I thrust my tongue right inside your cunt. Now tell me what you're going to do for me, Kelly."

The muscles low in her belly tensed, and her core pulsed. Just the thought of seeing John's head between her legs, made her whimper. And to remain silent while she exploded? It seemed an impossible task.

Kelly took a deep breath. "I'm going to be still, and I'm not going to make a sound while I come for you. But I won't climax until your tongue is deep inside me."

"Inside where?" John demanded.

Kelly felt her face heat, and it wasn't from embarrassment. It was from arousal. Who wouldn't be turned on from John's raw erotic words, not to mention the thought of his tongue *there?* But he obviously wanted her to use steamy words, too.

She cleared her throat and said, "Inside my cunt."

"Good girl."

Kelly knew her engorged clit was sticking out for him, just begging to be touched. John didn't touch it. Instead his diabolical thumb circled her aching nub, sending a bliss-filled zing throughout her body. Her instant moan became strangled as she pressed her lips together and all sound cut off.

"Thank you, Kelly," he said, when she'd subdued her impulse to move and make noise. "It's quite difficult isn't it? To remain motionless and soundless when your natural inclination is to do both? Don't speak – those were rhetorical questions," he added while still fondling her in a delicious manner. His touch seemed calculated to send her up into the clouds on an erotic high. "You're so good, Kelly. I don't expect that you will be able to do it, and I won't punish you if you can't. I just want to watch you try," he said.

It wouldn't take long to climax, for she was much more than half way there. John nipped the tender flesh of her open thighs.

Then he spread her nether lips with both hands, and licked her with the flat of his tongue, greedily lapping at her feminine entrance as if he wanted to drink every body fluid up that she had.

Oh God, she thought when her entire body rebelled with a crazed need to call out and move. *How can I do this? Impossible! And yet more than anything I want to please John.* It was torture. It was agony. But somehow she controlled herself.

His skillful tongue moved right from her perineum, all the way to her clitoris, but he neglected that completely, circling around it but touching never upon it. His teasing nips and licks were driving her mad. John clearly didn't plan to make this easy for her.

Kelly's whole body trembled wildly, but she held back her moans and whimpers and remained as motionless as humanly possible. She felt dizzy, giddy and unsteady, but all her attention was focused. *No sound. No movement. It was vital to make HIM happy.*

His fingers were deep inside her, twisting toward her public bone, pumping and rubbing as he penetrated her. Suddenly he curled his talented tongue around her clit.

With an internal mental scream of pleasure, Kelly clenched her jaw and bit back a moan. Her body lurched, only slightly. She was proud of that.

Relentless, John licked and sucked her clitoris. This time she gave an uncontrollable little buck before she was able to stop herself. When clever suction pulsed her clit, he almost sent her over. A pre-orgasmic throb rolled through her, and she stiffened and shuddered.

John began to fuck her then, thrusting his tongue deep inside. Abruptly it was all too much. *Thank God,* she thought. *He wants me to come.*

Kelly made a low keening sound – for a moment she couldn't prevent it. But she pressed her lips firmly together and the noise stopped. With his tongue deep in her cunt, John held her hips to steady her. If anything her violent orgasm seemed stronger than ever in her urgent need to hold all sound and movement back.

It was the difference between setting off a bomb outdoors – or in the confines of a small room. In the latter case, the room would be decimated.

In this case Kelly was decimated.

Her orgasm took her suddenly. It exploded from within, while all her concentration was focused upon holding still and keeping silent. It was a fierce battle and her climax seemed to be particularly long, going on, and on, because she simply couldn't bear it. All that pleasure had to be contained and experienced in silence and stillness when all she wanted to do was thrash and scream.

John stood up and held her tightly, which was just as well as her legs were going to give out. Her entire body shook; sweating, trembling and breathing raggedly. Her mind fogged, and occasional aftershocks pulsed through her – delirious spikes of added rapture that were almost too intense to endure. Finally her violent waves of pleasure eased.

John held her, patting and coddling her for long minutes, while she came back to herself. And all that time his husky voice praised her, saying "Good girl. You did so well. You tried so hard." Soft kisses covered her neck and face. "I felt the severe strain you were under. Thank you, Kelly. You did that to please me, didn't you?"

"Yes, John," she said. "I want to please you more than anything."

The sound of his sudden laugh surprised her. It was a carefree joyful sound. "You're like a mirror, Kelly. My God I see so much, just from looking at you." He kissed her soundly. "Because more than anything I want to please you, too."

This admission rocked her, but she didn't have much time to think about it. As she was strong enough now to stand, John wanted to continue his inspection.

"Turn around and put your hands on the foot board railing of my bed. Then spread your legs and bend over." As she did so he ran his hands up and down her torso, stroking her back, flanks and buttocks, and down along her hips. Her feminine fragrance filled the air, and arousal dripped down her thighs.

He moved her legs further apart, by nudging each with his feet. Once more he touched every part of her, commenting and examining. Sometimes just staring at her for minutes at a time, telling her how beautiful she was, and how much he wanted her.

"I love the color and texture of your skin, so creamy and silky," he said, stroking her hips. "And those freckles of yours are amazing. I want to kiss each and every one of them."

This interesting news thrilled her, shifting the way she saw herself completely. She had freckles everywhere, and she'd always hated them. But John liked them! A moan escaped her mouth with the idea of him kissing them all.

He chucked, aware of her thoughts, or at least of her arousal. "I'm going to spank you sometime tonight or tomorrow, and I just know I'll leave bright red hand prints on your pale flesh. I give a ruthless spanking. I want to see you squirming and writhing across my lap, suffering the sting of my hard, sharp slaps right until you climax for me. Do you want me to spank you until you come, Kelly?"

Jesus. I could climax just hearing him talk like that, she thought.

Kelly's face heated with arousal and embarrassment, and she was glad she wasn't facing him. Her pussy clenched, gushing with desire. Somehow she felt so vulnerable, ashamed to be such a deviant as to enjoy a hard spanking.

He gave a low chuckle. "Never mind, I see that you do." He rubbed her back, in a soft, comforting motion, because once more it seemed he had read her mind. "There's nothing wrong with you, Kelly Flynn. Please don't ever be ashamed of anything with me. You're perfect in every way – you just have to trust me on this. You're perfect. I know what you want, and I plan to give you everything that you need."

"Thank you, John," she managed.

Kelly hardly knew this man, but she'd fallen pretty hard for him. He however, seemed to know her so completely. His praise, his appreciation would crack the most stubborn heart. The pessimistic part of her mind whispered, yes, but how many women has he told these things to? Be careful. This is how he gets people to love him.

But she knew that it was already too late.

I'm totally in love with John Taylor, she thought.

Chapter 6

Horny

Caressing lower, John smoothed both hands over the white globes of her buttocks, squeezing, stroking and fondling them possessively. The man was in no hurry.

Kelly bit a lower lip when John spread her butt cheeks and quietly studied her for some time, once more making her squirm with conflicting emotions: need, shyness, embarrassment.

"Has anyone had you here before?" he asked, softly rubbing the tip of one finger around the ring of her puckered anus, and then lightly pushing down against it.

"No, John." His touch on that forbidden place was sexually stimulating and a little scary, but Kelly didn't mind. Everything he did felt good. She felt unable to deny him anything.

"Good. You'll only feel my tongue and my thumb there tonight, but sometime soon I'm going to want to push myself into that tight little hole, Kelly." His fingers brushed lower, sliding between her dripping folds, and she moaned. "I'm going to have you in every possible way," he said.

"Yes, John," she whispered, helpless to his desire.

"Kelly, did anyone tell you that I never swear?" he asked with a casual hand on her buttocks.

"Yes John."

"Well, it's true. I don't usually swear. I was told as a child that "cursing is a sign of a lazy mind and an impoverished vocabulary." He snorted. "Maybe that statement is accurate. But I'm going to swear with you, Kelly. These are the words I'm going to use. First I'm going to use the word cunt."

John cupped her pussy, and began to finger her, probing lightly between her folds, squeezing and stroking. Kelly whimpered. "Nothing can describe this beautiful part of your body better than that word. You've a ripe, succulent cunt, Kelly. Swollen and needy, you're just aching for my cock, aren't you?"

"Yes, John," she said breathlessly, her heart pounded and her sex twitched. The raw, erotic way he spoke was incredible foreplay. She could listen to his deep seductive voice all day, but when he spoke with raunchy vulgarity in such a polite, conversational manner it sent her mad with shameless lust.

"Ass is another word, Kelly," he said and he put both large hands on her round globes, squeezing and massaging, stoking and caressing. "You have a magnificent ass – tight and round with a nice shapely curvature. It's a plump, firm, compact little ass. Do you think you'd like me to spread these lovely butt cheeks of yours sometime, and thrust my cock deep into your ass, Kelly?"

She gave a soft moan. "Yes, John. Yes," she said, to her surprise and amazement. She'd never, ever gone there, but again, she felt like going everywhere with John. Anywhere he wanted to take her.

"That's good," he said in a husky, seductive tone. "Because I want to push inside you there. I want to be your first. It's going to feel so good, Kelly, you won't believe how good I can make it feel. You'll like having my cock deep inside your tight asshole, pumping hard until I come, filling you up with my seed."

My God, a woman could orgasm just from his voice, but not just that voice – the things that he says, she thought.

Kelly restlessly shifted her feet, her body explosive with wanton lust and need. John's reaction was immediate.

Slap! Slap! Slap!

He gave her three hard, painful spanks on her buttocks – fast and shocking as machine gun fire. She called out and stilled, yet each strike from his hand made her core clench and gush with a pulsing wave of desire.

"I told you not to move, Kelly, while I finish my inspection," he reminded her.

"I'm sorry, John. I lost focus there for a minute. Please forgive me."

"Of course," he said coolly. "I understand perfectly. You're very horny and you really need to come again, don't you?"

"Oh, yes, John," she said. "But only when you want me to. I want to come for you, but only when you say I can. I want to please you, John."

"Thank you, Kelly," he said, gently smoothing his hands over her heated, smarting behind. "I understand, and you *are* pleasing me. Very much. And I was right. My hand has left lovely red marks on your white buttocks. So, so beautiful. Now can you recall what I was telling you?"

"Um, swear words, John. You were telling me what words you were going to use."

"Good girl," he said. With one hand on a butt cheek for balance, he petted her lightly between her legs, in soft, regular strokes with his free hand. She bit back a groan and did all she could to remain still.

"Finally, Kelly," he said. "I'm going to have to use the extremely crude word fuck."

He went to his knees then. Using his thumb and fingers he spread her butt cheeks and her nether lips at the same time. He vacuumed her clit into his mouth, biting and sucking making her want to scream. Then he licked from her clit, along her swollen empty pussy, right up to caress her tight anal ring with his warm, velvet tongue.

"Oh my God," she whimpered.

"You look amazing," he said. "Such delightful, delicious feminine holes. I'm going to fill them with my cock. I want to fuck you, Kelly. There's simply no other word for it. I'm going to fuck you all night long. That's why I'm trying to start slow. I'm sorry, Kelly, but I am going to pound into you so many times, and so hard you're going to have trouble walking in the morning."

"Yes, oh yes, John," she almost sobbed.

"Up on the bed now, Kelly. Lay down and masturbate while I undress. I want to watch you play with yourself, but you aren't allowed to come. The next time you climax will be when I've got my cock deep inside your needy little cunt. Do you understand?"

"Yes, John," she said, jumping up onto the middle of the bed. The soft white cotton sheets smelled like him, adding to her pleasure. He slept here every night. She wanted to roll around in those sheets like a dog, soaking up every bit of his scent.

She'd thought that it would be embarrassing, touching herself in front of another, but it wasn't. John was watching, and she was doing this *for him* after all. She shut her eyes to concentrate, and began to masturbate, the way she always did. After very little time she felt the slow, heavy pressure of an orgasm beginning to build.

The bed depressed and she opened her eyes and looked over to see John on his knees beside her, his cock near her face.

"Thank you, Kelly. It's beautiful watching you play with yourself, and extremely hot. What were you thinking about?"

"You, John, I was remembering the first time I sucked you off."

He smiled down at her, making her chest hurt. He had the most angelic expression sometimes. Kelly had met lots of good looking guys – she'd gone out with some, too. The man was hot, but it wasn't just his appearance. What was it about him that sent her so crazy with sexual hunger?

"I remember that, too." He put a hand on her breast, casually flicking and tugging a nipple. It was a natural, possessive action and her whole body quivered. John acted just like he owned her, and this gave her a huge sense of fulfillment and joy. It just felt so right.

Yes, she thought. *I belong to him.*

Chapter 7

Connection

⚮

"Arms over your head now, Kelly. Leave them there. Now spread your legs as far as you can, then pull up your knees. I want you fully exposed."

Oh God, she thought, her whole body thrumming with frisson of arousal as she obeyed his authoritative demands. *Finally he's going to fuck me.*

"That's right, good girl. Take a moment now. I want to feel that mouth and tongue of yours on my cock again. Just to soothe the ache, before I push myself inside your wet, wanton, little cunt."

Kelly drew in a deep breath as her body reeled with explosive tension. Nerves quivered under her skin with John's erotic language. His erection was large and well formed, with numerous thick veins. Kelly felt transported, just to see the most male part of him bob eagerly toward her lips, pulsing and red with his desire.

With his cock in his fist, John guided it to her mouth. "Lick it, Kelly," he ordered in a low voice.

Kelly both saw and smelled the shiny evidence of his lust. She nodded with an "um" of agreement, responding instantly to this imperative demand. He exhaled harshly as she dipped toward him and touched him with her tongue.

Kelly found herself whimpering as she licked pre-cum off his rigid shaft, carefully cleaning every drop.

"Christ, I love the feel of that sweet tongue of yours," John said. "That's good. Now suck it."

"Ummm," she hummed and nodded. Kelly sucked greedily on the silken rounded head. More blood shot into his cock in response and he swelled thick and long. John smelled and tasted so male, and his hardness radiated heat and musk. It was divine.

"Thank you," John said in a husky voice, making Kelly want to purr with pleasure. He couldn't hide how much she affected him – he craved her as much as she craved him. He put a condom on and moved to place his body between her legs. "I've never wanted to fuck anyone the way I want to fuck you right now, Kelly."

She moaned. "Yes, yes, John, please," she heard herself say. Her entire body ached and felt feverish, as if she was ill and his strong male flesh was the only possible cure.

John mounted, stretching himself on top of her, his hard cock like a steel bar at the juncture of her legs. The weight of his body immobilized her against the bed, flattening her breasts with his solid chest. Then he began kissing her with deep, intoxicating kisses penetrating her mouth just like he intended to penetrate her dripping sex.

Kelly felt she could drown in John's kisses, or perhaps get drunk from them. Their tongues battled together, until she caught and sucked on his. Then it was his turn to moan. John's hands feverishly touched her body, running up and down her torso, squeezing and fondling her breasts and pinching her nipples.

The feel of his hard male flesh, hot against her sex made her desperate. She wanted him inside her, stretching her. Filling her.

Ah, ah, ah, ah," she began a mindless litany, writhing with desire. Her hands above her head fisted and tore at the sheets. Kelly couldn't help her responses, and she hadn't been ordered to be still or quiet. Somehow being able to move and make noise felt all the better for having discovered what it was like to manage without sound and movement.

"Look at me, Kelly," John said, with his large body pinning her to the bed.

Her eyes flew to his face, and when they met his, everything stopped for an instant as they stared at each other. Their connection was beyond anything. Shocking. Intense. Their bodies remained skin to skin, hearts pounding, breathing each other's breath. Lungs rose and fell simultaneously, as if they were one person.

My God I need him, she thought with raw desire. *Right now John owns me, body and soul. But does it work both ways? Because I feel like he's mine. He belongs to me, too.*

Kelly stared at him, and her core turned molten. His striking features were harsh with lust, his eyes dilated and heavy lidded, his body taut. This beautiful man's need seemed so strong that even his formidable control seemed frayed. They both were sweating and panting.

He pulled away for a moment, reaching across the bed, and bringing two pillows over. "Lift up," he directed her.

Kelly did, and John slipped the pillows under her backside, raising her hips and pelvic area higher, and putting her lower back into a deliciously sexual tilt. She'd thought she was exposed before, but now she was really open to him.

His eyes glittered and his lips curved slightly in a stern smile. "That's better. You look amazing." The tight smile left him, and his features grew implacable and firm. "I can't be gentle, Kelly," he growled in warning.

"I don't care," she said, and she meant it.

With his hands holding her inner thighs, she felt the firm heated head of his cock at her entrance. John's coarse pubic hair rubbed roughly against her sensitive, distended clit.

He entered with one strong thrust, invading her, making nothing of the slight resistance of her swollen flesh. He rammed into her, right to the hilt, slamming Kelly down against the mattress *hard.* Air was pushed from his lungs with the force of his thrust and he grunted. The feel and sound of his heavy testicles slapping her buttocks added to her shock.

A harsh broken cry tore from her throat. The strength of his need simply took her breath away.

John's hips pressed against hers, abrasively chafing, grinding and crushing into her, possessing her body completely, taking everything he wanted to take. Her legs wrapped around him instinctively, and he made an animal sound of approval.

Kelly felt John's cock throb and twitch against her internal walls. He was so big, rigid and thick inside her, giving her a stretched – too full sensation. It gave her a feeling of being whole. *Completed.*

He pulled back and drove in again, penetrating right to the end of her, slamming into her cervix. It created the most exquisite pain and blissful pleasure she'd ever imagined.

Kelly's mind and body whirled with pleasure. John's bedroom smelled of sex, a heady, musky scent. The sound of ragged breathing, pounding heartbeats, moans, whispers and whimpers echoed in the confined space. Two people thrashing, joined together in the most ancient dance of all.

For a moment she wondered if the urgency of their coupling may have seemed violent to an onlooker, more like vicious combat, rather than an act of passion and love.

Tears coursed in a hot stream down her temples. It all added to the influx of astonishing, overpowering sensations. "Um, ah, ah, ah, oh! John! John! Johnnnn!" Kelly cried out, sobbing his name.

Every single muscle from her stomach and buttocks to her entire pelvic region seemed to contract at once. Unexpectedly she climaxed, her throbbing channel clenching in pulse pounding waves, her body tightening and convulsing as if connected to an electric current. John continued riding her hard and fast, grunting with each merciless thrust.

"Good, yes, come," he gasped. "That's right, Kelly. Squeeze my cock – God!"

He grabbed her ass, and his fingers bit into her as he lifted her up further to meet his thrusts, pounding inside her again and again with bruising force, his chest heaving. And then he came, too –

his entire body corded with strain and hardening into an inflexible male, muscular wall against her.

John's big body shuddered as he ejaculated, straining and reaching, pushing himself deeper with each wave of pleasure.

He collapsed upon her, arms around her, gripping her torso tightly, and Kelly buried her face into his neck. She heard the pounding of his heart, and both of their ragged breathing. They were keeping tempo with the sound of spring rain, falling on the roof of his house, and running down the gutters.

Daringly, Kelly violated John's order to leave her arms over his head. With only love in her heart, she curled her arms around the man she ached for. Nuzzling into him, she and zoned out in languid, post orgasmic bliss.

Chapter 8

Free

∝ ∾

Everything has changed, yet nothing is different, John thought. It was here in front of me all along, I just couldn't see it. He allowed himself an internal snort. More like I couldn't feel it.

The evening and early hours of the morning were an eye-opening shock.

At twenty-six years old John was only just beginning to understand the pleasure and essential intimacy of the sexual act. For years he had observed people engaged in every possible form of sex. Logically he was aware of their primal driving need for intercourse. He'd caused others, both male and female, sexual pleasure and orgasm, and had seen that the act itself caused intense gratification. But never once had he experienced it himself.

It was a revelation.

I'm like an adolescent having sex for the first time, he thought with a wry smile. *And I feel like one, too. I don't think I'll ever get enough.*

For years he'd pleased others through sex and pain, forging a connection – the only kind of bond he'd been capable of. But now, with Kelly he understood, and had discovered so much more.

Throughout the night, each time he recovered, they had sex again, and again and again. John took her from behind, bending her over the bed. And he took her when she lay flat, also from behind, immobilizing her with his body, nuzzling her neck and back, whispering erotic suggestions in her ear. He had her face to face with her legs up over his shoulders, and again face to face against a wall, with her legs wrapped tightly around him, while trapping her arms above her.

John still had a queasy aversion to having her hands on him. Kelly enjoyed restraint, which was just as well, because he preferred her bound. He didn't really want her to touch him.

John had been rough and edgy from this greedy newly discovered sexual need. He'd taken her like an animal, insatiable, and savage. André, his mentor, would have been shocked by his complete lack of control and finesse, yet he knew André would be happy for him, too.

John loved everything about Kelly's body, especially her responses to him. He remembered the feel of her swollen, needy clitoris as it pulsed against his questing fingertips. It had been pulsing as hard and strong as the carotid artery of a neck. Her little whimpers, cries and moans that sent him mad. The smell and taste and feel of every part of her.

Sex with Kelly was wondrous. John had even allowed Kelly to be on top, telling her to use his body as she wished, as long as she kept her hands behind your back. That was another real first. It was so strange, to obtain pleasure from letting her be in control of an intimate scene.

When under tutelage with André, John had hated subbing. He despised loss of control and found it difficult to trust. Trusting Kelly came naturally to him. With him deep inside of her, and her hips undulating above him, John actually enjoyed her playing Top. Especially as he could so clearly see how much it amused and pleased her, not to mention watching her sweet breasts bounce and swing.

Anything that pleased him, pleased her, and vice versa. At one point John had gone to the kitchen and brought chocolate and Diet Coke, building up their strength, eating and sitting companionably with each other. Kelly chatted then, enthusiastically talking about nothing in particular.

John loved that about her, her ability to talk.

It wasn't that he preferred silence. It was more that unless he was dominating a scene, he simply couldn't think of what to say. Kelly was like a trusted friend, playmate and lover all rolled into one vital person and he didn't want the night to end.

"…and that's why my mother sometimes drives me nuts," she said, her pale blue eyes flashing.

John saw Kelly's cute little nose crinkle up in distaste. Her orange hair was tousled, and the black make-up around her eyes had run from all her tears, so she looked a bit like a raccoon. She was sitting naked and cross-legged on his bed, unconscious of her nudity, chattering away, and John thought she was the most beautiful woman, and most important person to him in the entire world.

He sat with his back against the bed head, his legs stretched out in front of him, drinking the last of his coffee. Kelly had finished hers, as well as peanut butter and banana on toast. He put the cup on the bedside table.

My, God. It was five in the morning and he'd never felt so invigorated. After being up all night, he didn't feel like he was even beginning to flag. Sex felt so incredible, and it made him mellow and glad inside. Or was it love, this overwhelming euphoric feeling of belonging?

He'd been taking a distance education course called, "The Philosophy of Religion and Ethics." It was something to do, to fill a gap. André had encouraged him to continue learning. His lips curved as he thought of the Bible verse he had discovered, *I once was lost, but now I'm found.* It clearly applied to him. He must have had an odd expression on his face because Kelly looked at him then.

"What?" she asked. "What did I say?"

He laughed and the sound was so foreign to his ears, this extraordinary happiness. John decided that he'd laughed more in this one night with Kelly than he had in his entire lifetime. She was so essential to him, alive and passionate.

An unexpected urge to touch her, kindled every nerve in his body. Instead of subduing all natural impulses as he habitually would, he succumbed to it.

"Come sit on my lap," he said and she scooted over and crawled up on him. John curled his arms around her, pressing her head against his neck, adoring the satiny feel of her soft feminine skin. "I love listening to you talk, Kelly."

"Really?" she said in an astonished voice. "Do you mean it?"

"Yes."

"I was trying not to talk too much, because I didn't want to be annoying," Kelly said a little breathlessly. He hid his desire to smile, because it was obvious that her tongue was still on overdrive. "I never would have thought it, but I kind of let my guard completely down with you. I'm so comfortable being here with you, and you're Father John, the guy with the bullwhip. Jesus you scare the crap out of me, but you're not just that guy are you? You're this guy, too, the man who's created this warm, welcoming room, who is polite and kind, and understanding."

She looked shyly up at him from under her eyelashes then, and added, "And you're the best lover on planet Earth."

Without conscious thought, John grabbed her arms and pulled them behind her back, holding her wrists there with one hand and staring into her hungry eyes – eyes that reflected his own need. His free hand went to a breast. She gasped and responsively arched toward him when he pinched her nipple.

John nuzzled into her then, biting her between her shoulder and her neck, sucking and stroking her with his tongue, crushing her body against his.

Pliant and welcoming, she moaned in his arms.

"I'm sorry," he said, pulling back from her. "I'm not looking after you very well, Kelly. You must be so sore. I wouldn't be surprised to find your poor overworked cunt was bleeding by now. It's a kind of madness, my need is so great. I simply have to have you again."

"Jesus, John, are you kidding? This is the best sex I've had in my whole life. You so totally rock. I love it." She laughed and the sound of it was light and musical. Carefree. Then her eyes met his. That connection was there again, and he felt his heart skip a beat. "I love everything about you, John Taylor," she said.

His own chuckle was joyous, but it turned into a growl, as he fell on her like an animal once more.

Chapter 9

Kelly

Kelly woke and stretched like a cat. *I'm in John's Taylor's bed*, she thought happily. *But I sure didn't get much sleep last night.* Every single muscle she had hurt, and she was sore in places she'd never been sore in before. Even her scalp was tender from him fisting her hair when he plied her to his will. John's tireless sexual energy had been awe-inspiring and untamed, but *yum* it had all been worth it.

Kelly looked down between her legs, seeing where John's unshaven stubble had chaffed her white thighs and shaved pussy into pale pink, not to mention her burning, sensitive breasts and nipples.

She put a hand to her cheek, skimming down her neck and throat. It was probably red there, too. Her jaw was aching from going down on him – but oh my God, she'd never experienced anything like that before. She sighed. He'd loved it, and so did she.

Kelly stood up on shaky legs, and she knew that only an axe could kill the grin she was wearing. She was pretty sure she had one or more hickies somewhere between her neck and shoulder. Putting her hand to her lips she traced her jack-o'-lantern grin and didn't care that she had a big manly jaw and orange hair. John thought she was beautiful.

She giggled. Even her mouth and lips felt bruised, and her insides certainly had been battered. Kelly felt well used, replete and never more satisfied in her life.

John was rattling around in the kitchen, and she thought she could smell French toast. She didn't recall nodding off – but that couldn't have been more than an hour ago. The last thing she remembered was John behind her, cuddled in a spoon position, his inexhaustible ever erect cock thrusting leisurely between her legs. Leisurely!

That had been a change. Man, the guy was some sort of sex Olympian, or a machine, ceaselessly pounding away like a pile driver. How did he do it? Was it just his age?

It was nine a.m. and even after little or no sleep, Kelly felt wide awake and invigorated.

Three paperback books and an ereader lay on the bedside table. Kelly picked the books up, one at a time. "*Man's Search for Meaning*," "*As a Man Thinkith*," and "*Screw the Roses, Send Me The Thorns*." She giggled over that one, as it was obviously a manual concerning the use of pain in BDSM play.

A large framed picture was also on the bedside table. It was of John when he was a child of six of seven years old, with an older woman – perhaps his mother or his Aunt. The woman was hugging him and he was laughing. He looked so cute.

She stood up and took a peek outside. It was overcast, but the rain had stopped. The call of nature had her moving to his bathroom, another room she'd approved of. John had renovated this too. It was now a luxurious and sensible place to attend to one's business. She freaked out when she saw her eyes.

Oh my, God! My mascara has run! How embarrassing.

Kelly washed her face and brushed her teeth. The bath looked inviting. The idea of soaking the poor sore muscles of her body sounded just about perfect. She considered starting to run the tub – but decided to wait to see if John wanted to have a bath or shower, because whatever they did, she knew they would do it together.

Kelly found a thin, dark blue cotton bathrobe behind the door and put it on. When she stepped out John still wasn't back, so she decided to join him in the kitchen. While passing a desk, she saw her name on a file, and came to an immediate stop.

KELLY FLYNN, it stated in big letters.

Her hand trembled when she reached out for the file. A typed summary was inside, and pictures and other details further in. She felt her entire body heat, and a strange roaring sound was in her ears. Feeling faint and weak at the knees, she sat down and began to read.

"Information as requested concerning Kelly Flynn." The date was a month ago, about the time when she started going to The Basement – about the time John had first seen her. What had he said? *You've been watching me, Kelly. Well, I've been watching you, too.*

Holy shit! The information he'd gathered was certainly comprehensive. What schools she'd attended, information on her HIV status and blood results, her parents, her siblings, even cut out articles of her when she played Little Orphan Annie when she was twelve years old.

Kelly abruptly remembered John's comment in his car after they left The Basement. When she'd said they should go to his house, he had replied, "Good. I live closer." At the time she had thought it an odd thing to say, but hadn't questioned it. Because of course he couldn't know where she lived. But now she understood.

Kelly's hand went to her heart, and her throat tightened with unshed tears. John had known her address. He knew everything about her – while she, in fact, knew *nothing* about him.

Instantly she felt stripped of all the pleasure she'd experienced in the last twelve hours with John. It had all been a trick, a lie. But why? Why would he do something like this?

Kelly couldn't take any more – an urgent need to escape boiled through her veins and she put the file down. Logically she realized that this spike of panic was simply caused by adrenaline, making her want to run. She struggled to remain calm. Still, her mind immediately flew to worst case scenarios.

Was Father John a complete nut job? Would he chain her up and keep her in some underground bunker? Or even kill her?

Quickly she got dressed. *Jesus, I have to get out of here,* she thought. *I've got to get away.*

Chapter 10

Unfeeling

John came in, just as she was about to leave the bedroom. His eyebrows rose just slightly with surprise when he saw that she was dressed. As she tried to brush by him, he caught her, with his hands on her shoulders. "Kelly, what is it?" he asked.

When she didn't reply he pushed her against a wall, and held her there, studying her face with his intent, unfathomable eyes. "Tell me, Kelly," he said. "What's happened?"

She just stared up at him, utterly motionless and still quite shocked. Dark eyes, strong jaw, thick dark hair and implacable expression. He was so beautiful. But it was all a mask, hiding the monster underneath.

John Taylor, the guy she'd been crushing on every day and night for the last month, was a fake. Now everything made so much sense. No wonder he knew everything about her, he hadn't been in tune with her at all – he'd hired someone to search her background.

Who does something like that? Did he have any idea of how creepy that was? And all that time he'd been pretending to understand his subs and read their minds!

A sudden anger helped her get control of herself. *What a mind-fuck this guy is,* she thought, despising him. *He's a cunning, manipulative sadist and a calculating sociopath. And he made me love him.*

There was no telling what John was capable of. As far as she knew, he could've even "arranged" to have the elevator break, to trap them both inside together.

She recalled what she'd been thinking earlier in the evening when she'd imagined that John's praise and appreciation would crack even the most stubborn heart. And her instinctive self-protective reflection, *Yes, but how many woman has he told these things to? Be careful. This is how he gets people to love him.*

Well, she'd sure fallen for it.

And her friend Rosslyn's comments: "Father John just oozes the Triple 'F' factor, crushing and breaking the heart of every woman who comes near him. The man is beyond reach but utterly captivating. You know, the "Fatal Female Flaw" when ordinarily sensible women fall madly in love with an unattainable man who can't, or won't love them back?"

My God, she thought, *I've been so stupid! Such a trusting innocent.*

"Kelly, you will tell me *right now*," he said in his deceptively mild Dom voice.

She was pinned against the wall, held by John's overwhelming strength and will. His eyes held a challenge, the opportunity for her to say no to him, or to fight back. Steps which they equally knew her submissive nature would find difficult to take. Either way, they both understood who would win. John's strong authoritative tone had her unconsciously opening her mouth – he almost had her talking.

No, she thought. *He's so clever, and I'm so gullible. He'll explain everything away and I'm so stupid! I'll believe it, because I want to believe it. God, I'm an idiot. I've got to get out of here. But how can I escape?* But then she remembered. She still had a safe word.

"Daisies," Kelly said.

John Taylor stepped back and away from her in one quick stride, as if he'd unwarily grasped a nettle, or a rattlesnake. His lips firmed and his face became even darker and more unreadable.

"I'm going home," she said.

He looked around his bedroom, and suddenly he seemed to comprehend. His cool gaze met hers, but his expression was remote and empty. A river of distrust had torn them apart. They were separate from each other now, he on one side; she on another. Nothing could bridge that gulf.

The connection they'd forged together disappeared completely – just like that. Now when Kelly looked at him, there was an insurmountable distance between them.

"Will I call you a taxi, or drive you to your car?" he asked in a soft, even voice.

"I'll get a cab."

John left her, striding back into the kitchen. Kelly only then realized that he was naked – she'd been so shocked by seeing KELLY FLYNN on a file on his desk that she hadn't even noticed. As he walked away from her she stared at him. Even from behind he took her breath away, his sleek muscular back, narrow hips and tight ass. Just looking at him was mesmerizing.

Shit, she thought. *He is soooo bad for me.* Dressed and ready to go, she followed after him into the kitchen.

John had his phone to his ear and was already calling, ordering the cab. "Yes. From Aloha to Hillsboro. Ten minutes? Thank you," he said and put his cell on the orange countertop.

He sat down at the small kitchen table and silently searched her face.

"I'll wait outside," she said, feeling uncomfortable.

"You must do as you think best, Kelly," he said with an utterly impassive expression on his handsome, once well-loved countenance. "You've found that file and drawn conclusions, without enough information to do so."

"What am I supposed to think?" she snapped back, feeling righteously angry, betrayed, hurt and insulted. John had tricked her. And he'd made her fall in love with him too.

Bastard! All men are bastards, she thought. *I'm soooo going to be a lesbian. At least with a woman I'll know where I stand.*

"I'm suggesting," John said mildly, "that there may be another reason that I would have such a file. A logical explanation."

Kelly shook her head. "Reeally?" she said, drawing the word out. The sarcasm in her voice was laid on thick as cloud cover on the Portland International Airport, after all flights had been cancelled and the airport closed. She was so angry at him she felt like she could spit, or claw his eyes out.

Kelly's pink and while daisies sat up in their vase, bright and cheerful, mocking her. Their colors clashed obscenely with John's ugly orange counter-top.

Just then, she never wanted to see another daisy again.

A horn honked outside. The cab was here.

John made no move toward her, not to stop her, not even to open the door for her. As she walked out onto the porch, he opened his mouth, and appeared as if he was going to say something. She held up her hand to stop him.

"No," Kelly said. "Don't even try to explain. You don't say much, but what you do say is always pretty smooth. I don't think there *is* an explanation except for an iniquitous one."

John still hadn't moved – he was a cold rigid statue of heartless stone in his chair. The last she saw of him was the remote and unemotional look on his face.

Unfeeling bastard! Kelly thought as she got into the cab and it drove off.

And then she began to cry.

PUNISHED 4

Chapter 1

Roller Coaster

"Discipline is very important, *mon ami.* Boundaries must be maintained for the security of both Dom and sub. These agreed upon limits become consistent and comforting parameters to work within. I do not use pain for punishment. I inflict only pleasure through pain, John. For me, such is associated with gratification and reward. If you genuinely wish to punish a sub, John, find something that truly hurts. Not torment to the body, *non.* Cause anguish to the mind, the heart and soul."

- André Chevalier, conversation with John Taylor

Kelly Flynn was on an emotional roller coaster ride from hell.

Saturday night she'd hit a freakish all time low when she'd been caught in a broken elevator. With a phobia of being trapped in small, dark places, Kelly had totally flipped out when the lights went out and the elevator screeched and jerked to a halt.

Luckily the Dom she'd been crushing on all month, John Taylor, was there to save her. One thing led to another and Kelly ended up spending the night with John and having the best sex of her entire life. Not to mention falling head over heels in love with the guy.

Who unfortunately it turned out, was a complete nut job wacko bastard.

So her twenty-four hour amusement park ride had finally come to an end. After experiencing huge emotional downs and wildly euphoric ups, her roller coaster slid to a stop and cheerfully let her off, depositing her safely and miserably on the ground. Now she was left feeling an unfamiliar all-time low.

Kelly drove her slate blue Infiniti G coupe along the curving tree lined roads on the way to her parent's home. She'd been given her car on her twenty-second birthday, and now, two years later, she still loved it. It was Sunday and the family tradition was to get together for dinner Sunday evening.

After mind-blowing sex throughout all of Saturday night and Sunday morning, Kelly had a multitude of odd marks and hickies that would be a dead giveaway to even an unobservant parent, not to mention her protective older brother. Consequently she wore jeans and a turtleneck sweater. She was so damn deliciously sore from her sexual marathon that even walking in a normal manner was difficult.

Driving into the circular driveway, she gazed up at the elegant two story Classic Revival mansion. The family home was huge, white with four pillars that went right to the second story, and pretty, contrasting dark shutters on the upper story windows. It had six bedrooms and six bathrooms, a pool, family room, home theater, a wine cellar and every mod con. She parked her car and went inside.

"You're late," Kelly's mother said with a disapproving glare, as she walked inside. Kelly recoiled slightly in surprise. Intercepting her at the front door was new. Usually her intrusive parent waited until she'd gotten further into the house before she began any verbal assault.

"And why are you wearing that God awful sweater?" her mother added. "One would think that you could find something better to be dressed in than that. Can't you afford nicer clothes on the salary from your newest new job? And what have you done with your hair?"

"Sorry, Mom," she said.

Kelly's mother, Marguerite, was a marvel. In less than thirty seconds she'd managed to remind Kelly that she'd gone through a succession of jobs like a 4th of July hot dog eating contest winner, went through hot dogs. She'd also criticized her clothes and her hair. Once her mother brought up Kelly's lack of a rich fiancé, then she'd have met most of her main targets. Man! She'd only just come through the front door, and was still standing on the white marble floor of the family entry. It was pretty good going, even for her mother, who was a master at pointing out both real and imagined flaws.

Kelly's mother had shoulder length black hair, and dark blue eyes. Kelly's orange hair and freckled complexion had come from her father, which was a real pity. Mother was wearing an elegant off-white silk blouse and tan skirt that was tailored to follow the line of her body. Around her neck was a single string of pearls. As always with her mother, nothing appeared out of place. Mom turned fifty, almost three months ago, although she still looked to be in her early forties.

So, she thought. *It being the weekend, Mom is dressing down today.* Kelly looked at her gorgeous, fashionable mother and thought for the thousandth time. *Why didn't I get her black hair?*

"We were just going to sit down," her mother added.

Kelly followed her into the dining room, and sure enough, everyone was already seated, except her dad who was fixing himself a drink at the bar. "Hey, honey," he called out, shooting her his customary genial grin. "You look beautiful."

"Hey, Daddy," she replied, walking up to him with a smile and giving him hug and a peck on the cheek. "You always say that, but I love you for it."

They all sat down and after saying grace, everyone talked together with a number of conversations going on at once. Kelly sat next to Richard her older brother and the family member she was closest to. She could discuss almost everything with him. Also at the table was Maria; nineteen, Katrina; sixteen and Jamie, who Kelly had suspected had been an unplanned surprise, and who was now eleven years old.

"Where's Heather tonight?" Kelly asked. Heather was Richard's long term girlfriend.

Richard leaned his long body back against his chair, chewing a mouthful of his turkey dinner. He had black hair and blue eyes like their mother. *Why did he get the black hair?* She wondered. *So unfair. Men looked good in any color.* He was a handsome, confident man at twenty-six, and Kelly loved him to bits. Richard had just finished a civil engineering degree and so far was enjoying his choice of profession. Swallowing, he said, "She's cramming for exams. Honestly the woman is such a stress-head over some things. I told her not to come tonight."

Kelly laughed. "Were you thinking of her when you suggested that, or of yourself?"

Richard mouth quirked in a sheepish grin. "Myself I think, but it'll be good for her to escape tonight, too."

They both chuckled, although Kelly's amusement was forced, as she was utterly distracted. The thought of Richard's girlfriend reminded her that she'd almost, kind of, had a boyfriend… just last night. Images of John Taylor naked, his beautiful eyes heavy lidded, dark with lust, and thrusting above her, competed with her vision of him the last time she saw him, cold and distant as she walked out his door.

Richard looked along the table, and when he was sure no one was paying any attention, he stared at her intently and then raised an eyebrow. "So what is wrong with you?"

"Man, I don't know where to start," Kelly replied with a frown. "But it would be good to talk later. I'm seriously screwed up at the moment."

It was a family tradition to go to church on Sunday morning, and have Sunday evening dinners together. She'd been escaping the church thing for some years, except for Christmas and Easter of course. After dinner the entire family would play games, and just hang out.

It was a non-negotiable mandatory weekly get together, and honestly except for her mother mostly being a pain in the ass, Kelly thought it was great. A lot of her friends had parents who were divorced, or had families that didn't relate at all. Kelly considered herself extremely lucky.

Kelly spent a good night with much laughter playing Pictionary. Who wouldn't laugh when playing Pictionary with her crazy Dad? Dad, a hobby watercolor artist, kept trying to make a work of art with his one minute turn. It was hysterical just watching.

Afterwards she and Richard had a tussle with Jamie, wrestling him to the floor and letting him win from time to time. Katrina and Maria joined in. Their mom then nagged everyone individually, firing a few shots at each child. But her focus, as customary, was on Kelly.

Kelly got herself together, prepared for a verbal battering, and sighed. This was the only painful part of these nights. As usual her mother hit her with constant questions such as, "Are you going out with anyone?" (Translation: Are you dating anyone with position and money?) or, "How long are you going to do that silly job you have? It's a dead end position and how will you meet anyone?" (Translation: You will never meet a man with the right kind of background and financial security there).

Kelly, barely able to hold her temper, pointed out that she was working for a dating agency, and if she couldn't meet anyone there, where would she meet them?

"I was married by your age, Kelly. Were you aware of that?" Mom informed her for the hundredth time just that month. "And you don't even have a suitable boyfriend."

"Why don't you pick on Richard? He isn't married," Kelly asked irritably, finding her patience was coming to an end. Richard, the favorite son, who was never the subject of such an examination, just grinned.

Her mother raised her chin, and gave her a regal look. "Your brother has a fiancé. He also has a good job, excellent career prospects, and will be able to support a wife and family."

"Oh, that's right, I forgot," Kelly said, as if she could. Mother sang Richard's praises whenever possible.

Kelly considered telling her mom that Maria had a boyfriend, and perhaps she should grill her about him. But that would just be mean, particularly as poor Maria still lived at home and was stuck with her Mother bothering her all the time. Regrettably all 'quality time' spent together with Kelly's mom was not unlike revisiting the inquisition. Thus Kelly sat back and just took the heat for all of them.

Why not? It was the perfect end, to a perfect day after all.

Chapter 2

Childhood Memories

Kelly's Dad eventually interrupted, suggesting they all watch one of the latest sit-coms. This was also a normal occurrence, Dad subtly attempting to re-direct her mother's attentions. He'd been doing so much of the night to no avail.

And thus the family party broke up. As everyone else settled into the home theater, Richard and Kelly went outside to the back yard where Kelly sat on the oak tree swing. The moon was completely full now, so there was plenty of light. There was little breeze, but the air was cool and damp. Kelly's brother, a patient fellow, waited for her to begin.

After some time, Kelly finally said, "So, I met this guy."

"Reeally?" Richard drew out the query.

Kelly spun her swing in a circle, and stopped suddenly. "Richard, for the last month I've had such a crush on this guy, a mad, crazy, freakish, died and gone to heaven crush. And last night I had sex with him, mind-blowing over the top best ever, ultra compatible sex."

"Seriously?" Richard said and shrugged. "A little TMI beloved sister mine, but hey, I can deal. So what is the problem? It sounds good so far. He likes you too, right?" In the bright moonlight Richard's handsome countenance could be seen to suddenly tense and he said, "Or do I need to kick his ass? I swear to God, Kelly, if so, point him out and just say the word."

Kelly laughed and hopped off the swing. The affection she felt for him tightened her throat. "God, Richard," she said, giving him a hug. "I love you. I honestly wouldn't have survived childhood without a big brother like you to look up to. Not to mention how you're forever protecting me from all bad things – not excluding our well-loved, but extremely annoying mother."

Richard laughed and Kelly thrilled to hear the 'no holds barred' sound of her big brother's honest happiness. "I'll always have your back, Kelly," he said. "You know that. Mom was a little rough on you tonight."

Kelly snorted. "You think? Well, she's probably going through menopause or something because she's like a broken record." With tacit agreement they both started back to the house as the night air was quite damp. "I can't see how Dad stands it," she added.

"He lays low. It's the only effective strategy," he said. They both giggled. "So what happened anyway?"

As they walked together toward the back door, Kelly told him how they'd been trapped in an elevator, and how John had saved her life, because she'd been in such a complete state of panic.

He stopped and abruptly grasped her by the shoulders. "Christ, Kelly. You, trapped in a small, dark elevator?" His tone communicated his shock and concern as he studied her face. He knew all about Kelly's claustrophobia. "You look like you survived it okay. Jesus, you must have gone absolutely ballistic. I'm just glad that guy was there." Richard released her and shook his head.

"Oh yeah," she agreed. "It was pretty tense. I seriously think I'd have gone mad if I'd been alone." Then she explained how she went to his home and how interesting and considerate he was, right down to the details of buying her daisies, and putting marshmallows in her hot chocolate.

"So what's the problem?" he asked. "This guy sounds like he has your back, too. I don't think I need to kick his ass. It sounds like I should shake his hand."

Kelly couldn't tell her brother about the intimate details of John's file on her, but she hedged and told him that he had a newspaper on his desk, from when she played Annie as a child. It had made her worry that he was a stalker, crazy guy. "So honestly,

NIKKI SEX

the second I found that newspaper I didn't even let him try to explain. I just took off like a scalded cat."

"So, do I know him?" Richard asked.

"I don't think so."

"What's his name?"

After that comment about cats, their cat turned up. The affable creature came out of nowhere to rub against her legs. Kelly gave a low chuckle and bent down to pick up their orange colored, de-sexed tom cat.

"Hey, Plasma," she said.

No one could remember the cat's original name. Dad had backed over it when it was a kitten. Thousands of dollars in vet bills later it was still going strong and at least twelve years old. That was how it got the name Plasma, because the poor injured creature had cost as much as their brand new plasma TV and surround sound system that they'd bought around that time.

"What's this paragon-come-stalker's name?" Her brother asked again.

"I'm sure you don't know him," Kelly said, with Plasma purring loudly in her ear as she made her way into the house, heading toward the games room where they could sit down. "He lives in Aloha of all places, and his name is John Taylor."

"What, not that weird guy who went to Riverdale with us?"

"No way," she said turning on the light in the games room. The pool table was uncovered, and most of its balls were out, in a half played game. "I think I'd remember if I knew him from school."

Richard frowned, picked up the cue ball, and reached for a cue stick. "The John Taylor I knew was in my year in grade school. Black hair? Dark eyes? Top student, with nothing to say? Weird? No friends? Any of this sounding familiar? He left and was never seen again at the end of year eight."

155

Bending over, Richard placed the cue ball down, and took aim. "Seven ball in the side pocket," he said, and took the shot. Three balls clicked loudly. He cheered as if he'd won the Open Championships when the ball went in, just as he'd called it.

He bent over for another shot, but looked over his shoulder at Kelly, and then stood up. "John Taylor's parents live up past Military Road," he said. "You know that house that looks like some sort of embassy in a Middle Eastern country because it has so much security? His dad is some sort of district judge I think."

Suddenly Kelly did remember a guy named John. A number of indistinct pictures came into her mind, and her knees went weak. Dazed, she sat down on the brown leather couch nearby. Was her John someone she'd known in grade school as a child? That might explain the Annie newspaper, but not the whole file.

Richard laid the cue stick on the table. He sat down next to her, and began petting the cat that had instantly settled comfortably in Kelly's lap.

"John was the guy that those shit head bullies McCarther, Jones and you know – what's his name? The other asshole that used to hang with that crowd – tried to beat up," Richard said. "They jumped John after school one day, remember? You and Linda Barker were walking home and saw the whole thing. John broke one of their arms, and they all lied and said that he'd attacked them."

The memories were returning, and Kelly felt a cold chill. Could the John of the past be the John of now? She put her hand to her chest as she felt herself getting back on the emotional roller coaster, and riding upward toward an exhilarating high of uncertainty, mystery and excitement.

What the hell? Could it be? She'd been in 5th grade and had been probably only eleven years old. The tension in her body must have disturbed Plasma, because the cat jumped off Kelly's lap, and trotted off toward the kitchen.

Her friend Linda had refused to get involved, but Kelly, burning with a sense of injustice went to the principal's office and

156

reported the whole thing. The three well known bullies had picked on the wrong guy. John Taylor, who was younger and smaller than any of them, had given one a bloody nose, and broken another's arm. The last attacker, deceitful coward that he was, had run off to tell on John.

"Well," Richard said, with a raised eyebrow. "Is it the same guy?"

"You know what?" Kelly said after a moment of heart-stopping reflection. "I think it is."

Chapter 3

Whip Practice

After Kelly left so abruptly, John ate the French toast he'd made for breakfast, and then had a long shower. Dressing in distressed jeans and a grey, heavyweight long sleeved cotton shirt, he picked up his phone, surprised to see that an unlisted number had left a message for him sometime last night. That was odd. No one ever left him messages. In fact, no one ever even called him. John didn't like talking, much less talking on the phone. Only three people had his number.

Hitting playback he heard an angry, older female voice say: "Mr. Taylor. It's Professor Lopez. I'm calling to re-iterate that, as discussed over a month ago, I'm no longer your counselor. I'm sorry but you simply must find someone else."

John frowned, puzzled. Maria Lopez had been his counselor for four years. The older woman, who faintly reminded him of his Aunt Brenda, was one of only two people he'd trusted with his family secrets. Just yesterday he'd phoned her, and confirmed his appointment with her for Tuesday. Why would she call him and leave such a peculiar message? He located the professor's number in his cell, and rang it. There was no answer, so he left a recorded message: "Maria, its John. I have my phone with me today and would appreciate hearing from you. Thank you."

John then sent a text to his friend and mentor, André Chevalier:

When r u available 4 me 2 call u?

After that he went on line, searching for a reputable jeweler. John made some phone calls while drawing a sketch using a pencil. When he found what he was looking for he hung up the phone and faxed the sketch.

John hadn't heard back from André, so he put on his swat boots and a jean jacket, and left the house to visit The Basement – taking Kelly's personal file with him. After a hugely physical evening, and an early morning with no sleep, he was still completely buzzed and wide awake.

John parked where he'd parked his car the night before, and his heart gave a tug at the poignant memory of being right here with Kelly, just last night. He'd been parking here every time he came now, as this spot was directly under the security cameras.

Twice in the last two months his car had been vandalized. Once he could understand, twice made it personal. But who would want some sort of payback on him? And for what?

John had reported both incidents to the police, going through the effort to detail and take photos of each event. Not just for insurance reasons. John's garbage bin when left out had been strewn over the lawn last week, another detail he'd carefully recorded. Not that he had that much garbage. Yet these unprovoked attacks made him paranoid with good reason.

Putting in the security code to the door, he took the stairs down to The Basement. He unlocked and entered the male changing area, turning on all the lights with the master switch. He unlocked his personal locker, opened it and took out his bullwhip and two thick plastic rolls – these were his human targets. Leaving the male target behind, he took the female outline with him.

John's manager, Colin, wouldn't be in until after twelve, but John went into his office and left Kelly Flynn's file on the manager's desk. Sunday was a pretty busy night, and they had a Masquerade party planned. John generally left those details to Colin.

The area he intended to practice in was well lit. John set up his plastic target against the clay covered seven foot plywood backdrop he'd specially made for this purpose. After each session he'd smooth the clay out, and then when he next practiced he could see how accurate his hits were.

To successfully use the bullwhip took time and the extensive ongoing disciple of practice, practice, practice. This was neither a challenge nor a hardship to John, as he enjoyed the sound of the whip, and using it. It allowed him to fully center himself and be in the moment. Nothing focused attention like cracking a bullwhip precisely on target.

With his phone placed on a table nearby, he heard when the text came in. John walked over and saw that it was from André.

"Available noon today."

Good, he thought. *I need to tell him about Kelly.*

Without warning John got an image of Kelly having an orgasm with his tongue deep in her most feminine hole, and it was so visceral that he could almost feel the soft texture of her skin and smell her unique essence. By his command, his poor eager sub had been trying desperately not to make a sound or move as she climaxed.

Afterwards he'd said to her, "Thank you, Kelly. You did that to please me, didn't you?" and she'd replied, "Yes, John. I want to please you more than anything."

He shut his eyes, absorbing the sensations that this memory provided. It was such a heady sense of belonging and fulfillment.

Kelly is mine, he thought, twisting his bullwhip between his hands with sudden savage intensity. *I would marry her tomorrow if she'd let me. No matter what the barriers, and there are so many. Too many. Kelly Flynn. She was kind to me even as a child. My first friend. My first girlfriend… almost anyway. My first real sex. My first love. And the last. For me, there will never be another.*

For now and for always, John knew he'd love Kelly Flynn.

Swallowing his violent emotions, he effortlessly blocked them off as he'd done all his life. Then he put on some safety goggles and gently swung his bullwhip over his head, making sure that he had adequate space and wouldn't hit anything while practicing.

He placed his thumb in line with the handle, and then brought the whip forward in a relaxed, fluid motion and flicked his wrist back, aiming for the floor.

Crack!

Yes, John thought, instantly feeling less off balance. *I love that sound.*

Once the whip was fully extended, he retrieved it by cocking his arm back and to the side, away from his body and head. He repeated this action a few times.

Crack! Crack! Crack!

He then began forward hits to the target. Practicing with both his dominant and non-dominant hands, John worked for about an hour until Colin came in about a half an hour before noon. By then, partially because of his heavy protective clothing, and largely because of his vigorous physical efforts, John had worked up quite a sweat. He took off his goggles.

"Hey, John," Colin Wilkins said, "Always glad to see you here honing your skills."

About forty-five years old, Colin was a stocky man, just under six feet tall, with brown hair and a thick dark, well-trimmed beard. The man had done most everything at one time or another, including working as a lumberjack in Canada, security; including armored car bank transport, and numerous laboring jobs.

Colin could strip a motorbike bike down and put it back together in half a day. He sported some tasteful tattoos on his muscular biceps, and was a consistent, experienced Dom. It was his Dom skills that had initially attracted John to him. The man didn't have a higher education but what he lacked there he made up in enthusiasm and his natural people skills and security expertise.

Rolling up his whip, John decided he'd had enough. He and Colin both wandered over to have a look at the target area. Colin snorted, after seeing the clay indentations underneath the outline of female breasts and vulva area.

"Ouch," Colin said.

John checked the indentations, pleased by how shallow they were. Not one of his hits would have been more than a brief kiss of the whip, which is what he'd been aiming for.

"True," John said. "But at this level it would only leave a welt. It's the psychological effect from the sound of the whip as much as ever increasing amount of pain that sends my subs off into sub space." He gave Colin a hard look. "Trust me," he said and held up his bullwhip. "A cane hurts way more than this does."

Colin raised his dark bushy eyebrows. "You sound like you know from personal experience."

John lifted one shoulder in an ambiguous shrug. As was customary from a lifetime of habit, he gave nothing away. "Let's go to your office," he said. "I want to talk to you about something."

As they both walked toward the office area, John reflected. The truth was he'd years of personal experience of being caned by his sadistic, sociopathic father. He still had the scars. All his life he'd never attended sports at school or swimming, or anything that would expose his father's shame… or his own. He'd never even worn a pair of shorts.

The doctor's note explaining John's "unusual and possibly contagious rash" sent to the principle of every school he'd attended ensured that all skeletons were safely kept locked away in the family closet.

John's jaw tensed. A bullwhip had nothing on a cane for pain. Not the way he used his bullwhip, in any case. And as for sub space? Well, he'd had plenty of personal experience with that, too. At one point, as a child, he'd felt the powerful craving for the dread, nervous excitement, and euphoric high that could be created from constant physical torment.

Pain was the ultimate high.

That was why he didn't often use the same sub twice, or if he did there were months between scenes. Severe pain addiction

John understood intimately. He never intended to find himself as the cause of it in someone else.

The words of his mentor, André Chevalier echoed in his head. "Pain must only be used as a means to ultimately add to your sub's sensation of pleasure, *mon ami*. To do otherwise is *un péché noir* – a black sin. It will tarnish your soul."

Tarnish his soul? John gave an internal snort, well aware that he couldn't afford to blacken his soul any more than he had already, sick perverse fuck that he was.

Like a military officer following orders during wartime, he'd always heeded André's advice to the letter. Thus when John dominated a scene his focus was always on using pain to increase sexual stimulation, with attention at all times directed toward orgasm.

Still, nothing gave John more pleasure than hurting a sub and making him or her cry from administering pain. He'd always sought that – a submissive that was willing to accept his torment in their desire to please him. Such tears were a profound gift. There was nothing more beautiful.

Except for Kelly, he thought. *I spent the entire night having sex with Kelly, and never even thought of hurting her, much less felt my customary desire to do so. I still don't want to hurt her. What I want to do is fuck her. That's the biggest change of all. Could loving Kelly have transformed me?*

If so, he was on board with it. Kelly was good-hearted. She was the best person he knew – and all that purity came naturally to her. Even as a child. That was what had drawn him to her in the first place. Kelly was like the sun, bright with joy, and love and happiness. How did she do it?

He was Kelly's opposite. For years he'd been buried in darkness and hate, that despite all his efforts, he simply couldn't exorcize. Sighing, John knew that he was still learning to like himself.

But if someone as good as Kelly wants me, he thought, *I can't be all bad, can I?*

Chapter 4

Suffering

The 'Managers Office' was clearly labeled and pleasingly fitted out in an office worker palette of blues and creams. Coming in directly from the dungeon-like BDSM play areas just outside this room could be a shock, but it helped to make the adjustment from play to work. Colin had a large wooden desk with an 'in,' 'out' and 'pending' basket on it, two cream colored filing cabinets, a high-back black leather executive chair, with two comfortable visitor's chairs in front of this desk. A small sink, kitchenette area was in one corner.

The only concession to this strictly office atmosphere was a framed poster on one wall, of a blindfolded and cuffed, naked female sub, lying across her master's lap, clearly enjoying a spanking. Underneath this erotic scene was inscribed:

'Sometimes what seems like surrender isn't surrender at all. It's about what's going on in our hearts. About seeing clearly the way life is and accepting it and being true to it, whatever the pain, because the pain of not being true to it is far, far greater.' Nicholas Evans, The Horse Whisperer.

John liked the quote very much and felt it was rather apropos to his own circumstances. Walking over to the small fridge, he pulled out a small bottle of water, twisting the top off and drinking every drop of it down. His mind remained on the words from the poster: *Seeing clearly the way life is and accepting it and being true to it.*

While John wanted Kelly Flynn, and needed her submission he knew the opposite was true as well. In his heart he'd already surrendered to Kelly completely. But he wasn't free to tell her that. Not yet.

John's manager had the drip-feed coffee maker ready to go. Colin put beans from the fridge inside, and flicked the switch to on. With the smell of fresh coffee brewing, they sat down together and discussed the evening's events.

"I won't be attending tonight," John said.

"No problem." The machine was sputtering, indicating the coffee was ready. Colin moved to pour cups for both of them, getting sugar and half-and-half out of the fridge. Everything edible was kept in the fridge so they didn't inadvertently attract pests.

"Has Kelly Flynn signed up for another month membership?" John asked.

"Not yet."

John's mug was red with green letters that said, *'Anal Sex: a pain in the ass.'* Hiding his smile, he stirred milk and sugar into his coffee. "I want you to contact her on Monday. Tell her to come in and see you Monday or Tuesday – wherever she isn't working, and is available." He took a sip, and realizing he was still thirsty, took another.

"Okay," Colin said, surprised. Then he frowned and narrowed his eyes, displaying a curious, calculated look.

The man was completely transparent to John, which was part of the reason why he'd hired him. That and his squeaky clean background check. In the Middle Ages Colin would have been a knight; he just had that sort of chivalry about him. Honest, hardworking, married with two children, and faithful to his sub – Colin was a 'what you see is what you get' kind of guy. He liked him for that and paid him very well. If the club made money, Colin did too, in the form of generous bonuses in addition to his salary.

John smiled, fully aware of exactly what his manager was thinking. Colin's response to his wry smile was to give him wide eyes. Colin rarely saw John smile.

"Colin, my friend," he said. "It's as you suspect. I've a thing for Ms. Flynn. I want her on a permanent basis. The woman is mine – she just hasn't realized it yet. I've got a plan however, to get what I want."

Laughing out loudly, Colin set his large dark green mug down. It had *'Bondage: Knot for everyone'* written on the side of it, in big red letters.

Colin's good-natured grin broadened and he settled back into his chair. "That's fucking fantastic," he said. "In the four years I've known you I've never seen you want anyone, ah… you know. Like that. Honestly you've always seemed a little lonely to me. I don't know where I'd be without my Donna. Anyway, you're a private person, John. No one even knows you own the club. But for what it's worth, I'm really happy for you."

Still smiling, John said, "Thank you, Colin. I appreciate it." He then explained about the elevator, and the events that occurred with Kelly because of it. Also he told him about her unfortunate discovery of her own personal file at his home.

"Wow," Colin said. "So she used her safe word, didn't let you explain, and now she thinks you are a stalker?"

John shrugged. "That about sums it up. But Kelly wasn't far wrong. In fact I rather think her Spidey Senses are absolutely correct. I did bring her file home to study. Have you ever known me to do that with anyone else's personal details?"

Colin laughed some more and slapped the desk in his enthusiasm.

"I want you to give Kelly a month free membership if she doesn't plan on signing up again," John said. "If she does plan on staying at The Basement, let her pay her own way, or maybe offer a discount. I don't want to show my hand yet if I can avoid it. Think of the best way to tell her that I own this club. Maybe leave her file and a few others out where she can see them? I rely on you in this, Colin. Talk it over with Donna. You know how to get the message across, but less is more when talking about me."

John swallowed the last of his coffee and stood up. "Oh, and get on to the manager of the building about that elevator. Nothing will happen today as its Sunday, but if you notify him, something will be done first thing Monday morning."

Colin stood up also and shook John's hand. "Leave it to me," he said. "And what are you going to do with Kelly? Wait for her to make the first move? Talk to her? What?"

He looked at Colin well aware that he'd made no attempt to hide what was probably an evil, sadistic little glint in his eyes. "I'm going to make that poor girl suffer," John said.

Colin just stared at him with a little frown between his eyes. Clearly his Manager was uncertain of how to take that remark.

Unfortunately, John thought as he left the office, *in punishing her, I rather suspect that I'll be suffering, too. But it can't be helped.*

Chapter 5

Phone Call

John walked to the car park, unlocked his silver Mercedes sports car, and got into it at exactly noon. He settled himself comfortably and then hit speed dial on the blue-tooth for his mentor, André Chevalier.

"*Bonjour! Oui?*" came the pleasant melodious sound of his mentor's voice.

"André? It's me, John."

"John, *mon ami, comment allez-vous?*"

"Good. I'm good. Do you have time to talk, André?"

"But of course."

"Well then," John said, "I wanted you to be the first to know. I love someone, André. I love her so much that it hurts."

"*Vraiment?* Bravo, John! And she loves you?"

There was a long silence. "She's confused right now, but I know that she loves me." John explained about the elevator breaking down, Kelly's panic, and how he'd handled it. Then he told him how he'd brought her home and had amazing sex all night long.

"Sex with is more wonderful than I could ever have imagined, André. I could never have conceived of such pleasure. And sex with someone you love…" He paused, recalling the joy he felt from giving and receiving pleasure. The silence grew, as he was unable to explain such rapture.

Aware of his difficulty, André spoke, "This is a cause for much celebration my friend, *n'est-ce pas?* You have made me – a very happy man – much happier. *Mon Dieu,* much more than I can say."

"Thank you," John said, feeling an unexpected ache in his chest. "Me too. I wanted to tell you first."

"And second?"

"My counselor. In time I'll explain it all to Kelly. I don't want secrets between us."

"*Ce qui est* excellent. It is best to begin a relationship in the manner in which you intend to go on. But your secrets, John? *Très difficile.* It is good that you do not mean to alarm her, by telling her too much, too fast. Do you still visit with your counselor, Maria Lopez?"

"Twice a month, André. On my honor, I've always followed your every instruction to the exact detail. You told me that this day would come. It seemed, how shall I say it? Well, unlikely. But I decided to have faith and trust that you knew what you were talking about. You did. I've so much to thank you for."

"You are most welcome," André replied warmly. "And does your Kelly enjoy pain, *mon ami?*"

"I don't care. If I need to, I'll teach her, but it doesn't matter, André. It honestly doesn't."

The sound of André's soft joyous chuckle filled John's car. "This very much sounds like true love, my friend."

"Yeah, well, she isn't really talking to me at the moment." John explained then about how Kelly had found a file with her name on it and all her personal details in his room. Also how she'd used her safe word and left in a panic.

"*Merde!* Why did you choose not to account for your actions, John? Of a certainty, it seems to me that this would have been a simple task."

"Kelly didn't want to hear it," John said. "There's a saying André, that it's a waste of breath arguing with someone who is angry. When people are angry they are simply not ready, or even willing to hear the truth."

"*Eh bien*, this sounds most sensible. And so, you are calling perhaps to ask my advice?"

"No. Only to share my happiness with you."

"*Merci beaucoup*. And Kelly? How do you intend to settle this issue with her?"

"I know exactly how to deal with a disrespectful sub, André. Trust me on this. You trained me, after all, and I'm a good student. I'll take care of this problem with Kelly."

When John hung up he was grinning.

Even as he hit 'end call' on his steering wheel he could still hear the deep, musical sound of André's laughter echoing throughout his car. John's mentor had been laughing at full volume in that playful, carefree, French manner that was uniquely his.

Chapter 6

Manager Meeting

Tuesday night, Colin Wilkins, The Basement's manager, had left word with Security at the entry to the club, to text him the moment Kelly Flynn arrived. Colin had called Kelly on Monday, and found that she intended to renew her club membership. They'd made an appointment to meet up together tonight, as she was working Monday, Wednesday and Friday this week, and would come to The Basement on the alternate nights.

Christ almighty, Colin thought, nervously pacing outside the ladies' change area. *I so don't want to screw this up.*

This was the first instance in the entire time that Colin had known John Taylor, that he'd seen his boss display actual interest in anyone – male or female. For all he knew his boss was gay, or bi, because he certainly never showed an obvious preference. John seemed to be the curiously peculiar kind of guy that could reach down someone's pants and be satisfied with whatever he found there.

Colin had gone over the plan of how to deal with Kelly Flynn in his mind, considering many different possibilities, discussing how to handle things with his wife, Donna. Donna had been a rock. She'd given him the female sub perspective on the best plan of action. After much discussion, they had decided to go ahead with her concept.

It's a simple arrangement, Colin thought. *So why am I so nervous?*

But he knew the answer. John Taylor was important to him, and not just because he was his boss and gave him a generous salary. Colin had grown to admire and respect him. The young man was twisted, bent out of shape by something probably from his childhood. Anyone with a drop of humanity could see that.

While every sub of both sexes wanted him, the young man remained totally self-contained and completely alone. Colin just knew that John was lonely.

He and Donna had had John over to their house for dinner, but just the once. It had been an excruciating and agonizing experience for all concerned. John was like a Redneck attending a Gay Support meeting, he sooo didn't fit in. Not that there was anything Redneck about John. Colin's boss just didn't seem to know how to interact with people outside the confines of the BDSM environment. It was as if he'd no experience with such normal, social, human activity.

Colin smiled. Donna of course immediately set about thinking of people that she could set John up with, the little matchmaker. "The right woman will iron out those peculiar little character flaws of his," she'd pronounced. "Someone social, with a bit of life and zest, will brighten that dour personality and make him laugh. The right woman would teach John exactly how to behave."

His dick twitched as he recalled the erotic spankings he'd given her as a result of *that* fixation. "You keep out of it," he'd demanded. "He'll figure it out on his own."

Donna simply wanted John Taylor to find the happiness that she and Colin had found together, which was completely understandable.

When Kelly exited the ladies' change room, Colin was pacing nearby, waiting for her as he'd been forewarned by text. Of course he tried to appear as if their meeting was casual and unexpected. "Kelly," he said, noticing the young woman looked a little drawn and pale. She was dressed in an olive and rust colored bustier, something new, and it really set off her hair and pale freckled skin. "Are you alright?"

Kelly gave him a wan smile. "Oh, I'm a little off my game at the moment, Sir. But I'm getting there."

"Love the new bustier," he said. "Yowza. You're looking pretty damn fine, girl."

"Why, thank you, Sir," she said, brightening. "See? I feel better already."

Colin placed his hand at the curve of her lower back to escort her. "I'm glad I caught you. Come into my office and we can go over the membership thing, alright?" he said.

"Sure thing, Sir," she said.

Colin was glad to find Kelly happy to attend to this business without demur. Naturally submissive, she'd a powerful need to please, which Colin as a Dom had instantly picked up on. Was that what John was attracted to? The woman was no beauty. Even as young as she was, compared to Donna, Kelly didn't match up to his own wife's good looks.

Meh, he thought indifferently. *Orange hair, plain round face, medium breasts, a zillion freckles.*

The girl had some meat on her, and that was good. Kelly was probably a size twelve to fourteen. Colin didn't like skinny women because he liked nice, soft curves. Unfortunately, she had more of a straight, boyish figure rather than the classic hourglass shape. One thing she did have going for her was that damn fine ass. Kelly Flynn would totally ace an international 'Most Perfect Butt' competition.

"How is the evening going so far, Sir?" she asked him, looking less pale and more herself. "All good?"

Colin laughed. "I have the best job in the entire world, Kelly. Who wouldn't want to be me? I love this place. I'd come to The Basement all the time, even if I didn't work here." He opened the door to his office for her, politely guiding her in. Gesturing to the nearest chair across from his desk, he motioned for Kelly to sit down. She did.

"Can I get you a drink? You look like you need one."

Kelly's pink lips curved and her pale blue eyes twinkled. "That depends," she said with a tilt to her head, and a mischievous expression. "What's on offer?"

Colin suddenly could see John's attraction to the woman. Kelly Flynn had something going for her alright. She was striking when she smiled with that ridiculously large mouth of hers. The girl did have personality, and when it showed, she could be extremely attractive.

Speed dialing his cell, Colin spoke to one of The Basement's regular bartenders, "Hey, Daniel, do me a favor and bring me a Rum and Coke and a..." He looked over at Kelly.

"Tequila Sunrise."

Colin gave a low chuckle, "...and a Tequila Sunrise. Thanks my man." He hit 'end' and said, "Well, that should take the edge off, Kelly." He went to one of his filing cabinets and made a show of rummaging around. "I wanted to talk to you because we always survey new members after their first month. I like to do the survey myself; just to see if anything can be done to improve your experience here at The Basement."

He looked over to her as he brought out two files – one of another recent new member and Kelly's own file, placing them casually on his desk. "I'm glad you're going to stay on with us," he said.

Kelly blinked and then recoiled slightly. In a very short moment the color drained from her face, making her naturally pale complexion whiter than ever. *Good,* Colin thought with approval. *She's recognized her own file from John's house. I can tick another step off the plan.*

Colin sat down in his own chair. Appearing not to notice Kelly's astonished reaction to viewing her file, he continued speaking in a chatty manner. "It's nice to attract young members to our club. In fact, we have a special at the moment, a thirty per cent discount. You'll be able to take advantage of that."

"I'm sorry, Sir," she interjected. "Do you mind if I ask? What is that file with my name on it?"

"What, this?" he said casually, picking up her manila folder. "Oh. Well you know how you signed a waiver allowing our security firm to perform a full security check on you? Including police records? This is simply what they give us back as a result."

"May I see it?" she said with a tremor in her voice.

Colin shoved it toward her, and across the desk with a shrug. "I don't see why not. It's all about you after all. You should know what's in it already."

Kelly opened the file with unsteady fingers, he observed, well aware of the stunned distress that was running through her. For a few moments she trailed through it, flipping pages and seeming more and more faint.

"What's wrong?" he asked. "Are you okay, Kelly?" *What the fuck? Where did I go wrong?* Because this wasn't the response Colin had been planning on.

Right now Kelly Flynn looked as if she was going to pass out.

Chapter 7

In Confidence

A knock sounded on the door bringing a welcome relief from the tension of the atmosphere. "Come in," Colin bellowed.

Daniel, a young, slim man and one of the bartenders slipped in with two drinks on a tray. He placed the rum and Coke in front of Colin and the orangey-red Tequila Sunrise, with a little pink umbrella in it, in front of Kelly.

"Thanks, Daniel," Colin said. "Put it on my tab, I'll fix you up later."

"You got it, Chief," Daniel said with a grin and a cocky three fingered half salute.

"Drink up, Kelly," Colin said, coming around to her side of the desk to sit in the chair next to her. "You don't look so good."

Tossing out the umbrella, Kelly took a large gulp, knocking back half of the liquid in the tall slender glass. Sitting down beside her, he patted her knee comfortingly. "Hey, what's going on, girl? You seem weirded out."

When she didn't respond Colin scooped her into his lap and pressed her head against his chest. Then he began to rub her hands. "Jesus, little girl, what the fuck? You look like you're going to faint. Never mind, you sit up here on me for a bit. Donna says I throw off heat like a furnace. I'll warm you up." He put his arms around her, wrapping her like a blanket, in the warmth of his bigger body. Kelly's skin felt so cold against his heat. "I've seen shock before. Something has upset you. Just sit here until you get it together, honey."

Colin couldn't help but feel a familiar, instinctive pull when Kelly curled trustingly into him, just like a little kitten. The woman was a soft ball of female flesh that had unconsciously sought his security and support. His protective Dom nature sparked from her helpless vulnerability, and he continued to rub and pat her back in a soothing circular motion.

Hummm, he thought. *Here are some more extremely attractive character traits, trust, need, dependence. This little sub might do very well for John after all,* he decided. But then he frowned. *Except that she most definitely isn't a pain slut. That could be a serious drawback for a man like John.*

When Kelly began to snap out of it, she sat up and winced with chagrin. "I'm so sorry, Sir," she said. "Donna would scratch my eyes out if she saw me sitting here on your lap."

"No she wouldn't," Colin said calmly. "Donna is a caring sort of person. She'd be angry with me if I *hadn't* picked you up. That woman has no earthly reason to be jealous of anyone." He snickered. "Donna has me by the balls and she knows it."

Kelly gave a faint smile at that. "That seems rather doubtful, Sir," she said.

"Okay, well she has my heart by the balls then – that is, if my heart had balls. Donna knows she's the only woman for me." To Colin's complete surprise, after that comment, Kelly burst into tears.

Man, he thought. *Women. Who could figure them out? If John comes into the Manager's Office right now the normally icily composed SOB would probably lose his shit. I'd probably get my ass fired, after a severe thrashing with that bullwhip of his.*

Well, there was nothing he could do for the present except relax and enjoy the ride. Consequently he simply continued to pat Kelly's back and said nothing. Luckily he had a box of tissues on his desk. She used quite a few of them while he patiently waited for her to calm down.

When Kelly finally got it together she said with her breath hitching, "I'm okay now, thank you." Sliding off his lap she returned to the seat beside him. "I'm sorry, Sir."

"No big," he said. "So are you going to tell me what's up? Is someone here bothering you or something? Is there anything I can do?"

Colin knew that wasn't the case, but he threw it out there anyway. Kelly's dilemma was his boss, and he figured that problem was going to get bigger before it was resolved. In fact he was certain more tears were on the way sometime soon, no doubt caused by her Dom. He just hoped he wasn't around when the dam broke. Cross fingers that John contained the whole thing with a spanking in a private scene.

"I saw this exact file," she said, with a catch in her throat. "This one with my name on. It was at John Taylor's house. Does he work for that security firm or something? Do you know?"

"Huh," he said with raised eyebrows. "I've never known John to take anyone home with him," he said, twisting the knife a little. Poor woman already feels bad, but it wouldn't hurt to make her feel worse for running out on the man. That's what he and Donna had decided anyway. "He must really like you, Kelly. Why don't you ask him?"

"I don't think he'll talk to me right now," she said in a small voice. When Kelly began to explain, Colin cut her off. "Look, Kelly – no offence, but I don't want to get in the middle of this. I don't think I'm the right person. You should talk to him. I promise you that John has had a very through security check. He's not a stalker or anything. And yes, there was a legitimate reason for him to have your file."

Colin felt like a heel, but he continued playing his hand, right to the end where he trumped everything. Kelly needed to beg to be told the secret that he already intended her to have: That John owned The Basement. It was a little painful, this complete duplicity, but he assured himself that it was for the best. It was the plan he and Donna had worked out between them.

"I don't understand. Why would John have my file?"

Colin shrugged.

"Can't you tell me?" she asked.

"Not really," he said drinking over half his Rum and Coke down, and swirling the ice in the glass. "It's a secret that's not mine to tell."

Kelly just gave him a long, pitiful, lost puppy look.

Colin stood and began to pace, as if tense with indecision. Finally making a big show of giving in, he faced her with his best 'Stern Dom' gaze. "Look Kelly," he began with a raised index finger. "No one knows this. *No one.* So if rumors get around I'll know who said something and I'll cancel your membership, bang!" he snapped his fingers loudly. "Just like that. I'll end it under violation of the confidentiality clause, understand?"

"I swear I won't say anything to anyone," Kelly assured him, eagerly sitting forward.

"Fine," he said. "John Taylor owns The Basement. In fact, he owns this whole damn building. He's a fantastic boss, and I don't want to lose my job. Now I'll have to make it clear to him why I told you, and he'll probably be okay with that. But the explanation is simple. You're a new member, and John personally checks every new member out. That's it."

"Oh," she said, and then she downed the rest of her drink. Colin felt the expression on the young woman's' face was priceless. Kelly looked as if she'd lost ten bucks, but found a hundred. So now she knew.

The question to Colin's mind was, what was she going to do about it?

Chapter 8

The Letter

～✕～

Kelly Flynn was back on the emotional roller coaster ride from hell, only it was twice as high and three times as heart-stopping and terrifying. Not only that, the lows were much worse than before.

What a terrible evening.

After talking to the Manager of The Basement, and finding out how wrong she'd been about John, she went to the sub's gallery and hoped to see him. Various friends had come over to chat with her, but she was too preoccupied to listen. Even Master Ron's perfect off-beat humor had failed to engage her – she was just too bummed. Kelly didn't explain her mood to anyone. They probably all figured she was suffering from PMS.

Master Ron, a really great guy, clearly had a crush on her, but she had a crush on John. Why was life always so complicated? More than anything she wanted to talk to someone about what had happened.

No, she thought. *I opened my mouth and put my foot in it already this week. Once was enough. Colin was right to not want to get involved. It isn't his business, and it isn't anyone else's business either. I'll just shut up and wait until I can talk to John.*

The resolution to keep her mouth closed was against Kelly's character, because she liked to talk. For her, talking was like breathing, easy, natural and automatic. What had finally settled the matter was imagining what John would want. He wouldn't want her gossiping about him, and about the time they had spent together. John was too private a person for that.

When Kelly first saw John Tuesday night at the club, after running out on him on Sunday, it was like getting a fist slammed right into her chest.

Kelly just sucked in a deep breath and stared. John was wearing his standard black leather pants that showed his utterly built, male body. Black swat boots, and black leather vest, his beautiful torso was exposed as he wore nothing other than his vest top. The magnificent virile Dom had a flawless, smoking hot, sculpted body. Broad shoulders, cut abs, thin hipped, great ass.

And he could fuck all night long.

Kelly subdued the sudden impulse to fan herself. Jesus John made her hot. Yet it wasn't just the sex. What was the inexplicable pull of the man? It wasn't the fact that he was simply gorgeous either, although that was a serious draw card. Now that Kelly knew him better from that one night with him, she wasn't in love with just a fine body.

No, John knew her, or at least he seemed to be able to read her mind. She'd adored every single thing about John, and had felt comfortable and able to tell him anything. The intimate moments they had spent together had been powerful, passionate and overwhelming. She really missed that connection.

Kelly stood up and tried to get John's attention, but he didn't seem to see her. On the pretense of going to the toilet she quickly moved down the sub gallery ramp and walked by him. With a strong, graceful, stride, he was going the opposite way. To her utter mortification John's eyes slid right past her without apparent recognition.

When she'd impulsively called his name out, he'd turned toward her with that implacable, dark, sexy gaze. She'd been pinned then, unable to move from his piercing look. With the smallest of shake of his head, he had indicated 'no,' an expression of finality.

Then he'd continued walking away from her.

The harsh, detached expression on John's handsome face was agonizing and beyond any pain she'd known before or could imagine. He didn't want to acknowledge her. John had refused to even talk to her.

Kelly thought her heart would break into a million pieces just from that.

Seeing John so changed from the smiling happy lover she'd known so intimately hurt as much as a knife in the chest. Why had he done it? Was this a test he had set for her? To prove that she deserved him? Or was he simply punishing her for using her safe word and running? And was this painful impasse temporary or permanent?

Kelly had gone into the change room and just kept on going after that, running home to the sanctuary of her apartment.

After her train wreck of an evening at The Basement, she decided to write a letter. It was after midnight, but she didn't think she was going to get much sleep anyway. Saturday night she'd known the most awe inspiring connection with another person in her life – and now it was gone.

She'd bought and worn the new bustier to please John. It was in the same colors as his bedroom, and looked good against her fair skin and orange hair. Kelly sighed. Now her credit card was maxed out and he hadn't even noticed.

Friend, savior and amazing lover, John Taylor radiated a palpable energy and devastating seductive appeal. Kelly missed him so much. She missed his body with his raw, intense sexual need, not to mention his fascinating, ever erect cock. It was insane. She'd do anything to get John back, even for one night. She wanted a re-do. Why had she run off like that on Sunday? So stupid. She felt like wringing her own neck.

Kelly was unhappy and horny and didn't want to cry again. She'd cried too much already. It wouldn't surprise her if her eyes fell out from already shedding an ocean of tears, but she simply felt so sad.

Kelly made herself a hot chocolate, with no marshmallows this time. The last time she'd had hot chocolate was with John and that thought gave her another painful pang. He was punishing her, and teaching her a lesson. That was the only explanation.

Surely he missed her as much as she missed him? He *must* have had the same feeling of bonding and union that she had. It hadn't been an illusion – it had been real.

Kelly, to a large degree, was experienced in love. She knew the deep feelings she'd had for her big brother and her father, and she loved all of her family – even her tiresome mother. As annoying as her mom was, Kelly knew that her mother wanted her to be happy.

The occasional crushes Kelly had experienced with the opposite sex had easily worn off, and she knew the difference now between actual love and infatuation. While love of family members didn't in actual fact compare, she could recognize the honest, genuine feeling.

Love as a concept, was not foreign to Kelly.

What she'd felt toward John, after that one night together…. Well. At first, before she knew him, it had been infatuation. But now it could only be love.

Sex with John was one thing – a wow, huge, never experienced before ultimate high, but it wasn't just that. Never had Kelly felt so 'herself' with another person. She and John had talked and laughed and reveled in each other's company. They had completely connected. This was the real deal. In her little heart of hearts she was certain of that – if of nothing else.

So, Kelly sat at the kitchen table and composed a letter.

Dear John,

(OMG a 'Dear John' letter, Kelly thought.*)* I wanted to write and thank you for your help on Saturday night. I honestly think I might have died, or gone insane if you hadn't been there to save me when I was trapped in that elevator. I owe you. A lot. *(Okay. Pretty good. So far so good.)*

John I had the best time last Saturday night in your lovely home, particularly your lovely bedroom *(No, can't write that! That sounds bad. Start again.)*

John, I had the BEST time Saturday night *(True, but this could be expanded.)* I've never felt such a wonderful connection with anyone *(Too cheesy? Maybe, but it's true.)* I'm so sorry I spoiled it all Sunday morning. Will you please forgive me? Can we start again? *(Pitiful, but I think it works.)*

I was really freaked out by finding that file on me on your desk when I left the bathroom I wasn't snooping, I swear — my name just jumped out at me. Your manager Colin explained why it was there, but quite honestly I simply panicked *(Actually I assumed he was a lying, sneaky, wacko pervert and was afraid for my life. Shit. I don't have to tell him that, do I? Jesus I know he'll get that out of me, he soooo always finds the truth. Shit, shit, shit.)*

(Okay, what next? Oh yeah.) So I think I've learned my lesson I'll not jump to conclusions, particularly about you. I'll not use my safe word when I don't need to I know you would have simply talked to me about it At least what I know of you makes me think that *(Jesus, I'm rambling.)*

John I really miss you and I'm thinking about you all the time. Will you please call me? Can we meet? *(Really pathetic.)* I spoke to my brother Richard about you He remembers you from grade school, and when we started talking, I remembered, too

Kelly sat back, and bits and pieces came back to her. John had been a strange sort of shadow in her childhood, but he'd been a friend. Once he had found her crying out in the back of the school. She'd been perhaps eleven years old. The other kids had been teasing her about her orange hair, and she'd taken it to heart.

Without even a hello, John had walked up to her and peremptorily demanded, "Why are you crying?"

It was just like him to accost her in that odd, frank way of his. Kelly had explained that all of the kids had been calling her 'carrot top.' She'd rambled on and on, pacing back and forth with anxious, restless energy. John had stood perfectly still and silently watched her with his dark, solemn eyes.

When all of Kelly's ranting had finally run out, and she had sat down dejectedly on some steps, John spoke. "They are all stupid," he had pronounced with authoritative contempt. "A carrot has a green top." At that she'd laughed and laughed and laughed. And she'd instantly felt much better.

Looking back, even then the young man, who was two years older than she was, had displayed dominant behavior. Was that what had attracted them to each other? Her budding submissive personality and his dominance?

John had watched her when she practiced and played Annie. Kelly knew he loved to hear her sing. The older boy had been consistently quiet, yet always there in the background.

He'd been a really strange kid from her perspective now. Why couldn't she see it? But she'd only been a child, then. John had been sad and lonely, already inherently guarded and isolated from everyone else, yet he'd been unequivocally on her side. At the time he had felt similar to Richard, like a big, older, protective brother.

Now he was anything but.

Kelly took a deep fortifying breath and continued writing.

John, I remember now. We were friends when we were children. I'd like to talk with you about that sometime (That was true.)

I miss you John. Will you call me please? (Pathetic again, but there you are).

I think I'm in love with you,

Kelly Flynn

Kelly finished by writing her phone number on the bottom of the page.

Now, she thought after re-reading it twice. *I'm seriously baring my heart and soul here. What if he doesn't respond? Or worse, what if he says he doesn't want to see me? God. Can I really give this letter to John?*

The answer was a definite yes.

Chapter 9

Unloved Puppy

Wednesday morning Kelly drove to John's home. He either wasn't there, or he didn't answer the doorbell. She considered the mailbox, but then slipped her letter under his kitchen door and left. Wednesday night she worked, and Thursday she went to The Basement and once more spent the entire evening in the sub's gallery, hoping for John to relent and speak to her.

Behind the railing up in the sub's gallery, Kelly felt like an unwanted puppy, forlornly waiting for someone to buy her and take her home. But she didn't want just any owner. Kelly wanted to belong to John Taylor. Kelly's friend Rosslyn sat with her, cheerfully watching the adventurous members in the BDSM world of The Basement go by.

"Hot damn," Rosslyn said. "Check out Mistress Cheryl."

Kelly's eyes obediently roamed to where Rosslyn had nodded. Mistress Cheryl had a red, skintight cat-womanish latex outfit on, and sexy thigh-high black boots with 'I'm sooo going to fuck you' wicked stiletto heels. Wielding a black riding crop with one hand and a black leash attached to her sub in the other, she looked dangerous. The intense commanding dominance of the woman even gave Kelly, a confirmed heterosexual, a little sexual buzz. *Wow.*

"She looks fantastic," Kelly murmured, awed because Mistress Cheryl was probably fifty but looked much younger. Her sub had on a black leather mask. Lots of people wore full masks around here. The Basement was a private club, expensive and extremely selective because people with high profile jobs needed to protect their identity. Intricate, difficult to meet membership standards, combined with a high price helped ensure privacy.

Mistress Cheryl's sub was on his knees, his masked face turned up reverently toward his mistress. The man had nipple piercings, and cock and ball rings all in red, matching her outfit. His jutting shaft was fully erect and wearing a condom, no doubt so he didn't drip pre-cum everywhere they went. Mistress Cheryl's submissive was clearly enjoying himself, and that made Kelly smile. Good for him. At least someone was happy.

Kelly felt sorry for male subs because of the stigma against them. So stupid to think less of a man for having submissive sexual needs. Why was it more acceptable for a woman to do so? One thing Kelly had discovered was that many powerful men outside these walls, men holding extremely key positions in society, were actually submissive sexually. Who knew? That man on his knees could be the chief of police, or the CEO of a multinational company.

The same was true for women of course. Confident, successful and dominant women outside the bedroom often wanted their partners to be in-charge during sex. There was no all-encompassing stereotype. People needed what they needed. Mind you, BDSM itself was such a societal taboo. For a moment, Kelly imagined her family finding out about her own sexual desires and cringed.

"Yep," Rosslyn said after careful scrutiny. "That outfit is tailor made and brand new. I bet her sub has a latex fetish and she got it especially for him, lucky guy. What an incredible figure. I think she must have had breast augmentation. What do you think?"

"I dunno," Kelly said doubtfully. "They look real to me."

Forty years old, Rosslyn Walker had recently divorced her vanilla husband that she'd married at nineteen. The split was as amicable as could be, and unfortunately unavoidable. At Rosslyn's age she was apparently at her sexual height, and vanilla just didn't cut it for her and never had. Few women understood their sexuality when they were nineteen. Kelly was just glad she'd worked out what she, in general, needed in order to be fulfilled.

As for the specifics, well, John Taylor fit the bill perfectly.

Rosslyn's blonde bob was, as usual, a faultless coiffure, and her thin shapely blonde brows were amazingly expressive. Having her around cheered Kelly up. This was the fourth day of her trials of living without the utter bliss and heaven she'd experienced from just one night with John on Saturday.

As if thinking of him caused him to appear, John Taylor himself began the walk up the ramp to the sub's gallery. His face was implacable, his firm lips set, and he walked with purposeful male animal grace.

Jesus, Kelly thought, her pulse kicking up and pounding loudly in her ears. *He must be coming to Top me, because he had Rosslyn recently, and everyone knows that John never takes the same sub twice unless there were months between scenes.* Kelly felt her face, neck and breasts flush red with heat. *Thank you, Lord! John has to be coming for me.* Could she even stand up? Kelly didn't think so, her knees felt so weak.

John stood in front of both of them for a moment, staring intently.

Kelly could feel the dominant power of the man palpably radiating from him. Father John was a tremendous force of edgy, barely-contained, male sexual energy. Shit, just being this near to him gave her goose bumps.

Then John focused solely on Rosslyn, and gave her a curt nod.

Rosslyn blinked from that unexpected bombshell, and trembled. At once she put her shaking wrists out to him. John tied them and pulled her to her feet. Then he turned and strode away, certain that Rosslyn would obediently follow. Rosslyn looked back at Kelly with a 'What the fuck?' shrug of shock, nervous anxiety, lust, and astonishment. And then they were both gone.

The world dropped away from under Kelly's feet.

John doesn't want me anymore, she thought with a silent, internal wail of pain. She was alone again, her eyes stinging while she tried unsuccessfully to fight back tears. Kelly was just one more unloved puppy, hoping, praying and waiting for her master to come and take her home. But her master didn't want her. What could she do now?

With her mind reeling, she zoned out somehow. Kelly wasn't aware of how long she sat there, trying to pull her shit together enough to get up and leave the club. It could have been five minutes; it could have been ten or even twenty. All she knew was that she was looking down and wiping her eyes when she abruptly became aware of John's familiar swat boots in her line of sight. The man had returned to the sub's gallery suddenly, completely taking her by surprise.

Kelly's head snapped up and she stared uncomprehendingly at John. "Where's Rosslyn?" she shot out without thinking. As per usual her mouth engaged before her brain did.

"I left her with Master T, not that it's any concern of yours," he replied in a deceptively mild voice that was filled with reproof.

"Oh. Sorry, John." After a long pause where his eyes remained unrelentingly upon her and he said nothing, Kelly finally murmured almost unintelligibly, "Did…did you get my letter?"

"Yes."

"Oh." *Jesus, I'm so lame. Why can't I talk?* It was just that there was so much she wanted to say to John, and it was all bottled up inside her. It was as if the backlog of communication was so large that only a trickle of incoherent sound was able to get through. Kelly, the girl who always had something to say, that everyone agreed could talk underwater, suddenly found that she couldn't speak at all.

Never had she suffered as much agony as she had these last few days, moving from joy and love and a sense of connection, to completely black despair.

John stood in front of her, large, confident, and utterly dominant. Fuck he was so beautiful, simply looking at him hurt. Kelly's stomach knotted. His handsome face appeared cold and merciless. The way he was studying her seemed detached and possibly even disdainful. It was so difficult to identify what he was feeling when he wore that impenetrable, impassive mask.

She simply couldn't bear his disapproval and disappointment. Unable to endure the dangerous intensity of John's scrutiny, her gaze lowered.

"Eyes up, Kelly," he ordered. Her eyes flew to his face. "I'm a Dom that prefers to see my sub's eyes."

Kelly felt such joy at those words that her chest, which had felt so tight, loosened, making it easier to breathe. A torrent of emotion swelled inside her. Her eyes welled, and tears trailed silently down her cheeks, but she ignored them. For the first time in days she felt a rush of hope. John had said, 'my sub's eyes.' Had he intended to do that? Did he still considered her his?

Impulsively she blurted out, "Will you forgive me, John?"

"When are you here next?"

"Saturday night."

"Good. I'll Top you Saturday night. Be here at seven, I'll be outside the ladies' change room door, so don't be late. No makeup, and have an enema before you arrive. Agreed?"

An enema? she thought. *Really? Shit.*

Kelly had never had anal play, except the small amount she'd experienced with John that one memorable night. Right now, however, she'd do anything to get back into his good graces. She recalled Rosslyn's words to her just last week: "You won't sing that tune when you fall for someone. There's nothing you won't do for your Dom then. You'll want to surrender any power you have completely, and let him do anything – just to see him smile."

Wow. Were those words prophetic, or what? Here she was, madly in love. Right now she was willing to endure absolutely anything for this man that she was completely gone on.

Motionless, John continued to stare at her. Kelly felt utterly exposed by his piercing gaze. What did he see when he looked at her? He was such a powerful Dom who seemed able to read minds. She had experienced that already. Did he have any idea how much he meant to her? But he'd told her that he'd Top her on Saturday. That was two days away. Two days to wait and to worry.

She licked her lips and swallowed. "Um, John, are we doing a, er, public scene?"

"I haven't decided, but that's none of your business now, is it?" His deep seductive voice was soft and menacing.

Jesus. Kelly cringed. Her core tightened and gushed. Actually, she'd become totally aroused the moment she'd seen John, but that voice of his, and the words he spoke! Wow. It was as if her body recognized him as the one who had given her so much pleasure, and was instantly ready to go there again.

She expelled a deep breath, wanting his touch, aching for *him*. She knew that no matter how John wanted to take her, she'd submit to him. She'd be glad to have his attention, any attention, even if it involved public humiliation or pain. Freely, willingly, and more than anything else in the world, she wanted to give herself completely to John Taylor.

Punishment would be on the agenda, and she deserved it. She knew she was due for some discipline, but exactly how much did he intend to hurt her? Kelly cleared her throat. "May I ask, John, um, are you going to use your bullwhip?"

"Again, that's up to me isn't it, little sub?"

"Yes," she whispered with her heart pounding loudly in her ears. "Alright, John. I'll be there at seven."

He gave her a brusque nod. Without another word, he turned and left.

Chapter 10

Discipline

~~~

Kelly arrived at The Basement a half hour early. Delaying anxiously in her car until a quarter to seven, she took the stairs down. Forcing a happy hello to Tom, she entered the ladies' change room. After using the toilet, and washing her face, she walked out to the main area and waited.

Was John going to be late, she wondered? Because she didn't think her nerves could stand it if he was. This entire week had decimated any emotional stamina she had. Every single day she had to get up and pretend that everything was fine. She'd had to go through the motions, to go to work, and be her normally cheerful self.

It had been complete and utter hell.

If John's intention had been to break her completely, to make her a total basket case, then he'd been successful.

John strode up to her right on time wearing his traditional BDSM attire, black leather pants, vest and swat boots. He stood in front of her, studying her face with that compelling, possessive gaze of his.

Now that he was here, Kelly met his eyes and she instantly felt so much better. The wait was over. John was in control. Kelly couldn't give any power she had over to him fast enough. Even the bullwhip didn't scare her anymore.

The last week had been a revelation, separating what was important and what wasn't.

Forget the bullwhip, intimidating open scenes with everyone looking on, and excruciating pain. Who cared about any of those things? Disappointing John, making him unhappy, or living without him was all that truly frightened her.

More than anything she wanted to see him smile. She needed to please him, to bask in his approval and his love. Kelly needed to be his, somehow. If he forgave her tonight then maybe they could get back to that wonderful loving bond they had forged together a week ago.

John pulled out a club tie and Kelly raised her hands. John bound her wrists, without touching her at all. Yet he never took his eyes from hers. Kelly shivered from his intense stare. Without a word, he turned, and she followed.

John took her to a room she'd never been in before. It was private, thank God, not that she cared anymore. Kelly found it liberating, not to care. All her attention was centered utterly on *him*.

During the last week her head had been full of stupid thoughts, rumination, mental self-flagellation and just plain noise. Now there was nothing, only tranquil peace. It was such a relief to be under his protection. To be *his*, if only for tonight.

The room was fairly normal, large king size bed, spanking bench, St Andrew's cross, and various toys, and tools. The only difference was the desk and lap-top at the side of the room, with papers on it. That was different. Was John planning on getting some work done?

He turned around. "Hands," he said.

Kelly raised her wrists and John untied them, again without even one brush against her skin. How did he do that? It made her desperate. She ached to have him hold her, to kiss her, and be inside her again.

"Take your clothes off, Kelly."

"Yes, John," she said.

He watched impassively as she undressed, making no attempt to tease. This was a punishment, and he hadn't asked for that. Still, Kelly knew her body was prepared for him already. Just being near John made her wet. Her breasts swelled, and her nipples hardened in the hope that he may yet touch her.

"Turn around. Hands behind your back," he growled with dangerous menace.

When Kelly complied he buckled on a pair of leather, fur lined cuffs and locked them together. She noticed that he wasn't saying "thank you" to every order she obeyed, as he had before. Man, John was still seriously pissed off. Well, that was okay. She'd work through it, because no matter what happened, she wanted to be his – if he'd have her.

She bit her lip. If he still wanted her. Kelly was mad crazy in love with John Taylor and that was all there was to it.

Chapter 11

Happiness

"Back now," he ordered, and she turned back, face toward him.

John stared at her with that intense gaze, that look that made her whole body tremble with a combination of excitement, apprehension and raw desire. They stared at each other for a long moment. It was a wordless exchange, yet profound and extensive communication occurred with that one look.

His eyes may have been saying, 'I haven't decided if you're beyond redemption or not. I'm going to punish you, and hurt you, and then we'll both find out.' She would've said, 'Anything, John. I surrender. I'm yours. I've screwed up, and I trust your judgement to help me make it right.'

Did John know how much he affected her? Kelly felt certain that he did.

"Knees," he snapped.

This dominant command blasted her into a heated state of shameless lust. Was it the tone of his voice? Or the rough demand? Or the fact that her lips and mouth would be level with his cock? She swallowed and carefully went to her knees, well aware that he wasn't going to help her.

John pulled out a blindfold and put it over her eyes, locking it in place with the Velcro attachment.

"Be silent and be still. I'm going to jack off in your mouth, Kelly," he said. "You don't get to touch me and I'm not going to touch you with my hands. You don't even get to see me. The most you're getting is my cock on your lips and tongue, and my cum in your mouth. I'm still seriously displeased with you. Wet your lips, and don't move."

"Yes John," she whispered, liberally coating her lips with moisture.

Kelly smelled his rich musky male scent, and then felt the heat of him near her face. She inhaled, simply wanting to breathe him in, intoxicated by the smell of him. She'd have to concentrate not to make a sound and to remain motionless, because just the thought of him made her entire body quiver with a primal, powerful need to take him into her mouth and lick and suck him.

John pressed his cock against her and rubbed the head of it around her wet lips. She felt a thrill of elation, because there was plenty of pre-cum there, so he wasn't as unaffected as he had pretended.

The memory of the first time he'd climaxed in her mouth while trapped in the dark elevator shadowed the present, and her body trembled. The sounds of pleasure he had made, the joyous kiss he had given her afterwards, with his heartfelt, "Thank you, Kelly." My God, she'd never felt so happy, knowing that she'd made him happy.

John loved her mouth, and he wanted to use it. Fuck, she really wanted to be used by this powerful Dom. *But only by him.* Kelly felt her entire body flush with heat. *I belong to John.*

Jesus, she thought, and once more she stifled a moan, her skin tingled from the magnetic pull of John Taylor. *If I spend the entire night without a single orgasm I'll be okay with that.*

For the first time in her life, Kelly 'got' the full meaning of a being a true sub with the Dom she loved. John's happiness was hers. His unhappiness was hers. It was a simple concept, but the simple things were often the most profound.

Yes, yes, this is perfect, she thought, there on her knees, with her hands bound behind her back, and her Dom using her body for his pleasure. Right there and then, Kelly knew what made her happy, and it wasn't anything at all to do with her.

It was *all* to do with John, and what he wanted. What he needed.

My God. I really am in love.

John's cock was hot and hard yet the velvet skin of it was soft. Kelly was desperate to please him. She couldn't see anything, and John was silent, withholding all sounds of pleasure.

She knew that he was doing this on purpose, to make the experience less for her. That was fine, because she trusted him. John knew what she needed. Already he'd taught her so much. The man seemed to understand her better than she understood herself. What else would he help her discover?

The rhythmic sound of skin slapping back and forth rapidly came to her ears, and she felt his cock jerking against her lips. Remaining silent and still was difficult. She craved him so badly, to lick, to taste and suck but instead she controlled her own ferocious physical responses in favor of his needs. John came first.

"Open wide," he ordered in a husky, lust filled voice.

Kelly opened broadly, which was easy with a mouth the size of hers. Mercifully, John put his entire cock inside her. His cum jetted and Kelly swallowed greedily as his twitching shaft pulsed and his hot seed sprayed again and again in intermittent spurts. As he came he made only one barely audible grunt, but to her it sounded almost as beautiful as a love song.

His semen flooded her mouth, and she gasped and gulped as she swallowed him down. She felt then, that her reason for living was to please John, and to make him happy. It was crazy, but somehow as mad as it sounded – it *felt* right.

This was why she was here. For him.

Chapter 12

Bullwhip

John reached around and took off the blindfold. Leaving her cuffs on, he detached them from each other, so her hands were free.

"Now," he said. "Up on the bed on all fours, ass in the air. Rest on your forearms." He followed her to the bed, checking her obedience. When she complied he said, "Arch your back so that ass is higher, that's right. And spread your legs further apart. Perfect. Stay there until I'm ready for you."

The position wasn't difficult to maintain. John went to his desk, and started doing paperwork, Kelly could hear him sometimes turning pages, or typing on the laptop. Okay, he was going to make her wait. Well, if it was going to make him happy, she'd wait for him as long as he liked.

A memory of the week before intruded. "I can't be gentle," he'd said with that raw animal urgency that had so astonished her. Kelly could almost feel the head of his cock at her entrance, and his coarse pubic hair rubbing against her sensitive clit. The powerful thrust as he rammed into her swollen flesh. She bit back a moan, and tried to remain still. Arousal trickled down her thighs, and heavy sexual heat pooled in her lower belly.

Jesus, John, she thought. *Waiting is hard.*

Kelly was an action person, not a sit-and-do-nothing kind of girl. Anything would be better than waiting, particularly when swallowing John's cum had made her feel so aching and empty and horny.

Fuck me, hurt me, do anything you want but please somehow at least do something, she thought desperately. When she began to feel so frantic that she considered chewing the bed sheets, she heard him get up from his desk and approach her.

"What's your safe word, Kelly?" he asked mildly.

"It's still daisies, John."

Kelly had decided to change it initially, but as the week progressed, she realized that she didn't need to. Daisies were still her favorite flower and it wasn't their fault she had misused the word. Yes, she'd called her safe word when she hadn't needed to. But she'd gotten past that, and she'd learned something important from the entire experience.

"Good," he said. He moved close to her head, looking at her turned face as it rested on the bed. "Kiss my bullwhip, Kelly," he said, and raised the curled whip to her lips.

Shit! Yet her compliance was instinctive and she kissed his whip.

"That's right, Kelly. You need to kiss my whip, because it will be kissing you. My bullwhip will enjoy touching your soft, untested flesh. You've never been whipped before have you?

"No, John." She swallowed nervously, and her pussy pounded, along with the sound of her heartbeat in her ears. Even though she hated the idea of being whipped, his dominance was sexually inflaming her, making her crave him. She felt desperate for his cock. She wanted it inside her, anywhere he wanted to put it.

Everything about John made her think of sex. His baritone voice by itself was an aphrodisiac; the sensual cadence, tone and quality. Simply the way he said her name sent her body into a thrum of arousal.

"You've never been punished except by hand? No riding crops? Nothing?"

"That's right, John."

"Good. I love breaking in a virgin," he said callously. "Now stay very still and don't forget to use your safe word if you need to." He moved back some distance, and while Kelly couldn't exactly see him, she could hear him. He was swinging his whip.

"Crack!"

Holy shit! It must have been a practice strike as the whip hadn't touched her. The sound itself was enough to scare her to death. Kelly trembled but she shut her eyes, gritted her teeth and didn't move. She didn't want pain, she didn't. But if this was how John wanted to punish her, then so be it. Whatever he wanted.

"Crack!" The sound came again.

"Are you going to use your safe word, Kelly?"

"No."

"Why not? I thought you were afraid of my bullwhip."

"I am, John, but right now I don't care anymore," she said in her frank, outspoken manner. "If you think I need to be whipped, then that's okay with me. I did wrong, and I'll accept any punishment you want. I need to make things right with you again, John. There's nothing I won't endure in order to do that."

There was a long pause while Kelly quivered, waiting for the first blow.

Unexpectedly Kelly felt John's warm fingers run along her back. The stroke of his hand was electric. It sent a current of joy running right through her, the instant she felt his warm male caress. Her eyes stung with fresh tears and her lungs expanded on a deep audible breath that was virtually a sob of surprise.

My God. I don't think that I can learn to live without his perfect touch.

John hadn't physically contacted her even when putting on the club tie or when ejaculating in her mouth. It was a cruel punishment but he seemed to have relented. God, she was so thankful for this mercy, for this kindness.

Kelly recalled when she was trapped in the elevator with him, when he'd said, "Do you feel my fingers?" while stroking down to her breasts. He'd made her body burn with an unfamiliar and utterly shameless sexual need. And now he was touching her again.

But why? Why hadn't he whipped her? Kelly wanted John to punish her, because how else would she earn his forgiveness?

Chapter 13

Spanking

"Come here, Kelly," he said quietly.

She opened her eyes and turned toward him. John's beautiful face was still utterly impassive and contained, yet his eyes seemed soft and bright.

He outstretched his arms, and Kelly jumped up and flew into them with a sob. Hard and muscular, John was like a big solid Oak tree – there was no give in him. He easily took her weight as she wrapped her legs around him, and clung on as if he were a life raft in a rough open sea. He stroked her and patted her and murmured soft sounds while she cried and cried, making his collarbone thoroughly wet.

"I'm sorry, John," she sobbed, her breath hitching.

He walked over to a comfortable chair and sat down with her on his lap, curled into him. "Beautiful girl," John said softly, running his hand through her hair in an absorbing sensation of tactile delight. He pulled a handkerchief out of his pocket and gave it to her. Kelly gasped and gave a strangled giggle when she saw it, remembering how he'd given her one in the elevator. Taking it gratefully, she used it to wipe her tears.

"I don't want to whip you, Kelly. How can your Dom punish you when you have already so thoroughly punished yourself?" he asked her. Her unavoidable response was more tears, and to squeeze him even harder. John was patient, and simply petted her and soothed her until she settled.

"Tell me what you did wrong, Kelly," he said.

"I should have trusted you," she burst out, happy to be able to get her transgression off her chest. "We had a connection. I know we did. I was stupid not to remember that. But I'm a naive person, John. I've been caught out so many times believing in people or things, just because I prefer everything to be happy. I can face a fight, and I can stick up for myself. It isn't that. It's just that I like happy endings, and soft furry animals, and I prefer to think of everyone in the world as kind and trustworthy. It's in my nature to be gullible, because I want to believe. I wanted romance, and love, and I wanted you. I know I'm rambling and I'm sorry, John."

"Kelly, tell me what you did wrong. Exactly," he said, reminding her of his question.

"I used my safe word."

"No," John said. "You did the right thing by using your safe word. Always use it when you don't feel safe, Kelly. That's what it's there for. You should've used for the bullwhip. That's a subject we will discuss later. I know you don't want that."

"I honestly didn't care anymore, John. What were a few painful welts, compared to the idea of losing you?"

His eyes softened, as he stroked her cheek with a knuckle. "Thank you, Kelly. I'm glad that you didn't change that word. Daisies suit you."

Kelly couldn't help it, she had to laugh. She covered her mouth and continued to giggle. "Yes, daisies are soooo me."

"Answer my question now, Kelly," John said his voice firming. "What did you do wrong?"

She inhaled a long breath and expelled it. "I should've trusted you. You were my Dom. I did trust you, John. You saved my life in that elevator. I just doubted everything when I saw that file."

"No. Your doubts were not wrong, Kelly," he said. "In fact your fearful reaction to seeing that I had a file on you was both intelligent and rational. Honestly? I admired your response. You were protecting yourself. I don't want you to blindly trust anyone, not even me. Why should you? I could have been a sociopath, how would you know? No, doubting me was not what you did wrong."

"Oh," she sniffed. "Huh. Well, thank you. That actually that makes a lot of sense. I didn't think of that."

"Think now, Kelly," John said, and an odd little smile played about his mouth. He gave her hair a gentle pull of reprimand. "Use that brain of yours that, I know you have, and tell me what you did wrong."

"I should have talked to you," she said. "Instead I just ran away."

"If you're afraid for your safety you should run, Kelly," he said. "It seems sensible. That file was a serious head trip. I'd forgotten that it was there. When I think about you finding it, and no doubt looking through it…" He shook his head. "Well, I'm surprised you didn't just jump out of the nearest window to escape."

Kelly giggled. "Really?" Man, he was making her feel so much better. She'd been beating herself up all week, when her actions hadn't been irrational or even that bad. But, what was her mistake then? Why was he disciplining her?

"Yes, really. Now what did you do wrong, Kelly?" he asked her, continuing to repeat the initial question. He gave her an unexpected pinch on the bottom. "You don't know, do you?"

Perplexed and frowning, she just stared at him.

With startling speed, John flipped her over on to her stomach and Kelly gave a little squeal of surprise. Lying across John's lap, she curled her arms around his strong male legs, feeling the strength in his calf muscles and pressing her face up against his leather pants. John smelled divine, and the scent of him stirred the memories of all the carnal pleasures she experienced a week ago in his bed.

"I'm going to spank you until you figure it out." His deep voice took on a dangerous growl.

Horny and already experiencing a building orgasm, Kelly began to throb and ache with the thought of a spanking. There was just something erotic about being spanked that made her body and her entire lower torso convulse with forbidden, wicked ecstasy. Unconsciously she moaned, but then his hand came down on her naked bottom.

Crack!

Kelly almost bit her tongue off she was so staggered. No warm up, nothing to get her ready. Wow. John really planned to punish her. Holy Christ Almighty! Was the man's hand made of wood?

Crack!

Kelly ground her teeth together trying to prevent a scream, and then shut her eyes while attempting to absorb the pain. She hadn't been counting, but it didn't take many of those hard blows before she was sweating, with her hands bunched in small tight fists.

Crack! Crack! Crack! Crack!

He wasn't giving her time to acclimatize, to focus and prepare for pain, and fucking hell, the man wasn't holding anything back! She began to scream, and thrash, and cry, "Owww! Oww! Ah! Ah!" Jesus, her ass felt like it was on fire.

"Kelly, tell me what you did wrong," he said, pausing for a moment and running his hand over her smarting backside. Strong male fingers moved in sensuous, slow circles on her throbbing, stinging buttocks.

Kelly was panting, and she saw the shine of sweat on her arms. Shit, that's right. She'd forgotten that she was supposed to be working out what she did wrong. "Ah, John," she panted. "I'm sorry but, um, I can't seem to think very well just at the moment."

"That's too bad," he said with a bark of laughter, "for you."

Chapter 14

Thank You

⁓

Still laughing, John continued raining down his sharp, punishing blows. Mercilessly he spanked her, left cheek, right, alternating strikes without a break. Her whole body was thrashing, John had to hold her down. She had no ability to control herself, and was breathless and screaming the entire time. *Fuck it hurt.*

He stopped, and his hands fondled her buttocks once more. "Kelly, do you want me to help you to remain still?"

So polite, she thought. The considerate question was just John all over. Kelly let out a long choking breath, aware that her whole body was shaking and her face was covered in tears. No wonder he'd said 'don't wear makeup.' It wouldn't have stayed on.

"Yes thank you, John," she said with a ragged sob.

"Hands behind your back," he ordered, and when she did as he asked he took her wrist cuffs and locked them together, holding them with one firm hand. "Thank you, Kelly," he said.

Her breath hitched with that courtesy, the one she'd become familiar with the week before. John had wonderful, nearly chivalrous manners. During the night they'd spent together he'd treated her with so much respect, and nearly reverence. As if her submission was the most valuable gift in the world, or as if she was. Something about that thought niggled at her.

John put his right thigh over her legs, holding them down firmly, his erection pressed against her hip. Trapping her between his hard male thighs confused Kelly's focus. She lost concentration and her trail of thought. She was bent over with her ass even higher in the air, but now she was constrained.

"Would you like a hint, Kelly, before I continue? So that you can remember what you did that offended your Dom?"

Despite the pain, she closed her eyes from a wave of intense pleasure because John had said, 'your Dom.' Oh God, she really wanted him. She needed to be his. Did he still want her, too?

John gave her time to answer. He continued to caress her burning buttocks, occasionally dipping his fingers down to find the wash of moisture between her legs, evidence that despite the pain, she was still majorly turned on. Kelly could feel the hard heat of John's massive erection in this position, and foolishly, even with the fires of hell scorching her backside, she felt so happy it was beyond ridiculous.

John had said, 'your Dom.' Those words alone were more than enough to send her into an upward spiral of euphoric joy.

"Nope," Kelly replied cheerfully. "I'm not desperate yet, John. I'll figure it out." She giggled, deciding to show him that she could take whatever he could dish out – as long as he could. John's hand must be smarting. And that aching erection of his would want relief, too.

Crack!

Shit it hurt, but she was okay with it. This was a punishment, and honestly it felt good to be spanked. She deserved this. It was cathartic. All would be as it was before; she just had to endure this. Kelly knew that once she got through the pain threshold it wouldn't hurt that much anyway.

Crack!

John began to strike her hard, harder, the flat of his hand hitting her rounded buttocks, making them flinch, wobble and shake. She focused on not tightening up, relaxing into the blows, and trying to accept it. This discipline was from John, and she trusted him, and she loved him.

Without thinking she raised her bottom up, wanting more attention from his cruel spanking hand that slapped and heated her buttocks so tantalizingly.

Crack! Crack! Crack!

John was a gentleman, and that seemed a strange thought because of the way he was beating her ass with such savage vengeance. But he was. Always please and thank you. Never impolite, or rude.

I belong to him, Kelly thought, and all her worries and pain simply went away. The ball of tension inside her eased, and her clenched fists released as she accepted and even sought his punishment. *Must be endorphins,* she thought dreamily. A future spread before her, one with John in it. It made her happy. A familiar sensation of lightheaded euphoria flowed through her, despite the ringing pain.

The answer came to her then. It was so obvious that she began to laugh. "I know what I did, John," she said.

All spanking ceased. His left hand continued to grip her wrists in the cuffs behind her back, and his right leg pinned her, holding her safe on his lap. *Safe.* Kelly realized that she felt safe and cared for. *Cherished.*

Right now she had nothing in the world to worry about, because she belonged to John. John would take care of her. Crazy but true.

"Oh, God," she said. "The way I spoke to you. I was so disrespectful. I'm sorry, John. I'd never normally talk like that to anyone, much less you. You really are so very important to me."

"Thank you, Kelly," he said. "That's correct, clever girl." And from her upside-down view of him, her heart skipped a beat when she looked up and saw John's handsome well-loved face.

"I forgive you," he said, giving her that mind-blowing, mesmerizing smile of his.

Chapter 15

Climax

Hard male fingers caressed and stroked her, soothing her abused flesh. "You told me once, Kelly," he said, "that you can sometimes climax with a spanking."

"Yes."

"I'd like to see that," he said, tracing her wet clit and slick folds, running his fingers just inside of her, and then cupping her pussy. "You feel so swollen, wet and ready for my cock, Kelly," he growled in that sexy deep voice of his. "Christ, I love your hot little cunt. I should just throw you down on the bed, and fuck you so hard, that you'll never want me to stop."

Kelly wanted to giggle, but she simply couldn't laugh after those fantastically seductive words. Not to mention the images those words conjured up.

"I don't ever want you to stop already, John," she said seriously. "Right now I'd like to spend at least a week in bed alone with you, ordering in room service, serving you as your sub, and making you as happy as humanly possible. I really want to make you happy, John. I love to see you smile."

He exhaled sharply, clearly affected by her words. Acute sexual tension buzzed in the air that surrounded them, almost palpably encompassing them both. The way John looked at her made Kelly's breath come short and fast and her pulse ratchet up another couple of notches.

"Yes," he said. "I'll put that idea at the top of my list." John's thumb was on her clitoris, circling seductively, then pulling back the hood and teasing her. Aching and needy, she whimpered.

"I'm a list person, Kelly. I've a list of goals, and I work toward them. I'm not a man who ever gives up, once I put something on my list." He inserted two fingers deep within her aching channel, and she moaned. An intense pulse of sensation rolled through her body.

"A week alone in bed together, sometime soon," he said confidently. "The thought of having you all to myself, with nothing for you to do, except serve me..." He blew out another audible breath. "And you already make me happy, Kelly. More than I've ever been before."

Abruptly he pulled his fingers out and spread her butt cheeks with both hands. Then he began to lick the round puckered area of her anus, probing and delving, curling his tongue inside. Taken by surprise, she gasped and jumped. The muscles of her stomach, pelvis and buttocks contracted violently, not to mention the sensitive nerves in her empty pussy where his fingers had been.

"Jesus, God!" she shouted, astonished by the naughty wicked pleasure of it.

John chuckled. "So responsive. You liked that. Good." He began stroking her tight hole with a finger, gently pulling the ring until he managed to push inside, perhaps up to his first knuckle. "You're very tight, Kelly, but I'll train you to take my cock. You're going to love it. I can tell."

"God, John," she moaned, squirming and desperate.

"You need to climax," he said. "That's pretty obvious. Shall I spank you until you do?"

"Yes, if you'd like to, John. Spank me until I come. I want to come for you."

"Very well," he said. "But this is not a punishment. This spanking is for your pleasure. Show me how you come for me, by my hand. You climax from my touch, no matter if it's gentle, or hard. You want me, don't you?" he crooned in a seductive whisper.

"Oh, God, yes," she said. "I want you more than I've ever wanted anything in my life."

"Good," he said. "Because I want you, too."

Crack!

Rhythmically his hand struck her, sending shockwaves through her body. Kelly felt her heated core contract with each one, her buttocks clenching to this new, seductive beat. This spanking was different. Sensual. Erotic. Was it simply his intention that made the difference? Or was it the fact that he'd said he wanted her? All the happiness in the world seemed to be hers with those words.

John kept up a steady, predictable rhythm, slow at first, and then faster. Like the strokes one might receive from a man during intercourse, solid, long, hard slaps, and then shorter, faster as he came closer to climax.

Her body quivered, her belly clenched and her womb wept and pulsed while John delivered blows to her ass. The pain was both terrible and wonderful.

Kelly felt his hard hand and his hard cock, and she knew that he was enjoying spanking her. *I'm making John happy,* she thought. She imagined herself as he'd see her, her white ass red with multiple handprints, trembling and shaking, while she squirmed against his strong thighs and cock, enduring his blows. Accepting everything.

For him. To please him.

Her whole body tightened with that thought. *Oh, fuck!* A shudder was growing, something huge within her molten core.

Crack!

"That's right," John said in a husky, lust filled voice. "You're going to come for me now, aren't you, Kelly? Let me hear it. Show me how much you love my touch, how much you want me. Come. Come. Now."

"Ah, ah, ah, ah," she sobbed. "Oh, God, Oh, God, Ooohhh God!!!" She was shaking uncontrollably. It was huge, it was too much – sensations overwhelmed her. Such exquisite pain, such exquisite pleasure. "Johhhnnnn!" Kelly wailed her frenzied orgasm, bucking and shaking.

John picked her up even before her climax had finished, and laid her across the bed on her stomach, her hands still cuffed behind her back. He left her there, as he undressed. Kelly was in a bliss-filled fog, winded and breathless, trembling uncontrollably and jerking with every aftershock.

When he returned, he gripped her hips. Kelly felt his hard thighs against her, and his knee nudged her, making her spread her legs further apart.

Gentle hands stroked her abused buttocks, fondling and squeezing. "You look amazing, Kelly," he said, positioning himself. She felt his hard shaft against her entrance and shut her eyes with the sensation of it.

"Such a perfect ass. I'm going to fuck it later, but right now I'm taking your cunt. I'm going to watch this burning red ass of yours move underneath me. It's so damn gorgeous. You're on the pill, Kelly?"

She gave a half laugh and murmured into the bed sheet. "It's in my file, John. I won't get pregnant."

"I know. Just making sure you're still taking it," he said. "I should have spoken about this before, but you're clean and so am I. I don't want to use a condom. I want to shoot my cum in you, Kelly. I want to feel it when I finger you, knowing my seed is up inside you, making you even slicker for me." His finger's gripped her sex, parting her folds and teasing her with his cock.

She moaned, incredibly aroused by his raunchy words, and the demanding way he said them.

"Would you like me to shoot my hot cum deep inside you? Marking you as mine? Because you are mine, aren't you, Kelly? You belong to me."

"Oh, God, yes," she said breathlessly.

"Good," he said with a possessive satisfaction in his voice. He was still teasing her, rubbing his erection back and forth against her entrance. Almost absently he fingered the small swollen bundle of nerves of her clit, rubbing it in sensual, circular strokes,

"You're so wet for me. My cock is bathed already, slick with your sweet arousal."

Kelly squirmed and sobbed, "Please, John. Please. I need to feel you inside me."

"Soon, beautiful girl," he said. "I'm going to fuck you so hard you're going to climax for me again. Only this time you will come with my cock deep inside your tight needy cunt, won't you?"

"Yes, John, yes," she whimpered.

"But you can't climax without my permission," he reminded her.

"Never, John, I'll only come when you allow it."

"Good." Without warning he thrust deep inside, stretching the sensitive, swollen walls of her sex. It felt so amazing that she shouted out from the pleasure of it. He was thick and hard and without the condom she could feel him so much better as his cock twitched inside her. He leaned over her body, and wrapped a hand in her hair, twisting it and pulling it back as leverage.

She called out, something incomprehensible.

John chuckled and his breath gusted over her ear. "You like that, don't you?" he asked in a seductive whisper. "When I pull your hair?"

"God, yes!"

"Good, because I'm going to have one hand yanking your hair, and one on your cuffed wrists. I need something to pull against while I ram my cock into you. This is going to be a hard, fast fuck, Kelly. I've had to wait all week to have you again, and I'm not waiting a moment longer."

She whimpered at that sexy, hungry demand and the internal walls of her sex clenched hard on his cock in a pre-orgasmic pulse.

He gave her hair a hard tug. "Not yet," he said.

She swallowed. "I'm okay, it's okay." She blew out a deep breath, barely able to stop her climax. Jesus she was close.

John began to drive himself into her then, in short, fast, rhythmic thrusts. She pushed back against him, feeling him deep, and right up against her cervix. It took only moments, it couldn't last long. Their hunger for each other was too urgent, frenzied, and greedy. Moaning and straining, both tried to push themselves into each other, reaching the pinnacle and about to go over.

Sensations had mounted, bringing Kelly's whole body into overload.

The burning feeling of her buttocks, with John's hard thighs and hips rubbing up against her hypersensitive, over-stimulated skin. The tingling sting of her scalp as he pulled her hair, needing the leverage as he strained to push himself even deeper inside. The stretched feeling of fullness from his thick cock, as her body trembled to accommodate his savage, hammering thrusts. The sensation of being bound to his will, with her hands cuffed behind her back.

John gripped her wrists hard, holding her, using her for his pleasure, possessing her completely.

"Yes," he shouted, putting a hand down between her legs and rapidly flicking her clitoris. "That's it. Come for me, Kelly, my beautiful girl. Let me feel you milk my cock." Pumping in fast, short strokes, he continued to drive his hard body against hers.

Kelly was well-versed in withholding her orgasms, but this devastating sensual onslaught had severely tried her control. Exploding with relief, she came instantly upon John's command in a vaginal and clitoral climax that made her entire body spasm and tighten.

The rolling orgasmic pulses went on and on. For a moment she thought she may black out, as she couldn't even breathe between such violent, euphoric contractions.

"Yes, squeeze me, Kelly. Fuck that feels good," John growled.

She felt a convulsive shudder move through his powerful frame. John's thick cock jerked against her internal walls as he sprayed his hot cum, emptying himself inside of her. With a ragged groan, he murmured, "Kelly" as he climaxed.

It was something he'd never done before.

When she heard her name sound out from John's beautiful lips, Kelly felt a wave of elation, and climaxed again from the sheer pleasure of it.

Chapter 16

Last Sunday

Head on John's chest, Kelly enjoyed the feel of his body lifting and dropping with each breath. His heart thudded in a slow, steady rhythm in her ear. She cuddled into him, playing with the crisp black hair that lightly covered his chest and trailed seductively down his abs toward his pubic area.

John didn't usually let her touch him, so she was taking full opportunity of the chance. Her hand moved to gently rest on his flat stomach. Jeez, he was beautiful. Kelly was happy just to look at him, drinking him in.

They were both completely fucked out, and temporarily exhausted. She'd only just landed back in the 'real world,' having gotten past the boneless, brainless, post orgasmic phase.

The musk of sex perfumed the air. John had spread her and licked her into another couple of mind-blowing orgasms. After that he had taken her twice more before stopping for a break. Pounding her into the mattress with frantic tension, he'd ridden her hard, telling her, "You're mine, Kelly Flynn," and "You were made for me."

He'd used her body exactly as he wished, his coarse authoritative demands creating heady spikes of burning sexual desire. Again and again John ordered: "Come now, Kelly, come for me," easily sending her over the edge and off into sexual oblivion.

It was insane. The man's ever ready dick simply never softened. Was it always that way? If so, just how did he sleep at night? But maybe he was only this ardent with her? Kelly hoped so. She'd never known such a keen, inexhaustible lover, or a better one.

"Tell me what happened after you left me last Sunday," he said.

She rolled over, onto her back, her mind recalling. It had been such a terrible week. He propped his head up on an arm looking down at her, and she smiled up at him, instantly diverted by his beauty. His bicep bulged just by bending and holding his head. His chest was muscular and sexy and perfect – in fact everything about him was utterly compelling. Her fingers trailed across him, tracing the ridges of his abdomen.

Why me? Kelly thought for the hundredth time. *What does this amazing commanding Dom see in me?*

John's dark expressive eyes were bright with interest, his body language indicating that Kelly had every bit of his attention. He ran a finger over her bottom lip. "What happened Sunday after you left?" he asked calmly once more, apparently undisturbed by the delay in her reply.

What had John said before? Oh yeah. "I love listening to you talk, Kelly." How lucky was she? She suppressed the impulse to giggle. Talking was one of her favorite things, sex with John was another. Did life get any better than it was for her right now?

"Last Sunday," she said, inhaling a deep sustaining breath. "Hummm. Alright, I'll tell, but I'm warning you, John. It isn't pretty."

Kelly explained how she had gone to dinner at the family home, and had spoken to her brother Richard. She told him how his manager, Colin, had explained everything on Tuesday night, and how upset she was. How she'd bought a new bustier to wear for him, maxing out her credit, and how he hadn't even noticed. Writing the letter, being ignored and rejected, him taking Rosslyn from the sub gallery, and not her, including the fact that she'd felt like an unloved puppy.

As she was feeling herself again, Kelly talked and talked. John never once stopped her verbal diarrhea, not that he ever had previously, even when she'd been a child. Instead he just watched her with that sweet faint smile on his handsome face. They were both online with each other again. She felt so comfortable being with him. It was as if she had known him forever.

"John," Kelly said finally finishing up. "That was the worst week in my entire life. I never want to suffer like that again. Honestly. It would have been kinder to just shoot me."

John had been stroking her hair, twisting it in his fingers and creating a heavenly tactile delight. After that last comment his finger moved to her face, tracing her eyebrows, her lips and even her eyes. "Kelly, that was the worst week in my entire life, too. When you get to know me better, you'll understand what I mean, but to say that was the worst week in my life is saying something."

"Really?" she said and sat up, propping her head on her hand so she mirrored him.

"Yes."

"Did you like my letter?"

"I want to frame that letter in gold and diamonds."

Kelly giggled. "Honestly?"

John smiled back at her and once more she felt almost dumbstruck by his beauty. Damn he was the most gorgeous man in the entire world. What did he see in her? But he was looking at her in that way again, that way that made her heart beat out of rhythm. It wasn't a smoldering desire for sex – though there was that in his face, too. It was that intense expression of connection again, and love.

"I noticed your new bustier," he said, "and it made me hard. Particularly when I considered that you may have bought it for me to enjoy."

She laughed. "I think everything makes you hard."

"And just so you know," John said. "I've never once taken a club member's file home."

Surprised, flattered, and shocked she said, "Seriously?'

"Yours is the only file I've ever taken home – and I read it more than once. Your intuition wasn't wrong, Kelly. The moment you became a full member at The Basement all my mind was focused on you. The night I joined you in the elevator, well, I actually did that on purpose. I'd finally gotten up the nerve to ask you out."

"Wow," she said. "That's just… well. I'm happy about it, John. I'm glad I attract you. I don't see why of course, but I'm grateful for that fact."

It was such a mystery. What did he see in her?

Chapter 17

Brave

John took a deep breath in, and she became a little alarmed when his expression became decidedly grave.

"I decided to punish you so cruelly for more than one reason, Kelly," he said. "I wanted to discover if you thought I was worth fighting for. You may have given up, you know, when you had time to reflect upon what you were doing. I'm Father John, the sadist, and you don't like pain, remember? It was a test. Because I thought it might be easier for you if you changed your mind. To come to your senses and to live without me…"

She began to interrupt in protest but John just put his finger on her lips, silencing her.

"Hush now," he said. "It's my turn to speak. I never intended to use my bullwhip on you, Kelly. But I fully appreciate the fact that you were willing to do something so terrifying… for me."

John picked up her free hand and bit the fleshy part of her palm *hard*, surprising her with a sharp twinge of pain. Then he licked and kissed where he had bitten it, sending a frisson of sensation right through her. *Wow.*

John didn't let go of her hand.

"My courageous girl," he said in a low voice. "Even as a child you were ridiculously brave. I was so surprised when you went to the school principle for me, did you know that? You didn't even know me then. Why did you do it? You shouldn't have done it, Kelly. You must have been frightened. Those bullies would certainly have exacted revenge if they found out." He shook his head in disbelief. "Who wouldn't admire your courage?"

Kelly's heart swelled so much that there was a strange ache in her chest. Her mind was empty of all thought, her throat became tight, and her eyes stung. She didn't have anything to say, even if John would let her speak. No words could express how she was feeling anyway.

As if well aware of her overwhelming emotions, John squeezed her hand. While his expression was still impenetrable, he gazed at her with softness in his eyes. "But I just had to keep pressing. And I tried to frighten you away with my bullwhip. By then I realized that I'd been intentionally pushing you away. I was expecting you to quit. A part of me wanted you to give up, to run away and escape me. Why didn't you? I know I scare you. I don't understand why you want me. You're an amazing person, Kelly, and you're far too good for me."

Bringing her hand to his lips, he softly nibbled and then kissed her knuckles. "I don't deserve you."

Kelly kept her mouth shut, because he'd told her to do so. Yet she knew that her frown was communicating to John her utter disagreement with what he was saying.

He laughed. "I should tell you to hush more often," he observed. "Then maybe I can get a word in."

To Kelly, who loved to sing, John's laughter was more beautiful than the music from an all-boys choir. The man needed to smile and laugh more often, she decided. If she was his sub, she'd make sure that he did.

"It's true anyway, however much you doubt it," he said. "I don't deserve you. I was pitiless and brutal to you last week. I made you face so much. I meant to make it difficult, I wanted you to run. But you never did. You never even faltered, my brave and beautiful girl."

"You really are remarkable." His knuckles grazed her face. "I began to hope then. I thought that if you could bear that punishment, then maybe you could take me on. I'm not going to be easy, Kelly. You'll have to teach me everything. I've no idea about social situations; honestly the only thing I know is how to dominate a sub. When you get to know me better you'll understand."

He squeezed her hand once more and gave her a fierce look. "I need you so much more than you need me."

He cupped her face, and his thumb rubbed her bottom lip again. "Do you really want me as your Dom, Kelly? I find that so difficult to understand. I'm damaged. I'm broken – and you're perfect." He gave her a teasing little smile. "And you can talk now, by the way."

That was just as well, as Kelly was afraid she'd burst if she had to remain silent much longer. "Do I want you?" She knew she was grinning like a jack-o'-lantern, but she didn't care. "Are you kidding? I'm bat-shit crazy over you!"

John frowned at that, and she couldn't read him. The man was such a mystery, but so what? They would sort it out over time. And whatever his flaws, or issues, they'd work through them together. She wanted him more than anything she had ever wanted in her whole life.

"Listen to me, Kelly," he said. "When I got your letter I almost cried. I didn't – but if I knew how to, I probably would have. You don't understand yet, but I can't remember ever being able to cry – except once after my aunt died, when I was with someone I trusted. Tears are something I just can't do. Normal human emotions are another."

John leaned over and kissed her. Kelly melted into the gentle, loving caress he gave her with his lips. It was a kiss of love, not lust. He gave her a faint smile. "But I suspect that you have enough emotions for both of us."

She snorted and grinned at that. "You got that right."

He cleared his throat. "Anyway, after I received your letter, I wrote you a letter back."

"Oh, John," she said feeling an excited little twist inside. "You wrote me a letter? That's so sweet."

He jumped up and got an expensive looking box out of his vest pocket. It appeared to be something one would get from an up market jewelry store. With an unreadable expression, he handed it to her. Kelly sat up, crossing her legs Indian fashion and took the box from him, frowning in confusion. "Where's the letter?"

"I'm not going to give it to you yet."

Kelly cracked up laughing. John was such a strange man, he honestly was. Yet she loved everything about him, even his unpredictable, inexplicable behavior. "Alrighty then," she said cheerfully taking this news in her stride. "I don't get my letter yet. Fine. So, what's in the box?"

John stood near the bed, standing apart from her, tense and stiff. Kelly could feel the change in him. Even though he was wearing his impassive mask, his face had darkened slightly, and she knew he was suddenly wound up tight.

Kelly reflected that she was actually beginning to read him better. What was his problem? Was he nervous? She rather thought he might be.

"It's yours, Kelly," John said in an unnaturally impassive voice. "Why don't you open it and find out?"

She paused. Jesus, sometimes the man really did freak her out. The way he was acting, it was like there was a chopped off human ear or something disgusting like that inside this innocuous little container. What was with the tension?

John was certainly making her uneasy, and a little frightened to open the box.

Chapter 18

What's In The Box?

Apprehensively, Kelly opened the box.

"Oh my God! Look at this! It's soooo gorgeous!" she exclaimed.

Inside was the most beautiful ring. Kelly had never seen anything like it before. Pink sapphires and diamonds were set in gold, creating a unique pattern. The circular focal point of the design appeared to be a gorgeous bouquet of pink and white daisies.

"Oh. My. God. It's beautiful, John," she exclaimed, bouncing up and down on the bed in her excitement. "Where did you find it? It must have cost a fortune. You bought this for me?"

John crawled back to the middle of the bed and sat back, resting against the headboard. Then he pulled Kelly across his lap. "I designed it and had it made this week. I gave the jeweler the order Sunday morning. Did you know some of the more reputable jewelers have a twenty-four hour phone service?"

"No," she said in a quiet voice, still shocked by his gift. "You designed and put an order in to have this made on Sunday morning? Right after I left?"

John nodded.

Kelly threw her arms around his neck and of course she started to cry. John's arms banded tight as rope around her waist, holding her as if he'd never let her go. She couldn't believe it. He must have been just as infatuated with her, as she'd been with him.

All week Kelly thought he didn't want her. Yet all that time he had suffered, too, while testing their relationship and giving her a chance to back out. What woman in her right mind wouldn't want John Taylor?

He remained silent, but his hands roamed over her back in a constant soothing caress. He patted her, and held her, until her crying and slowed.

Man, was this guy full of surprises or what?

The ring was so thoughtful, and it communicated so much. Daisies – her safe word. John always wanted her to be safe. He also understood how much she loved daisies, a plain, unpretentious and cheerful sort of flower. Daisies were sooo her, and John knew that, too. It was the most wonderful ring in the world, and he'd designed it, and had it made *for her*.

"What kind of ring is it?" Kelly sniffed, still feeling really emotional. She was just so happy! She pulled back from him to examine it from within its box once more. "Is it like a friendship ring, or what? Do you know what finger I'm supposed to wear it on?"

John shrugged. "In time, if it all works out, I was hoping that someday you might use it as engagement ring. If you decide you still want me… after you get to know me better."

Kelly turned on his lap to look directly at him, confused, astonished, and stunned. *Am I hearing things?* she thought. *Did John Taylor just propose to me in a totally bizarre, ass-backwards way?* With an intense look of naked longing, he returned her gaze. *Wow,* she thought. *There it was again, that amazing sense of connection.*

John added with quiet certainty, "I already know that I want you, Kelly, now and forever. I'll never want anyone else."

Kelly squealed, closed the box, and dropped it on the bed. Then she threw her arms around him again, kissing him passionately with her heart bursting in a mixture of enthusiasm, love, and hilarious indignation. Wouldn't you know it? John definitely needed her to teach him some social skills. That was no way for a man to propose!

Once more Kelly felt too emotional to even speak – which in her case was really saying something. She was only just beginning to understand the depth of his need for her. They fit together perfectly. What they had felt *so right*.

What started as a loving 'thank you' kiss – quickly fell into an all-consuming sexual need.

She LOVED the way John kissed. The high-handed man simply took over her mouth, and acted as if he would like to crawl right inside. His raw desire radiated with that bruising, passionate kiss. The man's focus was incredible. Intense. Absolute. It was as if he didn't kiss her *right now* he'd die, and didn't that make her feel special?

Kelly felt as if having John's firm demanding lips against hers, with his tongue in her mouth was the only thing real in the entire world.

Swollen and bruised, she thought fleetingly. *My mouth may never recover... ah, but what a way to go.*

Aware of John's response last time, Kelly sucked his tongue hard in a pulsing, milking manner. She imagined it was his cock, remembering how much he loved it when she went down on him. That was just as well, as she loved it, too. There was nothing better than hearing John make those little sounds of pleasure as she worked his hard thick shaft with her mouth. Sucking, tasting, nibbling, licking, and drinking him down.

"Kelly, you drive me crazy," he said, inhaling in a long breath. "Let's talk about the ring later. Right now I need my sub to serve me." He grabbed her hand, and thrust it down between her legs, making her cup her own mound. With his large male hand possessively covering hers, he squeezed her sex firmly.

"This is my cunt, isn't it?" he demanded in an abrupt, harsh voice. His dark eyes flickered dangerously, as if daring her to deny him.

Kelly heard herself moaning, "Yes, John, oh, oh, yes, it belongs to you. I belong to you, too. I want to give you whatever you need. Whatever you want."

He growled at that, crushing her to him. "You're mine," he rasped.

"Yes," she agreed.

Jesus. It was like pressing a button, and then having her whole body become instantly, desperately horny. Everything about him made Kelly think of sex. Trembling with anticipation, she realized that the rawness of John's male animal need for her was unquestionably the most effective aphrodisiac that she'd ever experienced.

Biting her ear, he licked and nuzzled into her throat. "I'm still deciding which of your luscious feminine holes I want to shoot my cum into first," he taunted deliciously.

He sucked on the skin of her neck, and a burning wave of arousal flowed through her, shooting sensation between her legs. Her clit responded instantly, it was as if he was sucking her *there*. No doubt she would have to wear a turtleneck sweater again to Sunday's family dinner, but she didn't care in the slightest.

"Your Dom is going to use every single part of your body for his pleasure, Kelly," he whispered seductively in her ear, sending a thrill of longing and lust down her spine. "Do you have any idea of all the things I want to do to you?"

Inflamed by his erotic words, she whimpered, "No, John."

He gave her a dark chuckle. "I've an entire bondage club here full of toys, an overactive imagination, and a lifetime full of fantasies, Kelly. And I plan to enact every single one of them with my very accommodating sub... starting right now."

"Yes, John," she said in a breathless, happy little sigh.

Chapter 19

Murder

Homicide Detective, Lorenzo Martin sat in the Portland Police Department and studied the file of available information.

The prominent psychologist, fifty-seven year old Professor Maria Christina Lopez had been murdered, bludgeoned to death in her residence Sunday morning, April 7th, between the hours of midnight and five a.m. Afterwards her documents were all emptied from her filing cabinets, and with petrol poured on the papers, her home was set alight. The fire department had prevented the entire house from going up in smoke, but there had not been much left as evidence. The good professor had been semi-retired, mainly writing, and had just one ongoing, active case.

His main suspect? John William Taylor, Professor Lopez' only client.

John Taylor was unemployed, the only child of a local district judge. A secretive, paranoid man, with documented mental health problems, his suspect had been estranged from his parents for years. Apparently he resided in Aloha only twenty minutes from the murder site. According to phone records, Mr. Taylor had called Professor Lopez the day before her death, and she had called him the day before she was killed.

Detective Martin stood up and checked his watch. It was late Saturday night, and he should've gone home hours ago. He needed to get some sleep.

Sunday morning will be soon enough, Detective Martin decided. *Tomorrow I'll have a word with Mr. John Taylor*, he thought with a grim little smile. *I'd like to find out if he can assist us with our inquiries.*

CONNECTED

5

Chapter 1

Colin Wilkins

"Do not be confused, *mon ami*, especially with your history. You of all Dom's must have this perfectly clear in your mind. BDSM first and foremost is about pleasure and fulfillment needs, for both Dom and sub. Physical pain is only one tool, and not even the most essential tool, necessary to achieve these goals."

- André Chevalier, conversation with John Taylor

Saturday night The Basement stayed open until 3:00 a.m. Just after that time, Colin Wilkins, the club manager was double checking that no one was still there. Using his security code, he keyed himself into the control room and shut the door behind him.

"What have you got, Jay? Anything?"

Stocky, muscular and fiftyish, Jay had gray hair, a crew cut, and the bearing of a military man. John Taylor liked Colin hiring ex-cops and soldiers, and he paid them really well. Colin sometimes wondered if John actually made any money from The Basement, because he seemed to put it all back into the club via excessive salaries, and constant equipment upgrades.

"Nope," Jay said. "Nada. Everyone is long gone, Colin. So long as you've checked room twelve?"

"Yeah," Colin said, feeling strangely comfortable with lying. "The monitor on that one is broken so no one was allowed to use it tonight – it's been locked up tight. I'll get it fixed this week."

"Right," Jay said standing up. "That's it then. See you tomorrow." Jay logged out by keying a code, which kept a record of the name of employee, and time of departure. With a heavy, booted stride, he left.

John Taylor, the man who owned The Basement, was a safety conscious businessman. When the club was open, a member of security monitored the close-circuit TV's in the control room. Twenty different screens needed constant review, thirteen separate scene rooms, the main area, four public play areas, the bar, and entrance.

Security Staff had an earpiece that kept them constantly updated from Control. Staff rotated into Control, and never spent more than one hour within its hallowed core. Everything was digitally recorded, and all of this was authorized within the membership contract.

John Taylor didn't want to take chances with "he said, she saids."

A person might suggest that his boss was paranoid, but Colin thought he was smart. The three contentious issues that they'd encountered in the four years since they had opened had been easily dealt with by playing back the security footage with the disagreeing parties present.

Curious, and also feeling a compulsion to check, Colin moved to the back of his monitor set up and plugged the viewing screen in. Then he switched on the monitor for scene room twelve.

"That's right, Kelly," Colin heard a husky voice say, "Take me deeper."

"Oh God," came a strangled female cry.

Then a male voice once more, a reassuring murmur, "Yes, yes. Perfect. Good girl."

Kelly Flynn had her hands bound to the bed board, cuffed together over her head, but those were the only BDSM trappings in evidence. Father John, the uncrowned king of merciless S & M games, was banging Ms. Flynn. This was no surprise. What was surprising was that John appeared to be having rather ordinary, and more or less missionary style sex.

Kelly's long, shapely legs were draped over her Dom. They rested just under his shoulders, her ass spread and lifted up high, to allow for really deep penetration. The woman was bent so far it looked like her bellybutton was pressed up against her backbone. She was going to have a serious vaginal orgasm in that position.

Hot damn, Colin thought.

The man was banging into her as hard and fast as a jack hammer. John's chest was heaving, his slim, powerful hips and thighs pumping. What Colin's boss lacked in the creative use of BDSM toys, he was making up in enthusiasm.

He was on his knees between Kelly's thighs with her ass tilted up in the air and man oh man was that boy giving her a pounding. The sound of flesh slapping against flesh, and the sight of John's balls swinging rhythmically, slapping into the woman's puckered anal ring caused Colin's own body to heat.

Kelly was curled upward, resting upon her shoulders. John was mounted, and pressed in close. Firmly squeezing one breast and nipple, the long fingers and thumb of his other hand were tight around her throat, in something like a collar, or perhaps he planned to use erotic asphyxiation? Cutting off oxygen and blood to the brain just prior to orgasm? The returning rush of blood and oxygen right at the point of climax could really spin a sub out, creating a unique high.

John didn't know her well enough to do something like that though – or did he?

"I own you, Kelly Flynn," Colin heard him say. "You're mine."

"Yes, John, oh yes!"

Kelly was sweating, whimpering, panting and keening, desperately holding back her orgasm no doubt by her Dom's command. Colin didn't know how long John had been edging his sub into this highly excited state, but Colin could tell by her eyes that she had been sexually tormented for an extended period of time. She looked mindless and euphoric – in a far off sub space of wanton sensual bliss.

Wow, Colin thought. *The man is good. How the hell had he learned Kelly's body so fast?*

Colin, a masterful Dom himself, knew that by carefully varying the intensity and speed of sexual stimulation, and by continually practicing with the same partner in order to intimately learn their responses, a sub could be held in a highly aroused state on the brink of orgasm. The entire process took keen observation and time, however, because no matter how attentive and watchful a Dom was, every woman or man was different, each unique to themselves.

"Who do you belong to?" came a gruff demand.

"You, John. I belong to you," Kelly sobbed, clearly desperate for release. Tears were running down her cheeks and Colin smirked. She was an emotional girl. He'd seen her crying before.

Colin gave a happy sigh. This erotic sexual denial could only improve the outcome. Kelly was going to have a massive orgasm – most likely multiple ones. Colin could tell. Ten to one she was a real screamer, too.

Chuckling, he sat down, and put his feet up on a desk with a broad grin. He may as well stick around and watch the show.

Chapter 2

Love and Scars

—⚮—

All I need is popcorn, Colin thought. *Or better yet, Donna. If my wife was here, I'd fuck her silly while we both watch, sitting right here in this chair.*

Colin expelled a sharp breath. Man, John was still working his sub *hard and fast.* He tried to recall, had he been that inexhaustible at age twenty-six? Kelly was off into the zone. At this point only the occasional, "Oh, God, oh, God," or "Please, oh please," was all she was managing to gasp.

Abruptly the woman convulsed and looked as if she was going to go over.

John eased for a moment, stopping all movement and bringing her back from the brink. "Good girl. You won't come until I tell you to, will you?"

"No, John," she panted.

"You have fantastic control, Kelly. You're the perfect submissive. I love watching when you come for me." The man began pumping again, but his thrusts were more directed, circling and twisting into different parts of his sub's cunt. "I love the way you come," he said. "The sounds you make, and the way your body explodes."

Kelly could only moan in response.

Colin noticed that no matter how close she came to climax, she kept her eyes open, staring at John. Her Dom had no doubt ordered that. The poor frantic woman was constantly keening now, in soft feminine sounds of exquisite, yet torturous, pleasure. Her cuffed hands were gripped into little taut fists, and her toes were tightly curled.

Whew! That woman is right at the end of her tether.

It was a simple basic scene, but Colin was blown away by the sexual heat of it, and unable to take his gaze off either of them. John was pounding fast again.

Smooth skin, young and firm, shining with sweat, and pushing against each other with a fierce almost combative need. Colin couldn't see John's eyes, but Kelly's were large, dilated and looking right into his with an amazing sense of connection.

Open-mouthed with ragged gusting breaths, from time to time their swollen lips came together as John gave Kelly a devouring, soul-wrenching kiss, a kiss of ownership, desire, compelling, powerful need, and love.

There was no doubt about it – even only able to observe him from behind – that boy was in love. And so was she.

"Do you want me to come inside you, Kelly? Do you want me to fill you with my cum?"

"Yes, please, yes, yes!" she wailed the pitch of her voice high in her frantic urgency.

After a particularly brutal thrust Kelly squealed, whether from pain or pleasure, Colin wasn't sure. Holy shit, the man was a God damned fucking machine.

"I'm so deep," John panted. "And your sweet cunt is going to get every drop."

"OhGodohGodohGod!"

"I'm going to come, Kelly," he said in a low, lust-filled growl. "And you're going to fly with me." One of his hands reached down between her legs and flicked her clitoris. "Now, Kelly, now. Come for me!"

Clearly on a hair trigger, she exploded instantly. Head thrashing back and forth, her narrow little hips were furiously bucking and thrusting as she cried out, "Ah! Ah! Ah! Yes, oh yes, Johnnnn!"

"Take it," he grunted, "take it all." His strong muscular buttocks and thighs clenched and unclenched through his first and second thrusts of ejaculation, his loins convulsing, no doubt with intense pleasure, as he pounded himself into his sub.

Their two bodies remained locked together savagely pushing and pulling themselves into each other. For long moments they teetered, enjoying a peak of powerful and concentrated pleasure. Then their simultaneous orgasm lessened and they slowly came down from their sexual crest together. John's subsequent thrusts diminished, as his violent climax eased.

Fucking wow, Colin thought. *That was some seriously hot sex right there.*

John released Kelly's legs, and she uncurled and lay flat. Both lovers entwined, pressing themselves close, with him covering every inch of her smaller body. John's larger hands reached up to lace into hers, bound to the bed board, and his head nuzzled affectionately into her neck. The man's cock was still inside her. Even post orgasm they both wanted to remain as physically close as humanly possible.

Colin's eyes narrowed and he stood up, looking closely at the screen. *What the fuck?*

He hadn't really looked before because the scene had so absorbed his attention, but John's back, buttocks and legs were covered in fine white scars. *Jesus.* The man looked like a soldier just back from a Vietnam POW camp. How the hell had he gotten scars like that? His boss, was no masochist, and he didn't believe in marking his subs. Surely the man wouldn't have willingly accepted such pain?

In a sort of mental re-wind, Colin recalled what he'd said to him about a week ago, when he had been target practicing with his whip. "Trust me," John had said, holding up his bullwhip. "A cane hurts way more than this does." Colin had replied with, "You sound like you know from personal experience." His boss had lifted one shoulder in an ambiguous shrug, giving nothing away.

John Taylor made sure that he was as separate from the BDSM Club as humanly possible. No one knew he owned it, and there were no paper trails. Colin had always thought that was because his boss wanted to protect himself. But maybe it was the other way around. Maybe John had actually been protecting the club from something in his own past?

Well fuck me silly, Colin thought.

All this time and Colin hadn't any idea. John was a private person, and now that he recalled, in the four years that he had known him never seen him without a shirt or vest. What was the secret of those scars? Did anyone know? And would he tell Kelly?

Colin, a practical, sensible man wasn't given to strong emotion, but God damn it! He felt a wash of conflicting feelings just now. John Taylor, self-contained as he was, really needed love, security and trust from the right woman. Colin sure hoped Kelly was the one for him.

Colin took one last look at the two lovers. Their chests were rising and falling in the aftermath of such an explosive expenditure of energy. Their breaths would be mingled, a soft sound in each other's ears. Kelly was still jerking and trembling with aftershocks and John was soothing her. Their strong young bodies were nuzzled close, with him stroking her and murmuring soft, incomprehensible words. Colin did hear him say one thing however. It was a grateful, and earnest, "Thank you, Kelly."

Wow. Colin thought. *I'm sure glad I didn't miss this.*

Colin decided that after he told Donna every single detail of these lovers' passionate joining, they were going to have some serious sex themselves.

Weird as the man had been, when he had come to dinner at their house, his wife had liked John Taylor. Donna would be overjoyed, and she'd no doubt agree that Kelly, a cheerful girl, was exactly the right person for the somber young man. Yet how was John going to manage the sadistic side of his personality? Had fucking his new sub taken John's craving to cause pain away somehow?

Colin left The Basement in a pensive mood, certain of two things. One: John Taylor had personal experience of being caned, probably over an extended period of time as a child. Whoever raised him and gave him those scars was a lousy evil bastard who deserved a slow, painful death.

That thought made him frown.

And, two: John Taylor, – the lonely young man that Colin had such a high opinion of – was very much in love.

And that thought made him smile.

Chapter 3

Early Sunday Morning

They were still at The Basement.

John sat in front of Kelly, just staring at her. She humbled him. How had he earned her submission? How had he gotten to this wonderful place?

Kelly was the girl of his dreams.

Blindfolded, Kelly was sitting naked in a chair, with her hands cuffed behind her back. Her ankles were hooked around the outer legs of the chair, leaving her pussy exposed to his view. He hadn't cuffed her ankles. He knew she'd do exactly as she was told. Christ, she was a fantastic submissive. So willing and eager to please him in any way he wanted. Kelly wouldn't deny him anything.

His cock twitched with lust at that thought.

He'd been fucking her anal passage with ever increasing sized crystal anal plugs all night, preparing her for his cock. For fun he'd made her climax multiple times while pushing the plugs in and out of her. He'd gotten her so hot that every plug slid into her rear entry with ease. Kelly was not a small girl, and he felt certain that she'd have no trouble taking him already. John wanted to make sure she had positive experiences and associations concerning anal sex.

Kelly had the most perfect ass that he had ever seen on any woman anywhere.

He didn't consider that he was particularly an ass man, but he may be. How would he know? He'd only recently enjoyed his first real orgasm in Kelly's mouth, and he still hadn't gotten over that. Kelly had a compelling mouth.

Her cunt was also fantastic, so probably her ass would be too. Everything about her stirred him with wonder and awe.

John wanted Kelly to experience anal sex because he needed to take her in every possible way. This was an instinctive desire, like a physical marking or branding. It was such a weird caveman-like longing. He wanted to plant his seed in every feminine hole.

"Tell me how you feel, Kelly," he said.

"Happy," she responded instantly, not holding anything back. "Cherished. Cared for. Loved."

"Put your legs together," he said. When she instantly complied, John drew his own chair nearer. Wrapping his legs around either side of hers, he captured her hips with his hands and moved closer. The tip of her tongue moved out to moisten her lips, and her body flushed with red heat.

He glanced lower and saw that she'd already flooded the wooden chair. God, she was always so slick, and ready for him.

"Thank you, Kelly," he said in a quiet, seductive tone.

Kelly rewarded him with a low moan, just as he was certain she would. *Yes. Yes,* he thought as a sense of powerful control flooded his body. John knew instinctively how to use his voice. For him, it was an integral part of being a Dom, to use soft whispers of seduction, or commanding authority in different volumes, pitch or tone.

Being with Kelly was both soothing and exciting, almost like practicing with his bullwhip or meditating. She centered him into a peaceful Dom space where they were joined, as Dom and sub, sharing a world alone together.

At times John felt as if Kelly was an extension of himself and in those moments he understood her emotions and her tears as if they were his own. An intense sensation of power and pleasure flowed through him, because he knew her so intimately. So completely.

He felt connected.

Kelly was *his,* everything she was, her breathing, her heartbeat, her body, thoughts, feelings, sensations and pain – it all belonged to him.

Running his hands up her flanks, John could tell that the blush that covered her skin was from sexual arousal. He was making a point of knowing Kelly's body. In time he intended to know it as intimately as he knew his own. How did that beautiful pink tinge arrive on her skin from out of nowhere? It was so fascinating. It usually started in her face, and then traveled down her neck, to her breasts and then even lower.

"What are you feeling and thinking now, Kelly?" John asked in a soft growl.

"Jeez, John," she gasped and her gasp turned into a giggle. "I'm feeling anxious and horny, and I'm wondering what your plans are. And you already know what I'm thinking, mind reader! I felt your legs against mine, and your hands on me, and I immediately thought of sex."

"Is that all?"

Kelly tilted her head and her lips pressed together. "No. I actually had quite a few thoughts," she said musingly. "I used to imagine that what I needed was restraint. Being dominated, having a Dom in charge of me during sex, and I guess that's still true. But it's different now with you, John. I don't need anything – just you."

Kelly's words slid over him, filling him with pleasure.

She paused for a moment and he didn't speak, instinctively remaining silent. John knew that she had more to say. Why did he know her so well?

Probably because Kelly had been in his thoughts forever.

"You know what?" Kelly said. "Plain old vanilla sex is more than enough with you. Don't get me wrong, I'm enjoying being vulnerable, blindfolded and tied up right now. Bending to your will makes me feel like I'm pleasing you. I belong to you. I'm your submissive, and that's important. It's also seriously sexy when you

control me, and take me. When you use me, exactly as you want."
She licked her lips. "Yum. But I've come to realize that I don't
need the trappings. Just you, and in any way you'll have me, is
perfect. You make me really, really happy, John."

"I'm very glad to hear that, Kelly."

He moved closer still, cupping her face and brushing her lips
with his own.

John loved Kelly so much that it actually hurt – but this pain
was exquisite. There wasn't anything in the world he wouldn't do
for her. He had often heard the expression, 'I'd kill for...' a
burger, or whatever – just fill in the blanks. He knew without any
doubt whatsoever, that if something threatened Kelly he was
completely capable of tearing whoever, or whatever it was apart.

With his bare hands if necessary.

"I'm glad that I make you happy," he said. "I belong to you,
too, Kelly. You make me happy, too, but more importantly, you
make me feel human."

"You *are* human, John," she snorted. "You're the kindest, most
wonderful human being in the entire world."

John just had to laugh at that. "Wow. I guess love really is
blind."

Chapter 4

What John Needs

John reached over and broke off a piece of food from the plate he'd brought in. Leaning in to her, he said. "Open your mouth, Kelly."

She obediently complied, and John put a little morsel of food inside, on her tongue, brushing his fingers against her lips as he did. A thrill of desire went through him. What was it about Kelly's mouth? Was it simply that the first orgasm he'd ever actually enjoyed and fully experienced came from those lips and that tongue? One look at her mouth was more than enough to make him hard.

Kelly began to chew and then her lips curved up into a smile, her cute little nose wrinkled and she laughed. God she was adorable.

"Meatloaf? Really, John?" she said. "Here I was expecting something seductive, like pancakes and whip cream, or chocolate. You're such a practical man. Where did you come up with meatloaf of all things? And how did you get meatloaf to be so damn sexy? Yowza. Pretty tantalizing, you, feeding me by hand with your own fingers."

"Yes," he said in a low voice, "it is. And protein is sexy, Kelly. You need your nourishment, because I'm going to use your body for my pleasure for many more hours yet."

With food in her mouth, she gave a soft, muffled moan. John said nothing, because he felt like moaning, too. God he needed to fuck her again. He'd lost count of how many times he had fucked her already tonight.

I'll never get enough of Kelly Flynn, he thought. And then an intriguing idea came to him. Maybe he'd change *his* last name when they married, if Kelly decided to have him. He'd no loyalty at all to his own surname. Perhaps he should be John *Flynn.*

John broke off another bite and placed it between her lips, this time running his fingers along her mouth in a way that made his balls tighten. She chewed once more and he watched, fascinated.

"My neighbor, Mable," he said, "makes me lunch five days a week. I go over to her house and pick it up, and I pay her really well. She was Aunt Brenda's friend, and she'd been having some financial difficulties. I doubt if Mable would take charity, and I do like her cooking. It reminds me of my aunt. Thus, meatloaf."

Kelly smiled. "You're a good person, John. I'm so totally gone on you."

John didn't reply, but he brushed her face and hair in acknowledgment. He could feel his throat swelling, just like his heart and his chest had. He was utterly gone on her, too. It was so obvious and simple that it felt complicated.

He shut his eyes and drew in a deep breath. No wonder people went crazy when they fell in love.

For some time he fed his sub by hand. Like a spoiled, treasured pet, Kelly enjoyed her early morning meal. It was a sensual, erotic experience that kept them both ultra horny and on the edge.

John cleared his throat. "My best friend and mentor is a man named André Chevalier. You'll meet him sometime, he lives in Las Vegas. Anyway, André told me that I would enjoy feeding my sub, and he was right. He said it was a pleasure that only a Dom could fully understand or appreciate. Do you want to know what I'm feeling, here now with you, Kelly?"

"Yes, John," she said.

"I feel that you're mine and that I'm taking care of you," he said. "As if I'm totally responsible for you and I'm protecting you and helping you to live. Like a pet – a kitten or a puppy – but more than that."

He blew out a gust of air in frustration. "I don't know if I can explain it. I'm not sure I understand it myself. I want to be the one to give you everything you require. It's like you're vulnerable and helpless and you need me to survive. Crazy, right?"

"No, John," she said in a soft voice, and he could see that his words had moved her. "Tell me more," she said.

He stroked her face with his knuckles. Then, because he couldn't resist her, he leaned in and gave Kelly another kiss. He pressed in close, took her mouth as his own while casually caressing her breasts, rolling, squeezing and tugging on both nipples. When he pulled back he noticed that her pulse had quickened, but so had his.

Where was his vaunted self-control? Kelly made it disappear every single time, like a piece of straw sucked away in a hurricane.

"You're a strong, capable woman, Kelly," he said. "And you can manage perfectly well on your own. Logically I know this. These are all my imagined realities, but right here and now, they feel so real. It's like some sort of overpowering male instinct. I want to make your life perfect. I want to pound all your enemies to the ground. I want to be the one you depend on, the person you trust and the only one you need. I want to dominate you, and protect you, and feed you, and keep you, and discipline you. I want to worship your body, and be the first in your heart. I want to own you, body and soul. I need to be everything to you, Kelly Flynn."

John pressed in close against her while she sat in the chair, arms cuffed behind her. It wasn't close enough. Lurching forward, Kelly was in his arms once more, the long length of her young naked body up tight against his.

"You *are* everything to me, John," she whispered, with a deep sigh of pleasure.

Her breath gusted over his ear as he reveled in the smooth tactile happiness he experienced from being skin to skin, and touching her. She kissed his neck, making small sounds of longing, licking and biting any part of him within reach of her mouth. John chuckled at her actions, knowing she was ultra horny and desperate, too. Every lick and bite sent a shiver of arousal down his spine.

"Whew," she said when he pulled back, and her whole body quivered. "What you just said. That's pretty comprehensive, John. Jeez Louise."

"There's so much that I need to tell you, Kelly," he said. "There's a lot you need to know about me. André told me that, 'It is best to begin a relationship in the manner in which you intend to go on.' I want us to be honest with each other, always. I've lots of secrets, and I swear that you'll hear them all in time. But I don't want to frighten you."

He took her blindfold off. "Oh," he said when he looked into her pale blue eyes. They were dilated and desperate with lust and need.

"We can talk later. Right now you need me to fuck you."

Chapter 5

Triggers

John slid his chair back and tugged her to her feet, pulling her naked body against his. His thick cock pressed against her stomach and he gave an unintentional growl of relief at the physical contact. God he needed her so badly.

"John?"

"Humm?"

"Do you mind if I touch you?" she said. "I really want to touch you sometime during sex. It doesn't have to be now, just sometime."

He wasn't at all surprised to find that he wanted to please her even more than he wanted to fuck her. He was the Dom, so why did it seem to him sometimes that she had all the power? And even more importantly, why didn't that fact bother him?

He pulled her body closer against him, and reaching behind her, he unhooked her cuffs. Sweeping her into his arms as if she was his bride and they were crossing the threshold, John sat down, and set her on his lap.

"Hands in front, Kelly. Lace your fingers together." She obeyed.

He sighed. "Do you know what a trigger is, Kelly?"

She frowned and then grimaced. "I don't really know the definition, but I do know enclosed, dark spaces are a trigger for me."

"Oh, of course," he said. "You have had a very real and personal experience with the subject." He had an arm curled around her waist, the other resting on her thighs. With a sympathetic squeeze, he pulled her into him.

"Okay, a trigger is of course, different things to different people," he said. "Basically it can be defined as that time, during specific situations, when a person becomes vulnerable. These situations are called 'triggers,' because they trigger an onset of unwanted symptoms."

"The odd thing is that sometimes triggers occur without conscious awareness, so people don't always know what creates or 'triggers' the negative reaction. For example, if you were bitten by a dog as a child, you may not remember the incident, but you do know that dogs make you nervous. Seeing a dog then would be a trigger for sudden, inexplicable anxiety."

John reached back to the table and took a sip from his can of Diet Coke. He held the can up, and raised his brows, offering Kelly a drink.

"No thank you, John. I'm good."

"Okay. Well, in my case, I have difficulty with hands," he said. "I don't like to be touched. When I'm touched I can sometimes feel nauseated, out of control and vulnerable. I was going to talk to you about this, because I want you to touch me. I want to get over this kind of 'hand phobia,' and I know that in time you can help me to do this."

Kelly smiled broadly, and her joy was so unexpected when discussing such a serious subject that John almost burst out laughing with relief. He had feared that she'd become quiet and worried.

"What are you so happy about?" he said.

"Oh," Kelly said. "It's just that I'm certain that I can help you, John."

"That's it?" he said in disbelief. "You aren't curious about where my trigger comes from, or why I have it?"

"Sure, I am," she said. "And you'll tell me when you're ready. But this time when we have sex, I'm going to ask if I can run my hands through your hair, or put them around your neck, and man, I'm kind of looking forward to it. I love your wonderful, thick wavy hair, John. I bet it feels silky and amazing to touch."

Laughing joyously, John swept Kelly up into his arms and took her to the bed, throwing her on to it. "My hair, huh?" he said. "For now, hands over your head, beautiful girl, and spread those legs, knees up. I'm going to eat you out until your scream for me to stop, because you can't take any more pleasure. And at some point, while I'm doing it, I'm going to let you touch my hair."

Much later, after he had licked and finger fucked her to orgasm three times, John had taken her twice more. Once against the wall, because there was just something about doing it standing up that appealed to him. He loved having her legs wrapped around him, and her arms held high above her head.

Then once while lying on their sides, with him coming from behind. Kelly's hands were naturally in front of her that way, and he could play with her breasts and kiss and caress her easily while entering her.

John had gotten around the hand thing by commanding Kelly to run her fingers through his hair. He had suffered a reaction, but he had pushed through the anxiety. While he didn't yet enjoy the experience, he was beginning to tolerate it.

Now they lay together like children, Kelly talking away and him smiling as he watched her. John didn't think he'd ever get tired of watching her. The woman was so alive, and irrepressibly cheerful. He wasn't the same person, now that he was with her. He was different. He was better... so much better.

It was impossible to be anything other than happy when he was with Kelly.

Not just happy, he thought with a sense of magic and wonder. *Happier than I've ever been before – lovingly, exultingly, joyously, lightly, effortlessly, happy! Without doubt, without darkness, without anger, or hate. Could I have ever imagined such a state?*

And John knew the answer: *Never.*

"So," he finally said. "We have to think of getting some rest. I suspect that it would be best if we both go to our own homes. With you in my bed, Kelly, I won't get any sleep. No matter how exhausted I am, I'm always hard for you. I think that even if I was dead I'd still be able to fuck you."

"Eww!" she laughed. "What a terrible picture! But yeah, I noticed that, too. Does that cock of yours ever go down below half-mast?"

"Not really," he said. "It's always been a problem for me. But now that I have you as my sub I'm not complaining."

My sub, he thought with a thrill of pleasure. *God, my beautiful Kelly.* It still amazed him that she was his. But could he keep her? Or would she run away when she found out what had happened to him?

Not to mention all the bad things that he'd done.

Chapter 6

Confessions

John stood up then, finally managing to show Kelly his scars. He had decided that that was the best way to let her know that he had childhood issues. Sitting cross-legged on the bed, Kelly had frowned and become very quiet. But not for long.

John had an internal snicker over that. His beautiful girl would never be quiet for long.

"Why didn't you tell anyone, John?" she asked. "Couldn't someone, a teacher, or a counselor have helped you?

He sat back down on the bed next to her, and explained that his father was a dangerous, and manipulative man, as well as a district judge. If he'd confided to someone, it wouldn't have solved anything. It would have only created problems for his confidant, or it may have even gotten them killed.

Only two people outside the family knew this family secret, and if anyone found out there would be terrible repercussions. He admonished her in the strongest degree to tell no one, and she promised she'd keep hush-hush.

"But, John," she said. "I don't understand. How did you get away from him?"

He smiled. "When I was thirteen years old I recorded what he was doing to me. I made copies, and hid them in safe places. Then I confronted him. I told him that if anything happened to me or my Aunt Brenda, that recording would go to the police. He used to threaten me all the time that if I told anyone, that he'd kill Brenda. It was an effective threat, because she was the only one who cared about me. I became afraid to talk to anyone. Unless I'm working a scene, or with you, talking still makes me nervous."

He ran his hand over her hair, loving the color and the feel of it.

"Then one day at grade school the indomitable little Kelly came to my rescue. I'm so glad that I broke that jerk's arm, and you went to the school principle. How would I have found you otherwise? You were like the sun to me, when I was in the dark. God, you were a happy child. So cheerful, so alive, and so beautiful. I was fascinated. I couldn't keep away from you. Didn't you think it odd how I used to follow you around and just watch you whenever possible?"

"Nope." Sitting side by side, she bumped shoulders with him. It was an affectionate, best friend gesture. "I kind of thought of you like a big brother," she added with a grin.

He chuckled over that. "I felt like someone from the stone-age who had discovered fire. Being around you warmed my empty, hungry soul."

"Oh, John," she said, in a sympathetic tone. "I had no idea."

Her eyes filled, and John watched fascinated for a moment, as a tear began to trail down her cheek. Awed, he touched it reverently with his index finger. Kelly *felt* so much. And she'd shed this tear for him.

Will I ever be able to cry, he wondered? *But it doesn't really matter now, because Kelly will cry for me.*

John put his arm around her, and pulled her close against him. "I told my father that the recording would be sent if anything happened to me, too, so my father and I came to an agreement. Basically I out blackmailed him, and then moved in with my aunt."

"I lived with Aunt Brenda for the first six years of my life, did I tell you that? My parents would visit me from time to time, when I was a child, but not often. I didn't understand who they were. They finally took me 'home' when I was old enough to not be a problem I guess. I cried to be away from Brenda, the only mother I'd ever known. And then the beatings started and the threats…," he swallowed and in the silence of the room the sound seemed loud. "... and the other things," he finished.

He sighed. "You're getting the short version here, Kelly. There's so much to tell, but the main thing is – my father is still an extremely dangerous man."

"While I haven't talked to him in years, we're in a temporary truce. My father has documented things about me, some of it made up – some of it not so much. His intention was to make people think that I'm mentally unstable. I suppose he anticipated that if my recording came out he'd convince people that it was fabricated. As he's a prominent man of the community, he could possibly make it stick. So the truce is uneasy, but it works."

They left The Basement at five a.m. as the cleaners were coming in at six. John planned to pick Kelly up at her apartment later that day. Against all his better judgments and objections, she'd finally convinced him.

John was going to have Sunday dinner at Kelly's parent's home, to meet her entire family.

Chapter 7

Family Dinner

<hr>

Sunday afternoon, Kelly and John visited her family.

John drove his silver Mercedes sports car into the circular driveway, with Kelly in the passenger's seat. He knew exactly where her childhood home was, of course, having walked by it many times as a child, on the way to and from school.

John hated catching the school bus, so walking had been the best option. 'Do anything, in order to keep away from people,' had been his motto. With the amount of anger and hate he had inside him as a child, the walking option was safer for him... and safer for them, too.

The weather was clear, damp, and cool, fairly typical for April. Mt. Hood, the highest peak in Oregon at over 11,000 feet could be easily seen as he had left his bungalow. The mountain was only about fifty miles from Portland, covered in snow, and shining in sunset tinges of pinks and purple in the late afternoon.

The common sardonic saying by Portlander's was, 'If you *can see* the mountain, it's going to rain.' That and, 'If you *can't see* the mountain, it's raining already.' John could tell it was most certainly going to rain later as it often did, particularly during spring.

Kelly patted his arm. "You seem tense," she said. "Just relax and be yourself. They're going to love you."

He parked near the front of the white, two story Classic Revival mansion, beside the two tall pillars that stood on either side of the front door. He switched off his car, and turned toward her.

"I hope we aren't making a mistake, Kelly. I've told you I'm just not good around people. Isn't this a little fast?" he asked again. "Don't you think it's too soon to meet your family?"

"Nope," she said in her naturally positive manner. "I don't care. We'll work it out, John. You're very important to me. My family will get used to you, and you'll get used to them, too. We have to start sometime, and I don't see any benefit in waiting. What for? 'Don't put off until tomorrow' and all that. It'll work out."

"You aren't going to tell them we're engaged, right?"

She laughed. "No, that would be a little too much. I don't want to scare them to death, but I do want to show them my ring."

Kelly held out her right hand, and smiled happily at the daisy ring that she wore next to her little finger. At great expense, John had designed that ring, and had the jeweler make it and deliver it within five days. Pink sapphires and diamonds were set in gold, all resulting in a graceful, circular bouquet of pink and white daisies. He couldn't have expected a better reaction to his gift.

An unfamiliar array of emotion washed over him whenever Kelly admired that ring; pride, joy, and pleasure at her obvious delight. It was particularly pleasing because *he* had made her happy.

I always want her to be happy, John thought. Kelly was a naturally cheerful sort of soul anyway, so making her even happier was the easiest thing in the world.

John felt that familiar tightening sensation in his chest, which he was beginning to associate with his heart. It seemed that just as André Chevalier had assured him, he have a heart after all. Being with Kelly had allowed him to discover it. Right now his heart was coming to life, and it was unreservedly centered on her.

"Find someone, John," André Chevalier had said, "and love them so hard that it hurts." Well, he'd done just that. Thinking of Kelly and seeing her happy caused that clearly recognizable and exquisitely painful ache in his chest.

"I'm really glad you like that ring, Kelly," he said. "And I'm pleased that you don't intend to tell them we're engaged. You need to know me much better before you decide to become engaged to me anyway."

When Kelly tried to interrupt, John said, "No, listen to me. It's just like jumping to conclusions about that file, Kelly. You don't have sufficient information. You don't know me well enough. I understand that we feel the same right now – we equally want to spend every minute together. We're both crazy in love, but that may wear off, Kelly. Not in my case – never in my case, but it might in yours."

She positively glowered. Kelly looked so insulted and mutinous that John wanted to laugh.

He'd laughed and smiled more with Kelly than he had in his entire life. She was such an angry, furry, soft little kitten sometimes. Yet she still seemed, so often, to get her own way. He hid a smile and thought, *except in bed.* By God he was in charge of her there, and didn't she just love being ordered around and utterly dominated during sex?

Yet there was nothing John wouldn't do for Kelly Flynn.

For a start, he really hadn't wanted to come to this family dinner, and somehow here he was. How had she done it? Manipulating him into doing something he so completely hated even the idea of? He'd have to be careful or she'd Top him, like Donna often seemed to Top Colin – when they weren't having sex anyway. Colin dominated Donna completely during a scene, but outside of the bedroom? Not so much.

John sighed. "Living with me, and being with me Kelly…." He took the keys out of his car and popped them in the pocket of his black leather jacket. "Well, the reality may be harder than you could have ever expected. My beautiful girl," he said touching her face with the tips of his fingers. "Don't get trapped by me, Kelly, not until you know what you're getting into."

"Okay, John," she said unhappily.

He just stared at her. She was so, so, pretty, with that long orange hair that he loved to fist with both hands. A vision of her on her knees came to him, a memory of her beautiful mouth wrapped around his cock.

John was stiff right now, but he was used to that. His mindless cock was often hard. But now at least the damn thing had good reason. Who wouldn't find Kelly the most gorgeous woman ever? But she was a little annoyed with him, and she looked so damn cute, especially when provoked.

Feeling an urgent need to make her understand, and to make her smile John leaned over, cupped her face, and gave her a light kiss on the lips.

"You're the best person in the whole world, Kelly Flynn. If you do end up staying with me, I swear that I'll spend my entire life just trying to be worthy of you."

At that, Kelly's demeanor changed. John was pleased to see that yielding, soft, absolutely female smile back on her face – not to mention the heartfelt devotion in her eyes. Why did she care for him? John still didn't understand it.

His chest tightened, and it hurt once again.

It was that sweet yet terrible ache of painful pleasure, simply from witnessing Kelly's heartfelt expression of love.

Chapter 8

Kelly's Plan

Kelly's mind was echoing with John's words. You're the best person in the whole world, Kelly Flynn. If you do end up staying with me I swear that I'll spend my entire life just trying to be worthy of you.

Wow. John Taylor took her breath away.

They both walked inside, and for once her mother wasn't nearby. John shrugged off his jacket and helped her with her coat. Kelly checked her watch, knowing everyone would've already sat down.

Decisions, decisions: To be late, which would annoy her mother? Or to make John suffer pre-dinner chats? Kelly had decided to be late, because John could settle down and become comfortable over dinner when everyone was eating.

Kelly had seen her mother's face peeking out the window as they drove in, no doubt checking out John's car. Mom would have decided that John might be okay if he could afford a Mercedes.

Dressed in a simple, yet elegant green sheath dress with high heels and with an orange and yellow scarf decorously hiding the hickies around her neck, Kelly led John into the dining room, holding his hand.

"Hey everyone, sorry we're late," she said, offering no explanation.

The formal dining room was designed in a traditional style, decorated in olive and white with a sparkling chandelier over the table. Rich dark wood flooring covered the area, broken up by a white carpet square. On the carpet sat a solid oak dining table with carved legs and matching white seating.

Another leaf had been put into the dining room table, and two chairs were empty. Her father was at the head of the table, Richard on one side of him, her mom on the other.

Kelly hid a cringe. She and John were placed directly across from her mother. She had John sit down next to Richard, because her brother would be nice to him in any case. The rest of the family, Maria, Katrina and Jamie, were seated in their normal spots.

Richard stood up and Kelly was pleased to see how warmly he shook John's hand.

"Nice to see you again, John," he said. "I'm so glad you were there to help Kelly in that elevator. I hate to think of what would have happened if you weren't there."

"What elevator?" Kelly's mom asked.

"Just a minute, mom, let me introduce John to everyone," Kelly interrupted still standing up. "Everyone, this is my boyfriend, John, and you all have to be really nice to him, or I swear to God I won't speak to any of you ever again."

The family laughed, and introductions were made, with some good-natured teasing of Kelly. She sat down, hiding her physical discomfort. Jesus, John gave a great spanking, but her backside was a little sore – both inside and out.

She glanced over at John, to give him raised eyebrows and a sardonic expression about her sore butt, hoping to make him laugh, but for once, he wasn't noticing her. Uh oh. He wasn't himself. Something was wrong.

John was looking extremely uncomfortable. Kelly supposed it didn't really show to anyone else but her. To everyone else, he just looked impassive, and ridiculously handsome.

Shit, he was amazingly hot in that crisp white, open necked Egyptian cotton shirt, with his charcoal colored Armani trousers and dark Berluti shoes. John had told her André Chevalier had gone shopping with him, and taught him how to enjoy quality clothes. There was no doubt about it – he was a fast learner. In everything apparently, except on how to deal with his anxiety over social situations.

Kelly observed her mom sizing John up: Expensive car, expensive clothes, and that TAG Heuer watch. She'd spent some time dressing John, making him look rich, but not snobby, or like a yuppie douche. It was an art, but she had managed it. Dressing John up had been as arousing as watching him undress, so they of course enjoyed lots of sex during the extremely erotic and pleasant interlude.

Kelly's mind flashed back and the memory of John's touch rippled through her.

They honestly had no time for sex, because they had to get ready to go to the family dinner. Yet John still managed to bind her hands, put her over his knees and give her a savage, mind-blowing, and erotic spanking. He hadn't let her come, and Kelly had wondered if anyone had ever died from not climaxing.

It had been a serious question, because she wasn't sure if she could survive being on the knife edge of orgasm for as long as she had been.

Unfortunately, John liked her there.

After that he'd tied her up with his expensive neck ties, naked, spread-eagle on her stomach, to his four post bed. John had wanted to fuck her ass for the first time. Utterly submissive to his wishes, frantic and desperate to climax, Kelly was up for anything.

"Do you think we have both gone a bit crazy, John?" she had asked him once she was at his mercy once more, his willing sex slave. "I mean, here we are having sex, when honestly, we should be getting ready and going off to Sunday dinner. You know I'm crazy in love with you. And I've heard that love is supposed to make you do irrational things."

Sitting beside her, John had been running his hand along her heated, tender buttocks, making admiring comments about his red handprints, nibbling, licking and kissing. His hands were an odd combination of rough and gentle, as he pinched and squeezed and caressed. Jeez, he really liked her ass.

"Ah, my beautiful girl," he had murmured with his mouth against her skin, "You're a fairly rational woman – as far as women go," he had replied calmly.

Kelly had given him an indignant gasp, and then giggled. "Was that a joke? That was a joke, right? I'd hit you if I weren't tied up," she threatened.

"Why do you think I tied you?" he had replied with a smirk.

Jesus, she loved it when John was playful. In the end, he'd gotten her so worked up, and so horny, that she couldn't see straight. The massive vaginal and clitoral orgasm he had given her had blown her mind. Wow. Just fucking wow.

Finding the right clothes and getting all dressed up had taken two hours. Kelly felt her body heat with the thought. God damn but the man was soooo sexy, and amazing in bed. For the first time she'd experienced anal sex, and it had been fantastic. John was the ultimate lover, aware of everything. The man knew exactly how to turn her on, and keep her turned on, no matter what he did to her.

What a distraction. John Taylor rocked her world. And being in love was the most wonderful experience. Kelly couldn't possibly be any happier than she was right now. If John could learn how to deal with her family, everything would be perfect.

They sat down and dinner was served. She knew her mother had gone all out, bringing in a cook and servant for the special occasion. Kelly never brought boyfriends home. She had dated plenty, but there was never that click of real possibility with anyone. Today, Kelly had called and told her dad that she felt John was 'the one' for her. Dad would certainly have passed that tidbit on.

It was a big pork dinner, with applesauce, and baked vegetables. Once everyone was served and eating, the inquisition began.

"Well, John, I understand from our son, Richard, that you both went to school together until year eight?"

"Yes."

Kelly watched as her mother waited a beat, but when no further information was forthcoming her mother said, "And your father is the Honorable Frank Taylor, a district court judge?"

"Yes."

Another pause, and again John remained silent. "And he and your mother live up on Hillside Crescent?" her mom asked.

"Yes."

Kelly's mother seemed to have accepted John's closed-mouth reserve. There was no gap now, as she continued to ply him with questions. "What does your mother do?"

"We are estranged. I haven't seen either parent since I was thirteen years old."

"Oh." Kelly could see the wheels turning in her mother's mind as she decided whether or not to pursue that ticklish question. Eventually her mother said, "So how did you and Kelly meet?"

"Marguerite, let the man eat," her father said.

Kelly noticed that John wasn't eating, but he was making a show of appearing to. Jesus he was nervous, or at least he certainly wasn't acting himself.

Kelly decided to take some of the heat. She began a fictitious story of how they met, explaining that they had run into each other across the road from the Plaza. That was one of the places she did her Speed Dating job. John had recognized Kelly from grade school, when she had accidentally dropped her keys and he had picked them up.

Kelly had quite an imagination and could really tell a story, so she embellished and carried on for some time. Then she explained how they had been trapped in an elevator together, and her Dad in particular warmed to him for 'saving my little girl's life.'

"What work do you do, John?" Kelly's mother persisted with her inquisition.

"I'm a student. I've finished a psychology degree, and am now studying the philosophy of religion and ethics."

"But how do you support yourself?"

"I invented a phone app when I was seventeen. It made me rich." This little nugget was a momentary conversation stopper.

"What app?" Maria asked.

"Violent Vipers."

"Seriously?" Jamie said. "That's my favorite!"

This was all news to Kelly, and she smiled at John. So. That's how he was able to get the financing to start The Basement. She was studying John closely and noticed that he was looking rather grey, or green. Holy shit. What was wrong with him?

Kelly jumped to her feet, because there was no question in her mind.

John was going to faint.

Chapter 9

Kelly's Solution

"Just one minute everyone," said Kelly, knowing that she had to do something fast. Lord, to her he looked as if he was going to throw up. "C'mon John." Kelly grabbed his hand and dragged him out of the dining room, through the living area and into the den. "Jesus, John, are you alright?"

"No."

"What's wrong?"

"I think I'm going to be sick," he said. "I've been worried that I may throw up. I really don't do people, Kelly. I do everything through the phone, and other than in a scene, I don't interact. I haven't for years."

"But why?"

"I'm nervous, and when I'm nervous I become wooden I guess, and even more emotionless," he said. "I'm pretty sure that if this constant interrogation keeps up I'm either going to pass out, or throw up, or both.

Kelly gave a bark of laughter and John frowned at her, either hurt or more likely surprised by her levity. "I'm sorry, John," she said, "I know it isn't funny, but it isn't the end of the world either. Here, sit down."

He sat on the black leather couch. "Why did you laugh?" he asked in that familiar peremptory way of his. *Ah,* she thought, relieved. *This is the John I know and love. He's clearly not insulted, but simply curious.*

"I don't know, it just seems funny," she said. "To my mind you're perfect at everything. I respect you so much. Somehow, you being anxious seems so odd to me. It kind of makes you fallible and human, John. I'm afraid that it makes me love you even more. What are you afraid of?"

"My counselor says that because my father always terrified me with threats if anyone found out our secrets, that I'm frightened to interact with others. It feels unsafe talking and telling anyone anything. You have no idea how scary my father is. He has all the power, Kelly, even now. He just does. I feel anxious even being here in case he finds out – that's how terrifying he is. I know it's irrational, but I just can't seem to get around it."

"This seems so unlike you."

"But this *is* like me, Kelly," he said. "I honestly can't do people. It's never bothered me before. I manage pretty well." He took her hand. "But now I'm worried that if I can't overcome this, you won't want me."

Sitting down on his lap, she said, "Well then, I guess we will have to figure it out." Kelly kissed his cheek. "But I won't give you up, so just forget that stupid idea. You know when you dominate a scene? Why can you do that so well, yet not be as capable when outside a scene?"

"When I'm dominating a scene the sub is mine," he said. "I'm in control, and they're under my care. Everything is my responsibility. It's hard to explain but I find it easy because my job as a Dom is to take them through their experience, to scrutinize everything about them, body, mind, soul, and to not let them get away with anything. I'm observant and particularly skilled at noticing a sub that's under my care, Kelly."

"You're the best," she said reverently, giving him a cheeky smile.

John smiled at that.

"Well that's it then," she said. "Just imagine everyone is naked and you have your bullwhip. Treat them like your subs, John. Observe them and ferret out their secrets. Have you ever tried that? Maybe that will work."

He appeared to be giving this consideration. "Alright."

They stood up. Fast and unexpectedly, John pulled her hands behind her back, and pressed her to him. Kelly's flesh melted against him, and her body went into instant overdrive, as he captured her mouth and kissed her. *Jesus.*

"Why can you be yourself with me, John?"

"I don't know. Even at grade school I could be myself with you, Kelly. You're the only one, I swear." He kissed her forehead and let her go. "By the way, you're an expert and extremely experienced liar. That story you told everyone of how we met?" He tugged a lock of her hair. "Don't ever try anything like that with me, will you?"

Kelly laughed and shook her head, placing her hand on her heart. "Never, John. But trust me, if you had a mother like mine you'd have learned how to tell lies like that, too." She giggled. "It's simply self-defense. If parents don't *want* to hear the truth, children learn not to speak it."

She put her arm in his. "Okay, well let's do it. Remember, John. They're naked, and you have your bullwhip."

When they returned, John did appear different. No one would have noticed, but to Kelly he seemed much better.

"Mr. Flynn," John said, "you must be very proud of all you've accomplished. You have this beautiful home, and your wonderful family. I don't know everyone here of course, but I judge by your daughter. You and Mrs. Flynn have obviously been outstanding parents to her. Kelly is quality, through and through – and she was even as a child. Kelly is the very definition of Class. I think she's a wonderful girl."

Kelly felt a flush of heat radiate across the skin on her face, neck and breasts. She wasn't embarrassed; she was flushed pink with pleasure. Wow. What a complement. Could there be any one more appreciative of her than he was?

Kelly's Dad was beaming. "John," he said. "You must call me Rodney, and thank you. I agree with you about Kelly. I'm so glad that you appreciate her. I promise you that I've never heard a single negative comment come out of her mouth, and that's from when she was little girl. Our little bundle of joy, that's what we called her. Always so cheerful and good-natured. Yes, John, I'm very happy with my life. I've been blessed."

"Your cup runneth over," John said, apparently recalling one of the bible quotes he had recently learned from his philosophy, religion and ethic's course. He'd never been to church a day in his life, but Kelly had told him that her family was Catholic.

"Oh," Kelly's mom said, apparently impressed. "What religion are you, John?"

"None."

Kelly's mother frowned, disturbed by this revelation. "But you believe in God don't you, John?"

He turned to look at Kelly, and she watched as his anxiety and tension seemed to soften even further. "I'm beginning to," he said, continuing to stare at her.

Awww, Kelly thought. *Wow. Underneath Father John the sadist, there is the heart and soul of a poet.* Her own heart was so full that her eyes stung, and she had to blink a number of times to stop herself from crying.

The rest of the dinner seemed to go well for some time. It was clear to Kelly that both her sisters, Maria, sixteen, and Katrina, nineteen, were pretty well in love with John. What woman wouldn't be? The man was so handsome, and fascinating. He was successfully hiding any nervousness. Kelly was sure no one noticed the way he had been acting earlier. Even Jamie loved him for inventing "Violent Vipers."

John asked Richard about his profession, and listened in that intent perceptive way he had. Amused, Kelly studied her brother as he replied. John coaxed numerous tidbits out, and she saw how Richard easily began to loosen and chatted away, telling John far more than he'd have intended to. Treating John like a trusted long term friend.

Kelly understood her brother's reaction.

With John's interested and attentive eyes upon him, Richard would feel as if he was the only person in the room. John could do that to someone, make them feel special and make them forget everything. Yet his interest wasn't in any way faked. Right now, John really was absorbing and fully assessing her brother, Richard's personality.

Kelly wanted to laugh out loud.

The fact that John usually did this in order to better sadistically torment a sub into mind-less bliss, had no real bearing on the matter.

Chapter 10

Faux Pas

Kelly's mom, unfortunately stuck in her old habits, began to talk about Kelly's faults. It started small, and went from there.

"So Kelly, when are you going to give up that silly job?" Marguerite asked loudly. "A woman with a degree can do so much better, don't you think, John? Even if it's only an Arts degree, I do think she could have done something more substantial educationally. And I wonder if you need me to go out with you, Kelly, so we can get some style into that hair. Would you like me to take you to my hairdresser? Jean Paul is a marvel. He could do wonders with that unfashionable mop top of yours."

At the end of that sentence John sprang loudly to his feet.

He shoved his chair back so ferociously that the rear feet of his chair moved off the white carpet, and scratched loudly on the dark wood floors.

Every single person looked up at him in shock and astonishment, as if he had just landed from Mars or turned florescent purple or something. John's lips were firm, his jaw tight. This wasn't her date, John Taylor, standing straight and tall before her family now. This was Father John, the stern, hard-eyed, and no-nonsense Dom.

Oh shit! Kelly thought.

It was a bit like watching a car whose parking-brake had disengaged roll down the hill and into a thick crowd of people who were all looking the other way. There sure was nothing Kelly could do about it, except scream *'Look out!'*

But screaming, *'Look out!'* wasn't going to help in this situation.

Oh. My, God, Kelly thought wildly. *You can't take her over your knee, John! That's my mom!*

"Excuse me," John said in an icy tone, his face turned toward Kelly's father. Kelly figured that John was addressing her dad as her mother's theoretical Dom. Little did John know, mom wore the pants in this family.

"I'm afraid I'm going to have to leave," he said, with barely disguised fury. "I can't sit here and listen to anyone criticize or malign Kelly in my presence, no matter who's doing it – even if the disparaging comments are coming from your wife, and Kelly's mother."

"Oh," said Kelly's dad, "Now just sit down, young man. I'm sure Marguerite didn't mean anything by it."

"Nevertheless, I can't stay," he said remaining standing without backing down in the slightest. "Neither Kelly nor I can remain here in your home without an apology."

John's head turned from Kelly's father, so his eyes could focus on Kelly's mom.

"You'll have to forgive me, Mrs. Flynn," he said. "Kelly is the best person I know. There couldn't be a more wholesome, honest, kind or ideal woman in the entire world. I won't have anyone belittle her achievements, or her beautiful hair, or any other single thing about her. Not while in my presence. Kelly is perfect exactly as she is, or exactly as she chooses to be. And an Arts degree is the ideal choice of study for an inspiring, creative woman, who sings like an angel."

There was a remarkably long silence, and just like the wax figures of Madame Tussaud's waxworks, not one person moved.

Kelly's mother had initially been white as paper, as the blood had drained from her face. But now her features were becoming quite red. Kelly wouldn't have been surprised to find that her mother's heart had stopped with shock, and then her mom's pulse had picked up again. Was she angry? Embarrassed? Just what was she feeling now?

Kelly had absolutely no intention of interfering. This was 'Father John' at his best. Stern and domineering, John, the man she loved, wasn't going to take crap from anyone. Kelly wondered how her mother would deal with the social faux pas. John was handsome, and clearly rich: Husband material. Kelly's mom wouldn't want to make him leave.

Mrs. Marguerite Flynn finally said, "I'm sorry, John. I meant no insult. None at all."

"Thank you," John said, giving her a curt nod.

Kelly was glad that John's fiery gaze was on her mother, and not her. Honestly, she had to give it to her mother – mom was meeting John's eyes. She hadn't looked away. That took guts. Kelly had encountered John's heated disapproval before, and she never wanted to endure it again.

"However," John said in that deceptively mild voice that indicated further discipline was on the way, "I believe that it's Kelly who deserves your apology, Mrs. Flynn."

Jesus, Kelly thought, uncertain if she wanted to sing 'Halleluiah,' or cheer John on, or hide her face with shock and mortification. Kelly's brother, Richard had wanted to say those things to their mom a million times, but he never had. It probably wouldn't have helped anyway. Even her dad didn't have the courage to make their mother back down, at least not in Kelly's presence.

"Kelly," her mom said after a long moment. "Please forgive me. You're a good daughter. I didn't realize that I was coming across so negatively."

All in all, Kelly thought, *it's not a bad apology.*

"Apology accepted, Mom. And I really appreciate it. I admit that for some time now I've been feeling like you weren't pleased or proud of me."

"Oh, darling," Mrs. Flynn said looking genuinely contrite.

Chapter 11

Kelly's Happiness

John drove Kelly home late that evening. Both of them were tranquil and companionably quiet together.

My family loves John, Kelly thought dreamily, while riding home in the car. *And so do I. And he's made mom stop and think about what she was saying for a change. And apologize! Could anyone be happier than I am right now?*

Of course if it wasn't obvious that John had piles of cash, it may have gone differently. Mother had this thing about 'financial security.' She'd been pretty impressed with the expensive ring John had given her, too. Taking everything into account – nothing could have turned out better.

Strangely, the rest of the family night had gone really well. With the event of her mom's misbehavior, John had clearly discovered his social persona. It had been an amazing experience for him. Kelly knew that he was still on a high. While he hadn't fully relaxed in the presence of her family, John had felt much more himself.

Richard had given Kelly the thumbs up as they left, when John wasn't looking. He'd call her later, and have *plenty* to say. Tackling their mother had made John a hero in a weird sort of way. Mom had been getting a bit out of hand, and to think that the dragon could be braved had been a revelation for everyone.

For the rest of the evening her mom had been actually a lot of fun. It made an impressive change, and Kelly hoped it would last.

"I've a list of what is important in my life, Kelly," John said, breaking the silence and giving her that beautiful smile of his, "and you're right at the top."

She laughed and patted his hand. "Man, you were terrific tonight, John. I'm so happy for you. You were great! The things you said about me. I guess we have a mutual admiration society going on here. The fact that you think I'm so incredible and talented, makes me think so, too. You make me believe in myself. Oh my God, when you said, 'Kelly is perfect exactly as she is, or exactly as she chooses to be.' Wow. Someday, when I sit down to remember every nice thing people have said to me over the years – it will be a long time before anything beats what you said about me tonight."

"Thank you, Kelly," he said in that sexy, well-mannered way of his.

Her mind went off into a blissful mental reverie of pleasure then, as he quietly drove for a while. John always said such amazing things. No one could sweet talk like he could. He didn't say much, but everything he did say was so heartfelt.

The words he had spoken just this morning came back to her: *I want to dominate you, and protect you, and feed you, and keep you, and discipline you. I want to worship your body, and be first in your heart. I want to own you, Kelly Flynn.*

Pretty comprehensive indeed.

John pulled up to a stop light. With his foot on the brake, he reached over and took Kelly's hand, and began nibbling on her knuckles, biting softly with his teeth and licking. She swallowed. Man, his every touch was like a brand, marking her as his.

How did it come to this? she thought awed by the way she felt. *Right or wrong, for good or bad, there's no escaping the truth. John Taylor owns me, body and soul.*

She'd known of her submissive tendencies for years, but with him it was totally different. Kelly craved him with a powerful, overwhelming need. She longed to obey his every command, to comply with his every order, and to do anything, and everything he asked of her.

She needed to please him more than she needed to eat, or sleep or breathe. Heat burned her face and body, and her clit began to throb, simply with the thought of making him happy.

"You kind of have an oral thing going on, don't you, John?" she said, trying to minimize her instant powerful lust with a casual comment.

He gave her an intent knowing look and said seductively, "What do you think?"

Kelly's hips flexed, as she remembered the last time he had been between her legs, licking her, fingering her and sucking her to completion. "Oh yeah," she sighed contentedly. "You really do. But so do I," she said, raising her eyebrows, looking toward the bulge in his trousers, attempting to make him as hot as she was.

"Hummm," he said, staring at her mouth. "I noticed that, too."

Kelly almost squirmed, his interest was so flagrant. The way that man looked at her mouth was shameless, and utterly X rated. John loved her going down on him, which was just fine, because she loved that, too.

The light changed and he returned his attention to the road. "What are you doing tomorrow?" he asked.

"I need to wash some clothes, and do some other household chores, but then I'm going to work in the afternoon."

"Good," he said. "I'm taking you home tonight, getting some sleep and then I'll get some study done. I'm running late on an assignment. We can afford to not see each other for some of the day tomorrow. But how about I come and visit you at work at the speed dating site? Would that be good or bad for you?"

"Oh I'd love it," she said. "Yes, by all means, break my night up. Come any time after 9 p.m. People are pretty organized and it runs itself after that." She went on to explain where she was located, as it was a different venue each day of the week.

As John dropped her off and gave her a hungry, demanding kiss good bye, Kelly reflected that sadly, she'd have to wait hours and hours to see him again.

As it turned out she was wrong.

Chapter 12

Homicide Division

Monday morning, April 15th, Detective Lorenzo Martin of the Portland Police Bureau felt incredibly irritated, and was doing his best not to show it.

As he sat at his desk, he stared for a moment at his new partner who was absorbed in some paperwork. The woman was smart, and she was also keen. Lorenzo had to give her that. Lucille Irwin was about five-foot eight, a slim woman with a stern face, and thirty-five years old. Her hair was brown, short and really curly. He figured it was permed that way, because it didn't look natural. It made him wonder, was the woman trying to look less attractive? She wore little make up and her brown eyes were piercing, somewhat like a predatory bird.

So far so good – no problem.

So what was it about her that got on his nerves? Because she irritated the hell out of him, that was for sure. Lorenzo felt it was some constant impression that the woman unconsciously projected. Her manner toward him almost seemed accusatory. He felt off balance with her, as if he had to justify his actions all the time, when he was the senior officer and far more experienced detective.

Upon being introduced, Lorenzo had disliked his new partner instantly, and didn't that just irritate the hell out of him? He'd been working though his natural antipathy ever since. Lucille had held her role as a detective for four months in Burglary but with the retirement of Lorenzo's partner six weeks ago, she'd been moved in to become his replacement. The woman was new to Homicide, but acted as if she knew everything already.

God, I miss my partner, Gelly, he thought. *I wonder if he misses me?*

Lorenzo gave an internal snort and went back to work. Gelly was probably out fishing, enjoying some peace and his own company for a change.

Lorenzo had planned to pay his chief suspect, John Taylor a visit on Sunday, but there had been a murder Sunday morning at 1 a.m., and he and Lucille had been called in. Tommy Kinsley a 28 year old white male had been shot to death on the corner of NE 22nd and Washington. Five eye witnesses saw the murder and heard gunshots. Police had apprehended the suspect with so much evidence against him that his defense attorney's only chance would be to get on his knees to the prosecutor and beg.

The killer, another under thirty white male, had a spotless record and was still living at home.

With no discernible connection to the victim, the perp had been diagnosed with drug induced psychosis, substance currently unknown. The blood test would sort it out. How he got ahold of his father's revolver was anyone's guess, and that wasn't necessary for Lorenzo's part of the investigation. Right now he was going to hand this file over to the assistant DA with a second degree murder charge.

The stupid idiot would regain his addled senses in Maximum Security with probably no memory of the event, wondering where he went wrong. Well. He'd have years to try to figure it out. With diminished capacity and no priors he'd probably be found guilty of the lesser charge of manslaughter.

Lorenzo signed off on the last of his notes, shut the case file and stood up.

"How ya doing there, Lucille? Ready to go see the twisted, sadistic, nut job? I'm thinking Taylor will enlarge both your experience, and mine. He looks like a real piece of work."

"I thought we were going to wait for the search warrant?"

"Nope." He checked his watch. "I figure we've probably two hours max, before the paperwork comes through. Meanwhile let's go rattle his cage and see if we can get some answers."

Lucille leaned back in her chair, pressed her lips together and frowned. "Are you sure? Wouldn't it be better if we waited?"

Lorenzo took a deep, steadying breath, getting a firm hold of his rising temper. "I'm not waiting. You coming or not?"

Standing up, she said, "But what if the search warrant arrives?"

"Then our forensic team members will turn up with it, and start searching. But we'll already be on site, scoping the guy out. C'mon. It'll be fun." He said coaxingly, not wanting to field any of her shit just then. "Let's go."

The drive to John Taylor's bungalow in Aloha took very little time. Lorenzo briefly went over the details of the murder, and the game plan with his partner.

"Now look, Lucille, this is your first serious case here, where the bastard can wriggle out of this. We have to do things properly, you get me? Right now we have all our little ducks lined up in a row. So when we're with this guy, you let me ask the questions, okay? Just listen to how I work things. Everyone does it differently, and that's okay, but while you're new, I want to you just watch and learn, right?"

Jesus, Lorenzo thought irritably. *She's making that face again, the tight mouth with prune lips of disapproval. Christ, this woman sends me nuts.*

"Fine," Lucille said, looking somewhat mutinous. "I'll take notes."

Chapter 13

John's House

Around 10a.m. Monday morning, John's doorbell rang.

He'd been sitting in front of the computer working on his assignment, so he stood up and looked out the window. A man and woman were outside, and he could tell immediately that they were cops. John never used the front door, because it opened directly into his bedroom, so he went through the side door kitchen area, and walked around to the front porch.

"Can I help you officers?" he said.

"Mr. John Taylor?" A crisp tenor voice sounded from the man.

"Yes."

"I'm Detective Lorenzo Martin of the Portland Police Bureau, and this is my partner, Detective Lucille Irwin." Both pulled out their badges to show John, and he nodded.

"How can I help you?"

"Can we come inside?" Detective Martin asked. John subtly stiffened, naturally resistant to having anyone in his home. Martin must have picked it up immediately because he added, "We need to talk, and it'd be better not to speak out here."

John nodded once more, turned and walked back through the kitchen and into his home. The detectives followed.

"Have a seat," John said. "Can I get you a drink? Coffee? Tea?"

"No, thanks," Martin said, as he and Detective Irwin sat at his small, square, four chair, wooden table.

John sat down too, and studied the obviously senior Detective, Martin.

The man was a couple inches shy of six feet, and thirtyish, the same age as John would guess his partner to be. Detective Martin was well built and wore the comfortable, commanding appearance of a seasoned cop. There was a Hispanic heritage somewhere in the man's background. Martin looked street-wise and dangerous with his strong no-nonsense expression, and dark intelligent eyes that raked the room.

John recognized and instantly related to the Dom tendencies of the detective. The man had a predatory aspect to his manner, the desire to hunt, to seek and take down a criminal. He liked him for it.

It was subtle in his body language, but John was well aware that Detective Martin clearly didn't like him. Now why was that?

With her lips pressed firmly together, the woman appeared annoyed. She was thin and her features seemed severe. John wondered if the two detectives had been quarreling, because she appeared to be in disagreement about something. She wore dark blue slacks over dark flats, a light blue uniform shirt. Her lightweight Portland Police jacket didn't hide the gun clipped to her belt. Detective Martin was dressed in a similar fashion.

John managed to maintain his customary impassive expression when Detective Irwin met his eyes, but damn. The woman *really* didn't like him. Hummm. This didn't look good at all.

"I understand that you have been the victim of some recent attacks?" Detective Martin asked.

"Yes," John said. "Twice in the last two months my car has been vandalized."

"And your garbage bin was strewn over your lawn last week?"

"Yes."

"And three months ago someone used red spray paint to write, 'Bad Seed' on your home. That was the first in this series of attacks?"

"Yes."

John had reported every incident, detailing and taking photos of each event. Even though he hated his father, one aspect had been impressed upon him as a child that he actually agreed with: Stay on the right side of the law. John faithfully reported any occurrence because of that. Also his father was a judge, and it was plausible that one of his father's disgruntled clients had it in for him.

"Do you have any idea why someone would want to do any of these things, Mr. Taylor?"

"No." John studied Detective Martin with slightly narrowed eyes. The man had his reports, and he knew who his father was. So why was he here? What was he looking for?

"Mr. Taylor, can you confirm for us that you're a client of Professor Maria Christina Lopez?"

"Yes." *Now this is an unexpected and disturbing line of inquiry.*

"When did you last see her? And when did you last speak to her?"

"I last saw Professor Lopez on Tuesday the 19th of March," John said, noticing that Detective Irwin was taking notes. "I last spoke to her around 3 p.m. on Friday the 5th of April."

"Did anything unusual happen when you saw her? Did she seem the same to you? What did you talk about?"

John gave Detective Martin a considering look. "You know that I see Professor Lopez in a professional capacity? She's my psychologist. I've been seeing her twice a month for four years, something that you must also be aware of. Nothing unusual happened on either date. May I ask what this is about?" he asked calmly.

Sitting perfectly motionless, John wanted to kiss Kelly again for teaching him how to manage people. He was a Dom, and these detectives were his naked subs and his responsibility. It made everything so much easier to imagine that he was the one in control, observing *them,* and noting their every thought or action.

Already he'd been analyzing both of these police officers, but what he discovered so far didn't bode well. Not for him, and not for Maria.

God, I hope Maria is alright, John thought. *With my all-encompassing love affair with Kelly, seeing my psychologist hadn't seemed as critical as it had been previously. I should have gone over there to find out why she didn't return any of my calls.*

Detective Martin rubbed his chin and then straightened, looking directly at John. "On Sunday morning, the 7th of April, between the hours of midnight to five a.m., Professor Maria Christina Lopez was murdered in her home."

John Taylor blinked, and remained utterly still and quiet. He found himself falling into that detached state of unreality he went into whenever he received a severe shock. It was a protective survival mechanism, and he knew this, too. His psychologist, Maria Lopez, had helped him to discover and be aware of the unconscious tools he used.

Maria's dead. Murdered.

Detective Martin said, "Mr. Taylor can you tell me where you were about a week ago, between midnight and five a.m. on Sunday morning, April 7th?"

John was experiencing a momentary mental fog. Maria Christina Lopez, had been a friend, and a confidant, and she had helped him, and now she was dead.

Maria, he thought. *I'm so sorry. Was your death my fault?*

"Mr. Taylor?"

"I'm sorry?"

"I asked where you were about a week ago, between midnight and five a.m. on Sunday morning, April 7th."

"In my home."

Martin's dark eyes were bright with interest as he leaned slightly forward and asked, "Can anyone substantiate that?"

John's first thought was for Kelly. Maria was dead, he'd put that aside and deal with that later. Kelly had been with him all that night. But did he really want to get her involved in this? Out of his depth, he decided he needed professional advice. There was no question in his mind that these detectives considered him a suspect in Maria's murder.

"I believe, Detective Martin, that I should seek the advice of counsel at this point," John said. "Do you have any objection if I call my lawyer?"

Detective Martin rolled his shoulder's, in a loosening manner, leaned back in his chair, and inhaled deeply. "Fine," he said. "You do that."

John told the two detectives to make themselves at home. Then he went into his bedroom, shut the door, and called his lawyer.

The firm who represented him didn't manage criminal cases, but knew a reputable firm that did. John instructed his lawyer, Marion Segal, to arrange everything. He explained that he had an alibi for the time of the murder, but as Kelly Flynn would be considered a hostile witness, he needed a professional to help her through the statement giving process.

The next consideration was Kelly's safety. John instructed his lawyer to get a 24 hour guard arranged for Kelly – the best there was, at any cost. If someone started by spray painting his home, then moved to vandalizing his car, and ended up killing his psychologist, they were clearly escalating. Kelly could be in danger.

The final priority was that he didn't intend to drag his club into this, so he didn't want Kelly to mention where they had met up Saturday night. John knew that Kelly wanted her sexual kinks to remain confidential so it was important that she tell only what was required and did not offer more information. His lawyer would help her there.

Ever since he'd began the enterprise, he'd kept his own life separate from The Basement – not for his safety, but for the club's protection. John didn't want his father to know that he owned it – particularly as they'd already rejected his father's membership application twice.

Due to a long term, uneasy truce, with his powerful and dangerous father, John was naturally paranoid and security conscious, so he never kept anything related to the club in his house. The money trail showed that he owned the building, but that was an investment. He'd bought the building in order to create a safe place for the club, but no one knew that.

John instructed his lawyer to call the club Manager, Colin Wilkins, to apprise him of the circumstances. If Colin wanted to contact him, then he'd have to go through his law firm. From now on, until this crime was solved, John would be on lock down and nowhere near The Basement. Colin could easily manage without him.

With the phone to his ear, John opened the door to the kitchen area. Despite his grief and tension he almost laughed out loud. The two detectives had clearly been arguing. Lucille Irwin looked as though she had been eating lemons. Lorenzo Martin was worked up enough to jump into a boxing ring and utterly destroy the crowd favorite.

"My lawyer is asking if I'm going down to the station with you?" he asked.

"Yes," Lorenzo growled.

John relayed this information to his lawyer. And then, to his complete surprise, a number of cops arrived on his doorstep.

With a search warrant.

Chapter 14

Lucille's Crusade

Lucille drove into the driveway of the elegant Flynn home in her own car and while off the clock from work.

Why is everyone so blind? she wondered. *Why can't they see what kind of man Taylor is?*

It was early Wednesday morning, two days after executing the search warrant on Taylor's lair. That evil man! Who reads books like, "*Screw the Roses, Send Me The Thorns?*" Not to mention the numerous quotes he had from the infamous sadist, the Marquis de Sade? His lawyer explained that Taylor was studying an ethics and religion course, and questions like that were not relevant in any case.

Not relevant? The man was a wicked sadistic murderer, and he'd been let off – all because of an impressionable young woman.

All the evidence from searching Taylor's home proved that John Taylor had killed Professor Maria Christina Lopez. There had been so much proof, all carefully hidden in the garage. Items from the victim's home, the woman's purse, the gasoline cans. Sure there were no fingerprints, but the man had obviously used gloves.

Then there was his psychological profile and his violent and utterly disgusting history. Yet the evil bastard had an alibi from Kelly Flynn, a twenty-four year old woman who was no doubt guilty of perjury. That was no surprise.

What woman hadn't been brainless and stupid when in they were in love?

Lucille got out of the car, carrying the file on the suspect, John Taylor. The asshole was impossibly attractive – there was no question about that. Young Ms. Flynn wouldn't have a chance against a handsome, inhuman, manipulative sociopathic monster like him.

As she mounted the steps and knocked on the door, Lucille reflected that she was breaking a number of privacy laws by doing what she planned. Yet her conscience was clear.

The door opened and Lucille met Kelly's parents. The mother was a graceful stunner with her black hair, deep blue eyes and pale skin. Elegantly dressed in a peach silk sheath dress, with pearls and an open toe high heel, she looked like she was about to dine at the White House. The father gave a genial impression with his stocky build, orange hair and pale blue eyes. He was wearing equally expensive, yet more casual clothes.

"Detective Irwin?" Kelly's mother held out one slim hand. "How do you do?"

Mr. Flynn also shook her hand and then added, "You said you wanted to see us on a matter of some importance?"

"Yes."

"Come with us into the study," he said. "We can be comfortable there."

Lucille Irwin followed them into a gracious and welcoming room, filled with books, leather chairs, expensive paintings and Oriental rugs. They all sat down, and Lucille told them about the recent murder, and how the police felt that they were certain of the perpetrator. However, there had been the issue of an unbreakable alibi.

"I'm sorry," Mr. Flynn said. "I can't see how this has anything to do with us. How can we help you?

Lucille then showed the Flynn's, John Taylor's police file. They, of course, knew nothing about how their daughter had been acting as an alibi for the man, and they were shocked to hear it. Kelly had given a statement saying that she was alone at John Taylor's home with him from midnight and five a.m., April 7th on a Sunday morning. This was also deeply disturbing, of course.

Lucille explained that all the evidence pointed to Taylor as the murderer, and how she felt certain that their daughter was lying to the police to protect him.

The file was shocking enough. John Taylor had an extensive psychiatric history. Right from a child he had been difficult: Breaking another child's arm at school, torturing hundreds of animals, being unmanageable and violent at home. Taylor's parent's, frightened for their life, threw him out of their house at age thirteen.

Three psychiatrists had diagnosed John Taylor with "Conduct disorder." This was a disorder of childhood and adolescence that involves long-term behavior problems such as defiant or impulsive behavior, drug use and criminal activity. In Taylor's case, he had been using and selling hard drugs. Statements written included the fact that John Taylor was an "anti-social personality" and was "manipulative and capable of violence, and perhaps even murder."

Taylor's early offenses had been locked away and couldn't be used in evidence. Yet, Lucille had felt that if she were Kelly's parents, she'd have wanted to know what was going on.

Mrs. Flynn, alarmed and indignant, confided to Lucille that she. "had always known there was something wrong with John Taylor." She made numerous statements such as "I knew it from the first, didn't I, Rodney? I told you so!"

Wearing jeans and a T shirt, with her hair back in a ponytail, Kelly arrived about an hour after Lucille had, walking into the study with a broad smile and a cheerful, "Hey, what's up? Is everything okay? From the message I got I was worried that the house was on fire." When she saw Lucille, she visibly paled.

"Kelly," her mother said. "We want to talk to you about John Taylor."

"Marguerite," her father said. "Let me handle this. Come here, Kelly, honey."

Lucille watched as Kelly's father showed her the file, and explained how Taylor was a charming, handsome man, but it seemed that they had all been fooled as he was actually dangerous and manipulative. Kelly, Lucille was glad to see, listened carefully to everything that her father said. She asked to read the file on her own for a bit. With her back to them all, while sitting on the large brown leather davenport, she read through the folder.

"Thank you," Kelly said somberly, as she gave the file back to the detective. Lucille could see that the young woman was extremely pale and shaken. God knows, Lucille herself, older and more experienced, as well as a police officer, had wanted to throw up.

"Now, darling," her father began. "Detective Irwin has come here wanting to know the truth. Were you really with Mr. Taylor between midnight and five a.m. on Sunday morning, April 7th?"

The young woman blushed very red. "Yes, I was, Daddy."

There was an incredibly awkward silence, and then Mr. Flynn cleared his throat and said, "But were you asleep? Could he have slipped out at any time?"

Lucille had to hand it to the young woman. Even flushed with embarrassment, Kelly Flynn still met her father's eyes.

"Daddy," she said, self-conscious, but with her head held high. "John and I didn't sleep between the hours of midnight and five a.m." She licked her lips nervously. "I was with him every single minute of that time."

Kelly's mother moaned, and her father, clenching his jaw, remained stoic.

"Silly, girl," Lucille burst out. "Why would you protect him? Can't you see what he is? Love is blind. He'll ruin you, honey. He will! Don't waste your life with an evil sadistic bastard like him!"

Kelly jumped to her feet. "I'm not lying for John," she said with her light blue eyes flashing. "I don't believe any of this stuff in this file. It's all lies! I was there when he broke that kids arm – there were three of them and he was attacked by older, bigger bullies. I don't know why that falsehood is in this file, but I know John. He's a wonderful man and I'm going to marry him!'

Lucille was shocked by the fury in Kelly's vehement reply, but before she could speak Kelly's mother cried out, "You will not marry him! I don't care how much money he has. I forbid you to see him anymore. He's an evil man."

The arguments went back and forth with so many nasty things said on both sides. Lucille began to feel that she had made a serious mistake in coming to the Flynn's house.

One couldn't get someone to see unless they agreed to open their eyes. Kelly Flynn, like so many vulnerable young women everywhere, had chosen to be blind.

As Lucille let herself out of the house, she overheard Kelly screaming, "I won't give him up! John is estranged from his parents. Well, now I am, too! I don't want to see either of you again until you accept that John is the one I love, and the man I'm going to marry."

God, Lucille thought, feeling a little tendril of guilt. *I hope I didn't make things worse. But what could be worse than being under the thumb of a manipulative, psychopathic killer?*

Chapter 15

Kelly Confronts John

Wednesday afternoon Kelly sat alone in her apartment in a weird and detached state of numb.

Kelly had a favorite chair. It was upholstered in corduroy fabric predominantly in various shades of green, with finer lines of red, white and yellow stripes, and a matching foot stool. She'd bought it on impulse, and its ridiculous colors matched nothing else in her apartment, but something about that silly chair always cheered her up.

Not that it was able to cheer her up now.

Chamomile tea with honey was what she was drinking. It was supposed to be calming, but also hadn't worked yet. A knot had formed in her belly, a hard tangle of emotions and anxiety. The words from the police detective repeated in her mind. *Can't you see what he is? Love is blind. He'll ruin you, Kelly. Don't waste your life with an evil sadistic bastard like him!*

How had that detective done it? How had she put so many grains of truth in those few hateful sentences? Because John was a sadist, and love was blind, at least Kelly certainly had found it to be so.

There was too much that was going through her mind, and so she had called work and begged to be allowed the night off due to a 'personal crisis.' The Speed Dating coordinator job wasn't easy to replace, and Kelly hadn't given them much time, but her boss, Tammy, said she'd fill in for her. Thank God.

She took another sip, trying to 'be in the moment' and enjoy her tea. At least she had caught up on her sleep last night. John had told her that he rarely slept well. Was that because his conscience bothered him?

Her phone buzzed, letting her know that a text had arrived, and she put her favorite yellow primrose flower cup down on the teak side table to answer it. It was from John and it said:

R u going to tell me what's wrong?

She instantly texted back:

Jesus, are you psychic?

When it comes to you, yes,

came the reply. And then:

I'm coming over.

John would know that she hadn't gone to work perhaps, from speaking with her security detail, and he'd have put two and two together.

Kelly spent her time while waiting for John while tidying up a few things, not that the place had been a mess. Being in love made her so happy that she didn't need to sleep, hardly needed to eat, and she had boundless energy, so her little apartment was immaculate. She was still in love, but she was confused and upset, too.

John buzzed and Kelly unlocked the apartment entry way. She unlocked her own door, too, but returned immediately back to curl her legs up under her, within the security of her favorite chair.

As John strode confidently through into her apartment, his authoritative eyes fastened on her, his gaze searching her face, noticing everything. Outside Kelly knew that she looked the same.

Inside she was different.

John shut the door and stood still with his arms at his sides.

Kelly just looked at him, aching to touch him, but the knot was still there, twisting in her gut and she felt uncertain. God, John was beautiful. Sooooo freaking beautiful with those dark intent eyes, his strong jaw, and thick wavy hair. What was it about his face? How could such pretty, almost feminine features look so masculine? Kelly was staring, once more ensnared by his dominant male energy. John simply took her breath away.

Kelly had been strong and angry and certain when with her parents, but later she'd begun to distrust her own judgment. Lies! That police file was full of lies. Or was it? How had she come to doubt John?

"Come here to me, Kelly," he said, opening his arms wide.

Kelly hesitated.

John lowered his arms. "I see," he said. Then he went to the breakfast counter and leaned against it with his arms crossed.

There were long moments where neither said a thing.

John inhaled a deep, lung filling breath. "Kelly, I can see you're upset but you're going to want to think about how you're going to deal with it," he said with a dangerous edge to his voice. "No matter what has happened, you're still my sub. My respectful sub, remember?"

The recollection of living without John for a week stabbed her, and the pain of that memory snapped her out of her anxious mental fog.

"I remember, John. I'm sorry. I'm just a little freaked out right now."

John smiled then, and his implacable, remote expression disappeared. "Good girl," he said. "Kelly, look at me." He waited until she had her eyes on him. "I'm the same person I was yesterday, and the day before. I still love you. I still want to marry you. You're still the best thing that has ever happened to me. Whatever occurred this morning changes none of those things."

John stood up, straightening abruptly, and Kelly unconsciously flinched. He noticed, of course, and Kelly felt terrible, but right now he scared her. He walked to the couch a good ten feet away from the colorful chair she had curled up into, and sat down.

"Tell me what happened, Kelly."

It took a little while, but she explained about the file and the detective who had come to see her parents. "So, I turned my back to them, John and I made a copy of your police record by taking pictures with the camera in my phone."

"You clever girl," John cried out and clapped his hands in admiration. "I should have known. Do you have any idea just how smart you are? Later, when you feel better, I'm going to reward your quick thinking in a more substantial way."

Kelly remained tense, still unable to uncurl from her chair. It was a sexual promise, and his warm approving smile made her want to melt, but she simply couldn't unwind. The knot inside her was still there. The reports on him had totally freaked her out.

"Show me the pictures you took," he said. "I want to see what has you looking at me like I'm Frankenstein."

Kelly came and sat down next to John on the couch, and showed him each of the photos she had taken. The more she showed him, the happier it seemed to make him – except for the dead animals. No one could be cheerful over that. This unexpected joyful response loosened something inside that she had been holding tight.

"Why are you so happy?" she asked.

John smiled. "I had a full police record check four years ago, when I was starting up the club. None of this stuff was in my police records back then. None of it. This is all juvenile stuff, and is supposed to be sealed. It was sealed. So who put it there? There's only one person who could have done it, my father. But why? It's a clear violation of our agreement. Isn't he afraid that I'll retaliate with the evidence of his abuse?"

John frowned and pursed his lips. "I don't like it. The balance of power has changed somehow and it was always a delicate balance." He put his hand to his chin, and rubbed it as he considered. "What could have happened I wonder?"

"Then it's all lies then, John?" she asked eagerly. "Something your father put in the file?"

"Not all," he said. "Just almost all lies."

"Oh."

"I've never taken drugs, probably because I've never had friends," John said. "I suppose I would have tried drugs and alcohol if I had been a normal sort of kid going to parties and such. The opportunity was simply never there. I certainly never sold drugs."

He chuckled, and shifted back further on the couch. "I've never even seen them. You know yourself that I broke that boys arm in self-defense. These accounts of incidents of violence can be easily challenged. They are all twisted stories, embellished to make me look worse. The psychiatrist's reports, well, let's just say my father has a lot of influence. I was seen by a crap load of psychiatrists as a child."

Kelly felt his penetrating gaze reveal everything she was thinking as he searched her face. She trusted him completely; at least she had until this morning. Would John lie to her? Could he? And if he did, how would she know?

But did she really want to hear the truth? That was the real question.

Noooo! A craven animal voice wailed from somewhere inside her. *I can't face it! I can't!*

Couldn't she turn back time and somehow un-know what she knew now? More than anything she wished Detective Irwin had never visited her parents. Then Kelly could have gone along as always, and nothing would have changed.

The truth – if it was what Kelly was afraid it might be – would be the one thing that could break her and John apart forever.

Standing up abruptly, John began to pace from the kitchenette, across the living room to the hall, and back again. "You're upset over the pictures of tortured animals that are in that file."

"Yes," she rasped in a hoarse voice. "You didn't... did you?"

Her turned and looked at her with narrowed eyes and an intense stare. "And if I did?"

Oh God, she realized suddenly. *If John has tortured animals, I don't think I can possibly love him anymore.*

Chapter 16

John's Greatest Sin

Kelly simply couldn't speak, and she couldn't move.

John was a sadist, she knew that. He enjoyed causing heightened anxiety, torment, and pain, and he particularly loved tears. He'd said that because he couldn't cry, his subs cried for him. Or was it begging he wanted? No, she remembered suddenly. What had he told her once? That he could only connect to people through pain.

"Kelly?" John said authoritatively. "Answer me."

"I don't know, John," she said, trying to find the words that would explain what she felt. "I think I'd look at you and not see you anymore. I think I'd just keep seeing those poor animals."

He strode back and sat down at the other end of the couch. With a large expulsion of air, he said, "My father tortured animals for a while. That wasn't his real kink. I think he did it partially to break me. I ran away once, not long after being taken from my aunt Brenda. The police brought me back. I tried to tell them about my father, but they didn't believe me. Why would they? Judge Taylor was well respected, and he had a golden tongue that explained everything. Who would believe a kid?"

"Besides," John explained. "My father kept telling me to do exactly as he said or he'd kill Aunt Brenda. I believed him. Even though I wasn't allowed to see her, I loved her too much to imagine a world without her in it."

He scrubbed his face with his hands, and Kelly realized she had never seen him display these anxious human reactions before. He was usually so calm, measured and self-contained.

"My father made me watch as he tortured cats and dogs, and he wanted me to do it, too," John said. "I have to say, I never once enjoyed it. They were under our care, they couldn't speak. It was wrong on every level. As dumb creatures they didn't understand, either. It's not like whipping a human being for punishment or pleasure. The most I did, was whip them, and that was over a period of about six months when I was eight."

Kelly noticed that John's voice had become dry and hoarse. He looked tense and uncomfortable.

Jumping up off the couch, he strode to the little kitchenette and before he could start looking for a glass, Kelly said, "Right hand cupboard over the sink. There's Coke in the fridge."

He got down a glass and turned on the tap. "Water's good," he said. Swallowing the entire glass full, John resumed his initial place on arrival, leaning with his back against the kitchen counter, but this time his hands were on either side of him, gripping the countertop.

"My father caught me playing with a puppy." John shut his eyes for a moment. His expression became grim and his hands on the counter whitened with the strength that he was gripping it. "It was a little brown mutt, and because of a dog's naturally generous nature, that little pup gave me unconditional love."

His voice became strange and strained, as if filled with some undefined, yet explosive raw emotion. It kind of frightened her. "I used to call it 'Pup' as if that was its name, and the trusting little creature came when called. It was my only friend. Animals are so much better than humans sometimes, you know? So generous with their affection and so loyal."

He ran a hand through his hair. "I don't think I ever saw my father so angry. I won't go into it, but it took three days before I did what he asked. He made me kill that puppy, Kelly, and I swear I did it willingly in the end – as quickly and as painlessly as possible. I refused to torture it. That's what he really wanted."

Kelly saw that John's face had become impassive once more. His eyes seemed empty, distant and remote.

"It was a turning point," he said, "and it was the last time I can remember ever being able to cry. I cried for hours over that puppy, Kelly, but I was simply unable to cry after that. It was like everything in me died. I was black and dead inside."

Kelly's eyes stung and she felt too shocked to move, or to speak, or to even make a sound. Tears welled and began to roll in warm trails down her cheeks.

John came back to the couch, and sank down into it with a defeated look. Like he was contagious or diseased, he sat at the other end of the couch, again as far from her as possible.

"I refused anything my father wanted after that, no matter what he did to me," he said. "I was cut off and completely disconnected. I think I went a little mad. I was an eight year old having a nervous breakdown, I guess. All emotion, sensation or pain seemed the same to me then. My father punished me, but he couldn't touch me, not the hidden person inside. The real me just went away, I guess."

John's hands were balled into tight fists and his body was tense, his expression empty. Kelly found that she was still afraid of him, frightened by the pain and violence inside of him.

"By then he had what he wanted," John said. "Evidence that I'd been torturing animals. Proof that I was screwed up and mentally ill. I had so many psychiatric interviews where I sat sullenly and couldn't speak or explain the dead animals. I wasn't able to tell, do you see? How can an eight year old explain that his dad, a prominent district judge, was the real psychopath of the family?"

"But those pictures," Kelly said, "of animals…?"

"Never," John said, leaning back against the couch, appearing as if he was trying very hard to force his tense body to relax. "I never cut one, or burned them or any of the other despicable things in those pictures. I did whip them for about six months, as I already explained. I still feel so ashamed and guilty for that, and for killing my only friend, poor little Pup. I planned to eventually tell you, but of all my sins, these are honestly the last ones I would have spoken to you about. These are the ones I burn with the most shame for."

"Trust me, Kelly," he said. "The disturbed, angry and hate-filled child that I was, is not who I am now."

She saw that John had more to tell her, but how much more could she take? Already she felt like throwing up.

Chapter 17

Vulnerable

⋞ ⋟

Kelly steeled herself.

John took a deep breath. "I'll not discuss this right now, but I'll give you an idea," he said. "My father made me call him, Sir. That's why I hate that title."

"You've probably guessed that not only physical abuse but sexual abuse was part of my childhood, too," John said, standing up and resuming his pacing. It was as if he was too full of explosive energy to sit still.

"It was pretty ugly, and until you came along, I'd cut myself off from sex. Sex was one big trigger. But this is what I want you to understand. You know what I've found in life, Kelly? It doesn't matter what was done to you. These things can hurt, yes. Being a victim is always difficult. It destroys any chance of self-esteem or self-love. Yet. in truth, nothing burns like knowing you've done wrong."

"Victimizing others hurts far worse than any pain you can imagine, Kelly. Was I ashamed to be sexually abused? Yes, but I was a victim and that dishonor belongs to my father and my mother. If I ever really want to squirm with humiliation and regret, I simply recall the terrible things I myself have done. Because those shameful things were my choice, no matter what the circumstance. Those were the moments I victimized another and made the decision to do wrong."

John looked up at Kelly and their gaze met.

"I learned not be a bully," he said. "It would have been so easy to go down that road, to take all the hate and violence I had inside and put it onto others. I wanted to cause pain to anyone and everyone, Kelly. I wanted them to hurt, just like I hurt inside. But the goodness of that puppy taught me right from wrong. That trusting, loving little puppy never doubted me, even as I killed it. Do you have any idea what that was like? I felt as if I was killing myself. Perhaps committing that sin against an innocent did kill a part of me. It was horrific, and it was shameful, but it was a lesson I've never forgotten."

John spun on one foot toward her suddenly, and Kelly, too stunned to think, didn't flinch this time. "Where's the bathroom?" he asked her.

Kelly told him, and she was left alone, while her brain processed all John had said. What would it take to make an eight year old child kill his only friend? Jesus, no wonder John had been seeing a counselor regularly. Was he screwed up or what? But he'd only ever been considerate of her. John cared about her, and sadist or not, he didn't hurt others. Not really.

John seemed to be spending a long time in that bathroom. Again, she suspected that he was doing that for her, letting her think over all that he'd said.

When he returned, he seemed much more composed. He sat back on the couch, again far from her.

"André helped me direct my needs, Kelly," he said. "He taught me how to use my sadistic nature to cause pleasure. That changed everything for me. I could control a scene, bring a sub to the bliss of sub space, and I could connect with others, finally. I needed the connection, Kelly because no matter what has happened in life, a person can't really be human without that vital link to another human being. Do you know what I'm talking about, Kelly?"

Mind reeling, she just stared at him and nodded.

"And now I'm connected to you," he said in a raw, low voice. "I always feel connected to you. I don't need to cause pain, I don't need anything anymore – I only need you. I've gone through the fire, and I've come out the other end. For the first time in my life I'm genuinely happy. That's all because of you, Kelly."

Kelly looked at John and her chest ached to see the openness in his expression. The tough, sadistic Dom, the man known as Father John, was defenseless because of her. He was vulnerable... but only to her.

The tight painful knot inside her loosened, and then disappeared.

Instantly Kelly felt an overwhelming all-consuming need to touch John, to ease his pain, and to make him feel better about himself. Ever attentive and aware of her desires, he put a hand out to her.

When Kelly took it she felt a burning sensation flow right through her, like scalding water – only it didn't hurt. It was a hyper-awareness and a strong, almost spiritual bond. It felt good.

This was her John, and she loved him. He went through so much as a child. It was a wonder he was sane at all.

Smiling sympathetically, as if knowing what she was thinking and how she felt, he pulled her gently toward him, and she came willingly then, cuddling up onto his lap. She melted into him as John stroked her back and hair, and gave her light, soft kisses on her head and neck.

Soothing, but not sexual. The images of dead animals were still vividly in each other's mind.

"Thank you, Kelly, for listening, and understanding," he murmured. "You really do make me feel human. You force me to accept my own goodness. You're enough to make me believe that maybe there is a God, because only God could create someone as pure and perfect as you. Perhaps God has forgiven me. I dare to hope that maybe I deserve to be happy, and to find peace. Did he send you to me, do you think, Kelly?"

"If he did, he knew that you were just the right person for me, too," Kelly said and her eyes stung as tears welled once more. "We make each other happy, John. I love you so much."

And with that they hugged each other. They pressed their bodies as close together as possible, and fully connected once more.

Chapter 18

A Walk in the Park

Homicide Detective Lorenzo Martin walked down the street, enjoying the mild weather. April in Portland was often wet or overcast and that had more or less been the case so far this month. Today it was sunny and a balmy fifty-seven degrees. Consequently Lorenzo was happy to take the mile walk to his favorite restaurant for lunch.

As he neared the Portland Police Bureau entry, a familiar silver Mercedes sports car pulled up beside him, and the passenger window rolled down.

"Detective Martin?"

What does this fuck head want? Lorenzo frowned, suddenly re-thinking the whole walk thing. "What do you want, Taylor?" Lorenzo said, making no attempt to hide his irritation.

"To show you something."

"Is that so?"

"Hop in."

"I don't think so."

Lorenzo's eyes narrowed as Taylor, the asshole, chuckled. "Okay, fair enough," Taylor said. "How about we go for a drive in your car then?"

Curious now, Lorenzo acquiesced and, using his ID badge, he opened the gates, letting his suspect, John Taylor, into the cops' private parking lot. Taylor parked and got out of his car. It beeped when he locked it.

"I would prefer not to have your partner in on this," Taylor said.

Lorenzo raised his eyebrows at that, but nodded his agreement. He was always happy to do something without a Lucille. "If you're going in my car, and not sitting behind the perp protection in the back seat, I'll have to search you for weapons."

Studying his suspect in his watchful cop way, Lorenzo caught just a brush of an odd shift in Taylor's features in response to this demand. It was a strange combination of possible emotions, anxiety, tension, and then resignation perhaps. Lorenzo had observed that stiffening tension earlier when he had acquainted Taylor with a physical search before taking him downtown.

Did the man have something to hide? Or did he just hate to be touched? Lorenzo wondered.

Without a word, Taylor obediently put his hands against the police cruiser 'assuming the position.' *Fast learner,* Lorenzo thought. Utterly motionless, Taylor allowed Lorenzo to search him.

"Alright, you're clean," Lorenzo said. "Hop in."

Lorenzo's jaw tightened as John Taylor, the most likely suspect for the brutal murder of Professor Maria Christina Lopez got into his police cruiser.

Chapter 19

Holladay Park

"Where to?"

"Holladay Park."

"Fine," Lorenzo said with another frown.

While on the job, Lorenzo had found there were bad criminals – the kind that were just plain BAD. And there were mad criminals, the real fruitcakes, and they were just plain MAD. But this guy, he had to be the full deal, both BAD and MAD. And they were the worst of all.

What was this good-looking bastard up to? Christ on a fucking cracker, the man should have been a model. Lorenzo never usually gave the subject much thought, but it seemed to him that a man like John Taylor would be a serious chick magnet. What was the saying? Beauty is only skin deep, but ugly cuts right to the bone?

Well, in that case John Taylor, the sociopathic murdering bastard, was both seriously beautiful and bone deep ugly.

Taylor was wearing blue jeans of some expensive type that was out of Lorenzo's pay scale. A shiny name brand button down shirt, and casual leather shoes and matching belt that also looked above his pay grade finished this ensemble. Casual as it seemed, John Taylor, with his dark handsome features and nice clothes, looked like he had just hopped off a catwalk.

Both men remained silent as Lorenzo drove, and he was happy for the peace.

Bloody Lucille drove him nuts with her constant complaining chatter. The woman would subtly grumble that he was late back from lunch, but tough titties. Lorenzo parked the white and black police cruiser and got out. Taylor got out, too, and without a word, started walking at a pretty fast stride. Where was the bastard going?

Well, that was okay with Lorenzo. He could use the fresh air. Keeping up with Taylor's brutal stride, Lorenzo walked behind him with an open careful eye.

Holladay Park could be a little sketchy at times as it had been the end of the line for MAX's Free Rail Zone (which was no longer free). It was also across the street from the mall. Mostly it was filled with harmless transients. There were also high school kids skipping class, or else hanging out there after school.

Lorenzo checked his watch, surprised to find that he'd been diverted from his job completely, just by enjoying a good pace and watching the people go by. Christ, they had been walking for over a half an hour.

"Hey, Taylor," Lorenzo said. "Alright already. Why Holladay park? What are you going to show me? Or are we here to talk? If so I think we're far enough away from anyone. No one can overhear us, you paranoid bastard."

Taylor laughed at this masterful and engaging description of himself. And despite having a casual stroll with a killer, Lorenzo found he was smiling back at him anyway. It was a nice day for it. As the weather was warmish, various people, mothers and their kids were hanging out and having a picnic. There were children playing near a fountain, screaming and laughing as kids do. The young kids were all running wild with the other kids. It was almost like summertime.

John Taylor drew closer, so that both men were walking together along a little pathway. "So," Taylor said. "I see that your partner, Lucille Irwin violated protocol and showed my file to my girlfriend's parents. That was rather overstepping her bounds, wasn't it?"

"Yeah? So? Make a complaint."

Taylor stopped suddenly, giving Lorenzo a crooked smile and a shrewd knowing look. "I didn't think you knew anything about it. Irwin went off on her own, didn't she?" Taylor clearly read Lorenzo's expression of chagrin. "Ha! I thought so. I bet you tore her a new one, didn't you? Well. Good for you."

Lorenzo tried to maintain a disinterested face, but this weird bastard was just a little too acute. How did he know? It was like he was a mind-reader. Lorenzo said nothing.

"Anyway, I should make a complaint," Taylor said, and his tone abruptly became fierce. "Your partner upset Kelly."

Lorenzo slowed his walk in order to study Taylor's body language. *Now that right there is the most honest and clear emotion I've seen from the icy bastard,* Lorenzo thought. *Lucille upset Taylor's girl. Interesting.*

"My lawyer feels, as lawyers often do, that suing the police bureau would be a good move," John Taylor added, once more using that calm, unreadable expression of his. "Apparently I could have her charged for some breach or another in the Privacy Act and she'd lose her job. It would all go to court, of course, and it would no doubt be pretty ugly. If I did that, some of that dirt may just fall on you."

Lorenzo came to a full stop. "Listen Taylor, what the fuck do you want? Are you trying to threaten me or something? Because I don't give a rats."

The truth was, Lorenzo did care. If this bastard went to court, it would begin a long tedious investigative process with numerous irritating and time wasting interviews – not unlike a witch hunt. No matter what the outcome, it would end up looking bad on his own record.

"Actually," Taylor added turning and starting the long walk back to the police cruiser. "Now that I've cooled down I've decided not to make an issue out of it. I was pretty happy to find out what was in that file. It made fascinating reading."

"Is that right?" Lorenzo growled. "Well I can't see how there would be any surprises. You ought to know what you've done, unless you're getting a bit demented. Do you think dementia is setting in, Taylor? Because maybe you should see a doctor. Oh, that's right, you'll have to find one first. You already killed your shrink."

Taylor froze abruptly and unexpectedly, and even with a totally emotionless expression, the well-built, slightly taller man looked scary.

Dangerous scary.

Lorenzo had to consciously prevent his hand from instinctively moving toward his gun. *Wow. I sure pissed him off.*

They continued walking and Taylor returned to his normal, inscrutable manner. When they got to the car, the drive back was silent once more. *What the fuck? Why did this guy drag me out there anyway?* Lorenzo wondered. *And why Holladay park? What was Taylor going to show me?*

Lorenzo parked his car in the police parking lot. John Taylor released his seat belt, making no move to get out of the cruiser. Looking at Lorenzo, Taylor met his gaze, eye to eye. From his top pocket, Taylor pulled out a USB stick.

"This is for you."

"Oh yeah?" Lorenzo said. "What is it? And why didn't the search warrant find it?"

Taylor just gave him raised eyebrows. "Listen to me now, Lorenzo," he said in a tremendously compelling voice. "This memory stick is full of information that no one has. It's extremely dangerous. If I were you I would view it in my home, away from prying eyes. I'd also treat it like high octane, safe and secure. Away from everyone. Don't say I didn't warn you."

"Oh, so we're on first name basis now are we?"

"Yeah. I don't know why, but I like you, Lorenzo," John Taylor said. "I think you're a good cop."

Lorenzo's hollow laugh dripped with scorn. "Well isn't that flattering? The sociopathic killer likes me. Thanks so much."

Unperturbed, Taylor gave him a sardonic smile and got out of the car. Taylor bent to look at Lorenzo through the open passenger door. "Watch that and get back to me," he said.

"Why me?" Lorenzo said getting out of the police cruiser and locking it.

Taylor unlocked his Mercedes with a beep, opened it, and got in. The driver's side electric window rolled down and Taylor leaned out of the window slightly to speak. He waited for Lorenzo to come closer.

"You want to know why you? I'll tell you. Because sometimes the best way to find out if you can trust somebody is to simply go ahead and trust them."

Lorenzo frowned and a long moment passed while he processed this cryptic little comment. *Well, shit a brick. So Taylor, the animal torturing killer has decided to trust me, huh? Why? Does he think I'll be flattered when any normal man would be sickened?*

"Are you listening to me, Lorenzo?" John asked breaking the Detective's train of thought.

Something in Taylor's commanding voice or gaze snapped Lorenzo into attention. He stared directly at the handsome, compelling murderer, sitting in the classy car in front of him.

"You really need to hear this, Lorenzo," Taylor said. "Only three people in the world have ever seen what's on that USB stick. I'm one. You know the other, and the last one is dead, recently murdered." Taylor's dark eyes stared into Lorenzo's intently, and Lorenzo felt a chill of threat and foreboding. "You'll want to keep that in mind, Lorenzo," Taylor said as the Mercedes purred to life.

"Hey, Taylor," Lorenzo spoke up as his suspect put the car into gear. "Why Holladay park? What were you going to show me?"

Taylor smiled broadly, and once more Lorenzo felt the mesmerizing charm of that smile. Fuck me. The man was definitely a chick magnet, Lorenzo decided.

"Oh," Taylor said in his deep, cultured voice. "Why nothing at all, actually. It's a nice day, Lorenzo. We went to the park because I wanted you to have a chance to enjoy the weather, and a pleasant outdoor walk in the sun. I thought you could use the break." Taylor's eyes narrowed and he intently studied the Detective, as if testing that possibility or uncovering all of Lorenzo's secrets. Then his lips twitched and he nodded. "I was right, wasn't I?"

Lorenzo watched as his main suspect, John Taylor drove off with his expensive clothes, in his expensive sports car.

This shifty bastard is too acute, the Detective. *Much too aware of everything and everyone.*

Chapter 20

Richard's News

❧

Kelly sat at John's kitchen table fascinated.

John really was an unusual kind of guy. Tonight he had made a kind of salad thing for dinner. It had fresh mango and cucumber in a bowl and on top were giant shrimp that had been fried with ginger, chili and garlic. Kelly who loved cooking was blown away. The meal was something she might have made, except the price of fresh shrimp would have put her off buying it. John had endless money so never thought like that.

"John," she said bubbling with admiration after her first bite. "You're amazing. I love this. So yummy. I've never tasted anything like it."

He smiled that smile of his that always made Kelly want to melt. Even his dark brown eyes had a laugh in them. As per usual, he was eye bleeding, lung collapsing, heart-stopping, drop-dead beautiful.

John was wearing a pair of blue jeans that accented his trim hips and waist, not to mention his perfect butt. He was wearing a dark blue button down shirt that he had tucked in, and his brown belt accented his perfect physical proportions. Something about the open neck collar, with a small scattering of chest hair drew her attention.

Kelly wanted to kiss that neck and chest. Jesus, the man was simply gorgeous. And he had her heart completely.

"I thought you'd like it," he said. "It's unique and creative, kind of like you, Kelly."

She just grinned at him. The man was constantly praising and flattering her, but everything he said was completely sincere. He took her breath away, and more surprisingly, he took her words away. For such a chatty person as she was, that was quite a feat. How did someone reply to a compliment as nice as that?

Her phone rang and she swallowed her mouthful and answered it when she saw that it was her older brother.

"Hey, Richard," she said. Kelly hadn't spoken to her parents for two weeks. Richard was the intermediary, and her poor brother hated being piggy in the middle.

"How are you doing?" Richard asked. "Any news?"

Kelly had told Richard everything. Other than her sexual kinks, she'd never kept secrets from her big brother, and he returned the favor. Richard knew the score. Maria Lopez's killer had to be found before that female detective got off their case, although after John had threatened to sue, all had become strangely quiet.

Had John's father killed Maria Lopez and set John up? It seemed likely, but why?

"Sorry, Richard," she said. "No news, except that John and I are formally engaged." Kelly looked at her daisy ring that she was wearing on her left hand, and smiled across the table, at John. He gave her an intense, proprietary gaze of ownership. It made her catch her breath. God, the man was such a distraction.

"Good for you, Kelly," Richard said. "Congratulations. I like him. Even in grade school he was weird, but he wasn't an asshole. I understand now. It's amazing he turned out okay, with all he went through. Anyway, I know how much he adores you. I don't think anyone could love you the way that man loves you, Kelly. You're the most important person in the world to him, and that's just as it should be. He's protective, too. Those security guards that follow you around are really something. But there was a murder, and one can't be too careful. I'm really, really happy for you."

"Thanks, Richard." John was in the kitchen, pouring himself a glass of mango juice. He lifted up a glass with a questioning look and Kelly nodded.

"So," Richard said. "Mom and dad got your second long newsy letter. I think they are chilling out a bit. This estrangement can't go on much longer – Dad will definitely crack. He misses you so much. You know he's always liked you best, you little favorite." Richard said this without any malicious intent or jealousy. Dad and Kelly had always been close, probably because they had such similar, naturally upbeat personalities. "Oh, Maria, Katrina and Jamie all send their love, too. Dad asked me for John's phone number, and I gave it to him."

John put a glass of mango juice on the table in front of her and sat back down. Kelly smiled her thanks, and took a sip. Kelly had given John's number to Richard in case he needed it. Her older brother, Richard, was completely on Kelly and John's side. The unwavering trust Richard had in Kelly's judgment and the love he had for her, his little sister, warmed Kelly's heart.

"I hope that's okay," Richard said.

"Oh," she said. "I think that's a great idea. I'll tell John." Kelly briefly explained what Richard had said.

With a considering expression, John nodded.

They didn't chat long, as Richard had simply wanted to warn John to expect a phone call. Kelly thanked Richard, told him she loved him, and hung up. John's eyes were bright. He looked happy, and that made her happy.

"It's all going to be okay, Kelly. I know it will."

"Yes," she said. "Because being together is the only option."

Kelly had given notice at her apartment and had already moved a lot of her stuff into John's house. It was stupid to have separate dwellings, because they spent every minute together anyway. That would never change. It may seem fast to some, but when it was right, it was right. There was no reason to wait. Kelly knew that she genuinely was in love with John from that first night they'd spent together.

Kelly now looked at life as 'before John' and 'after John.'

'Before John' was a stupid, pointless existence with anxious petty problems it seemed to her. Kelly had spent so much time worrying about what her mother said or thought. She had felt anxious about her profession, needing to do something interesting that would be acceptable. She also wasted time putting herself down, and being hypercritical of her boyish body, her mouth, her manly jaw, or her hair.

In the 'after John' Kelly knew what was really important.

John's constant genuine praise made her self-esteem soar. Why had she been focused on her physical imperfections? And on what others thought? Now she was considering continuing in a musical career, perhaps joining a choir, because it was what she wanted to do. Not for the money, or her mother – but because it was *her*. And as for her mother… well, everything with her family would work out in time.

John had finished his meal. Kelly continued eating, while he intently watched her take in each mouthful. There was unconcealed lust in his eyes. Jesus, could this man turn her on or what?

He was always the mind-reader, but she knew him pretty well now, too.

John was studying her lips, and imagining his cock sliding between them. He saw her awareness, and gave her a sexy, seductive smile, an acknowledgment that she was right. John planned to have her on her knees, in front of the mirror in his bedroom, right after dinner. Yum. They simply couldn't get enough of each other. Ever. They were still screwing ten or twenty times a day. Would this mutual sexual craving and obsession of theirs ever go away?

I sure hope not, Kelly thought. *My life might be falling apart because I've disowned my parents, my boyfriend is wanted for murder, and there's a psychopathic killer out there who most likely has me on the top of his 'To-do' list. But other than that – things couldn't be going better!*

Chapter 21

John and Lorenzo

John stared at Kelly, smiling.

He knew, that she knew, that he was going to have her on her knees in front of his bedroom mirror – right after dinner. The sense of connection he had with Kelly was continuing to grow, and seemed more powerful with every passing minute.

John's cell phone rang – something it never did. Kelly had his number, but she was right here. Brenda Lopez had his number, but she was dead. Colin Wilkins had his number, but he'd been told not to call. That left André Chevalier, but this number was unlisted, so it couldn't be him.

Was it Kelly's dad calling perhaps? Alert and prepared for anything, John went ahead and answered his phone.

"Mr. John Taylor," a familiar tenor voice said. "Nice video you gave me. Christ, I haven't slept since I saw the damn thing."

"Detective Lorenzo Martin," John said with a low chuckle. "Sorry about that. It isn't funny, but in a strange way, it kind of is. Welcome to my world. I lived that video, and I haven't been sleeping well for years."

A long, loud sigh came through the phone. "We need to talk. I know it's late, but can I see you? I'm thinking of the coffee shop just north of Holladay Park, called Café Olé. My cruiser will be parked outside."

"Right now?" John asked, looking at Kelly with an upraised eyebrow. She gave him a 'sure' kind of shrug.

"Yes."

"I'll be there in fifteen," John said and disconnected.

He'd explained earlier to Kelly how he had given the video to Detective Martin with the hope of enlisting some help on the case. As his father had broken the truce already by putting false information into his police records, John thought a little bit of tit for tat couldn't hurt.

John called the security guard into the house from the man's car outside. The guard was all muscle, an ex-Marine and was doing the two to ten shift. John asked the guard to stay inside with Kelly while he was gone.

When John was sure all was well, he kissed Kelly, and whispered in her ear to be ready for him because when he got back he fully intended to have her in a number of different ways. John got into his car, waved good bye to his blushingly aroused sub, and left for his rendezvous with Detective Martin.

Why now? he wondered, as he backed out of his driveway and on to the road. *Why is my father creating trouble now? It's been thirteen years since I suffered under his hands, and the truce has held all that time.*

John's father represented what John despised most in a badly trained or malicious Dom. The man's inconsistency and unpredictability had been relentless. He punished John if he climaxed, he punished him if he didn't. The safest option was to remain emotionless, and this had become a survival mechanism and a habit.

John had felt nothing – except for anger and hate. As time went on he'd become as André had said, 'cut off,' from people, incapable of feeling, or climaxing in front of others. He had only been capable of making a connection with others, during a scene.

Without Kelly, he mused, pulling up to a stoplight, *I'd still be living that dark, loveless life.*

The familiar grief hit him, as he remembered what he'd confessed to Kelly so recently. Other than once with André, a moment he could hardly remember, the last time John had cried was when he was eight years old. Kelly now knew the worst of his sins, and she loved him anyway.

John easily found parking on the street and walked into Café Olé.

The cafe was set out in the reds and gold's of a Spanish theme, and there was a mix of small tables, bar seating, comfortable couches and chairs and a restful atmosphere. Wi-Fi was available, and a few people, judging by the number of plates and cups around them, looked like they had camped out and spent most of the day here already. The noise level was a pleasant buzz, with seventies background music.

It seemed a busy place for a Thursday night. When John walked in, Lorenzo raised a hand, and John told the wait staff that he already had a seat. The detective had nabbed a quiet little corner out of earshot of other patrons. Lorenzo must have gotten here a while ago, as he'd already eaten what looked, and smelled like pancakes and bacon.

Detective Martin was on the job, and wore a light blue uniform shirt and a Portland Police jacket. Even without the wave, John would have picked him out quickly. The alert eyes of a cop, combined with his dominating persona were hard to miss. John sat across from Lorenzo in his booth, and for a full minute, they simply looked at each other.

"So, John," Lorenzo said after taking a sip of his black coffee. "Maria Lopez saw that video?"

"Yes. Four years ago."

"I owe you an apology," Lorenzo said. "I'm thinking that we may have been chasing the wrong psychopath, but ya see, here's the problem. Unless this video comes out, no one will believe that Judge Taylor is bent."

John shrugged. "It sucks."

"Why'd you give that to me?" Lorenzo said. "What do you want me to do about it? I've got some ideas, but I dunno. A whole lot of shit is going to hit the fan and blow back in all our faces. And you know what? I'm pretty sure it's the sticking kind, that don't wash off."

"Do you believe Kelly's statement now, that she was with me at the time of the murder?"

"Yes."

"All that evidence against me had to have been planted by the real killer," John said. "It would have been easily done. My garage isn't secure."

A waiter came and took John's order. He asked for a double shot espresso, because he planned to be up for a while tonight. Kelly was waiting for him at home and they were going to exhaust themselves. He'd an entire scene planned out already. John's cock twitched, and these days when it twitched it actually felt good. He never knew what living was, until he and Kelly found each other again.

"Maria Lopez helped me so much," John said. "I owe her. You have no idea, or perhaps you do now, of how screwed up I've been all my life."

Lorenzo rolled his eyes and John laughed.

It was strange how easy it was for John to laugh now. Kelly did this to him. She brought out the joy of life that he had known for a short space of time when he was an innocent child, living with his Aunt Brenda. John had thought that he'd lost that joyfulness forever.

Would he ever be worthy of Kelly? Probably not. But if the woman had one flaw, it was her attraction to a damaged person like himself. John hoped that Kelly would never come to her senses and leave him.

Lorenzo was looking at him, and the poor fellow had nothing to say. John imagined the man's shock at seeing that recording. What could anyone say to the victim after seeing something like that?

"Double shot espresso?" A waiter asked looking between John and Lorenzo as he brought a mug of coffee over.

John raised his hand and the man put it down in front of him. Yes, that video. That was a real face tightening conversation stopper right there. John decided to give Lorenzo a break and change the subject.

"Unfortunately," John said, "I do think that somehow I got Maria Lopez killed. But the thing is I just can't figure out why."

John detailed the truce he had made with his father at age thirteen, and how he'd had a police record check four years ago, and had passed with flying colors. John pulled a copy of the police report out of his pocket, and gave it to Lorenzo. His lawyers had faxed him a copy, as the original had been lodged with them. A duplicate had been left in The Basement records.

"Ha," Lorenzo, said his eyes brightening as he read the certified results of John's police record of four years ago. "So you're not a violent, drug dealing, animal torturer? Glad to hear it. Holy fuck, the guy has real clout to create this kind of misinformation and manage to put it in your police records. How did he do it? That's a trail that maybe I can trace down. I'll let you know what I find."

"Okay, but the thing is, Lorenzo," John said. "The balance of power has changed somehow. Why now? Maria saw that video years ago. How does it serve my father to suddenly cause this trouble? And why would he kill Maria? Maybe he wanted to frame me and put me in jail? He should be killing me, really, except that I've instructed my lawyers to release that video upon my sudden demise. Is Judge Taylor about to be investigated or something?"

"Nope," Lorenzo said. "I've checked into that. Status quo as far as I can see. What about your mother?"

John frowned. "What about her? She's a complete puppet, and will do anything, and I mean *anything* my father says."

"Oh yeah?" Lorenzo raised his eyebrows, but kept his gaze unflinchingly upon John. "You don't say. Well, I noticed that, too."

Feeling unexpectedly ashamed and humiliated, John shook his head. The video had him on the St. Andrew's cross as a child, getting a caning that left a pool of blood on the floor. What he had neglected to remember was what his mother's actions were at the time.

"I'd forgotten what was on that video," John said in a quiet voice. "It was a strange way to grow up. My good friend, André Chevalier, you remember him?"

"Sure. I interviewed the Frenchman. Likable guy."

John smiled. "Yeah, he's the best. André said that in time I'd find myself and become who I was meant to be, but it would take a little longer to do so because of my parents. Do you know, Lorenzo, it's finally happening. My whole life is coming together right now. I'm completely in love. Kelly and I are going to marry, and I've never been so happy. But I can't move forward until this murder is solved. How can I be content, when I have to worry that someone is going to go after Kelly next?"

Lorenzo shifted and leaned back in his seat. "I see you got security in. That was a good move. The company they work for is the best so you shouldn't have any trouble there."

"What can we do?" John asked, taking a sip of his espresso. The coffee was hot and strong. Just what he needed.

Lorenzo shrugged.

"I could have the video given in confidence to the courts," John said. "But you know that wouldn't work, and it would never prove he killed Maria anyway. My father would suppress it as evidence. I'm telling you, Lorenzo, my father is the scariest man I know. He's really smart, charms everyone, and is super manipulative. I think he'd just get even, and probably kill me and Kelly anyway. Right now the only thing holding him back is that video."

"Yeah, and even if that video anonymously ended up on the internet, the resultant bullshit would change your life, John," the detective said. "I've been around, and seen some fucked up shit." Lorenzo shifted restlessly in his chair, and frowned. "But of all the fucked up shit I've seen, yours is right at the top of the pile for child abuse, sexual perversity and gratuitous violence. You must have a shit load of scars."

"Yes," John said. "I never did get a chance to learn to swim, and I've always wanted to. I couldn't take my shirt off, and had to wear long pants to hide the scars. And as for u-tubing that video? I just can't do it. Kelly's parents couldn't look me in the eye again. The whole world would treat me like a freak. I'd have to change my name, and move away, but I can't do that. Kelly is really close to her family."

John frowned at Lorenzo and had another sip of coffee. "Now that I think of it, until your partner interfered, Kelly's parent's liked me too."

"Sorry about that," Lorenzo said and his manner was sincerely apologetic. "My new partner, Lucille Irwin, is a stupid, fucking bitch. I'm virtually not talking to her since that happened, I've been so pissed off. I haven't reported her however. Reporting one's partner goes against the unspoken code."

"Ah, well, you should probably cut her some slack," John said. "Father, forgive them, for they know not what they do," John quoted from the bible verse he had been studying on his course. It was the line Jesus said when the Romans were crucifying him, and just now as part of his assignment, he was supposed to analyze what the ramifications and practical applications of that quote were in real life.

"Cut her some slack?" Lorenzo demanded, sitting up straight, with wide eyes and self-righteous ire. "No way. Talk about not knowing what she's doing! That's Lucille all over. She has no clue, but the bitch of it is, that woman already thinks she knows it all."

"Lucille Irwin certainly had no clue in my case," John said, "but the evidence against me was pretty compelling. No doubt she thought she was doing the right thing. You have to admit, Lorenzo, that what she did took courage. Who would have the guts to do something like that? The woman broke the law, because she wanted to save Kelly from me. I have to say, I actually like her for that."

Lorenzo, who was drinking a sip of coffee, almost choked and he began to laugh. "You should try working with her. You won't like her then. You and your bat shit crazy religious studies degree and bible quotes, John!"

"I never went to church, Lorenzo, and I'm trying to catch up on what 'normal' people do," he explained.

"Holy shit, John," Lorenzo said. "I had enough of your bible quotes during your interview back at the station. For a man who's never once gone to church, you sure seem to have nailed the subject. What are you doing with Lucille then, turning the other cheek?"

"No, not in the least," John said, finishing up the last of his coffee and setting the mug down. "I just know that however stupid and professionally suicidal Lucille's actions were, she did have Kelly's best interests at heart. I simply have to like her for that. I'm not a really a bad person Lorenzo, but I'll never be good enough for Kelly. Have you ever been in love?"

Lorenzo laughed. "Yeah, sure I have, but it hasn't ever stuck."

"So there you are then," John said and his lips curved up in a happy smile. "Regardless of my rather regrettable childhood, and all the terrible things that are currently going on, I feel incredibly fortunate. I'm madly in love with Kelly, and she loves me. You should be so happy, Lorenzo." John stood up and took twenty bucks out of his wallet. "My treat," he said. "That should cover the tip, too."

"Thanks. But I figure that it's the least you can do after the nightmares you gave me."

John laughed. "You know what, Lorenzo? Nightmare childhood or not, right now I feel like I'm the luckiest man in the world."

Chapter 22

The Planned Scene

"Strip, Kelly," John ordered from where he sat on his overstuffed bedroom chair, fully dressed in jeans, button down shirt, and shoes. "Make me want you."

Kelly had dressed up for him in her newest olive and rust bustier, with black stilettos and fishnet stockings. Displayed for his pleasure, she wanted to please him, and she also wanted sex. John could smell the scent of her feminine arousal already.

"Can I touch you, John?" she asked. "While I strip?"

John felt unable to deny her anything. "Yes, Kelly," he said, "but don't touch below the waist. Soon, but not yet. Just one hand at a time, and go slow. I want your hands on me, Kelly, and I'll learn to love it, I know. It's just that I was touched without my permission for so many years, it still kind of freaks me out."

Kelly shot him a broad grin and said, "Thank you, John."

John reflected that she was such a naturally happy soul that even when he said no to her, she only thought that someday his 'no' would soon be a 'yes.'

Talk about an optimist.

Kelly strutted across the room, rolling her hips in a sex walk and John found he was smiling. Yes she was sexy, but she was also just so damn adorable. She moved all the way around him, trailing a hand across his chest. Well, that was okay. He was distracted by her captivating body enough that her hand didn't disturb him.

She spread her legs and bent over so that her ass was right near his face. The bustier hid nothing, and John, admiring her creamy skin, was getting an eyeful. Then she turned around and pulled the cups to her bustier down, and holding each breast with a hand, she placed her breasts right onto either side of his face.

John bent his head and inhaled, loving the feel of her soft skin and her heady feminine smell. She took one breast and offered it to his mouth, and he obediently suckled, and then nipped her.

Kelly gave an 'umm' sound of pleasure and writhed, and her other hand moved through his hair. A tingle went down John's spine, but it wasn't unpleasant.

Kelly put a foot up on his chair, giving him a view of her pussy, barely covered with a thong. John saw that her thighs glistened. She was dripping, but he withheld his desire to touch or lick. If he started, he knew wouldn't be able to stop. John could spend hours just eating her out and making her climax over and over and over again.

Kelly disengaged the garter belts, on one leg. After that, she dropped that leg down and put the other up, doing the same.

With one sweep Kelly then took the bottom of the bustier in her hands and with a sexy little wiggle, she pulled it over her head and off – leaving only the thigh high stockings, thong, and high heeled shoes behind.

John was up onto his feet in an instant, before he was aware that he intended to move. He snatched her wrists and put her hands around his neck, holding them with bruising strength before he realized it, and loosened his grip.

"Keep your hands there, Kelly. You may touch my neck and hair, as you keep telling me you'd like to do."

John smiled down at her, but he knew his smile was tense and forced. "Lose the shoes." When she did, he added, "And rise up on to your tiptoes, high as you can get. I want you to feel it in the muscles of your groin."

Kelly did as he asked, suddenly looking down and blushing. Arousal? Embarrassment? Or both, he wondered?

"Good girl," he growled. "Now look at me. Do you know what I want?"

Kelly looked up through her lashes, and man, she was seriously turned on. Well, so was he. This was nowhere near the complex, intricate scene that he had planned, but he couldn't help it. What was with this raw, physical urgency? He was trembling with desire.

God he had to fuck her *right now*.

Before she could reply he clasped her in his arms and quickly walked her backward to the wall, pushing her against it, slamming her hard against it. The air left her lungs in a rush, pushed out of her from the unforgiving muscular force of his solid, bigger body.

"Oh, ah, um," Kelly moaned.

John felt her sweet breath swirl against his face and neck, and her soft breasts hard against him. Kelly's fingers flexed, gripping his neck and hair, and that firm, desperate feminine touch was not unpleasant.

In fact it spurred him on.

John ravished her then, with a bruising, open mouthed kiss, one hand between her legs, enjoying the flood of her moisture and one hand on her breast. It was always difficult to tear himself away from Kelly's lips. Every time, each kiss they shared together was so much more than a kiss. It was more like a soul-wrenching molding of their mouths, a joining that melded and forged them into one person. Kelly moaned with pleasure and that just made him harder.

This was sex, but it was also love. How had two such separate things come together as they had?

John finally pulled away, biting her bottom lip and licking across her throat and neck where her pulse furiously pounded. He had a 5 o' clock shadow and he felt it brush roughly against her soft skin, marking her. John felt a quiver of need ripple through Kelly's body and like an electrical conduit, her desire transferred to him. She sagged downward in a blissful fog.

"Oh, no you don't. Up on those toes," he admonished.

"Oh, sorry, John," she said and rose up again.

John's broad hand ran along her leg, squeezing her inner thighs and the juncture of her sex. "Do you feel it now, Kelly?" he whispered seductively. "The strain pulls, doesn't it? But it's such a sweet pain. Your groin and thighs are filling with blood to manage this extra work." John's hand grasped her pussy, his thumb circling, and caressing her distended clit. "Feel how swollen you are?"

Kelly whimpered, making helpless little noises from the back her throat.

John licked her neck where her pulse was pounding, and bit and sucked. His thumb and finger had moved to her nipple and he tugged and pulled, while his other hand moved to her ass to cup her buttocks and thrust against her with his rigid shaft. He moved against her, pushed against her sex and she moaned even more, uttering wanton sounds of need.

The alluring feminine noises she was making, the smell of her arousal and the feel of her squirming, soft body under his made him realize that he couldn't wait.

John's mouth trailed down to her breast, and his hand returned between her thighs. Taking a nipple in his mouth he laved and caressed, and then suddenly bit it hard, feeling her instant flood of arousal. Kelly squealed and thrashed. They were both breathing rapidly with ragged panting lust. He licked and suckled her throbbing flesh.

"I'm going to hurt you tonight, Kelly," he said in a sensual threat, "and you're going to love it. Now hold still and be quiet while I bite your other nipple." She did exactly as he ordered, and her utterly submissive compliance made his balls tighten and his cock throb.

"Good girl," he growled, "You like to obey me don't you, Kelly?"

"Oh God, yes, John," she gasped.

"When you do as I say I reward you, don't I?"

"Yes, yes!"

John unbuttoned and unzipped his jeans, pulling them down enough to free himself. Reaching down, with a loud snap he broke her dripping thong and it fell away. The smell of her arousal was intoxicating. He felt his cock press lightly against her hot, soaking opening and this time he groaned.

Kelly reacted to the feel of his cock, too. She couldn't move as he was holding her still, but she was sure trying to. And the frantic, desperate little sounds she was making? Wow. The feel of his cock had ignited her completely. Kelly writhed, wanting him inside her. Damn she was hot. That internal combustion of hers would soon make her explode.

"How shall I reward you my sweet, sweet sub? Tell me what you want."

"Oh God, John," she whimpered. "Fuck me, please."

"And?'

"Let me come for you," she begged. "I want to come for you. I need to come." Sexually inflamed, and trembling, Kelly was frantic. Whimpering and moaning, she was making so much noise it sounded as if he was flogging her.

"Shush, shush," he soothed. "I'll take care of you, Kelly."

John had intended to torment her, bringing her close to the brink of orgasm a number of times, and then denying her a climax. But he didn't have the control for that right now. How could he deny her? When he had no power over himself? With his body pressed against her, his cock at her wet, welcoming entrance, John reached down, his palms tracing to her thighs, and to the back of her knees. Then he pulled Kelly's legs up around his waist, and while he did so he thrust inside. He penetrated her right to the root, his balls slapping loudly against her.

Kelly cried out, and the walls of her sex pulsed, but she didn't climax.

John hissed, and bit his lip. *Shit!* The muscles of her cunt had tightened like a vice and he almost shot his load. Warm, wet, swollen.

My God, this feels like heaven.

The sensation of his shaft deep in her heated, molten core made him throb and twitch. John was barely able to withhold his orgasm. He remained perfectly still, certain that he'd climax if he moved at all.

Kelly gasped and moaned, "Oh, John. Yes! Oh, please, please, please," she sobbed and begged, trying to thrust against him. He simply pushed her more firmly against the wall, holding her still.

"You have amazing control, Kelly," John praised, well aware that she may yet lose that control at any moment. "You're doing so well," he encouraged.

She was panting when she gasped breathlessly, "Thank you, John."

"Is there anything else you want your Dom to give you, Kelly?" he said, his throat raw with sexual urgency.

"I want your cum, John," she said desperately. "I love your cum. I want to eat it, drink it, and swim in it. I love the smell, the taste and everything about it. I love it because it's yours, John, and it pleases you when I take it. Oh, God!"

That last was punctuated with another roiling pre-orgasmic pulse, the walls of Kelly's sex squeezing him so tight that once more he almost ejaculated.

"Don't move," he snapped.

"Yes, John," she whimpered and he saw tears of longing and desperation running down her face. It made him smile. She was such an emotional girl.

Panting and sweating, John held her pressed against the wall and shut his eyes, struggling with his powerful urge to climax. He hadn't undressed, and between his sweat and hers, his cotton shirt was drenched.

Kelly made a continuous keening sound, so he held her jaw with his fingers and put his thumb in her mouth. The noise stopped instantly as she immediately began to eagerly suck him, working his thumb as if it were his cock.

Doubting his control, he counted to twenty, trying to catch his breath, while concentrating on *her*.

Kelly was so, so soft and feminine. Soft to his male hardness. Light to his dark. Kind and happy to his anger. Cheerful and positive compared to his years of hate and despair. She was all purity and goodness, to John's shadowed, evil past. Kelly balanced him. She made him see himself as someone better than he had been. Someone good.

John could feel her beautiful body quivering with desire. Her small feminine hands were holding his neck, pulling against his hair like a lifeline, and her sexual excitement and raw lust tried his control.

This perfect woman wanted him, and she needed him. Could there be anything more arousing? Or more fulfilling?

He took his thumb from her mouth. With a tenuous hold of his once formidable control, he cupped and fondled both of her breasts, tugging and pulling on her nipples. Kelly whimpered, and he liked the sound so much he pulled and tugged some more, this time twisting, eliciting a number of strangled female cries. Satisfied, his hands brushed down to grip her buttocks.

John's lust was all consuming, and if anything his resistance was worse than ever. It was because of Kelly. She tested him like no one ever had before.

She tested him in sex, in life, in everything.

"Kelly," he said in a husky voice. "You're going to come for me not long after I start fucking you, within a few strokes. Can you do it?"

"Oh, God yes, John! Jesus, I'd come right now if you told me to."

He chuckled. "Me too," he confessed. "But I want it to last a little bit longer, to see if we can go together."

Expelling a large breath of relief, like letting a bull off a chain, John let himself go. He began to thrust vigorously, pressing her against the wall, slamming into her, his hands gripping her buttocks with bruising strength, one firm, pussy-moistened finger, intentionally pressing roughly up into her puckered rear.

Kelly sobbed and keened in a melody of diverse and desperate cries.

Her soft flesh was willing and pliant against him, because she was his sub, and completely dominated by his will. John worried for an instant that his fiercely gripping hands may blemish her pale skin as he squeezed and pulled and strained against her, but he couldn't stop himself. His fevered hunger was frenzied, urgent and insatiable.

Mine, he thought. *Kelly is mine and I'll take her anyway I want. Every bruise is a mark of my attention. Kelly will love anything I do, because she belongs to me.*

"Oh God, John," she gasped. "Oh, please!"

Savagely pounding into her in short, fast strokes, John ground his pubic bone into her thick, distended clit and grunted, "Come, Kelly."

Kelly arched her hips even higher and they thrust together, her legs tightening around him and her internal walls gripped him, exerting a powerful pressure that squeezed his cock in a pulse of spasms.

"Uh, uh, uh, oh yes, John!" she sobbed as she tensed and then thrashed like an animal caught in a trap. Kelly wailed and shrieked as she came, and came, and came.

John shuttered and groaned, his entire body tingling from her body's climax. Chest heaving, John felt the cramping and then release of his balls and groin. Heat and pleasure exploded within, extending outwards to his entire body, thighs, buttocks, and back.

His head flew back and his hips thrust forward as he convulsed with a powerful orgasm. Kelly's body jerked with aftershocks as she continued to convulse around him, milking his seed.

Panting, John rested his forehead against Kelly's, both of their faces damp with perspiration. Every single time, sex astounded him. Who could have possibly conceived of such pleasure?

Kelly's legs dropped to the floor, and John secured her with his grip, intuitively aware that she was languid, weak, and unable to stand.

Careful, he thought holding her tightly, compelled by an urgent protective instinct to keep her safe. *Boneless and exhausted, Kelly will drop to the ground like a rag doll if I don't hold her up.*

Primitive male satisfaction slammed into him, almost taking his breath away. It was sudden, unexpected and overwhelming. It followed right behind, coming at the end of his powerful orgasm. Yet this primal natural pleasure had nothing to do with his climax.

It was his job to hold Kelly, and to keep her from falling.

Right then, in his heart John knew why he was here, and what his reason for living was. No matter what happened, if the walls fell down, and the earth stopped spinning, and the entire world came to an end, John was certain that nothing could stop him from holding Kelly, and loving her, and keeping her safe.

Now and forever and for always.

Chapter 23

Trapped

It was the sound that woke Kelly. A loud crackling, combined with odd little explosive noises. It was pitch dark, and smoke was everywhere, and she heard coughing, too – hers, and John's.

Kelly's brain lurched into action.

"Fire!" she yelled and felt him in the bed beside her and began to shake him. "John, wake up!"

"God! Kelly!" John shouted as he gripped her arm. "We've got to get out!"

Flames surrounded them then, flickering bright burning light that could be seen through the smoke. The noise was unbelievable. Kelly felt him throw the heavy blankets around her, and pull her to the floor. As she fell, she heard glass break and felt the picture of John and his aunt under her hands.

John will be so sad if he loses every picture of his beloved Aunt Brenda, she thought.

Instinctively Kelly picked up the frame. The glass was broken, but she clutched it against her naked body, determined that she'd take at least this one photo out of the fire with her.

John and Kelly crawled toward the front window, staying low to the floor where there was still breathable air. The window and all around them was surrounded by flames.

"Kelly," he screamed. "It's going to hurt, and we're going to get burned, but we have to simply run. If I break the window first, the fire will explode from the extra oxygen. It'll kill us. I think we should use our bodies to break the window as we jump out. That way we'll be outside when the fire explodes. Does that sound like a plan? Do you have a better idea?"

"No, John. Let's go with that."

He wrapped himself around her with the blankets covering their head. "When I say run, we stand up, and sprint right through the window together, okay? I'll be a little ahead of you, my body can break the glass for both of us, okay?"

"Okay."

"Take a few deep breaths, as many as you can. Now hold your breath. Ready? Run!" Together Kelly and John stood up and bounded forward in a sprint. His hard body hit first and cracked the window as they both propelled themselves through it.

Snap! The window fractured, and then shattered.

Kelly felt burning pain on the soles of her feet, and up her legs.

As soon as they broke the window a roar sounded, and flames exploded inside the house from all the oxygen in the air that rushed in through the broken window. But they were outside. The blankets were smoldering, the house was ablaze, and fuck! Her skin burned as if it was on fire, but she and John were outside and safe.

Coughing, Kelly and John took lungfuls of fresh air, stumbling blindly away from the surrounding heat. Unexpectedly arms banded around her, and pulled her away from John. Then one strong arm circled her neck.

Confused, Kelly tried to see behind her.

Bang!

The sound of a gunshot surprised and confused her. How could she have heard a gun? It made no sense. This was a house fire. Somewhere in the back of her mind, she tried to process this, but she was breathless and her ears were ringing and nothing made any sense.

She looked over and saw John, down on his knees, holding his shoulder. Kelly was too confounded from smoke and burning pain to even scream.

What the hell?

"Hold still or I'll shoot you, too," came a female voice behind her. She felt the cool metal of a gun shoved under her throat, and saw the black barrel shining in the light of the fire from her peripheral vision.

Kneeling about ten feet away, John had lost his blanket and was completely naked. Kelly could see blood dripping from his left shoulder like red paint slashed across a white canvas. The sight of all that blood really frightened her. Jesus, he could bleed to death right in front of her eyes. While her own life was in danger, all she could think of was John.

I won't let this crazy woman kill John, Kelly thought in sudden, urgent resolve. *Where are the emergency services? Where's my security guard?* John was down and injured. She began to realize that everything was up to her. But what could she do?

John looked up at Kelly and at the woman with her arm around her neck, who held a gun to her head.

"Mother," he yelled. "What are you doing?"

The woman behind Kelly gave a maniacal laugh. "John William Taylor it's time to die! You're a bad seed, aren't you? You thought you would get away with it, but you won't."

Holy fuck, Kelly thought in astonishment, *the nut job who just shot John and is threatening my life is John's mom!*

"Mother," he said in a forced, calm voice. "I'm sorry. I don't really understand. Can you tell me what's wrong? Maybe I can help." He put a foot up, preparing to stand, but his mom didn't like that.

"Stop," she snarled. "Stay on your knees. You ruined everything, you bad boy. Master has been displeased with me. I tried to understand where I went wrong. All I ever wanted to do was please Master. Why couldn't you be a good boy? I should have left you with my older sister. I should never have taken you home."

"Mother," John said, and Kelly could hear the desperation in his voice. "Please let Kelly go."

"No," she said with an almost childish petulance, squeezing Kelly's neck and making her wince. "You made Master hate me. I tried to get rid of you. I put Master's information in your police file, and I killed the woman. I made her call you, she told me that she wasn't your counselor, did you know that?"

Kelly worked to filter this. John had played back Maria Lopez' phone message, but neither of them could make sense of it. Now she understood. John's mother must have been holding a gun to Maria's head at the time.

"That woman was lying. I was going to kill her anyway," John's mother said with a giggle. "I put all the evidence in your garage. But the police were stupid. Why couldn't they see it was you? You're the one who's always ruined everything!"

In her peripheral vision Kelly could see Mable, John's next door neighbor. Surely Mable had called the police? With a sinking heart, Kelly knew that the police wouldn't get here in time to save her and John.

"It all started when you wouldn't come," John's mother said, and her childish voice was heated. "Why wouldn't you climax for Master? I sucked you good! I fucked you good! He fucked you good, too! But it was never enough for you, was it? Stupid, naughty, boy. Master loved only me. Then you came. I wish you'd never been born. You made Master unhappy."

Kelly's stunned mental state could hardly take it all in. John had told her that there was sexual abuse in his childhood, but she had always assumed that it was *from his father*. Now it seemed that his mother was part of it, too.

"Where is the security guard, mother?"

"I killed him in his car," she snarled. "And I poured gasoline all around Brenda's house. You both should have died in that fire, but this is better."

Numb with fear and shock, when John's mother said the name Brenda, she suddenly remembered Brenda's photo. It was in the frame in her hand. Kelly touched the glass, and pulled a long sharp shard of it out of the frame, holding it like a dagger. The hope it generated washed over her in a thrilling river of possibility.

Oh God, she thought in a fervent prayer. *Please let me use this as a weapon. I'll only have one chance. I need to thrust this right into this insane woman's neck.*

"What are you going to do, Mother?" John asked.

"I'm going to kill this girl, because you want her, and then I'm going to kill you," she said, and this time her bizarre childish voice was cheerful, calm and determined.

Kelly looked at John with wild, urgent eyes, widening and blinking, desperately trying to communicate her plan, holding the glass knife out slightly. He understood. Kelly saw immediately that he understood.

Oh, God, I love you, she thought, shutting her eyes for a moment with relief and gratitude.

Of course her wonderful true love understood her, gorgeous, lovable mind-reader that he was. When had he not understood her? John was so observant. He spent all his time watching, learning and working to be aware of everything about her, just so that he could love her more completely, and make her happier.

John knew what to do, because he always did.

She held her makeshift knife in her fist, ready. She felt the jagged ends of it cutting into the skin of her hand and fingers, and shivered with the thought of its sharp edges slicing into flesh. Could she really do this?

Kelly felt no uncertainty or moment of indecision. Even if wielding this makeshift knife cut all her fingers off – she didn't care. She had to save John. But could she successfully thrust it up into his mother's neck? Because she knew that she'd only have one shot at it. It had to be done right the first time.

Only seconds had passed.

With perfect understanding, John and Kelly both knew when the moment of truth had arrived. Distracting his mother, John put a foot out in order to stand once more.

His mother swung the gun toward him, and away from Kelly's head and neck.

Without any hesitation Kelly thrust the glass shard upwards with all her might. The desperate force of her thrust sliced into her hand, and severed the tendons in her thumb and two fingers. But it also severed the carotid artery in John's mother's throat.

John jumped up, and the gun went off again, but the shot was wild.

A spray of blood erupted from the woman's neck, soaking Kelly's face and chest with warm, dripping heat and the coppery smell and taste of blood. John's mother crumpled to the ground, like a broken doll.

The murderer, whose mind was broken, lay still. The lifeblood of her unconscious body pumped out with every beat of her heart, until it slowed, and slowed... and then stopped all together.

Chapter 24

Brenda's Help

Kelly ran to John as he fell back to his knees.

"Oh God, baby," she said, in a panicked tone, wrapping her blanket around him and pushing the cloth of it into his wound. "Sit down, Jesus, please don't bleed to death will you? I need you, John."

He looked up at her with an emotionless expression and asked, "Baby?"

Kelly laughed really loudly and it sounded totally hysterical to her ears. Of course, she had just killed someone, and was covered in her victim's blood. Also the man she loved was bleeding to death, and something was wrong with her thumb and fingers because they hurt and wouldn't move properly, and fuck, her feet and legs were burning like the very fires of hell.

Who wouldn't be a little hysterical after all that?

"Yes, baby," she said, wrapping her arms around him. "You're my baby and I love you."

"Kelly," John said in a weak voice. "How did you get the glass shard? I don't understand."

She went and got the photo and the frame, and showed it to him. "I felt this picture as I got to the floor, just before we left the house, John. The glass was broken, but I couldn't bear to leave Brenda there, because I know how much she means to you. I was afraid that you wouldn't have any pictures of her left after the fire, and I knew that would make you sad. So I took her with us when we ran."

John smiled up at her and his eyes were shining. "My beautiful, clever girl," he whispered. "You saved us both, Kelly. You and

Brenda. How grateful I am, to have been loved by two of the most wonderful women in the world."

Three fire trucks pulled up at the house, and men jumped out, wielding their fire hoses and getting instantly to work.

"He's been shot," Kelly said to a firemen as strode toward them. It suddenly struck her, but she was stark naked.

"An ambulance is on its way," the man said, handing her blanket, and taking over the first aid care of John.

"Call the police, too," Kelly said. Mable came up to her with a white terrycloth bathrobe in her hand, and Kelly gratefully put it on.

"I called the police," Mable said. "I saw it all Kelly, but I didn't know what to do. I didn't want to get involved and somehow make things worse."

"Will you call a man named Detective Lorenzo Martin for me? He'll want to know what happened here. He'll take your statement."

"Of course," Mable said. "I'm so sorry I couldn't do more for you, sweetheart."

"You did plenty."

There were crowds of people around now, all wanting to help. Kelly's whole body was trembling, but John was too weak to say much, so it was up to her.

"That crazy person over there tried to kill us," she told them. A sudden flash of memory hit her and her pulse quickened. "Oh, Jesus!" she cried out, in a loud, shrill voice. "Check the street everyone! There's a man in a car somewhere around here. He may still be alive. That crazy woman over there told me that she shot him."

A stretcher arrived and John was lifted on to it. "I'm coming with you," Kelly determinedly informed the emergency services officer.

The woman gave her a kind smile. "Sure, come along, honey. Hey, wait a minute," she said when she saw in the light all the blood on her face and neck. "Christ almighty, were you shot, too?"

"Oh," Kelly said with a shaky laugh. "That isn't my blood. But my hand is sure sore," she held it out to show the woman, "and my feet and legs were burned and they are absolutely killing me."

Bringing the picture of Brenda with her, Kelly got into the ambulance and sat near John's feet as they drove with lights and sirens to hospital. The ambulance officer gave her a cotton bandage and some ice for her burns, but the woman had no time to attend to Kelly's injuries. They'd notified the hospital that a gunshot wound was coming in, and that the victim had lost a lot of blood.

The treating officer put a line in each of John's arm's, and began pumping liquid into him as fast as humanly possible. John, pale, sweating and trembling, was no longer able to talk.

By the time they got him to hospital, he was unconscious.

Chapter 25

Hospital Two Days Later

John studied Kelly's face. He still felt a little woozy, but he was alive, and able to sit up slightly in bed. Today he'd been told that he'd be allowed visitors for short spaces of time.

Kelly bent over and kissed him lightly on the lips, and then took his good hand and squeezed it. John lightly curled his fingers around hers.

"Are you okay?" John rasped,

"Never better," she said.

John smiled at her. "My heroine," he rasped again and then because his throat was raw, he whispered. "Thank you, Kelly. You saved my life."

She pressed her soft lips carefully to his forehead. "You're welcome," she said. "But you helped, John. You knew exactly how to distract her."

His throat felt sore and dry. "Will you get me some water?"

"Oh, of course!" There was a straw in his glass, and Kelly brought it to his lips. John leaned his head forward and drank gratefully, resting back on the pillow when finished.

"That's better," he said. "Do you have any idea how many times you've saved my life, Kelly? Once when you were only a child when you gave me hope. And then as an adult. I really wasn't living before I met you again. And finally you literally saved my life from someone who wanted to shoot me." He shook his head. "It's going to take years to repay you."

Kelly raised her eyebrows up and down suggestively. "I like the sound of that."

"You called me, baby," he said, flashing back to that moment and remembering her endearment suddenly. He knew he hadn't been thinking that clearly at the time, but he recalled that because it had surprised, and kind of pleased him.

"You *are* my baby," she said and her pale blue eyes were soft and bright.

John didn't know what to say, but his throat felt thick just knowing that Kelly wanted to call him a special endearment. He'd have to learn about the expected boyfriend, girlfriend customs. Maybe there was something about it on Google. Should he perhaps call her sweetheart or something? But then John remembered that he already called her 'beautiful girl' from time to time, so maybe that was okay.

"How's the hand?" he asked.

"Well, as you can see I've had surgery, too." Kelly held up her right hand that was in a splint and sling. "I've damaged the flexor tendons in my thumb, and two fingers. I have to wear this splint for two months. Actually my leg and foot burns hurt more, how about your burns?"

"This patient controlled anesthesia is great." He gazed over at the small mechanical device that was connected to the drip in his arm. "I'm now an official fan of morphine," he said, with a faint smile. He didn't want her to worry.

"I'm sleeping really well. Honestly, that's a first for me. Nothing hurts much, and if it does, I just press the button. I don't have to press it often."

"That's good," Kelly gave him her big beautiful grin. "Oh," she said, "my security guard wasn't dead, isn't that great? He's in critical condition, but is expected to recover."

"Good."

"Want me to read your cards? Lots of people have called."

"No."

She smiled at his brief answer, but John could see that underneath there was something making her just a little bit gloomy, and uncharacteristically low. "What's wrong, Kelly?" he asked, knowing that she was pretending to be happy for his sake. "Tell me."

"Oh, well," she said with a little sigh. "You've lost your lovely home, and it's sad that you no longer have all your photos of Brenda." She looked at the framed picture of John and his aunt that was sitting beside his bed. "Except for this one."

"Anything else?" he prodded.

There was a frown on her face when she said, "I know it's silly, but I realized this morning that now I'll never get to see the letter you wrote me. You know the one in reply to the one I wrote you? I was looking forward to reading that someday."

"Is that right?" John asked, feeling a bubble of joyfulness burst inside. He was ridiculously happy, because he knew that he was going to make Kelly happy. And making Kelly happy was one of his favorite things.

Picking up on his mood, she gave him an open, curious expression.

"Kelly, Kelly, Kelly," John said with a chuckle. "I'd have thought you knew me better than that. Am I the kind of man that leaves things to chance? Don't you know by now that I'm paranoid, obsessive, and look at least twelve steps ahead in everything I do? I've a flame proof safe buried under the floor boards, hidden so well that even the forensic police missed it. Your letter to me is perfectly safe, and so is mine. And I still have all of Brenda's photos."

Kelly's eyes lit up, and she burst out laughing while doing a little happy dance. "God I love you," she said.

A nurse came in, and put a hand to John's wrist, checking his pulse. "Sorry Mr. Taylor, but that's all for now. You're too weak yet, for extended visitation. You need your rest. I've told that police officer he isn't allowed to come in, either."

John said, "Alright. I am tired. I think I can sleep, but Kelly will you bring me a pen and paper and money? I've a few things to attend to."

"Sure," she said and kissed him good bye. "I'll be back soon with the stuff you want, and after that I'll see you tomorrow."

John heard Lorenzo's tenor ice speaking to Kelly as she left, and her cheerful inaudible reply. *Good,* he thought. *Let those two compare notes.* And then he slept.

~~~

When John woke again he had a pen, note paper and his wallet on his bedside table.

Hospital catering had left a meal on the table by his bed, but he'd been sleeping and they had let him sleep, bless them. John lifted the lid that was on the plate, keeping his meal warm. Ugh. Pureed food. It looked disgusting, and he didn't feel the least bit hungry.

John settled for a large drink of water, and then he began to write. The important thing in this situation was to strike without hesitation, and to show no mercy. He knew from personal experience that it was always better to kick one's enemy when they were down.

Lucky for him his mother had shot him in the left shoulder. It hadn't affected his writing hand.

Father,

It is clear to me that the terms of our treaty are irrevocably broken.

I submit that your sub was acting on your behalf. Her murderous actions are in the hands of the police, and the media will be fully informed. I'm writing to tell you that I've given the video of your actions to my solicitor and have instructed him to take legal action in both civil and criminal courts.

After judging others for so long, are you now prepared to be judged?

My intentions are to:

1. Cause you to lose your position.

2. Take all your money from damages (pain and suffering).

3. Make you irrevocably lose any shred of reputation you once had.

4. Have you incarcerated as the sadistic pedophile that you are.

I'm writing this letter to serve as warning.

May you rot in hell.

John

John folded the paper over and addressed it with the number of his father's home. Then he checked his wallet, happy to see plenty of cash.

John used the phone then and called FedEx to arrange pick up. Within the hour a man about forty years old arrived to take his letter away. Wearing a dark blue uniform, the courier was smiling with a professional air of competence. The man was blond, about six feet four, and looked like a wrestler.

Well, so much the better. "I want you to deliver this letter immediately," John said.

"I'm sorry, Sir, I don't think…" the man began, but he pulled out a $100 bill as a tip, and held it out to him. The courier grew quiet, but took the money.

"Dunthorpe is only twenty-five minutes from here," John said. "If you deliver that now, and return to me before six p.m. today, I'll give you another $100." John paused to let that information sink in. "All I want in exchange is for you to describe how the recipient looks, with a confirmation signature and details of how this was received. My father will be at home, I assure you. When he sees the FedEx truck arrive, he'll take your letter. This courier job is not irregular in any way, except for my urgency for him to receive this letter. Can you do it?"

The older man grinned. "Sure thing. I'll do it right now."

Chapter 26

The Next Day

−−−−∗−−−−

John Taylor's father committed suicide overnight.

First thing the next morning, Kelly came in and told John all about it. "Detective Martin called me, and asked me to tell you about the death of that evil pig you lived with as a child. He wants to see you when you're up for it."

"Good," John said, smirking from the way she had described his father. "I want to see him, too."

John told Kelly about the letter he had sent, and her reaction was one of unholy joy as she raised her one good hand in the air and did a little dance of joy. "I shouldn't be so happy, and I shouldn't gloat, I guess, but John, you're a genius! I swear I wanted to go kill that man myself for what he did to you. But it's even better that he killed himself."

"Thank you, beautiful girl."

"Well, he was a bastard, and I hope he's rotting in hell right now."

John smiled, because that had been his exact thought, too. Not very forgiving of him, but he wasn't a saint by any means.

A member of the hospital kitchen staff, in a light green uniform, brought a meal in, and Kelly busied herself arranging his tray. Taking the cover off, she removed the fork, knife, and spoon, from their wrapper first.

His father was dead, and the relief of it was still flowing she though John in light-hearted waves. How could his father have coped, without his mother to blame and torment? John's father, a man who found it pleasurable to cause mental and physical pain, had no ability to endure similar anguish.

347

A true bully, John had hoped that his father would take the coward's way out. That he'd kill himself once he received his letter. And he had been right.

Kelly was messing with the little salt and pepper containers, and she was humming because she was content. That made John content, too.

John's mother was another matter. It had taken years, but his father had obviously driven her mad. Had his mother once been a sweet and attentive sub, not unlike Kelly? Had it been in his mother's nature to need and want to please her Dom? John would never know, because the woman had been irretrievably damaged and broken by the time he had come under her care. Was it years of gradually worsening abuse that drove his mother into tormenting her own child?

The thought gave him chills.

It made it even more important that he make every effort to always be a good man. Yet sexually submissive or not, Kelly was a strong woman with her own moral compass. She'd never allow him to fall into such wickedness. Kelly made John feel safe from himself.

"Okay John," Kelly said, brightly. "My turn to feed you. Runny scrambled eggs, probably powdered. How sexy is that? Yum. Open up."

John chuckled, and she continued chatting, mainly about the soft diet he was on, and how she planned to sneak him in some real food. Real food would probably make him ill, but he didn't say anything. John took his time chewing, as his stomach was rather unsettled.

One thing John had learned in life was that bullies were weak, cowardly people who caused mental or physical pain in order to get their own way. Yet that observable behavior was only the tip of the iceberg.

John intimately understood the impulse and compelling need to act out one's own personal pain, self-hate and aggression by directing it at others.

I've been there. Who could better understand the behavior of a bully than him? But what anguish had caused his father to become so evil? Not that anything could excuse or justify his father's actions. In the end it was every man or woman's personal choice, no matter what had happened to them.

A bully's real weakness was in blaming others, in taking no responsibility, and refusing to look at themselves. 'Never underestimate the power of denial," the saying went. How true.

André Chevalier had helped John to look and learn. André had started him down the road to responsibility and understanding. The ancient Greek quote: 'Know thyself' was easy to say. Overwhelmed as he had been with pain, anger and hate, it had been extremely difficult to do. John knew that he had further to go, but Kelly had been the cornerstone, the final key to everything.

Wearing a big grin, Kelly put another spoon full of egg into his mouth. He didn't want it, but he was enjoying her enjoyment, so he made no objection and obediently continued to eat but very, very slowly.

I'm nothing without Kelly, he thought while gazing at her cheerful expression and recalling his empty existence before she came into his life. John's lips curved. *But with her, I'm everything.*

John used the phone after breakfast, and called Detective Martin.

"Hey, John," Lorenzo said. "How's it hangin'?"

"All is well," John said. "Are you working? Can you visit? I know the nursing staff chased you off yesterday, but we have some business to finalize."

"I'm working, but I feel perfectly justified in stopping by on the government's dime. Will they let me in to see you?"

"They seem fairly pleased with my progress, so chances are."

"Alright," Lorenzo said. "Hey, thanks for solving and finalizing that sticky case. I gotta say, I had your father pegged, not your mother."

"Thank Kelly."

"I already have," Lorenzo said in a tone filled with admiration. "That's quite a girl you have there, John. I don't think there are many people – men or women – that would have had the wits or the ability to have done what she did."

"Yes," John agreed.

"Anyway, I'll be there in ten."

"Thank you."

Sure enough, Lorenzo walked in about ten minutes later, bringing John an expensive bottle of Scotch.

John laughed. "What, no flowers?"

"Sorry buddy, but you're a man," Lorenzo said.

Lorenzo's eyes brightened when he saw Kelly, and he gave her little hug of greeting. They exchanged a few words, but then she left them alone. Lorenzo and Kelly had already spoken this morning, and he'd taken her statement the day after the fire. The nursing staff was funny about only one visitor at a time with John, because they didn't want to exhaust him.

"So," Lorenzo said after Kelly left. "I guess your old man decided to take the garbage out. Finally the asshole did something right."

John chuckled and told Lorenzo about the courier, and how it was John's letter that helped his father decide to take the easy way out. He also made Lorenzo laugh concerning his philosophy that if one wanted to win, it was best to kick a man while they were down.

Giving a low, appreciative whistle Lorenzo said, "Judge Taylor. What a chicken shit bastard with his basement torture chamber, the disgusting pictures, and illegal porn. Yech. They are dropping everything, hiding the truth, and closing the case. I think the PR line will be that he committed suicide from grief over the mental breakdown and death of his wife. If they let out the information about the Judge's kinky crimes, then every case he sat would have to be questioned and perhaps reopened."

"Excellent," John said. "You know, for a while there I studied the cases he presided over. I honestly think he was a fair judge. Isn't that strange? If he wasn't, I suppose I may have been compelled to risk my own safety to stop him sooner. It just shows that no one is all bad all the time. Hitler was Time's "Man of The Year" in 1938. He invented freeways, did you know that? President Eisenhower copied him after he saw the autobahn."

Lorenzo snorted. "Jeez you're full of some serious bullshit, John. And you're fast making my list of people I'd take on a boat with me, when the ship is sinking, simply so I wouldn't be bored."

"I would consider taking you, too," he said, with a straight face.

"Gee, thanks! So enthusiastic. By the way, you may be interested to know that my partner Lucille is pretty quiet. Being wrong in a big way, has done her some good."

"That's the business I want to discuss."

"Oh?" Lorenzo's eyebrows raised at that.

"Yes." John explained that he wanted to personally deal with Lucille Irwin's transgressions. The minute he was well enough he planned to come to the station and speak with her, on her territory. Lucille would feel safe talking to him there.

"Why?"

"As I told you," John said, "unfinished business. Tell her for me that I've decided not to take her to court concerning her breach of the Privacy Act, as long as she gives me just an hour of her time."

Lorenzo's flat, alert cop's eyes narrowed as he rocked back on his heels. "You worry me, John Taylor. Is my partner about to commit suicide, too?"

John laughed loudly. "Nothing like that. She's still really concerned that I may yet take her to court, right?"

"Oh yeah," Lorenzo confirmed. "Lucille ain't sleeping, that's for sure."

"Good," John said. "Let her know how you discovered that my police records had been altered, can you? That my record check was clean four years ago?"

"Sure." Lorenzo shrugged. "No problem."

"And tell detective Irwin what's on that video I gave you. If you still want to punish her, for making your life miserable, feel free to let her watch it. That will really keep her up at night. But then destroy it, will you?"

The detective frowned, and then blinked, possibly with an inner vision of what Lucille's response would be while watching that video. "Okay, okay," Lorenzo said. "I'll do everything you want, but what exactly are you up to, John?"

"You'll see," John said schooling his face into an unreadable expression. "After all that, tell her that she's first on my agenda when I get out."

Lorenzo shook his head and tsked. "You're a cruel man, John Taylor."

John laughed. "Lorenzo my friend, you have no idea."

Chapter 27

Moving Home

───── ∞ ─────

The day John was due to leave the hospital, André Chevalier unexpectedly arrived.

John was sitting in a comfortable chair, under Kelly's careful eye. Using her left hand, her right in a sling and splint, Kelly was packing John's few possessions. She was going to drive him to her hotel. Luckily, her Infiniti G coupe had automatic transmission so she could drive with one hand.

Kelly's parents had wanted them both to come live with them, but even though everyone was getting along fine, and they'd both accepted her engagement, she didn't want to push it. Besides, living with her parents would seriously curtail their hopefully soon to be resumed sex life.

"*Mon ami!* You are well?" André asked as he strode with confident elegance into the room.

"André," John shouted and struggled to his feet. The two men hugged and kissed both cheeks in that French way. Kelly was surprised because ordinarily John didn't like people touching him, but that was clearly not the case with his friend.

"André, may I introduce you to my fiancée, Kelly Flynn?"

"The beautiful Kelly, *je suis enchanté*," André said and his grin flashed white against his tan skin. He captured her hand, lifted it, and with sexy male grace, and kissed it.

Kelly's eyes bugged out of her head and she felt a little zing of awareness when André took her hand. *Whew.* The famous André Chevalier! John's best friend in the whole world. Talk about sexual magnetism. This guy had it in spades.

"C'est un très grand plaisir de vous rencontrer. Vous avez été un bon ami pour l'amour de ma vie," Kelly said.

André's eyes lit with surprise and pleasure. *"Mon Dieu, vous parlez français! Bravo!"*

"Okay, you two," John said. "I only got a few words of that. English please."

André's eyes sparkled, "Your clever woman said that it was her very great pleasure to meet the good friend, of the love of her life. You speak French well, Kelly. And you, John, my young prince, I see that you have found your rose."

Kelly grinned with happiness. John spoke of André all the time. The man was well dressed and handsome. Not John Taylor movie-star handsome, of course, but he had an appealing and unmistakable Dom presence. Kelly had felt it almost like an electric shock, the moment he'd touched her. She'd instantly fallen under his spell.

André wore perfectly tailored charcoal slacks, with a well ironed, crisp white shirt with a black leather jacket. Whatever that scent he was wearing was, it smelled heavenly

André was healthy and fit with a flat stomach and broad shoulders. He looked to be about the same height as John. Dark hair, dark eyes, and a pleasant face. Kelly thought his eyes were amazing. There was keen intelligence in those eyes – and natural authority.

"What are you doing here?" John asked.

"You have lost your home, *oui?* And you need a place to stay?"

"Kelly and I were going to live in a hotel until we find something, but what do you have in mind?"

"One of my clients works in real estate here in Portland," André said. "He has friends who have departed on a round-the-world tour, on the ocean liner, and they will be away for months. They have a house that they wish to have reputable people live in. I desire for you, *mon ami,* to have a beautiful, restful home, in which you can recover your health. There are gardens, and oh, many things that you will both enjoy. I am told that it is a big house on a lake near here, *comprenez vous?*"

"Lake Oswego?" Kelly asked.

"*Oui, oui*, the same."

John shook his head. "André, you never cease to astonish me. How did you work that out?"

Giving them both a boyish grin André said, "Me? I am very clever. When I heard you lost the home, I immediately asked my friend, *et voila!*"

"Your timing is amazing," John said with no attempt to hide his awe.

"*Eh bien,* this is assuredly true," André agreed with a mischievous glint in his eyes. "Oh, many, many, have told me this already, *n'est-ce pas?*"

They all laughed at this boasting sexual reference.

John, Kelly, and André left the hospital together, André carrying their belongings, and teasing them both playfully about their injuries. Kelly had her right hand in a sling, and John had his left hand in a sling. This was fortunate however, André explained to them, because if they needed to row a boat, all would be well, as long as they both sat on the correct side.

The home was a mansion, directly on Lake Oswego just past Northlake Drive. They passed through the gated entry and when Kelly saw the house, she knew it must be worth ten million dollars or more. Adorned with Columbia River Rock, and copper clad windows, many of the internal walls were covered in walnut. It had boat lifts, an elevator, high ceilings, a full bar, dedicated media room, billiard, workout room, and a six car garage.

Oh, yeah, Kelly thought. *We can definitely rest and recuperate here.*

Chapter 28

Lucille's Confession

Lucille Irwin came into the police interview room, looking slim and pale. Her normally stern face seemed softer, less combative, yet more lined. John mentally chastised himself, genuinely troubled. He had made the woman wait to see what would happen for weeks, and that was far too long to torment anyone.

She wore her usual light blue uniform shirt and dark blue slacks, but those slacks looked loose on her now.

"Mr. Taylor, I wanted to say that I'm sorry," she began.

"Please," John said. "Sit down." He gestured to the chair across the table from him, and Lucille sat. "May I call you Lucille?"

"Of course."

"Thank you. You may call me, John. Please tell me why you're sorry, Lucille," he asked her in his best, soothing, yet compelling Dom voice.

"What I did was wrong, it was against the law."

"No," John said. "You already knew it was wrong, Lucille. You were aware that your actions were against the law, that you could get in trouble, and even lose your job. Yet you did it anyway. So, that's not why you're sorry. Tell me why you're sorry."

Lucille expelled a deep breath. "Lorenzo showed me your police record of four years ago." John saw that the woman was deeply upset. She looked like she might cry. Lucille cleared her throat. "And then he let me watch that video of you, your father and your mother."

There was a long, long pause of a full minute or more while Lucille got her breath back. John remained motionless, his face schooled into neutrality, while she regained her composure.

"I'm sorry for your rotten childhood, John," she said in a breathless rush, as if she was running to get speed up, in order to jump a hurdle, or perhaps a number of them. "I'm sorry you were raised by monsters, and I can't believe that you're a normal person after all that you went through."

"Thank you, Lucille," John said quietly. He didn't think he was exactly 'normal' but he wasn't going to tell her that.

"And I'm sorry that I added to your pain, by upsetting your fiancée, and her parents."

"Thank you." John stood up and began to slowly walk back and forth across the small interview room, his left arm was still in a sling, and the other was in his pocket. He stopped from the other side of the room and faced Lucille. "You risked your career. Why? Why did you do it, Lucille? I really need to understand."

"I don't know why."

John paced up until he stood directly in front to her. "Yes you do," he said mildly.

"I don't!"

"Liar," he said without any heat.

John backed off, once more walking the length of the room. Generally there was a good reason for an individual's inexplicable behavior, even though it may not be an obvious reason at the time. "Do you think that if you tell me, that I'll judge you, Lucille? Or that maybe, I won't understand?"

"No," she said in a small voice.

"I assure you that I will understand," he said. "You risked your career, Lucille without any reason at all?"

"I was thinking of Kelly."

"Thank you," John said, with genuine appreciation, coming back toward her. "Very good. What about her?"

"I thought that you were manipulating her, that she imagined that she was 'in love' when in fact you were an animal-torturing sociopath. I wanted to help her to see that," Lucille said.

"Excellent." John sat back down across from her, at the interview table. "Now we're getting somewhere. You do know that Detective Martin felt the same way that you did?"

"Yes, of course."

"But he didn't feel compelled to break the law," John softly reminded her. "This was personal for you, Lucille, wasn't it? Why was that? Did someone manipulate *you* and break your heart?"

The woman remained silent.

John stood up and began pacing once more, letting her turn that last question over in her mind. His movements were uniform and intentional, like waves against the shore, walking toward her and then withdrawing and walking away. He'd get his answers. With patience and persistence, like chipping rock into sand, John knew he'd wear the woman down. He was Father John, the confessor, after all.

He stopped and studied Lucille. Her breath, her pulse, her movements, her skin… Lucille Irwin was trapped with him in this room, helpless and vulnerable from the big very stick he was wielding – the very real threat to her career.

The woman was an open book to a knowing and experienced Dom, and John was going to force her to tell her secrets, whether she wanted to or not.

But, why? John thought. *Why am I doing this?* The answer came to him and he suppressed the impulse to laugh. *Because making people squirm and own up, forcing them to tell me their secrets, is serious fun for me.*

John walked toward her and stopped three feet away. "I was watching you from the first moment you came to my home, Lucille, did you know that?" he said softly. "Shall I tell you what I observed? I saw a woman who was in disagreement with her partner, who was irritated and argumentative, and I wondered if you had both just had a fight. But the next time I saw you, you were exactly the same. I came to the conclusion that you act that way with men in general. Am I right, Lucille? Who hurt you? Are you going to tell me?"

It didn't take much longer before Lucille Irwin crumbled and with the break came the tears. What was it with women and tears? How did they do that? John felt as if crying would probably make him feel better, too. If only he could figure out how to do it.

Yes, Lucille explained in hitching breaths. She had been in an abusive relationship. And, yes she'd loved him, and he was cruel to her, and broke her heart.

"When was this?" John asked, moving to sit back down across from her.

"Over a year ago. I knew it was a mistake to get close," Lucille said, roiling between anger and grief. "It was stupid to believe that Jonathan loved me. I learned long ago never to depend on someone, because they will disappoint you, or hurt you, or not be there when you need them. I knew that I could only depend on myself."

John waited, but it appeared that for now, that was all Lucille planned to say.

"Lucille," he said, leaning toward her, placing his arms on the table in front of him. "I'm talking to you now because I think you deserve another chance. You're smart, you're keen, and I think you can be an excellent detective." He leaned back in his chair.

The detective had her hands folded in her lap, and was looking down at them.

"Look at me, Lucille," he ordered in a commanding tone, and her eyes snapped to his face. "You know my history. I've had experience with such treachery myself."

Lucille nodded, and she colored, but she continued looking at him as requested.

"I can tell you this," John said. "A year is taking far too long for you to recover from this betrayal. You're a young woman. You should've bounced back by now. Do you know why you haven't?"

"No," she said.

"You're still upset, Lucille, because it was not Jonathan that upset you."

She recoiled back in her chair, and her eyes flashed in disagreement.

Leaning forward, John said, "No, Lucille, listen to me. I know what I'm talking about. Your problem is coming from a betrayal, by an earlier man – a father, a step-father, a brother, uncle, perhaps a male relative of some sort. I don't know who it was. Yet, I do know that he was an important man in your life. This man destroyed your trust, probably from when you were a child, and you've never recovered from it."

Lucille Irwin had suffered childhood abuse – John knew this without one ounce of doubt. Was her abuse physical? Mental? Or perhaps sexual? Maybe she had suffered abandonment, or neglect, which was the most devastating form of abuse of all. A man had done this to Lucille. A man who'd betrayed her.

It was men that she didn't trust.

John studied the woman in front of him, watching as the gears seemed to shift in her mind. Her eyes widened, brightening with sudden understanding.

He nodded, when he saw that she understood. "You know what I'm talking about, don't you, Lucille?" he said, gently.

"Yes," she said in a low voice.

"Father?"

"Step-father," she whispered.

"I see," John said. "Thank you for telling me, Lucille. You're an amazing woman."

When the detective frowned, and looked confused, he said, "It was brave to speak to me of your pain. And what you did in going to the Flynn's home, with my police record? Well, that took an extraordinary amount of courage, or madness, or both. You broke the law, Lucille, and you risked your career, because you wanted to save Kelly from me. I think your intentions were good. You had her interests at heart."

John gave her the warmest smile that he was capable of. "I simply have to like you for that."

"Oh," Lucille said, and her eyes welled once more. "Thank you, but I was so wrong."

"Have you heard the expression, 'If the only tool you have is a hammer you tend to see every problem as a nail?' Abraham Lincoln said it."

"Yes," she said. "I'm not completely sure what it means in this case. Do you think it applies to me?"

"Absolutely," he said. "It means that if your knowledge is limited, you try to fix every problem with the same solution. And you do that because that's all you know. In your case, you've been behaving as if all men are untrustworthy bastards, because that's what you know. You treat men differently than you treat women, Lucille. I suspect that your conduct is largely an unconscious, yet consistent habit. Anyway, I'd like you to get some counseling. Does the Police Service arrange for that?"

"I think so," she said. "I've never looked into it."

"Well," John said, "counseling is a stipulation of my agreement not to proceed with any complaint. I don't want to cause trouble for you. As I say, you were brave, and I like you for what you tried to do for Kelly. But I also know that you're going to screw up again without professional help."

"I see," she said, her brows furrowed in thought and she anxiously bit her lower lip.

"I hope you'll get counseling, because you want to sort yourself out."

The woman stared at him, lips parted, but she didn't reply. Was she uncertain about getting counselling? Perhaps she was hoping to avoid facing her childhood fears?

Lucille looked vulnerable, confused, and utterly exposed. John reflected that the detective seemed quite beautiful like this. She looked very much like one of his subs early in a scene; when he was stripping away masks, and discovering the person beneath.

Lucille Irwin, knew in her heart, that she couldn't trust men. She ran her entire life with that misguided premise in mind. But John intended to help her, and this truth flew in the face of Lucille's lifelong convictions. How was she supposed to act, when a man genuinely offered assistance, understanding, and support?

No wonder the poor woman was confused. John felt the soft tendrils of human connection. The heady power came from his natural inclination to protect, to care for, and to dominate her. He liked her. He wanted to help her, and he admired her courage.

"But either way, Lucille, you're going to get help," he said, smiling kindly to lessen the blow. "You're going get a crap load of counseling, until you work this thing out. Do you know why? "

She shook her head.

"Because I say so."

Lucille Irwin's brown eyes widened. He saw when she realized that he'd left her no choice. Taken by surprise and relief, she burst out laughing.

Chapter 29

An Effective Gag

Kelly just kept talking in one long flow of words.

She'd returned home from shopping, having bought, as far as John could tell, a ton of almost all unnecessary stuff. He'd stayed in bed this morning, his body tired and heavy, needing more rest. By 11 a.m. Kelly, who was buzzing like the Eveready battery bunny, had burst through the door with her mouth in overdrive.

God she was adorable.

She was wearing a rust colored, button down sweater. It was left open, over a cream colored, super lacy, feminine blouse. It was so, so, girly. Her black jeans were straight-legged and man, they did things to that ass of hers that was both suggestive and obscene. No one could have as nice a butt as Kelly did.

They both were still wearing slings. John, because he couldn't afford to wrench his left shoulder. Kelly because her right hand had to remain elevated. Besides that, her splint was really heavy.

One handed, Kelly had unpacked numerous things in the kitchen, fresh fruit, a box of chocolates, including a bouquet of fresh flowers. She explained that they didn't have daisies, and that her favorite chocolates were on special, but she couldn't find a ripe cantaloupe and there was no point buying a hard one, didn't he agree? But it had stopped raining just as she went to the car, and that was just as well as she had forgotten to take her umbrella, not that she had a hand to hold it with anyway, but she must be living right because the rain seemed to have stopped just for her.

The way his Kelly jumped from subject to subject impressed and astonished him.

John was standing in the living room, having followed her there, where she had placed a warm wool throw rug, because it was important for him to keep warm.

How in the world John wondered, was he going to get a word in? "Kelly," John snapped, in a sharp, commanding tone.

Kelly swung around, lips parted, blue eyes wide. John was pleased to see that his Dom voice had captured her attention.

"Come here."

Kelly came instantly, and stood just in front of him. Every bit of her attention was centered on him. Now wasn't her automatic obedience a turn on? A beautiful blush of arousal was rising, coloring her pale skin with red. That, plus her instant submission always made him hard.

"You may place your hand on my hip."

Kelly did so. With her right hand in a sling, John didn't want her to lose her balance.

"Hold still," he said in a quiet voice. Then with his one good hand he held her jaw, and pressed her mouth to his in a bruising kiss of longing and need. John loved Kelly's mouth, her soft, pliable lips, and the way she melted into him wherever he kissed her. Kelly kissed him back of course, with equal enthusiasm. She was making soft noises of arousal by the time he pulled away.

John threw a pillow on the ground from the overstuffed chair that was right behind him, and then pointed to the floor. "Kneel, please, Kelly," he said.

He helped her with his good hand, as being in a sling did make it awkward. "Thank you, Kelly. Now unbuckle and unzip me. I want my pants down. You may free my cock, but don't touch it."

Working with her left hand, she did as he asked while her tongue slipped out and touched her lips. Unconsciously, she licked them with greedy longing. John's cock jutted out in front of him, and he knew that Kelly wanted to lick and touch it, but she also knew that she wasn't allowed.

Well, she'd have to wait.

John sat down in the chair, capturing her body between his legs. He was still weak from his injury, and felt unable to do this standing up.

"You may put your good hand on my thigh, Kelly," he said. "That's right. Leave it there." John had a sudden impulse to laugh, but he suppressed it. His erection, as usual, glistened with pre-cum. Kelly's lips were wet and her mouth was slightly parted. Her eyes were focused on his cock – it seemed to be entrancing her. Kelly clearly craved it. Badly.

John tapped her chin, and her pale blue eyes flew to his face. "Beautiful girl," he said. "Keep looking at me. Good. Now open."

Kelly opened her mouth. Because his cock was so erect, it pointed up. Using his fingers, John pressed the swollen shaft down, toward her mouth, and inserted it.

"Close now, Kelly."

Kelly closed her mouth on his stiff male flesh, and immediately started to work it, licking and eagerly sucking.

"Uh, uh, no you don't, Kelly. Don't lick and don't suck," he admonished, and she stopped instantly. "I want you to simply hold my cock in your mouth. No moving, and try not to swallow as much as possible. That's right. Just like that. Thank you, Kelly."

John just stared at her for a few minutes. She remained on her knees, doing as he commanded, with her eyes on him, alert to his every need. He allowed himself an internal smile, because all the signs were there. Kelly was seriously aroused. Too bad. She'd have to wait.

"You're absolutely perfect, Kelly," he murmured, stroking her hair with the fingers of his good hand. "I'm grateful and honored by your obedience. I don't think I'll ever take you for granted. Every single time you submit to me, it feels like the very first time."

Her blue eyes blazed with pleasure, at his words and he smiled at her.

John stroked her throat and her mouth, then his fingers traced where her lips were pressed against his cock. How sexy was that? Feeling where her lips met his cock? He took his time, simply enjoying looking at her and touching her.

Kelly swallowed; she must be salivating like nothing else. She was so desperate to suck and move. Poor girl.

"Well," John said. "Now that I have your mouth otherwise engaged, I wanted to tell you some things. I love to hear you talk, Kelly. Who wouldn't admire your ability to just open your mouth and keep speaking as you do? How do you do that? It's a gift."

Kelly's eyes were bright with laughter now, and he cupped her chin, and then ran the pad of his thumb over her cheek. Seeing her like this, willingly bound to his will, made something low in his belly tighten.

"This form of gag looks beautiful on you, Kelly. And although it's distracting, you have to admit it's also very effective."

His hand gripped the back of her neck, holding her in a casual form of ownership. He always felt powerful and complete when acting as a Dom to Kelly. It was utterly satisfying and fulfilling to know that she was his.

"I called my neighbor, Mable today," he said, "and I repeatedly assured her that she did all she could for us. She's still pretty upset. I think older people find it harder to come back from a severe shock like that. Anyway, Mable is going to make double the food order while André is here with us. That will take her mind off of things, hopefully. I've given her the name of a courier, who will drop her meals here daily. We should take the time to visit her, when we next go into town."

He smiled down at her. "Nod, if you heard and understood me, Kelly." She did so.

"And my safe should arrive today. I've contracted some people that the insurance company recommended, to dig it out and bring it along." He caressed an eyebrow, and traced the shell of her ear. "Want to see what's in my safe?"

Kelly's eyes brightened with interest and curiosity. She nodded.

"Also, I spoke to Colin Wilkins," he said. "He and Donna are coming over tomorrow morning to catch up. I thought we'd have them for lunch, and order in something as neither of us can cook right now. Is that okay with you?"

Kelly nodded.

"Colin says André has taken The Basement by storm, which is no surprise. He's wanted by every sub there. You know how I introduced Lorenzo to him?"

Kelly blinked, and nodded.

"Well," John said. "It's just as I thought. Lorenzo Martin is a repressed Dom. His natural tendencies had been blunted by upbringing and culture, I guess. But André's on the case, and Lorenzo dominated his first woman last night at club. According to Colin the detective caught on quickly, probably from all his experience as a policeman, ordering people to comply. The man will never be the same. Lorenzo is on a total high according to Colin. Isn't that great?"

Kelly nodded, and as she did so, she swallowed. Her lips tightened on his cock unintentionally, and his rigid flesh throbbed and twitched.

Wow. That felt good.

John smiled down at her. "I don't have much more to tell you Kelly, thank God. You test my control, beautiful girl. You're the only one who ever has."

Her eyes brightened further and tears of emotion or strain started to trail down her cheeks.

Awed, John stilled. Kelly's tears always fascinated him. How did she do it? He wanted to understand. Nothing made him harder than seeing a sub cry. A submissive that was willing to accept his torment, simply to please him. John was unable to cry. His subs cried for him.

In the past, during a scene was the only time John felt connected, when his sub was in sub space, and he was in Dom space. That bond had been what he lived for, where his submissive was almost like an extension of himself.

When his submissives cried, John felt something. He could nearly grasp the elusive understanding that had always seemed just out of reach, that overwhelming emotion displayed by tears.

He still couldn't cry, but she did. And he was connected to Kelly. With her, John felt as if his own true humanity was almost within his grasp. Would he ever be able to shed a tear? From the current cultural perspective, the ability to cry was a stupid thing for a man to desire.

Why did one always want what they couldn't have? Dom nature notwithstanding, John wanted to remember how to cry.

John recalled what André's had told him four years ago: *You are cut off, mon ami, oui, but you are not an evil man. Your past has taught you to hide, even from yourself. But do not despair. You came to me, n'est-ce pas? That was an act of valor. Continue with such courage, jeune home. Life, for all its trials, is a healing process. Trust in what I tell you now. All will resolve in the fullness of time.*

John looked down at Kelly, aware that he had lost track of her, for just a moment, distracted by her tears. She constantly made him search his soul. That was one of the thousands of reasons that she was so good for him.

"I love you, Kelly Flynn," he said, looking into her eyes. Their connection was right there, that joining that he always seemed to have with her. It was such an ultimate high. "I know you know this already, but I don't think I could possibly tell you enough. *You* are the best thing that has ever happened to me."

Those tears! Kelly nodded, but those tears were really running now. His breath caught with the pleasure of it. God she was beautiful.

"Do you want me to come, Kelly?"

She nodded violently, and John gave a low chuckle.

"Okay, but we're going to try something new," he said. "For you, Kelly. Only for you. If you go slowly, you may use your hand on me. Other than the first time in the elevator I don't think I've ever let you touch me there, have I? So go ahead beautiful girl. I think I'll be alright, just don't grab, okay?"

Kelly nodded, and instantly began to suck and lick his cock with her mouth, moaning loudly. John tapped her chin and her eyes looked up and met his. "You're supposed to be looking at me, Kelly."

Kelly stared at him. John knew what she wanted, so he gave in.

"I'll allow you to watch what you're doing this time," he said. "I know you've wanted to see and touch my cock. Knock yourself out, beautiful girl."

John studied her, unable to prevent the stiffening tension in his body. That hand was there, and he fought to relax, yet his erection had softened slightly.

This is Kelly's beautiful hand, he thought. *And touching me is making her happy.* The thought of her pleasure did the trick, and he hardened fully once more.

Kelly reverently caressed his shaft, kissing it, pulling back his foreskin and pressing the rounded head against her moist lips, delicately licking his pre-cum. Taking a deep breath, her mouth vibrated with an "ummmm" sound, and her eyes, already heavy-lidded, drifted shut with pleasure. They opened again, and she studied his cock once more, softly rolling his balls and tracing the thick veins of his flesh.

She slowly worked him, and John suddenly became aware of something. Kelly had watched him stroke himself before, and she was doing it just like he did, clever girl. Kelly had been attentive because she loved him. Something in John's chest tightened. It was that aching feeling he got, when his heart was full.

Kelly began working him faster, with her hand, her mouth, and her tongue, making small helpless little sounds from deep in her throat.

"Oh, Kelly. That feels good," he said, astonished, because it did.

Kelly went down on him then, until his cock was deep inside, touching the back of her throat so that her nose was pressed up against his coarse pubic hair. Her hand was caressing his balls, and desperate for air she pulled back. Everything she was doing felt wonderful, even with her hands on him.

"Yes, yes," he said, fisting her hair. John didn't control her, he just wanted to hold on, to feel her bobbing, and moving side to side and up and down. "God I love your mouth, Kelly. So warm, so wet. You feel amazing."

Tears were running down Kelly's cheeks from happiness, or the strain of taking him, or a combination of both. John saw that she'd found a dreamy place, where all was peaceful euphoric joy.

"Ummmm," she moaned in a continuous little hum, drooling and utterly transported to be sucking her Dom off. Their bond was intense. His pleasure was her pleasure. John almost came right then with that thought.

"Do you want me to come for you, Kelly?" he asked in a low lust-filled voice.

She moaned, her desire making an inarticulate 'uh uh' sound around the thick cock that filled her mouth. Her soft sensual lips were wet and swollen.

"I'm going to shoot right down your throat. I love you taking my cum, Kelly. I want you to swallow every drop."

She moaned even louder.

John longed to give his sub exactly what she wanted, exactly what she needed. Serving a Dom this way was a real pleasure for a sub, and making Kelly happy was one of the most important things in the world for him. The sensation of her wet lips tight upon his shaft, her tongue flicking, and her mouth sucking him, and even her hand upon him, all contributed to his sensual and erotic joy.

"Yes, Kelly," he said, blood rushed into his cock, pulsing and swelling his shaft, until he was as large as he could get. John's fist tightened in her hair, as he felt that rigid, pre-ejaculation tightening of his body. "Take it my beautiful girl. Take it all."

John's buttocks, hips and thighs flexed *hard* – while his testicles contracted. His throbbing shaft convulsed, and semen shot into it. And then he came, shooting inside her again and again and again. He shut his eyes from the incredible pleasure of it.

When John opened his eyes, Kelly was watching him attentively, her face shining with a kind of euphoric rapture. She was still gagged. Her mouth was still full of his ever stubborn erection. John caressed her cheek, with the palm of his hand.

"Thank you, Kelly," he said holding the nape of her neck, in a casual, yet proprietary grip. "That was amazing."

Chapter 30

Letters

Kelly rested at John's feet between his legs, while he stroked her hair. There was something compelling about having her sit at his feet, captured between his legs, where he could pet her and touch her as he liked. She sat peacefully, her face an expression of serene bliss.

He kissed the crown of her head. "What? Nothing to say now?" John asked quietly.

Kelly giggled. "I'm just sitting here, zoning in my own little happy place, John. That was fantastic. I'm so glad I got to touch you, and it didn't bother you did it?"

He put a finger over her mouth. "No, I told you it was amazing. Do you want to come?"

She laughed, a carefree, lighthearted sound. "I always want to come, but I can wait. Making you climax, seeing your beautiful cock, being able to use my hand, and drinking you down was really fulfilling. I just want to sit here and enjoy the buzz."

The doorbell rang, and both John and Kelly looked out the window. Neither of them had noticed a car drive in, but they might not have noticed an earthquake either.

"It may be my safe." He helped Kelly to her feet and then pulled up his jeans, tucking himself in. They both couldn't stop smiling at each other.

As it happened, it was his safe. John had the men place it in the garage, and signed the receipt. The contractors and their large truck left.

Kelly giggled. "I'd have thought that one of us would have noticed them coming down the driveway. Do you think they saw anything?"

"Yes," he said, with his arm around her. "I can't imagine that they could have missed it. I'm sure it made their day."

John crouched down on to his heels and opened the safe. There were various papers, a few piles of cash, and memory sticks. One of those had his University assignment on it, but he was definitely going to need an extension. It was already overdue.

He took out two pieces of paper and locked the safe back up. "Let's go inside."

They both sat companionably together on the couch. "Here's the letter you wrote me, Kelly," he said, "and I am going to frame it," he squeezed her hand. "I'll read this out loud for both of us to enjoy."

Dear John,

I wanted to write and thank you for your help on Saturday night. I honestly think I might have died, or gone insane if you haven't been there to help me when I was trapped in that elevator. I owe you A lot.

John, I had the BEST time Saturday night. I've never felt such a wonderful connection with anyone. I'm so sorry I spoiled it all Sunday morning. Will you please forgive me? Can we start again?

I was really freaked out by finding that file on me on your desk when I left the bathroom. I wasn't snooping, I swear — my name just jumped out at me. Colin explained why it was there, but quite honestly I simply panicked.

So I think I've learned my lesson I'll not jump to conclusions, particularly about you I'll not use my safe word when I don't need to I know you would have simply talked to me about it At least what I know of you makes me think that

John I miss you and I'm thinking about you all the time Will you please call me? Can we meet? I spoke to my brother Richard about you He remembers you from grade school, and when we started talking, I remembered, too

We were friends when we were children I'd like to talk about that sometime I miss you John Will you call me please?

I think I'm in love with you,

Kelly

"I was completely gone on you, right from the start," he said.

"You could've told me."

"No, I couldn't have. That was the problem." He smiled at her. "You've no idea of the effect that letter had on me, Kelly," he said, hugging her to him. She cuddled into his chest with a happy sigh.

She asked, "So, do I finally get to read mine?"

"Of course. Here's my letter back to you. I wrote it immediately after I received your letter. I had to get my thoughts down."

"Okay," she said taking the letter in her hand. "I'll read yours out loud, too."

Kelly,

To me, you're the most beautiful woman in the world.

I've always loved you. Even as a child I loved you. You were my first real friend. I still don't know how you got through to me back then, I was in such darkness. When you selflessly stood up for me against those bullies, it was as if I became aware of light and goodness and hope. For the first time there seemed to be a reason to feel something other than anger and hate.

"Oh, John," she said in a broken voice. She sniffed. "I'm so glad I'm good for you. That's so sweet."

When I first saw you at The Basement I thought you were a hallucination. I'd imagined you so many times. But I never tried to look you up or find you. I never anticipated that you might want me, too.

"Awww," she said.

John could see tears forming in her eyes, and his chest tightened just to be able to witness her emotions. She was so pure, so kind, and giving and good. Kelly was the most wholesome thing in his world.

> I've never had a girlfriend. Until you I never once enjoyed sex. I usually only want to hurt people, but I don't want to hurt you, Kelly. I promise you that. If you have me as your Dom I swear I'll never hurt you (unless you want me to, of course.)

Kelly giggled at this, and John smiled at her.

"Oh, baby," she said. "You can do anything you want to me. I trust you and know you'll only do things I need, or want, too."

"Thank you, Kelly." John hugged her, still coming to terms with the baby endearment. He called her beautiful girl, and that made sense to him because Kelly was a beautiful girl. The same couldn't be said of her calling him baby. What did he have in common with a very young child?

She continued reading out loud.

> I don't need to give pain with you, Kelly. I don't even want to. Just being with you is all the connection I need.
>
> I love you Kelly Flynn, now and forever.

I would marry you tomorrow, but you're too smart for that.

John

By the time Kelly had finished his letter she was bawling her eyes out. As soon as she settled, she looked up at him and said, "That was a beautiful letter, John."

He rubbed her shoulders. "I'm glad you liked it."

Kelly sat up, and checked her wrist watch. "Oh! Look at the time. You know what? I forgot something. I'm going for a drive but I'll be right back. Will you be okay?"

"Of course."

Chapter 31

Surprise

The weather was mild, the sun was out, and the rain had stopped, so John took a walk outside along the lake.

He thought about the last few months, and how so much had changed. All because Kelly Flynn had come to his club, and back into his life once more. John Taylor was a rich man. He had money, but he had that before. Now he had the kind of wealth that really made him happy, like the love of a wonderful woman.

John was also rich with friends; Colin and Donna Wilkins, André Chevalier, Richard Flynn, and Lorenzo Martin. For the first time in his life, John had a real family. Kelly's family was amazing. From time to time they fought and bickered as all people do. But they were also fun, and affectionate with each other. They'd also accepted him, and now they seemed to care for him, too.

There was no one on the lake, as it was the middle of a work day, and school wasn't out yet. The breeze off the water was chilly, so he went back inside for a thicker jacket.

John decided that he'd continue to use his bullwhip. Practicing was soothing, and Kelly probably wouldn't mind him working a scene with other Dom's and their subs. He would still flog or spank Kelly, but only in order to give her amazing and powerful orgasms. Pain was really good for that. But the compulsion and sadistic need to cause pain was simply no longer there.

John had a connection now, one that never went away.

He thought about Lorenzo, happy that his new friend was discovering his naturally dominant desires. Maybe the detective would meet someone.

Thinking of Lorenzo reminded him of Lucille Irwin, and how well that matter had turned out. It would have been easy for him to hate Lucille, but for many years now he'd made supreme efforts to be done with hate. Detective Irwin had been genuinely grateful for his intervention. It had made her head spin, of course, accepting help from a man. But it had started her down an untraveled path, on what would hopefully be, a road to happiness.

John smiled. André would be proud of him.

It was Aristotle who said, 'In life, be kind, for everyone you meet is fighting a hard battle.' Lorenzo no doubt would tease him for quoting Aristotle, but Lorenzo would probably also shake his head and look at John in the calculating way that he often did. He'd then say, "Well, ain't that the truth?"

With a leather jacket thrown over him, John went back outside, but the sun had gone behind a cloud now and the breeze had picked up. It really was too cold. Well aware that his health was tenuous at the moment, John returned to the warmth of the mansion.

He wondered if Kelly would like to live here. Not in a massive mansion like this one, of course, but in a more simple home by this lake. It was pleasant to look out at water, and watch people go by on their boats. It they lived here, maybe John would even get the chance to learn how to swim.

Kelly had been gone for about forty minutes, and John wondered where she went. She'd that look in her eye, like she was planning to surprise him. His stomach fluttered with anticipation. What could that beautiful girl of his be up to?

John sat down on a soft leather couch in the den. With cream walls, decorated in light browns with high, cathedral ceilings, and arched windows overlooking the lake, it was the perfect place to sit.

Aunt Brenda would be so happy for him.

How had he come so far? He could never have done it without the support, care and affection of two wonderful women, his Aunt Brenda, and Kelly. His beautiful girl, who loved him and believed in him. And André Chevalier of course. André started him on the first few steps to finding himself, and to discovering happiness.

Integrity, John thought. *I'm not at war any more. I don't hate myself, or despise who I am. Kelly thinks I'm wonderful, and I'm beginning to believe that maybe I'm not so bad after all.*

John heard the door open, and he was surprised, because he hadn't heard a car, he had been so absorbed in his reflections.

Kelly walked into the room, still wearing her sling. She bent over, put something down on the floor, and then she looked up at him with her big, beautiful smile. "I got you a present, John, a little black Labrador. You can't go wrong with a Lab," Kelly said. "His name is Max, and he's ten weeks old."

John stared in shock and surprise as a little black ball of fur jumped and leapt, barking in excitement. *Kelly got me a puppy,* he thought, and his brain simply froze.

Oh! John was experiencing such a mix of emotions that he couldn't even respond.

He'd never owned an animal before, and particularly and especially not a dog. Dogs and puppies would always remind him of his shame, and of a terrible place in his past – a period of suffering, madness, hate, and despair. A horrible time during his childhood, that had almost destroyed him.

John didn't deserve the love of a dog, not after the evil he had done.

But the alert little puppy had spotted him now, and it was excited to see him, bouncing and barking with delight.

Full of life and energy, the happy little creature bounded across the floor and jumped up toward him, attempting to get on his lap. John was simply too stunned to move. He was aware that he was feeling something, some powerful, inexplicable emotion, but what?

Kelly calmly walked over, reached down, picked Max up, and put him in John's lap. The little creature's response to his new friend was to lick John's face with furious enthusiasm. John automatically began to stroke the puppy's soft rolling fur, and to hold it with his good arm.

Head tilted, and her blue eyes bright, Kelly stood beside him. When John met her gaze, her lips curved, with a knowing little smile. His heart ached to see such joy and love in her expression.

Kelly bought me a puppy. Max began to chew on his sling, and John's attention returned to the mischievous little ball of fur.

The exquisite pain in his heart grew, moving to include all of his chest, and his throat. John felt incapable of speech. Conscious of his inner turmoil, Kelly patted and rubbed his shoulder. She knew him better than anyone in the whole world could ever know him. Kelly, of all people, would understand all the impossible and overwhelming feelings that were roaring like a tidal wave – surging through him, body, heart and soul.

John Taylor was a man who was incapable of shedding tears.

Once, when he was eight years old, John had cried for so long and so hard that something inside him had broken. From that moment on, he'd disconnected from everything and everyone, and he'd lost the ability to cry.

Only on one occasion since then had he wept, and that was with André four year ago. But that was an exception, a perverse anomaly, and a dark time of grief that John could hardly recall. Everything was black to him back then, after Brenda had died, when he'd first met André.

Like an evil dream that's barely a shadow of awareness in one's waking consciousness, John could hardly remember that time.

Yet, because of Kelly, he'd reconnected to his body, and to his heart, and soul.

John couldn't take his eyes off the little puppy.

It was so healing to have this soft, innocent, puppy, wriggling and alive, safe on his lap, and in his hands. It reminded him of another animal he'd once known, many years ago. Pup had been a trusting, loving, little creature. At that time, Pup had been his only friend, single light in a world full of darkness. And instead of pain, somehow Pup's memory, now only brought him pleasure. *This squirming little ball of fur loves me already,* John realized with awe.

The vast wash of feelings and emotions within him were far too powerful for any human being to contain, even for a once broken soul such as his. John's heart was so full he didn't think he could possibly hold in, or express all the happiness he felt inside. And as it turned out, he couldn't.

Right then and there, while being thoroughly licked by a Labrador puppy, John Taylor, the man who couldn't cry, began to weep with happy tears of joy.

The End

Connect with me for free promotions and new releases!

Facebook: www.facebook.com/onlysexystories

Website: www.NikkiSexStories.com

Twitter: @NikkiSexAuthor

CPSIA information can be obtained at www.ICGtesting.com
Printed in the USA
LVOW10s1825240215

428165LV00036B/2601/P

9 781500 629045